Liath Luachra: The Seeking

Also by Brian O'Sullivan

The Beara Trilogy:
Beara: Dark Legends

The Fionn mac Cumhaill Series:
Fionn: Defence of Ráth Bládhma
Fionn: Traitor of Dún Baoiscne
Fionn: The Adversary
Fionn: Stranger at Mullan Ban

The Irish Woman Warrior Series
Liath Luachra: The Grey One
Liath Luachra: The Swallowed
Liath Luachra: The Seeking

Short Story Collections
The Irish Muse and Other Stories
Celtic Mythology Collection 1
Celtic Mythology Collection 2
Celtic Mythology Collection 3

Liath Luachra: The Seeking

BRIAN O'SULLIVAN

Irish Imbas Books

ISBN: 978-0-9951303-5-7

DEDICATION

This book is dedicated to Ruairidh Morrison and
Melanie Brown

(faraor, ar an taobh eile don domhan).

Glossary:

A pronunciation guide for names and common terms in Irish used in this book can be found at the Irish Imbas website (irishimbasbooks.com):

Members of Na Cinéaltaí (The Friendly Ones):

An Giobach
Biotóg
Feirgil
Liath Luachra
Mochta
Murchú

Tribal Groups:

Clann Baoiscne
Clann Morna
Éblána
Na Gréasaigí
Na Brígiantaí
Uí Bairrche
Uí Cailbhe
Uí Loinge
Uí Laoire

Placenames:

Briga
Dún Baoiscne
Inbhear Ciúin
Luachair
Poll an Iubhair

Common Terms (used throughout this book):

Bandraoi - A druid (female)
Banfénnid - A female fénnid

Beacáin scammalach – Literally, 'cloudy mushroom'. A fungus with hallucinogenic properties.

Bod – A cock/prick

Conradh – A champion/ battle leader

Draoi – A druid

Éclann – A person without a tribe

Faoi nocht – Naked

Fian – A band of warriors or war party

Fénnid – A member of a fian. The noun can be plural or singular.

Fulacht fia – a water-filled pit used for cooking (plural: *fulachtaí fia*)

Gaiscíoch – A band

Gallán – A standing stone

Gléas Gan Ainm – Liath Luachra's sword. Literally 'Tool Without a Name'

Imbas forosnai – A prophetic ritual

Léine – Upper body garment (like a shirt but heavier)

Lis – Circular courtyard of a *caiseal* or *ráth*

Marbhán – A corpse

Margadh – A deal or arrangement

Óglach – A young, unblooded warrior (plural: *Óglaigh*)

Ráiméis – Nonsense talk

Rí – A tribal leader/chieftain

Ríastraid – A battle frenzy

Rígfénnid – Leader of a fian

Síd – Ancient burial mound, usually containing a passage grave

Chapter One:

Some days the valley throbbed with a silence so profound she'd stand still, fearing to break the spell of it. Other days, strong westerlies would whip through the mountains and fill the void with a mournful, hollow moan.

For Liath Luachra – the Grey One of Luachair – such variances made little difference. Whatever sounds started the day, it invariably closed with the silence of the cave, the crackle of the fire and the maudlin ghosts that awaited her there.

Within five days of her return to Luachair, the winter landscape had started to consume her, the still, bleak terrain eroding the reserves of strength she'd built up while away. In Luachair, the landscape seemed to drain her soul and her loneliness was an endless falling where she never actually struck the ground. A constant sensation without respite; the only way to stifle its impact was to numb it through *béacán scammalach* – cloud mushroom – or sheer physical exhaustion.

For the first few days, occupying herself with the practical tasks of staying alive meant that the latter approach was more practical. Cutting wood for the fire, carrying it to the cave, feeding the fire, setting the snare lines, checking the snare lines, collecting the bounty, curing the bounty or cooking it: these tasks successfully drove her body to comatose levels of fatigue. By the time darkness fell, she was already curled in her furs, her mind closing down, too weary to form coherent thoughts, too dull to feel emotion.

And beyond the cave, winter beckoned.

***

On the fifteenth day of her return, she discovered the valley wasn't as lifeless as she'd first imagined. With the onset of dusk, she'd developed a routine of standing in the lee of the cave entrance before retreating inside for the night. There, staring out across the valley at the gloomy view of the eastern marsh, she'd mull over her existence before hunger and exhaustion drove her back inside. On the evening of the fifteenth day however, that routine was broken by a low hoot coming from a stand of yews off to the left of the cave mouth.

Startled by this unexpected expression of life, Liath Luachra studied the yews closely, struggling to work out where the sound had come from. Unlike many of the other trees, stark and stripped of foliage, the

1

evergreen yews retained their leafy mesh. Combined with the fading light, they effectively concealed whatever was hidden within their upper levels.

Cailleach Oíche. Old Hag of the Night.

That it was an owl, she had no doubt, although she did wonder what kind. Out in the Great Wild, each bird had its own pattern of behaviour and, as with other wild animals, there was much to be learned from observing them. Those patterns consolidated survival techniques over many generations and recognising any variation could mean the difference between life and death. For an owl to hoot while she was present went against established patterns and she was curious to understand why.

Moving towards the tree, the woman warrior climbed agilely onto its lower branches then slowly hauled herself upwards from bough to bough. She found what she was looking for about half-way up, a large bole hole on the western side of the central trunk. Perched inside the little cavity, regarding her with serious eyes, was a long-eared owl, the two ear tufts above its facial disc giving it a distinctively feline appearance.

Ceann cait. Cat Head.

Liath Luachra's teeth flashed briefly in the darkness, pleased with her success but also conscious that she'd had the luck in finding it. Even for owls, the Cat Head was notoriously secretive. Rarely seen in daylight, its grey and dark russet plumage merged effortlessly with the Great Mother's mantle and it was often impossible to distinguish it from the surrounding background.

The owl continued to watch her stiffly as she edged along the branch, advancing lithely towards the bole hole. When she was within two or three paces, the bird suddenly flared its wings, pulling its feathers inward in a manner that caused its body to elongate. Narrowing its eyes to thin slits, it glared at her, clacked its beak and swayed aggressively from side to side.

Liath Luachra paused to consider the bird without alarm. When threatened, the *Ceann Cait* often strived to make itself look bigger and far more menacing than it really was. Nevertheless, she continued to be intrigued by its general behaviour. *Ceann Cait* preferred the deep woods. Finding one on the very edge of the exposed marshland was unusual, as was the fact that it wasn't gathered in some communal roost – normal behaviour for that time of year. Strangest of all however, was the fact that the bird hadn't flown away as she'd approached, a natural reaction given her predatory size.

An unexpected, metallic-sounding squeak offered some explanation for that particular irregularity.

Startled, Liath Luachra pulled back, wondering if she'd misheard but then that unmistakeable squeak resonated hollowly from the bole hole once more.

Chicks!

Bewildered, the woman warrior leaned back against one of the moss-strewn boughs, propped herself securely between two converging branches and peered closer. The owl continued to watch her gravely from the nest of leaves inside the bole hole. Behind it, on either side, she saw flutters of movement. The owl had chicks. Three chicks.

Which made little sense.

With the coming of winter, the breeding season had already long passed. The dwindling food supply and dropping temperatures were highly impractical for raising young.

The woman warrior felt an unexpected flush of disappointment.

They won't last the winter. They'll be dead in days.

Deflated, she slowly started down the tree and returned to the cave.

***

After thirty-three days, Liath Luachra started to lose the physical momentum that had kept her safe and sane. The daytime temperatures had plummeted even further and snow now permanently layered the tops of the surrounding mountains, its white substance blunting the usually jagged contours. Most mornings when she ventured outside, the grass was white with hoar frost, and chopping firewood left her hands numb and raw. Fortunately, by then, she'd already amassed a sufficient supply inside the cave to keep her through the winter.

The low temperatures also meant it was harder to walk the land. With the arrival of the snow, hunting was exhausting and rarely productive with most of the wildlife leaving the valley, hibernating or simply going to ground. The task of managing her snare lines became more of an effort but, every morning, without fail, the warrior woman forced herself up and out to the frozen world beyond the cave. Despite the layers of clothing she wore, the wool cloak and hood, the scarf, double tunic and leggings, the icy wind cut through them effortlessly, as though they weren't even there. Her feet, wrapped in strips of wool and enveloped in the double coating of her winter boots, grew numb on the icy ground and she could no longer feel her toes.

On the morning of the thirty-third day, the woman warrior left the valley's south-western cliffs where the cave was located. Walking south through deeper forest, she eventually reached a pass in the western foothills where a murky stream flowed through to feed Luachair's sluggish river. The entry point of that tributary was where one of her snare lines began and, starting there, she slowly worked her way back north, following the grassier patches of land that ran parallel to the riverbank. The snares were set at intervals of about four hundred paces, their locations chosen from previous evidence of wildlife passage or natural run-throughs where animals were likely to pass. She stopped to check each one, readjusting them where necessary but the pickings were slim, the yield consisting of a single hare stretched cold and stiff on the frozen earth.

Continuing north past the cave where the forest grew thinner, she soon came upon a clearing. Set on the western riverbank overlooking a small strand of gritty shingle, it offered a clear view across the water to the misted reeds of the marsh on the other side. Liath Luachra paused to enjoy the beauty of the little glade, the weak touch of liquid winter sunlight caressing her cheek without the slightest trace of warmth. This clearing had always been one of her favourite places within the valley. Free of the usual towering trees, on a summer's day it was filled with light. Sunny and sheltered, it was a pleasant place to sit and muse or simply fish for trout. Years ago, she'd spent a lot of time here, swimming with her brothers and ...

Stop it!

Leave them. Don't disturb the ghosts.

Subdued and apprehensive, she quickly moved on.

Still headed north, she eventually struck an area where the river curved sharply east, merging and emptying into the marsh. Avoiding the perilous clumps of suffocating reeds and sucking mud, she maintained a northerly direction, moving further from the waterway to regain more solid ground.

A little further on, another of her snares yielded a second hare and that success prompted her to dig for wild tubers, collect a smattering of herbs and wade ankle-deep in a nearby pond to gather water cress for the meal she intended to make. By the time she'd completed her harvest, her hands and feet were completely numb and she shivered, conscious that she'd let herself get too cold. It was time to return to the fire.

Three more snares. Just three more.

Her mouth began to water as she continued north, thinking of the feast she'd make that night, visualising herself going through the actions of cutting the meat, frying it in a pan or browning it in a pot for a stew with the tubers and watercress. If necessary, such a meal could keep her

in food for several days, provided she ate sparingly and supplemented it
with the porridge she'd been subsisting on for the last three days.

Her winter existence was far more difficult now, of course. In
previous years, on her return to Luachair, she'd always had the luxury of
calling on an elderly couple who lived further south in the forest, for
help or supplies. The only other survivors of the raid that had
slaughtered the valley's occupants several years earlier, they'd spent the
latter part of their lives hiding fearfully on their little patch of land.
Childless, gentle people who'd been close friends with her mother,
they'd cried when she'd returned so many years after that raid, ruthless
and hardened from the experience. Although they'd approached her
with kindness, Liath Luachra had rejected their overtures of friendship,
wincing when they used her old name and refusing to answer to it.

The previous year, succumbing to age and a lifetime of toil, neither
survived the brutal winter. When she'd found them, Liath Luachra had
buried them together in the earth floor inside their little home before
setting the building ablaze.

Over the subsequent year, she'd thought about them far more than
she'd expected. She'd never really understood what it was about the
couple that had disquieted her and it was only when they were gone that
the realisation finally struck her. It had been the genuine affection
between the couple, that and the connection to the girl she used to be:
two things she could no longer allow to touch her.

Her mind must have wandered for a time for, looking up, she realised
she'd walked much further than she'd intended. Startled, she pulled up
short, her gaze quickly sliding towards a broad stand of oaks about three
hundred paces directly north of where she was standing.

The woman warrior stood in silence, the wind whipping her cloak as
she stared at the trees, a tightness catching the back of her throat. The
stand of oaks marked an invisible boundary, an unconscious limit she'd
set herself from venturing further up the valley. It also marked the edge
of the rough ground farmed by her family, a section of the valley she
hadn't approached for many years. Her childhood home was screened
by those trees, although by now she doubted it was still standing. After
so many years without maintenance, it was more likely the structure had
collapsed, the thatched roof rotted away, the mud-wattle walls
swallowed up by the encroaching vegetation. The fields she'd worked as
a child would also be overgrown, of course.

Even now, she felt no desire to get any closer, the fear of coming
across some physical remnant of her brothers enough to set her heart

pounding. One day, she reasoned, the Great Wild would reclaim that space completely, erode any markings, obliterate anything and everything recognisable. On such a day, she might finally venture further north. On such a day she might finally return home.

Exhaling heavily, Liath Luachra dragged her eyes from the trees and forced herself to turn, putting one foot in front of other until she was moving at a steady pace towards the western foothills. Like the old homeplace, she'd not set foot in that location for several years but at least there were no burning ghosts to haunt her and having already come this far, she decided, she might as well keep going.

The route up into the foothills was a barren track that led deeper into the mountains and she moved cautiously on the frozen ground for it was spattered with patches of treacherous black ice. Ascending the side of a bare rock canyon, she followed a rough trail that eventually terminated on the high cliff ledge known as Céim na Macallaigh – The Step of Echoes. Standing on that exposed spot, she considered the stark grey cliffs that loomed to every side where the canyon cut deeper into the mountains, their bleakness magnified by the lack of colour and a complete absence of wind. Turning, the woman warrior looked back towards Luachair, her view restricted to the southern section of the valley. In the mildewed gleam of a weak winter sun, that landscape looked pallid and lifeless. Stained with a myriad of variant greys and faded browns, its muted palette was relieved uniquely by the occasional slash of red from a strand of dead fern.

Standing in that perfect hush, Liath Luachra experienced an unusual sense of self-detachment and found herself wondering whether she too might be as dead as the landscape, working her way towards the Dark Lands while completely oblivious to the reality of her own passing. In her mind, at that moment the possibility did not seem too farfetched and it was easy enough to imagine her body strewn on some bloodied hillside, rent with wounds, dreaming of this existence as her life's blood leaked away. In truth, the concept held a disturbing appeal. The Dark Lands would mean a simple drift to nothingness, an end to all her thoughts and sentiments, an end to all pain.

To test her theory, the Grey One cleared her throat and called out tentatively. The sound of her voice rang softly off the rock in the immediate confines of the ledge, reassuring and yet, in some ways, disappointing.

Unsatisfied, she advanced closer to the edge of Céim na Macallaigh and peered carefully downwards. Shaded by the surrounding cliffs however, the base of the precipice was shrouded in shadow. Unnerved by the drop and the heady view, she hurriedly stepped back to position herself more securely. Bracing herself, Liath Luachra lifted her head, filled her chest and howled: a powerful, primal ululation, loaded with a savage rage that ricocheted off the faces of the grey cliff, amplified one hundred-fold.

She sustained that howl for as long as her voice could hold but, finally, choking, broke off and staggered backwards, completely breathless. Spent, the woman warrior dropped to her knees on the hard stone and listened, fascinated by the power of the roar she'd unleashed, and which now rang through the mountains: provocative, challenging and utterly defiant.

Eventually, of course, that furious clamour faded and when it did, the valley felt lonelier and emptier than ever before. Deep inside however, Liath Luachra knew that she'd given vent to something exceptional, cast her fury at the world and challenged its response.

And no-one had dared to answer her back.

By the time she'd returned to the lower slopes, the sunlight was fading, smothered by a slab of solid cloud that slid in above the western mountains. Returning south, the woman warrior could feel the temperature plummet, the cold becoming an almost constant throb of piercing icy discomfort.

Picking up the pace, she succeeded in making it back to the cave before the rain spilled over, although when she was in sight of the cave mouth, Father Sun's mounting anger erupted in a rumbling reverberation and a distant streak of lightning cracked the sky. Hurrying towards the winter cave mouth, Liath Luachra glanced towards the yew trees. Since discovering the *Ceann Cait's* nest she'd regularly deposited scraps of meat at the foot of the tree, mocking herself for the futility of such foolish gestures. The Great Mother's plans for the Great Wild were hardly hers to influence.

Nevertheless, she'd been quietly pleased to see that the scraps had disappeared overnight on several occasions, although whether that had been the owl or other animals, she could not tell.

Despite the incoming storm, Liath Luachra abruptly veered left towards the yews. Approaching the tree where the nest was located, she leaned against the cool bark of the trunk and peered upwards but, as usual, could see nothing in the upper foliage.

With a soft grunt, the woman warrior turned to go but then paused as her eyes were drawn to an odd shape lying among the desiccated leaves at her feet. Reaching down, she brushed the dead leaves aside to reveal what was lying amongst them.

It was a dead owl chick.

Liath Luachra stared at it for several moments, then wordlessly turned and made for the cave.

***

That evening, after cooking one hare and smoking the other, she succumbed to the pull of the *beacán scammalach*. Retreating to the fire and the comfort of her furs, she lay chewing the desiccated fungus until her mind began to soften. As usual, the mushroom's effects kicked in without her truly noticing, loosening the knots in her stomach, pulling her down to a realm of imagery that gripped her consciousness completely.

Left to herself, she'd probably have remained within her furs and dreamed herself to oblivion. Fortunately, the intermittent but insistent reminders of physical discomfort meant that between long periods of dreaminess, she did what was needed to stay alive. She rose from her furs to urinate or shit, to throw wood on the fire and, if she remembered, to eat.

And, of course, consume more *béacaán scammalach*.

The dreams formed one endless series of visions, living memories from her childhood in the valley, of her mother's voice, of her brothers giggling over mud pies. Softening her sharp edges, the visions were so vivid they were hard to distinguish from memories or living moments. Most were light and airy although, on occasion, they swung to darker places that startled her awake. Anxious and panting, she sometimes came to, conscious that she was mumbling, expelling words of complete gibberish.

On one occasion, she found herself standing in the outer passage with a ladle dangling uselessly from her right hand and no clear memory of what she'd intended to do with it. On another occasion, she woke up unable to move, her body still and unresponsive to the commands her mind tried to send it. For a long time, she lay wheezing in silent terror, convinced she was paralysed and trapped in those shadowed confines forever. During her darker moments, she imagined a lost traveller happening across the cave one day to discover her lonely skeleton.

A moment later, forgetting she was paralysed, Liath Luachra got up and ate some stew.

***

8

When the dreams finally petered out she wasn't sure how long they'd lasted. All she knew was that one morning she drifted back from dream to lucidity, her thoughts sluggish but clean, her mind blank but calm. Her body, on the other hand, stank from days without washing. She felt ravenous and dehydrated.

Attempting to rise from her furs, Liath Luachra fell onto the floor of the cave, her leg muscles stiff and unyielding after a prolonged period in the same position. Regaining her feet, she worked her way over to the wooden frame where she'd hung the smoked hare and used a knife to carve off the last slivers of meat. Stuffing them into her mouth, she chewed furiously on the tough and smoky texture, struggling to produce saliva in the parched tissue of her cheeks.

The bucket in which she kept her drinking water was empty, lying on its side, the ladle at an angle to the stone floor. Gasping from thirst, she unthinkingly made for the passage, her mind filled with images of clear water from the river south of the cave. Emerging from the passage however, an icy gust slammed into her side and sent her stumbling back into shelter, blinking in shock at the bitter cut to the wind. Raising her eyes, she regarded the grimness of the sky and smelled a definite edge of snow to the air. She also realised that, in her fug, she'd left her cloak and fur layers back in the cave.

Unable to deal with the prospect of returning inside, the woman warrior hunched her shoulders against the icy wind and stumbled determinedly onwards, working her way down the gentle slope towards the distant waterway. Reaching the slow-moving river, she dropped to her knees and drank greedily, taking several long swallows from water pooled in her hands before her thirst was sated. The icy bite to the liquid numbed her fingers and made her teeth ache but it also scraped the worst of the miasma from her mind.

Moving further down the riverbank, she came across a series of rock pools by a collapsed section of the bank, where she could crouch more comfortably to wash her face. Looking down at the still water, she stared numbly at her own reflection, observing the gaunt face framed by high cheekbones and the dull eyes without emotion. Over the winter period, she'd allowed her hair to grow far longer because of the cold and now she could also see its thick, tangled strands.

Over her years as a *fénnid*, prolonged periods had often passed when she'd had no opportunity to see her reflection. On occasion, whole seasons could pass where she had no memory of her own facial features. That wasn't something that particularly bothered her but, on those few occasions she did happen upon a reflective surface, it was always something of a disappointment to see her own likeness.

Without thinking, she lashed out at the pool, sending liquid tremors across its surface. Before the water had settled again, she was already up and turning away.

She breathed in deeply and exhaled a stream of warm vapour. That visible evidence of the low temperature reminded her body of how cold it really was and, almost immediately, her teeth began to chatter. Although loathe to return to the claustrophobic confines of the cave, she knew it was too cold to remain outside.

Muttering under her breath, she started back, still too groggy to feel any true resentment at her situation but cursing out of habit. Slipping her hands under her armpits to keep her fingers warm, she was about to start up the incline towards the cave when a movement further along the base of the cliff made her stop in her tracks and stare. A black horse and rider in a hooded cloak had appeared out of nowhere, rounding a large boulder that had concealed their approach until that exact moment.

With her instincts dulled, the woman warrior remained staring numbly, conscious that she was in a vulnerable position yet lacking any ability to respond with urgency. Instead, she found herself walking once more, continuing back up towards the cave, conscious the trotting horseman would probably reach it before her.

Fortunately, her luck held for, hunched over his mount against the cold, the stranger wasn't looking in her direction and didn't appear to notice her, even as their paths converged. He looked up quickly enough, all the same, when he came upon the entrance of the cave and caught sight of traces of her activity there: the chunks of chopped firewood, the empty wood frames used to stretch and prepare deer skins, a few discarded tools and implements and, of course, a diverse selection of tracks.

Driven by instinct rather than any conscious intent, Liath Luachra quickly bent down to scoop a fist-sized stone up from the rocky ground and concealed it adeptly by cupping it in her hand with her knuckles turned forward. It was hardly an effective weapon but it was better than nothing.

Looking around, the hooded rider finally spotted her, just as she arrived within ten paces of the cave mouth: stone throwing range, had she been in a fit enough state to throw accurately.

Raising one hand, the rider brushed the hood from his forehead. A good-looking young man with dark eyes and several days growth of beard about his lower face stared down at her as she came to a halt in front of the horse. His face broke into a wide grin.

'I see you Grey One.'

Murchú!

The woman warrior stared at him, too stunned to respond to the traditional greeting.

Murchú remained atop his horse, fidgeting with the bridle as she continued to stare, growing visibly discomforted by her extended silence. 'Will you offer no hospitality or welcome?' he asked at last.

Realising that she must present something of a bedraggled state, the woman warrior gestured meaninglessly with one hand. After so much time alone, it was remarkably difficult to speak. 'I don't have fresh food to offer you,' she managed at last.

'A fire would serve well enough. It's been a cold ride. I'm frozen to the core.'

And he did look frozen, pale and shivering atop his horse. It must indeed have been a cold ride from *Uí Loinge* territory in this mid-winter weather.

'How did you find me?'

'My uncle once told me you lived in the Luachair valley.'

Bressal.

The mention of her old *rígfénnid*, the sly ex-leader of *Na Cineáltaí*, was enough to make the Grey One wince. With his tricks and his bullying, he'd tried often enough to pry the location of her winter refuge from her.

'He didn't know its exact location,' continued Murchú. 'But you told me once that you lived in the shadows of *Cnoc an Óir*. An old tracker I know confirmed the valley's rough location.'

The *Uí Loinge* man paused, then, swinging one leg stiffly over the horse's rump, slid inelegantly to the ground. He stood awkwardly, flexing his legs while he patted the horse's shoulder.

'I found the valley this morning but I wasn't certain of your ...' He paused and glanced uncertainly towards the mouth of the cave. 'I wasn't sure of your abode's siting. I've spent the day searching its length to find you.'

Liath Luachra became conscious that she was grinding her teeth and that an extended silence had passed without any response from her.

'You have a horse,' she said, unsure what else to say.

'Yes.'

'Yes,' she repeated. Having reached the end of the sentence she wasn't quite sure where to go next.

'You can't bring the horse inside,' she said at last.

***

The cave that served as her winter quarters was a spacious grotto located less than twelve paces inside the western cliff face. Consisting of irregular, but smooth, granite walls, it retained a surprising brightness, primarily due to a wide crack in one of the upper arches through which a thick sliver of grey sky could be discerned.

While a short, curving passage sheltered the cavern from the worst of the wind, the Grey One had also constructed a rude leather flap where the passage connected with the inner chamber. This had proven effective in eliminating the worst of the draughts. Brushing that flap aside, she gestured for Murchú to follow.

Entering the cavern with the *Uí Loinge* warrior, Liath Luachra saw it for the first time through the eyes of a stranger and experienced a sudden and unfamiliar sense of embarrassment. The space in which she lived was chaotic, a maelstrom of discarded clothing, abandoned bowls and drinking vessels, bones and erratically placed 'islands' of firewood strewn across the stone floor. Most prominent, however, were the piles of discarded weapons that stretched along the base of the northern wall: knives, battle axes, slings, swords, some of them well maintained, some in obvious need of repair. One pile consisted of a stack of at least twenty javelins, an impressive number that she'd manufactured during a particularly cruel winter the previous year. Confined inside the cave for more than a week by snowdrifts, she'd thrown herself into the manufacture of the missiles with an almost rabid intensity to prevent herself from going insane.

Conscious now that her habitation exposed much of her own internal disorder, Liath Luachra moved brusquely towards the fire where she stirred the flames furiously with a broken sword, the short blade blackened and bent from heat. Feeding the flames with a fresh supply of fuel, she tugged a nearby cloak over a heap of little wooden animals lying off to the left of the blaze, feral figures she'd carved at that fireside every winter over the past five years. Shifting some of the other rubble aside, she also made room for her visitor on a long log she'd placed there as seating.

Murchú sat and although there was plenty of room for two, the Grey One moved around to the far side of the flames, dragging an upturned wooden bucket to use as a seat. Leaning forward, she pulled a metal pot from the cinders, scraped the congealed porridge it contained – now

12

days old – into two bowls and passed one to Murchú. The *Uí Loinge* man
dug into it like a man who hadn't eaten for days.

As he focussed completely on shovelling food into his mouth, the
young warrior's preoccupation allowed Liath Luachra to study him
unobserved. Murchú looked older since she'd last seen him. But then,
their previous tasking in the Lonely Lands had aged them all one way or
the other, she supposed.

As she watched the starving man, the woman warrior felt the first
stirrings of resentment at his presence in this, her most intimate refuge,
a personal sanctuary she'd always guarded jealously. Recalling the
disabling influence of the *béacán scammalach,* she scowled at her own
stupidity. In hindsight, she knew that had she been more lucid, she'd
probably have sent him away.

'What are you doing here, Murchú?'

The *Uí Loinge* man looked up, a thin line of wet porridge gleaming
across his upper lip. 'I've come to seek your help, Grey One. I have a
tasking for you. For *Na Cinéaltaí.*'

The Grey One looked at him without expression, saying nothing.

'These eyes see snow on the mountains well enough. And this head
knows the *fian* season doesn't start till spring but … but this is a tasking
of some importance. I'd ask you to hear me out.'

Liath Luachra stirred her own porridge several times, twisting the
spoon in slow viscous curls as she thought his answer through. After the
horrific violence of their previous tasking, she'd genuinely not expected
to see Murchú again. A well-liked *Uí Loinge* stalwart, everyone knew the
young man was being groomed for leadership by his father – the *Uí
Loinge* chieftain – and his uncle, Bressal. Having already proven himself
in battle there was no longer any reason for him to put his life in danger,
particularly given his increasing tribal responsibilities and the woman
warming his bed back at Briga.

Finally, she tapped the spoon on the side of the bowl and put it aside
untouched.

'Tell me.'

Sensing her deep-rooted reluctance, Murchú hurriedly grasped the
sliver of opportunity she offered. 'The tasking is a Seeking, Grey One.
We need *Na Cinéaltaí* to find my sister.'

Liath Luachra reached down to pick up the bowl once more. This
time she ploughed the spoon through the porridge, raised it to her lips
and took a mouthful. Keeping her eyes on the fire, she chewed on the
gritty material as she chewed on his words then chewed a little more.

'Where is your sister?'

'She was taken, snatched by a *díberg* – a raiding party – passing through *Uí Loinge* territory.'

'In winter.'

'Yes.'

Liath Luachra grunted in surprise. A *díberg* passing through their territory at this time of year seemed strange. Nobody travelled in winter if they could possibly help it. Not only were such expeditions more dangerous and unpleasant due to the cold and the rain, there was always an increased likelihood of a route being blocked due to flooding or storms.

'And you're certain she still breathes?'

'A trapper spotted her with the *díberg* from a distance some days ago. She was shackled but most certainly alive.'

'How many warriors?'

'He wasn't sure. It was dense forest. He thought, five or six.'

Liath Luachra remained silent, conscious of the most likely outcome in such circumstances. Of her own experience in such circumstances.

'And you're not already out there looking for her.'

The words were uttered as a statement, not a question. His presence at her fire spoke for itself.

'We can't follow the *díberg*.'

'The *Uí Loinge* have no trackers?'

'We've trackers enough but the tracks lead through *Clann Baoiscne* territory.'

Liath Luachra wordlessly munched the tasteless gruel. She knew little of the *Clann Baoiscne* people, a tribe based to the south east of *Uí Loinge* territory. When she'd first gained control of *Na Cinéaltaí* – The Friendly Ones – their chieftain, Tréanmór, had offered her a potential tasking but her disastrous attempt at vengeance on Garrad Mór, his vicious right hand, Gadra, and the other *Uí Cailbhe* raiders who'd enslaved her had put paid to that potential interaction.

Beyond that, through various conversations, she was aware of their fractious relationship with Murchú's people but little else. People said that there'd been constant tension between the two tribes over the previous decades: feuds over territory, historical grievances and imagined slights. For that reason, Murchú probably had the right of it. Any foray by *Uí Loinge* into their territory would inevitably trigger hostilities and bloodshed.

'Why not offer trade to go through *Clann Baoiscne* land?'

'Tribal pride,' said Murchú simply. He shrugged but she sensed shame beneath that apparent nonchalance. 'My father knows that following the trail is likely to start a war and that's something he won't risk. At the same time, the Elders refuse to let him approach *Clann Baoiscne* as they do not wish to lower themselves negotiating for passage through their territory.'

She thought that through. The *Uí Loinge* Elders' opposition to negotiation seemed unnecessarily heartless given the ramifications for their chieftain's daughter and the cruel fate they were condemning her to.

And yet Murchú was here. That could only mean one thing.

Murchú and his father intend to skirt the Elders' dictates.

'Should a *fian* such as *Na Cinéaltaí* enter *Clann Baoiscne* territory, a *fian* with no direct associations to any tribe …' Murchú lifted both hands, palms out in emphasis. 'Any connection to *Uí Loinge* can be easily denied and *Clann Baoiscne* sensitivities appeased.'

Liath Luachra nodded. It was clever thinking. 'Was this Bressal's plan?' It seemed the kind of sly, sideways manoeuvre he'd come up with.

Murchú shook his head. 'My plan,' he answered simply, the words devoid of any pride. 'There wasn't time to consult with my uncle.'

The woman warrior said nothing. She wasn't accustomed to offering compliments, nevertheless she was impressed by Murchú's inventiveness.

But then, he's never been a fool.

In fact, over the years she'd led *Na Cinéaltaí*, he'd been one of the few *fénnid* she could count on.

She sighed. At heart, she knew Murchú was an honourable man, nevertheless, extending her trust outside of *fian* activities wasn't something she had it in her to do.

'There's mutual benefit to be had here,' the *Uí Loinge* man pressed. 'The completion of this tasking would rebalance the relationship between *Uí Loinge* and *Na Cinéaltaí*. It would mend the frayed ties between both parties.'

Liath Luachra looked at the ground and nudged the ashes of the fire with the toe of her boot, scraping its stain across the hard, stone floor. She couldn't imagine a workable tie with *Uí Loinge*. Not while Bressal continued to hold a position of influence, at least.

She stood up abruptly.

'Finish your meal and warm yourself,' she said. 'I'll occupy myself with your mount.'

Murchú nodded gratefully, visibly relieved that she wasn't asking him to leave and return to face the cold.

'And the tasking?'

'My mind's too worn to offer an answer. You'll have to wait till morning.'

'Of course.' He nodded again.

'But don't hope for the answer you seek.'

She didn't wait to see his reaction to that parting comment but, as she left the cavern, she took time to grab a spare cloak, deliberately leaving her favourite behind. Moving the latter would have meant exposing the carved animals and, although she respected Murchú, that was a part of herself she had no intention of sharing.

Naturally, as soon as she stepped beyond the shelter of the passage walls, the wind seemed stronger and far colder than it had earlier. The horse had also moved since they'd gone inside. Fortunately, hobbled, it hadn't wandered far, and she soon found it behind the yew trees, seeking shelter from the wind.

Reassuring the animal with several long strokes to its flanks, Liath Luachra took a moment to look up, hoping to catch a glimpse of the owl but finding her view obstructed by the dense foliage. Shrugging, she undid the horse's binds and led it into the shelter of the rocky passage, hobbled it once more and then cut a few pieces of gorse for it to chew on as it settled.

Reluctant to return inside while Murchú was there, the woman warrior remained in the passage. The prospect of company in her winter cave left her unsettled and anxious and to recover her equilibrium, she fell back on her routine of standing at the cave mouth and looking towards the east. On the far side of the valley, the marshland was barely visible, its damp and spiralling tendrils merging comfortably with the vapours of the tumbling gloom.

A solitary hoot from the yew trees drew her gaze and she studied their mottled greens and browns with concern. In the silence of the valley, the bird's call had sounded unnaturally sad and forlorn and her stomach curdled as she recalled the tiny corpse at the bottom of the tree.

Not dead yet, then.

But only a matter of time.

She exhaled heavily.

And you're a fool to care.

A rattle of stone from behind alerted her to Murchú's approach. Appearing by her right side, the young *Uí Loinge* warrior sidled past to approach the horse. Leaning forward, he patted its rump with obvious affection.

'This is not my mount,' he confessed softly, as though revealing a great secret. 'It's my cousin's. A great beast and one he loves dearly but, knowing I'd need it to save my sister, he offered it without question when I asked.'

He turned his head to look directly at her. 'Cairenn is the name on her.'

Liath Luachra kept her silence, unsure whether he was talking about the horse or his sister and wondering why he would mention it in either case. Averting her eyes, she silently poked at the ground with the toe of her boot. She assumed the *Uí Loinge* man had joined her because her parting comment had alarmed him but she sometimes got such assumptions wrong. Feeling her way through a conversation was often as challenging as feeling her way through the forest at night.

Murchú pulled his cloak tight around his shoulders and moved to stand beside her at the cave mouth. He too peered out at the grey hills, the grey sky, the distant marsh, the descending haze.

'This is a bleak place, Grey One. Bleak and lonely and …' He paused. 'You know, if you agree to help me, I could negotiate the acquisition of better land from *Uí Loinge* territory if tha-.'

'I don't want your land, Murchú.'

The *Uí Loinge* man stiffened. He shifted his weight restlessly from one foot to the other. 'Then what *do* you want?'

She heard the growing desperation in his voice as the realisation hit him, that he'd most likely wasted his time coming to seek her help, time he could have spent in other ways to save his sister.

The reaction was a marked contrast to the assured tones of his uncle. Bressal Binnbéalach – Bressal of the Sweet Tongue – had also offered her *Uí Loinge* land once but there'd been a price to his generosity, of course. One she'd not been willing to pay. Murchú's goals, although far more altruistic, were undermined by his own honesty. In his place, Bressal would have known what to say or would have claimed to know, even if he hadn't. He'd have lied and bluffed, worked his conniving patter on instinct alone to obtain an angle or an edge of leverage to make her do his bidding. That obvious distinction between the two men suddenly made Murchú more dear to her.

'I want to be left alone.'

She recognised the irony of what she was saying, even as she said it. It was true that when she was with others she sought solitude. Nevertheless, when restricted to her own company for extended periods, that never seemed to work out so well either. Swinging wildly between reclusiveness and loneliness, there never seemed to be any alleviating balance.

'To live alone? To die alone?' The woman warrior couldn't tell if there was a trace of bitterness to his voice or not. 'That seems a singularly dismal existence, Grey One.'

'It's the existence I have, Murchú.'

Murchú averted his gaze but his eyes flickered back towards the cavern and she could tell he was recalling the chaos he'd seen there, registering it fully for the first time. Although he made no comment, an awkward silence followed that glance. Unintended though it was, the *Uí Loinge* man's embarrassment for her cut surprisingly deep.

'I thought you'd understand,' he blurted suddenly. 'Given your own history, I thought you of all people would understand my sister's plight.'

'Go back inside,' she told him sharply. 'You're fading on your feet and I need to check my trap line before nightfall.'

Hearing the hardness in her voice, Murchú made no response but it was obvious he was starting to regret his decision to seek her help. Disconcerted and visibly crestfallen, he started back in the direction he'd come from.

The woman warrior waited until he'd gone before she allowed her bitterness to spill through. What did Murchú expect of her! They weren't friends. Their sole connection was through the *fian* and any interaction beyond that was an imposition she'd never encouraged and one she certainly didn't welcome. Did he truly think she'd give up everything to try and save another woman just because …

Give up everything.

She cackled cynically at that.

Closing her eyes, she rested her head against the stone wall of the passage, felt the freezing firmness of stone, cold and hard against her cheek. With a growing bitterness, she recalled the day she'd stood at Céim na Macallaigh, the power of the howl she'd released on that occasion, the visceral sense of angry potential that had filled her heart as she'd vented her soul to the void. For a fleeting moment that afternoon, she'd truly felt as though she could take on the world, confront any threat or challenge that faced her. But, as always, such moments were fleeting, passing from her grasp before she knew it and, ultimately, fading from memory.

Another plaintive hoot sounded from the yews.

Liath Luachra suddenly straightened up and yanked her cloak close about her. Fists clenched, she stepped out of the passage and stalked determinedly downhill over the frosting ground, in the direction of the river.

***

Darkness had fallen when the Grey One finally returned, venting hard puffs of breath into the frigid air, her bounty tucked in the crease of her cloak. Nearing the cave, she swung left towards the yews, coming to a stop at the base of the tree with the *Ceann Cait's* nest. Ignoring the burn of the cold against her palms, she reached up to grasp the lower branches and started to climb.

Familiar with the position of the owl's nest from her previous visit, Liath Luachra scrambled up through the lower branches with ease, manoeuvring agilely between the heavier boughs until she was perched at a level adjacent to the bole hole. Approaching the owl's refuge, by the gleam of the moon she could see the *Ceann Cait* regard her anxiously, the two remaining chicks hiding sluggishly behind her.

The owl clacked its beak furiously, backing away as she reached her hand inside the woody cavity, Unmoved by the threat, she deposited part of her catch from the traps: five mice, five shrews and two legs from a hare, the greater part of which she'd retained for herself.

Drawing back from the bole hole, she shuffled onto a more secure perch to observe the bird's reaction. The owl's gaze switched from the little carcasses to the woman warrior and back, wariness competing with hunger as its round eyes snapped from one to the other. The two chicks however, demonstrated no such reserve. Slipping swiftly around their mother, they threw themselves onto her offering and started to gorge.

The *Ceann Cait* continued to regard her warily, refusing to drop its guard.

'The midwinter's passed,' Liath Luachra told the bird evenly. 'The cold's not done by any measure, but from today the days will lengthen. You have food and your little wood cave but from this moment on, your survival is up to you alone. There's no-one else to save you.'

With that, the woman warrior twisted about and started her descent.

Due to the cold and the dark, going down turned out to be more precarious than her initial climb but she quickly reached the ground safely. Shivering from the cold, she glanced up the trunk one last time but the upper branches were absorbed in shadow. There was nothing to be seen.

Retrieving the remains of the hare from the ground where she'd left it, she started towards the cave mouth. She couldn't tell if the *Ceann Cait* was watching her or not. She suspected it was otherwise occupied.

***

Murchú was asleep on some furs beside the fire when she entered the cavern. He wasn't particularly pleased to be woken when the Grey One sat on the log alongside him and poked him with a stick. Bleary-eyed and hazy, the *Uí Loinge* warrior stared up at her in confusion.

'I've made my decision,' she told him. 'I will help you find your sister.'

Chapter Two:

They rose at first light to make ready for their departure, Murchú blearily untangling himself from his blankets while Liath Luachra went outside to get a sense for the weather. A fresh smattering of snow had fallen overnight for the layers of white powder along the crests of the eastern hills were thicker than she recalled. Although the air was still, it was also bitterly cold and the sky was obscured by a grim layer of cloud. Flat and dreary and grey as slate, its broody aspect aligned perfectly with the bleak palette of the valley.

When Murchú emerged to occupy himself with the horse, Liath Luachra returned inside. It didn't take her long to gather what she needed but it took some effort to locate her wicker backpack amongst the other debris. She found it eventually, wedged between the wall and the stack of javelins and, dragging it out, she set it upright for filling.

There was little enough to place inside it. Having travelled from Briga, Murchú already had the essentials for cooking and camping. In terms of food supplies meanwhile, apart from the porridge and the hare meat – now wrapped in dock leaves – she had none to speak of.

In the end, she filled the backpack with a spare tunic and leggings, her sleeping roll and, of course, her faded red battle-harness. On top of that, she placed her little supply of food, an empty waterskin and the pouch that contained her fire-making kit. Sealing the cover tight with leather fastenings, she selected three javelins from the stack and slid them into the loops on the pack's outer surface. The missiles were a compact fit but she secured them more rigidly with leather ties so they couldn't shift about while she was moving.

Rising to her feet, the woman warrior strapped on the solid leather belt and scabbard that held her sword, *Gléas gan Ainm* – Tool without a Name. Once it sat comfortably on her hips, she wrapped her sling expertly around her left arm and knotted it firmly in place. A leather bag of shot went inside her tunic while her two knives were sheathed separately, one in her boot, the other – far smaller – in a separate sheath at the rear of her belt. Both knives were new, unblooded and therefore unnamed.

Pulling on her warmest cloak, she wrapped a woollen scarf around her neck and settled a pair of woollen hand wrappings into the inner pocket of the cloak. Glancing down at the fire, now little more than a low pile of ash and embers, she retrieved the water bucket and emptied its contents over the embers. Steam billowed up in a furious hiss but quickly dissipated.

Liath Luachra took one last look around the cavern, gauging her own reaction for any trace of regret, any hint of misgiving at her imminent departure.

There was nothing.

Emerging from the cave, the warrior woman found Murchú already mounted and waiting below the yew trees. Swaddled against the cold in his black cloak, he had the lower hem drawn up and held in place beneath his inner thighs. The sight of the *Uí Loinge* man poised so casually astride the animal took Liath Luachra by surprise. Too dazed to take note when he'd first arrived, she'd assumed Murchú had managed to make it to Luachair on horseback only through a combination of good fortune and determination. The restful pose and the relaxed manner in which the reins dangled loosely from his fingers however, suggested he was a more than competent horseman.

She was even more surprised when he reached down with one hand to help her mount. Looking from the hand to Murchú, then back at the hand again, she firmly shook her head.

'I'll run.'

'All the way to Briga?' He adjusted the folds of his cloak. 'That could cost us days. Days we don't have, Grey One.'

The woman warrior frowned and regarded the horse with a measure of distrust. She didn't know much about horses and had always viewed them with wary circumspection. They were beautiful creatures to look at and had their obvious uses but they were also skittish and could let you down when you needed them most.

And, of course, they were also rather high.

'I've not ridden a horse before.'

'It's not difficult,' the *Uí Loinge* man assured her. 'On certain terrains, riding a horse is far faster than running and we'll need to move at speed to have any chance of helping my sister. By the time we reach Briga, the *díberg* will already have ten days and more on us.'

He held out his hand once more.

This time, gritting her teeth, the woman warrior reluctantly grasped it and used the leverage to clamber up behind him. Seated on the horse's back, she was suddenly struck by the level of control she'd unintentionally surrendered. Powerless to control the animal on her own, she was dependent on Murchú's knowledge and skill to get them to Briga.

Mistaking the woman warrior's disquiet for fear, the *Uí Loinge* man attempted to bolster her by offering further instructions. 'Use your knees and legs to grip and keep your balance, Grey One. If you feel that you're falling, grab hold of me for support.'

Satisfied that this sage advice was sufficient to soothe her concerns, he nudged the horse's flanks with his heels. The animal shifted forwards with a jolt and the woman warrior hurriedly grabbed Murchú's waist with both hands to keep her balance.

'*Fóill ort!*' she said. Wait!

Murchú drew back on the reins and the horse came to an abrupt stop. Liath Luachra peered up at the yew tree, searching through the leaves and branches but, once again, the thick vegetation prevented her from seeing the owl or the bole hole. Murchú, meanwhile, had twisted around to see what was troubling her.

'Never mind,' she said. '*Ar aghaidh linn.*' Let's go.

Before he could react, a sudden hoot from the yew tree caused them both to look up. 'There's an owl up there!' the *Uí Loinge* man commented. He sounded surprised.

Liath Luachra shook her head sharply, marking her lack of desire to discuss the matter further. Shaking his head, Murchú nudged the horse's flanks with his heels once more and the animal took off at a canter.

At first, following the Grey One's advice, they rode south-east, eventually striking that section of dense forest where they were obliged to dismount and lead the horse. Later that morning however, the trees cleared sufficiently for them to ride once more.

To the Grey One's surprise, travelling on horseback turned out to be far more efficient than she'd anticipated. It was true that in such rough and forested terrain she'd probably have been able to surpass their current pace but she was realistic enough to recognise that she wouldn't have been able to sustain it. Travelling on foot, she'd eventually have tired and been obliged to stop and rest. With the horse however, even riding double or taking it in turns to run alongside it, the travellers could continue moving provided they didn't overstrain their mount. Travelling in this manner, slower though it was at times, actually allowed them to eat up the landscape at a steady rate and cover more ground than they would have on foot.

By mid-morning, the travellers had cleared the valley and covered a respectable distance beyond it. Towards noon, they halted at a peaceful riverbank beside a flat section of pasture and, while the horse rested and picked at the grass, consumed the last of the cold porridge. After wolfing it down, they foraged through the surrounding forest,

successfully gathering some young nettles, wild garlic and *arán glas* –
navelwort – to keep their hunger at bay until nightfall.

For the rest of the afternoon and into the early evening, they
continued south-east, leaving the mountains for the lowlands where the
terrain gradually levelled out. With Liath Luachra contributing little in
terms of conversation, Murchú passed the time by singing, crooning a
low song with an achingly melancholic air. The *Uí Loinge* man had an
impressive voice and the sad melody rang strong and true, even within
the confines of the trees.

Bored, the Grey One closed her eyes, lulled by the melody of
Murchú's song, the comforting warmth that radiated from his back and
the steady rhythm of the horse's trot. In a rare moment of drowsy
introspection, the woman warrior realised that she was completely
relaxed in both a physical and intellectual sense and would have been
content to remain in that moment of perfect harmony forever.

A sudden jolt as the horse cleared a low stream jerked her back to
reality. Roused from her stupor, the warrior woman realised, with a start,
that she'd drifted off and was slumped forward against the *Uí Loinge*
man's back. Pulling back sharply, the movement was enough to upset
her balance and slipping sideways, she grasped Murchú's waist with both
hands to prevent herself from tumbling off. Murchú pulled the horse to
a sudden stop and glanced back over his shoulder.

'What? What is it?'

Irritated at her own clumsiness, Liath Luachra shook her head
furiously.

Murchú sighed. Glancing up at the darkening sky, he then turned his
eyes down to regard the small wisps of water vapour drifting from the
horse's nostrils. 'It'll be dark soon,' he said at last. 'And there's a frost on
the air. We should find a place to make camp.'

They found a suitable campsite just inside the treeline of a small clearing
where an enormous rock protruded upwards through the forest canopy.
At the southern section of that solitary, granite mass, a low overhang
that faced the clearing offered an effective shelter against rain or snow.
The bitter cold however meant that they'd still need a fire to survive the
night.

While Murchú rummaged through the forest floor for dry firewood,
Liath Luachra busied herself constructing a rude fire-screen of
deadwood and brush, three paces out from the base of the overhang.
She did her best to ignore the stiffness in her thighs while she worked,
the inner muscles strained and aching from the unaccustomed action of

riding. By the time Murchú returned, arms full of fuel, she already had a fire started, the fire screen was completed and she'd settled back against the face of the overhang, working the blade of *Gléas gan Ainm* with a whetstone.

Having partaken of the Grey One's hospitality the previous evening, Murchú offered to prepare that evening's meal. Pleased that she didn't have to cook, the woman warrior sat back and watched as he prepared the food, appreciating his smooth competence as he deftly cut the hare meat into slices, wiped the metal pan with fat and adjusted its height above the fire to the level he desired. Tossing in the slices of meat, he flipped them repeatedly so that they fried evenly on each side. When they were browned to his satisfaction, he added the water cress, grassroots and a quantity of water, then sealed the lid of the pan.

Leaving the resulting stew to simmer, Murchú tended to the horse, accurately timing it so that when he'd finished, the stew was about ready to serve. Removing the lid, he lifted the steaming pot with the hem of his cloak and poured half of the contents into two wooden bowls. Carefully laying the pot aside, he handed one of the bowls to the woman warrior, then moved over to take a place alongside her. Both sat against the rock, warm from the heat of the fire reflected back against them by the Grey One's screen.

They ate in silence, preoccupied with their own thoughts. Despite the heat of the stew, Murchú scooped it into his mouth without thinking, as though directly fuelling the intensity of his preoccupation. Liath Luachra, for her part, just picked at her meal, her mind occupied with practical logistics as she worked through the journey ahead, mentally calculating the number of days it would take to reach the *Uí Loinge* stronghold and the supplies they'd need to get there. Despite their lack of food, she felt optimistic. The distance they'd covered on horseback had impressed her and she estimated that it would only take five days to reach Briga if they maintained their current pace.

But, as Murchú had already pointed out, that was another five days in which Murchú's sister remained a lone and terrified prisoner of the *díberg*.

'Tell me of your sister,' she said suddenly.

Murchú turned his head to look at her. 'Cairenn? What do you wish to know?'

'Why did the *díberg* take her? Most raiders would have had their fun then cut her throat and fled. Why didn't this *díberg* behave like that? They must have known there'd be a pursuit.'

A shadow passed over Murchú's face, as though the evening sun had abruptly moved behind the clouds. He held her eyes intently for several heartbeats. 'I don't seek to know their reasons,' he said sharply. 'I just seek to catch them.'

Liath Luachra returned his gaze without expression. She understood his resentment at the bluntness of her questions but she also needed to understand the detail of whatever she was getting involved in.

'Was …' She quickly corrected herself. 'Is there anything different about her? Anything distinctive?'

The *Uí Loinge* man mulled over that for a moment and the tension in his face eased a little. 'Only that she's a good person. She's gentle, well loved …'

'Has she had her red cycle?'

Startled by the question, Murchú stared at her. 'Yes,' he said at last. 'She's shared a dwelling with Cnes and I over the last year. In those cramped circumstances, naturally, their cycles aligned.'

Liath Luachra nodded.

Not that it would have made any difference.

The brutal thought slipped into her mind completely unbidden. Disturbed, she stared down at her feet. 'Is Cnes your woman?' she asked, more out of a desire to change the topic than out of any true interest.

'Yes.'

'And that is why you didn't accept Mical Strong Arm's offer of a winter's hospitality?'

Murchú finished the last dregs of his stew and laid the bowl aside. 'I accepted Mical Strong Arm's hospitality for five days. Then I chose to return to Briga. Unlike the other *fénnid*, I have familial and tribal responsibilities to uphold.' He reached out and absently tapped the side of the bowl with his fingertips.

'And then, of course, I also had to explain to the *Uí Loinge* elders why I hadn't taken leadership of *Na Cinéaltaí* from you.'

Liath Luachra stared deep into her bowl, studying the slivers of meat floating in the stew to avoid his eyes. Noting the tension in her shoulders, Murchú diplomatically moved the conversation to safer topics. 'But what of you, Grey One? After the rigours of the Lonely Lands, I thought it certain you'd winter with Mical Strong Arm and the *Uí Bairrche*. You were close friends with their *bandraoi*, were you not?'

The woman warrior's response was a noncommittal shrug but before she looked away, she caught the thoughtful expression in his eyes. Intuitively, she understood that he was thinking of her shambolic winter refuge, no doubt wondering at the rationale of her decision to winter there rather than in the comfort of Mical Strong Arm's residence.

'And Dubba,' he asked. 'You've heard the news of Dubba of Carna?'

Liath Luachra continued to stare into the cooling stew, stirring it absently with the tip of her forefinger. 'What news?'

He stared at her in surprise.

'The news that he's missing. Dubba ventured out from Carna to visit his mines – a normal practice by all accounts – but on this one occasion he never returned. They found his mount in the forest a few days later but without its rider. There's been no sighting of him since.'

'Perhaps he was swallowed by the Great Wild,' she answered sardonically.

Murchú made no response to that but, from the corner of her eye, she saw how he studied her. Whatever suspicions he harboured however, he decided not to voice them.

'At least, now, Grey One, you need not fear the blood price he placed on your head.'

Lifting her bowl, Liath Luachra swallowed down the last of the stew and wiped her lips with the back of her hand. 'We have an early start in the morning,' she said, putting an abrupt end to the conversation. 'And a full day's ride to follow. Let's settle for the night and dream of an easy route.'

That night however, instead of an easy route, Liath Luachra once again dreamed of her childhood in Luachair. On this occasion however, without the tempering effect of the *beacán scamallach*, those dreams steered to unpleasant corners and dead ends strewn with thorn and brambles.

The first indication of something awry was when her brothers called her by the name 'Liath Luachra', something that even in her dream state, she knew had never happened before. That simple irregularity marked a sudden but substantial shift in tone. One moment she was playing in the fields with her siblings, the next she was back alongside the standing stone, down on her knees, shackled and beaten beneath a sky of leaden grey. Writhing in agony from the lash marks across her back, her senses were further overwhelmed by the stench of burning and the high-pitched screams borne up on the westerly wind.

And the heavy tread of footsteps approaching from her rear.

Liath Luachra jerked awake, her heart pounding, mouth flooded with the metallic taste of terror as she fended off the chill friction of ghostly hands against her skin. Stumbling to her feet, she stared about in alarm before her surroundings congealed to familiar forms and she understood it had been a dream.

Doing her best to ignore the growing hollow in her chest, she mechanically added wood to the fire and stared into its rising flames, her mind still numb and blunted from the dream. Glancing to her side, she saw Murchú curled into a ball beneath his blankets, oblivious to the ghosts that circled their campsite.

There was no possibility of recovering her rest of course. Fortunately, dawn was a glowing smear on the eastern horizon so she wouldn't have to wait the night out. Pulling on her cloak, the warrior woman stumbled past the treeline, pushing deeper into the forest, penetrating the damp and dark interior until she reached a point where it was impossible to see, and she could no longer hold a coherent thought.

She wasn't sure how long she remained huddled in the forest's shadowed depths but, even there, the daylight eventually filtered through to rouse her self-awareness. Rising stiffly to her feet, she shook off the cramp and started back to camp. There, Murchú was already up and about, loading the horse and impatient to make a start. He seemed irritated at her impromptu disappearance but when he asked where she'd been her responses were monosyllabic and stunted. Knowing from previous interactions with the warrior woman that there'd be little chance of further reply, he ignored her and refocussed his energies on his own preparations.

A few moments later, mounted on his horse, he trotted over to where she was standing. When he reached his arm down, the woman warrior wordlessly took it and climbed up behind him. A moment later, they were once again headed south-east.

***

For the next three days, they travelled without incident, Murchú maintaining a restrained trot to avoid exhausting their mount, Liath Luachra alternating between riding double and running alongside the animal. By the third day, that exercise had worked the worst of the muscle pain from her inner thighs. By the fourth day, that discomfort was assuaged further by the sight of landmarks familiar to her from previous travels through the *Uí Loinge* tribal lands. On the fifth day, just before mid-day, all remaining discomfort was discounted when they crested the summit of a low hill and looked down on the settlement of Briga.

The *Uí Loinge* stronghold was an enormous *ráth*. Circular in shape, it consisted of an earth embankment topped with wooden palisades and surrounded by a deep ditch. Entry to the stronghold was through a single causeway and a stone gateway on its north-western face. Set on a stretch of flatland adjacent to a broad, slow-moving river, most of the land to the south and southwest had been cleared for cereal crops. With the long shadow of winter still clinging to the land however, that area was now occupied by livestock feeding on the vegetable residues.

A thriving settlement, Briga marked the central point of *Uí Loinge* influence, its tribal territory radiating outward in every direction for up to at least five days' travel, and in some places for more than that. Housing a resident population of fifty to sixty people, that number could swell dramatically when the surrounding families congregated for tribal gatherings and celebrations.

Slipping sideways off the horse, the Grey One landed softly on the hill's grassy summit, wincing at the pinch in her thighs. Staring down at the settlement, she considered the three plumes of smoke spiralling up from inside the embankment, the absence of wind causing them to rise in towering vertical columns before finally dissipating into the air.

Turning to glance up at Murchú, the woman warrior was struck by how worn he appeared as he stared stonily down at his homeplace. The physical strain of their rapid trek and concern for his sister had left its impact on his features. Nevertheless, beneath that bone-deep weariness, he exuded a tangible sense of relief that they'd finally made it home, that they could finally start the task of recovering Cairenn in earnest.

Sensing the Grey One's eyes on him, the *Uí Loinge* man turned to face her.

'The *díberg's* incursion prompted a summoning of the closest tribal Elders before I left. It's unlikely they'll all have made it to Briga as yet, but those that have will be settled in my father's dwelling.'

He turned back to cast a fresh glance at Briga and exhaled a plume of moist breath towards the settlement.

'Given your uneven history with *Uí Loinge*, we'll need the Elders' approval for *Na Cineáltaí* to fulfil the seeking. I'll request an immediate hearing once we get down.'

Liath Luachra chewed silently on her lower lip and looked down at the ground, poking a solid clump of sod with the toe of her boot. 'Murchú, my name is unwelcome in Briga. If their permission is truly required, perhaps I sh- '

'No,' he interrupted firmly. 'Their approval will be a formality. My father will ensure there is no opposition.'

'Bressal will oppose it.'

An awkward silence followed her words. Any mention of their old *rígfénnid* had been studiously avoided over the previous days of travel but, for Liath Luachra, the prospect of facing Bressal remained like a septic splinter beneath the skin. Although she'd feared attempting to address that inevitability, now that they were here in Briga, it was a reality she could no longer ignore.

Murchú sighed: a long, weary exhalation. 'Yes. It's true Bressal would most likely oppose the suggestion but his lands are far to the south-east. As the most distant tribal Elder, it's unlikely he received the summons.'

Relieved, Liath Luachra was almost able to smile at that. 'You didn't send him word,' she said.

'Let's just say, I know my uncle's … limitations. Besides, it would have made little sense. By the time he received the summons it would have been too late to respond.'

The *Uí Loinge* man paused then, as though reflecting on the process ahead. 'Would it offend you if I speak to the Elders alone? Bad blood still lingers from the loss of *Na Cinéaltaí* and the Elders have long memories your presence might rekindle.'

Liath Luachra looked at him then tossed a careless shrug from her left shoulder.

'Do as you think best, Murchú. They're your people.'

***

Descending the gentle slope to the *ráth*, the travellers approached the stone entrance at a trot. As they drew closer, two bearded sentinels on the ramparts above the gateway scrutinised their approach, javelins held loosely but ready to be cast at a moment's notice.

And probably several others close to hand.

As they approached the gateway however, the tension in the sentinels' shoulders eased perceptibly once they recognised Murchú. One of them even raised a hand in greeting. Their eyes lingered firmly on the warrior woman however and as they passed below, to enter the short passage into the *lis,* she felt the full weight of their hostile attention.

Within the settlement, that critical scrutiny continued but then, she'd expected that. A frequent visitor to Briga in the past with *Na Cinéaltaí,* her unique status as *éclann* and *banfénnid* – female *fénnid* – had always meant she'd provoked more interest than she'd desired. A conspicuous source of difference, the woman warrior had also been a source of curiosity and speculation and for the *Uí Loinge* men, she'd held a particular fascination. During her previous visits to Briga, they'd ceaselessly watched how she moved or held her weapons, debated the flatness of her chest and openly speculated at her performance beneath the blankets.

The female members of the tribe had also displayed a degree of curiosity although their interest had been far more proprietary. On occasion, they'd approach to take a closer look at her, mostly to assess her comeliness in terms of a potential competitor. Invariably, they'd leave, sniffing in disdain, their wagging tongues producing a flurry of rumour and unguarded derision.

The song that Bressal had commissioned: *Amhrán Liath Luachra* – The Song of Liath Luachra – had done much to garner her reputation as a vengeful killer and a woman with an insatiable sexual appetite. The dissolution of the *Uí Loinge fian* and her subsequent reassembly of *Na Cinéaltaí* had cemented that early notoriety even further. As a result, seeing her returned on the back of Murchú's horse, people now stopped to stare with open disapproval and several *Uí Loinge* women pointed outright, whispering unhappily behind raised palms.

'Pay them no heed,' growled Murchú, sensing her growing discomfort. 'I'll bring you to my residence where the other *fénnid* are gathered. Cnes will offer you hospitality while I seek an audience with the Elders.'

Liath Luachra made no response as she scanned the interior of the *ráth*. Broad and spacious, the *lis* comprised three individual clusters of roundhouses, each with their own firepit. One of those clusters included a rectangular longhouse markedly larger than the buildings surrounding it: the residence of Congal, *rí* of the *Uí Loinge* and Murchú's father.

Murchú diverted the horse towards the smallest cluster, a pair of roundhouses with a single lean-to situated close to the eastern embankment and separated from the nearest cluster by a distance of ten paces. As they drew closer, a pretty young woman emerged from one of the roundhouses and calmly stood watching their approach. Clad in a brightly coloured, chequered *léine,* her luxurious black hair was tied up in complex braids. She smiled up at Murchú as he pulled the horse to a stop.

'Safe home, husband.'

Her eyes flickered briefly to the woman warrior at his rear, evaluating her with brief, incisive interest before returning, once more, to Murchú. 'You found that which you were seeking?'

'I did.' Murchú slid easily from the horse and stepped aside to allow the Grey One space to dismount. 'This is Liath Luachra.'

This time the young woman turned to face the Grey One directly. 'I see you, Liath Luachra. A welcome to you at Briga.' She smiled again but her lips didn't curl fully at the corners and the Grey One detected a subtle stiffness to her stance.

'I see you, Cnes. I thank you for your welcome.'

While the women were speaking, Murchú brushed past to approach the empty firepit and stared at the cold ashes in dissatisfaction. 'What's this? No fire for our guests?'

'The internal fire is lit,' Cnes answered, gesturing back at the roundhouse from which she'd first emerged. 'As for our …' She hesitated. 'As for our guests, they are now warm and sleeping.' She raised one hand to indicate the second, smaller roundhouse. 'They were absent these past three days and made no return until dawn this morning.' She made no effort to disguise the reproach in her voice.

'And do you know of my father's whereabouts?'

'He's in his longhouse with Áed and three of the other Elders. It will please him to learn of your return.'

Murchú grunted and mulled over this update for a moment or two before turning to Liath Luachra. 'Rest yourself, Grey One. I'll go to update the Elders and seek permission to commence the Seeking. My cousin Mochta will pass by here soon with supplies.'

Preoccupied with internal deliberations, Murchú took the horse by the reins and started to lead it away in the direction of the longhouse at the far side of the *lis*. Once he'd departed, the two women considered each other in silence. Cnes gestured towards a pair of stools by the firepit. 'As an honoured guest, you should put yourself at ease,' she said. 'I'll fetch you something to eat and drink.'

Without further ado, she turned and entered the larger roundhouse.

Liath Luachra, left to her own devices, pulled her backpack close and settled onto one of the stools. She regarded the ashes in silence.

An honoured guest who warrants a cold seat by a dead fire.

It was a calculated insult of course, but the Grey One didn't really care. It suited her to avoid the effort of small talk, something she'd never been particularly skilled at. Making herself as comfortable as possible, she drew her cloak tighter, pulling her hands up into the heavy folds to avoid the chill. Sitting alone, she looked about the *lis*, observing the comings and goings of the *Uí Loinge* as they went about their daily business. One or two individuals stopped to stare at her but for the most part they ignored her.

Closing her eyes, the woman warrior imagined herself back in the forest, enveloped by the deep green where people seldom ventured. Just as her mind was starting to calm, those peaceful thoughts were scattered by the sound of unrestrained laughter. Her eyes snapped opened as two young girls with wild hair came careering around the side of one of the nearby roundhouses. Screeching in excitement like overtired seabirds, they surged towards her, stumbling to an unsteady halt when they realised she was stranger. Staring at her shyly, one of them, a pretty thing with scraggly bronze hair, smiled and waved and although Liath Luachra wanted to wave back … she couldn't.

A female voice, calling from somewhere beyond the other roundhouses, had the two girls scampering off again but whether they were running back towards that individual or away from her, the Grey One couldn't tell. A tepid smile tugged the corner of her lips but her good humour faded when two hard-looking *Uí Loinge* men appeared around the side of the neighbouring roundhouse cluster. She could tell immediately that they'd been informed of her presence for they halted to regard her with purpose and, once they saw that they had her attention, started mimicking a whole series of sexual movements, thrusting hips and simulated oral sex. Finally, tiring of her lack of response, they slapped each other on the back and started walking away.

The Grey One wordlessly watched them go, her jaw clenched as they wandered toward the roundhouses and out of sight.

'Now, there's a glare,' said a gruff voice to her rear, 'that would knock a bird from its perch. A glare that would carve calm through the wild waves of a stormy sea. A glare that would grind solid stone to powder.'

Liath Luachra turned to face the source of the voice: a solid pillar of a man with a long, unruly beard, a mass of curly brown hair and several white battle scars carved in parallel down the left side of his face.

'An Giobach,' she said calmly.

'Grey One.'

The big man stood before her, his great arms folded, the bulk of him blocking the slanted light of the late afternoon sun, his face a fearsome sight of mashed lips and missing teeth. 'Early start for the *fian* season,' he commented.

'Murchú had you fetched from Mical Strong Arm's then?' she asked.

'He did. Feirgil and I arrived some days back. Biotóg was already here. Murchú was off fetching you, of course.'

She kicked the second stool towards him.' Sit,' she said. 'You strain my neck making me look up at you.'

With a grunt, he took his seat, the bulk of him barely fitting on the wooden seat's circular upper surface and making it look childishly small beneath him. Pulling a sliver of smoked meat out from inside his tunic, he bit off a chunk and chewed as he regarded her.

'You're content to accept this tasking so early in the year?'

An Giobach's laughter was open and loud.

'It was time. I was wearying of the unaccustomed luxury, of doing nothing but grow soft and fat at Mical Strong Arm's expense.' He patted his stomach although Liath Luachra could see no signs of a paunch. 'Besides, it's Murchú's sister' he added, the tone of his voice suggesting that this had been the critical factor in his decision.

The *fénnid* jerked his head towards the smaller roundhouse. 'Biotóg and Feirgil are snoring in there but they hold similar views.' He turned her a curious look then, his bushy eyebrows curving down to overshadow his eyes. 'It's pleasing to see you here, Grey One. I didn't believe you'd come.'

Liath Luachra looked away, directing her gaze to the gateway, to the roundhouse clusters, to Congal's hall, anywhere to avoid the big *fénnid's* eyes.

'Murchú's woman said you were absent these past three days.'

'Cnes? She has a sour tongue but I suppose we were a little loud on our return.' He sniggered briefly, amused by some personal joke. 'We'd travelled south to the site where Murchú's sister was taken. I felt it wise to mark any tracks I could find so as to be ready when you and Murchú returned.'

'And did you find any?'

He shook his head. 'Not many. There's been a fine harvest of rain these past few days. We did find their campsite: traces of a fire, sign of between three and five people although my gut tells me there were four. We followed the trail as best we could for the better part of the day. Murchú had the right of it. They were headed south-east for *Clann Baoiscne* territory.'

Liath Luachra mulled over the big man's assessment. 'Do you have relations with *Clann Baoiscne*?'

An Giobach shook his head. 'None that I know of. Although I've heard rumours enough about them, including one that their chieftain, Tréanmór, speaks to The Dead.'

Liath Luachra pulled back a little at that. 'Truly?'

He shrugged. 'If it is, I suspect we'll find that out for ourselves.' He paused, then tugged thoughtfully on the end of his beard with his left hand. 'Feirgil has relations with *Clann Baoiscne*. His father's sister lives with a *Clann Baoiscne* man.'

Liath Luachra rolled her eyes in displeasure. Trying to draw information from Feirgil was like trying to draw milk from a tree, a surreal, challenging and ultimately dissatisfactory experience. 'May as well ask the clouds,' she muttered.

An Giobach snorted at that. 'When do we leave?' he asked.

'Have you finished eating?'

An Giobach stared at her, unsure whether she was being serious or not.

'The *diberg* already have more than ten days lead on us,' she explained.

The *fénnid* looked at the well-gnawed morsel of meat in his hand then abruptly tossed it aside. 'Well, yes then.'

She sniffed and rubbed her nose. 'We leave as soon as Murchú returns, presuming he's obtained the Elder's approval of course.'

The big man nodded and from the absence of questions she surmised that he understood the practical and political ramifications. 'Very well,' he said. 'I'll rouse the others. They'll be ready once I've revived them with a few kicks to the arse.'

Chuckling, the big man got to his feet and started back towards the roundhouse.

The Grey One remained on her stool for a time, drawing her cloak tighter against the cold as she continued to regard the activity within the *lis*, the *Uí Loinge* coming and going and carrying out their routine chores. Murchú's sister would probably have sat in this very same spot on occasion, she realised. Carrying out her own activities, dreaming of … whatever girls her age dreamed of.

The woman warrior paused, struck by the realisation she no longer remembered what girls that age dreamed of.

Why did they take her?

The question slid back into her head, the same question that had been troubling her since leaving Luachair. She struggled to understand why the *diberg* would have kidnapped a single young woman in that manner, particularly when they seemed intent on travelling some distance on the tail-end of winter. It bothered her when she didn't understand something.

Could they have taken her to use or sell as a slave?

For a single girl in hostile territory that struck her as an onerous burden. Perhaps their leader had simply taken a fancy to her.

Like Garrad Mór and Gadra took a fancy to you.

Rattled now by where her thoughts were taking her, the woman warrior rose to her feet and looked towards the second roundhouse that Murchú shared with Cnes. Cairenn had spent some time living with them. Perhaps there was something she could learn there.

Moving towards the little building, she paused briefly outside the doorway and coughed loudly in warning before lifting the leather flap and stepping inside.

Murchú's home was compact but comfortable and pleasantly warm from the heat of a small fire crackling in a pit by the eastern wall. Circular in form, one section of the interior had been partitioned off with a screen constructed from sections of cow skin stretched across a rectangular wooden frame. Through gaps in the skins, Liath Luachra caught snatches of a wide sleeping platform covered in furs and blankets.

Cnes was standing by a low wooden table in the centre of the dwelling, her expression sober as she cut chunks of dry tuber onto a tray that also held a goblet and a clay pitcher. As Liath Luachra entered, the *Uí Loinge* woman looked up, her eyes going hard as she recognised the woman warrior. Liath Luachra was momentarily taken aback by the unadulterated hostility she saw in that gaze.

This woman despises me.

'I want to see where Cairenn slept,' she said bluntly. There seemed little point in maintaining the pretence of cordiality now that Cnes' antipathy was out in the open.

The other woman looked at her coldly and, for a moment, the Grey One didn't think she'd respond. Then, she abruptly jerked her head towards another low sleeping platform at the base of the wall opposite the entrance.

Skirting the table and the irate *Uí Loinge* woman, the Grey One approached the sleeping platform and crouched to examine the flat surface of the bedding: a single wool blanket and a covering made up of several hare skins cleverly stitched together in a patchwork pattern. Rummaging through the bedclothes and the reed mattress, she found nothing of relevance. Chewing on the inside of her cheek, she turned her attention instead to a small wooden chest at the end of the platform where Cairenn presumably kept her things.

Opening the little chest, the woman warrior carefully delved through the girl's few belongings: a favourite grey *léine* that had been carefully and painstakingly folded, a bone comb, a string necklace of small shells, some dried flowers, coloured stones and ...

Buaircíní Bó!

Reaching deeper into the box, Liath Luachra pulled out the two objects that had caught her eye: a pair of large pine cones. Each had four small slivers of wood slotted into the horizontal base as legs, another smaller one on the upper side holding a small wooden knob in place to represent the head.

Buaircíní Bó. Cone cows.

She held the toys in her hand, looking at them and wondering why the girl might have kept them before deciding that they probably held some emotional attachment. She too had owned a similar toy when she was very young, one of the few presents her father had ever given her – and, in hindsight, had probably manufactured – before the darkness and the dream mushroom took his mind.

She frowned, again discomforted by the direction in which her thoughts were taking her. The subtle pattern of Cairenn's story now overlapped enough with her own to prompt that recurring constriction in her chest, the growing burn from the scars on her back.

Think of the girl. Think of the tasking.

Breathing deeply, she focussed on the sleeping platform.

It was perhaps good fortune that Murchú chose that moment to return, his arrival announced by the angry slap of the doorway's leather flap being brushed aside. Both women looked up in surprise as he entered and, in Liath Luachra's case, with some relief. The *Uí Loinge* man was far earlier than she'd expected but all the more welcome for the distraction he provided.

Of the two women, Murchú's eye first sought out Liath Luachra. 'We have the Elders' consent,' he announced. But there was something in the hesitant manner in which he said it that put her on edge.

'Tell me.'

Grabbing the pitcher, Murchú poured some water into the goblet and swallowed it down before he answered.

'It was a difficult gathering. My father and I had to tread a precarious path through tribal divisions and the Elders' self-interest. But, we succeeded. We not only obtained approval for *Na Cinéaltaí* to undertake the Seeking but negotiated a substantial reward to boot: ten dairy cows, a two-week supply of food and the choice of a new weapon from the *Uí Loinge* smith for every *fénnid* on their return.

Liath Luachra regarded him but said nothing. The other *fénnid* would be pleased of course but, as *rígfénnid,* it was her place to negotiate the elements of any tasking price. Murchú and his father had overstepped themselves, despite the fact that the reward being offered was far in excess of anything she was ever likely to have received.

Or dared ask for.

'What is it, Murchú? What are you not saying?'

Murchú shifted uncomfortably. 'Uargas Longfoot was present.'

Liath Luachra felt her heart sink.

Uargas Longfoot.

A confidante of Bressal and one of his strongest supporters, she'd seen the two of them huddled together on many occasions, their conspiratorial discussions broken only by the occasional bellow of raucous, drunken laughter. If Uargas had been present at the Elders' gathering, he'd almost certainly have been defending Bressal's interests given that they aligned so closely to his own.

'Uargas informed the Elders that Bressal has called for a *slogadh* – a hosting – for warriors to join a new *Uí Loinge fian*. Apparently, the candidates are due to be selected at Poll an Iubhair. He also argued that it was more appropriate for an *Uí Loinge fian* to fulfil this Seeking than a rag-tag group of *éclann.*'

Liath Luachra snorted. 'Any new *fian* Bressal establishes will be untried. They'll not function well together.'

'Yes, and that's the very argument we used to counter Uargas' proposal. Nevertheless, his words rallied the support of the other Elders, particularly with his claim that you'd done Bressal – and, through him, *Uí Loinge* – wrong by causing him to lose face when he lost *Na Cinéaltaí.*' He paused, briefly averting his eyes.

'For that reason, the Elders have imposed a condition on *Na Cinéaltaí* if they obtain the tasking.'

The woman warrior felt a harsh flutter inside her chest. 'What condition?'

'The Elders demand that you must travel to Poll an Iubhair. Fortunately, Bressal's settlement is close to *Clann Baoiscne* territory so it's not too far out of the way.'

'It's proximity to *Clann Baoiscne* means little to me. Why must I travel to Poll an Iubhair?'

Murchú hesitated but apparently there was no way to soften the blow for he came straight out with it. 'So that you can seek out of Bressal Binnbhéalach and ask his consent for the tasking. Only then will *Na Cinéaltaí's* right to the tasking be recognised.'

She looked at the *Uí Loinge* man, her face hard as stone. 'Murchú, you ask too much.'

From his strained expression, she could tell Murchú had no doubt of it.

'I'm not asking you to accept this condition, Grey One. I'm begging you. For my sister's sake. Accept the condition, lead the *fian* and you have my father's word – and mine – that your sacrifice will not go unheeded. Before meeting Bressal, we can seek some adept solution to the problem.'

Liath Luachra's stomach roiled with a congealed mixture of nausea and disgust but she felt her eyes tugged over to Cairenn's bed and the two *Buaircíní Bó* atop it.

'I will consider the Elders' condition,' she said at last.

'Murchú!'

Both turned to look at Cnes, her resentment at her exclusion from the exchange evident from the flaring of her nostrils.

'Do you truly intend to pursue this *díberg*?'

'Of course.' Murchú looked at her as though she had lost her senses. 'They have Cairenn.'

'With the Grey One as *rígfénnid*?'

'Yes.'

'Do you not believe such action reckless?'

'What?' He looked at her in bewilderment. 'What do you mean?'

'Could it not be more obvious?' The other woman's voice grew huskier, warmed by the heat in her words. 'Everyone knows you sniff the Grey One's musk like a hound in heat. Even here in Briga, your own people mock you behind your back.'

'Then they are wise,' Murchú responded coldly. 'For were they to convey such accusations to my face, there'd be swift and bloody resolution.' He inhaled deeply, struggling to contain his anger. 'There's no truth behind whatever whispers you're hearing, Cnes. My efforts in this Seeking are for Cairenn alone but for it to succeed I have need of the Grey One.'

The *Uí Loinge* woman was not convinced.

'Your interaction with the *éclann* diminishes your standing, husband. It puts your future leadership of the tribe in jeopardy. And it dishonours me.'

'How does this Seeking dishonour you?' This time there was a dangerous edge to the *Uí Loinge* man's voice, an edge the Grey One had never heard before.

'Because I know you'd slap buttock skin with that filth-stained *éclann*. Our bonding was made to cement the relationship between our families and the *Uí Loinge* dynasty. That should be your immediate priority.'

'So, you would leave Cairenn to her fate?'

'Much as I love her, if the alternative was to threaten our familial line, then, yes. Yes, I would.'

Murchú regarded her in shock. 'Then, I'd not understood the true price of your affection.'

There was a harsh silence as the pair regarded one another. Liath Luachra looked from one to the other, heartily wishing she was somewhere else, anywhere else.

That silence was abruptly punctured by the high whinny of a horse from outside the building. Murchú glanced to the doorway then back at his woman. He took a deep breath before speaking.

'That'll be Mochta with his horses and supplies. We'll be departing Briga on the instant to rescue my sister. Should you wish further words with me, they can be shared on my return.'

Without another word, the *Uí Loinge* man departed the roundhouse.

In the ensuing silence, the two women eyed each other until Liath Luachra turned to retrieve her cloak and leave.

'*Nach tusa an mealltóir, mar sin?*' snarled Cnes, the bitterness tainting her voice. '*An maighdean meallacach.*' Aren't you the temptress, then? The beguiling maiden.

Standing with the cloak in her hand, Liath Luachra regarded her coldly. 'I don't h-'

Cnes spat in her face.

Caught completely off guard, the woman warrior took an unconscious step back, wiping the smear of spittle from her face as she struggled to control the combat fury coiling up inside her, resisting the instinct to retaliate with violence.

'Know this, Grey One. When you're out there in the wilderness, whatever occurs between you and Murchú will make no difference. On his return to Briga, Murchú will fulfil his duty and cast you aside to deliver the progeny our tribe demands.'

Advancing on the warrior woman, she pushed her face aggressively close and gestured at the bed beyond the cow-skin screen. 'When you're back out in the wilderness, rutting in the dirt with your other *fénnid* savages, know that he'll be writhing beneath me on that fur-lined mattress, thrashing in pleasure like a landed fish as he sows his seed within me.'

Without warning, she suddenly reached over to the table, grabbed the clay pitcher and cast its contents directly into the Grey One's crotch.

Startled, the woman warrior stumbled backwards, ineffectually trying to brush the cold liquid from the sodden cloth around her groin, while fighting the urge to attack and obliterate the *Uí Loinge* woman.

Cnes glared at her brazenly, sensing the woman warrior's inherent hunger for violence and daring her to give into it.

Despite the fury clouding the space behind her eyes, the Grey One somehow managed to keep her rage in check. Cnes was intentionally goading her, provoking her so that she'd attack, no doubt intending to use the excuse of physical assault of an *Uí Loinge* member – of the *tánaiste's* woman – to foil any chance of the Seeking proceeding.

Puffing out her cheeks, Liath Luachra exhaled softly then turned and started for the doorway.

Plans thwarted by the Grey One's control, the frustrated Cnes resorted to one final insult.

'You'll die alone in the forest, Grey One. For all the pull of your disease-ridden arse, you'll die alone and forgotten.'

At the doorway, where she'd just raised the flap to leave, Liath Luachra stiffened. Turning her head to look back at the furious *Uí Loinge* woman, her eyes were flat and lethally cold.

'If you truly intend to reap *Uí Loinge* seed on that mattress Cnes, try at least to make pleasure for Murchú. It's the least he deserves, fucking the sagging, flea-riddled crotch you offer.'

Without another word, she stepped through the doorway.

Chapter Three:

They left Briga in the mid-afternoon, following the trail south in the direction of Poll an Iubhair. Although the route was rugged, weaving a circuitous path through steeply undulating forest, regular passage and interaction between the two settlements meant its established contours had long been ground into the landscape. As a result, it was an undemanding trail to follow and, with Mochta's horses – a strong roan and a bay – to carry the supplies, *Na Cinéaltaí* travelled at a rapid clip.

Leading the *fénnid* from the front, Liath Luachra was conscious the *díberg* would not have had the luxury of such a well-established trail. Knowing this route was well-travelled by the *Uí Loinge*, the raiders would have avoided it and found a separate one further off in the forests to either side – a safer but far slower path. That, of course, meant the *fian* were moving much faster than the raiders when they'd passed through this same terrain. After so many frustrating delays, there was a visceral satisfaction from knowing they were finally closing the distance between themselves and the *díberg,* and that the pursuit had begun in earnest.

Liath Luachra set a relentless pace for the remainder of the afternoon, relieved to lose herself in the physical action of running, for it allowed her to avoid reflecting on Briga. The abuse from Cnes had been humiliating and especially harrowing as it had come from another woman. Fortunately, returning to the wilderness offered a liberating sense of being absorbed into something far greater than herself, something that dismissed the petty associations of the human world. As a result, although traces of rage continued to smoulder deep down inside her, the altercation with Cnes now seemed reduced and very far to her rear. With a clear tasking to hold her focus, she finally felt unburdened and completely free.

Despite their growing fatigue, the woman warrior kept the *fian* at that same unyielding, driven not only by a desire to further reduce the raiders' lead but by the more pressing need to reach Loch na nEasa before nightfall. A well-known resting place between Briga and Poll an Iubhair, although she'd not been there herself, she'd heard it said that Loch na nEasa was an area of immense beauty and one that offered all the amenities for a comfortable camp: fresh water from the lake, a teeming supply of trout, abundant shelter and, of course, a copious supply of firewood.

Daylight was waning when *Na Cinéaltaí* finally emerged from the trees onto a stretch of rocky shingle that ran the length of what looked like a sheltered inlet. As they followed the curve of it around a thick stand of ash, a broad body of water opened out before them and the woman warrior knew they'd reached their destination.

Loch na nEasa – Lake of the Waterfalls.

Wheezing raggedly, Liath Luachra sank to her knees on the gritty sand at the water's edge, drinking in the spectacular view as she and the other *fénnid* fought to recover their breath. The lake was broad and flat, its dark waters reflecting the mountain range at its northern shore. Several tiny islands, puffed with vegetation, seemed to float on the water directly offshore. East of those islands, the lake curved around a high outcrop crowned with ash trees, where it abruptly disappeared from view.

It didn't take them long to find the area commonly used by *Uí Loinge* travellers. A flat section of ground little more than a hundred paces east of where they'd struck the gritty strand, it was well marked by the remains of several campfires under the oak trees at the water's edge. Keen to explore the lake a little further, Liath Luachra left the others to set camp while she followed the shore to the base of the outcrop. Clambering up its steep western slope, she crested the summit to discover an even greater body of water on the other side, its distant north-eastern shore barely visible in the hazy pre-gloom of dusk. This section of the lake also held a number of islets but they were far smaller than those on the western side, coating the oil-black liquid like a sprinkling of green jewels.

Three to four hundred paces from the base of the outcrop, the land flattened abruptly at a small clearing, sandwiched between the water and a dense stretch of oak forest. Another three hundred paces further on, the ground rose sharply again, framing the lake with a long curve of high cliffs. Atop those cliffs she spotted the source of the lake's name: three separate jets of water streamed out over the precipice, tumbling down the granite face to strike the water at its base.

Descending the eastern slope, Liath Luachra crossed the greater part of the flat, pausing every now and again to look towards the falls, drawn by the tumbling movement of the water and the clouds of vapour below. Following the shoreline, she reached the edge of the grassy clearing adjacent to the closest cataract. There, stripping out of her clothes, she unbraided her dark hair and let it spill onto her bare shoulders.

Stepping into the shallows, she felt the water lap cold and light above her ankles but ignored the icy bite as she pushed forward into the spray. Although quickly drenched, she was surprised to find that the force of the falling water wasn't as intense as she'd expected, the height and limited volume resulting in a deluge that was more mist than liquid by the time it hit the lake.

All the same, that icy wetness was too cold to endure for long. Scurrying out of the spray, the woman warrior quickly retraced her steps as goosebumps broke out on her skin. Back on the grassy shore, her hands numb from the cold, it took several attempts to tug on her leggings for the material clung to the wet patches of her skin. Finally, hauling them up over her hips, she hastily gathered her other belongings and retreated further along the shore to avoid the watery mist blown towards her by the rising breeze.

On the green flat in front of the forest, the woman warrior paused to draw her cloak around her, shoulders trembling as she absorbed the beauty of the lake. Staring out at the distant islets, she couldn't help wondering if she'd be able to swim out to them, even as her teeth chattered from the cold.

Foolish.

Dismissing that fantasy, the woman warrior transferred her attention to a trio of distant swans visible towards the eastern edge of the lake, midway between the falls and the last of the islets. Drifting languorously on the still surface, the birds were reflected in flawless mirror images. Entranced, she watched as they suddenly took to the air, the sound of their flapping wings clear and distinct across the still water. Rising, the birds circled gracefully around to the south, slid over the trees and disappeared.

The sudden sound of a snapped twig from the woods to her rear yanked the woman warrior from that silent contemplation. Whipping around on one heel, she dropped everything except *Gléas gan Ainm,* wrenching the weapon sharply from its scabbard before discarding that as well. Advancing at a crouch, she hurried forward into the trees, penetrating several paces past the outer treeline before dropping low in the shadows of the lofty oaks.

For several moments she listened intently, hearing nothing but the creak of boughs shifting stiffly in the breeze and birdsong that, to her ears, sounded unusually restrained. That there was a human presence somewhere within the trees, she had no doubt. The subdued nature of the forest told her as much and she knew it took a substantial weight to snap a twig as loudly as the one she'd just heard. Out in the Great Wild, even the larger animals weren't that careless.

Sure enough, it wasn't long before she heard the distinctive rustle of someone pushing their way through the undergrowth, the crackle of vegetation being roughly brushed aside growing steadily louder as the source of the noise closed in on her position. Spotting a sliver of movement in the shadows ahead, she rose to a crouch, adjusting her stance so that she could thrust the blade of her weapon forward at chest height. Moments later, the vegetation in front of her shook violently and as she prepared to lunge, the bushes parted and a bedraggled, bearded figure stumbled out.

'Grey One!'

Liath Luachra took a frantic step backwards to break the momentum of her attack. Shuddering with the sudden release of tension, she slowly lowered her sword.

'Feirgil.'

The wiry, surprisingly slight, warrior stood grinning at her, calmly rolling backwards and forwards on the balls of his feet, hands clasped behind his back as though he was out for an evening stroll.

'What …?' she began but found herself suddenly distracted by a disconcerting gap in the *fennid's* front teeth that, to her recall, hadn't been there that morning. Frowning, she tried again. 'What are you doing skulking about in the woods?'

Feirgil raised one hand to brush a tangle of black curls from his forehead.

'I was seeking you out.'

She squinted at him. 'Why?'

Feirgil's eyes glazed as his focus turned inward, seeking the answer to that question. A moment passed and, failing to find a suitable response, he raised both hands in an expression of complete helplessness.

Liath Luachra inhaled deeply, struggling to repress her growing frustration. Feirgil had his occasional periods of lucidity but it was at times like this she regretted her decision to accept him into *Na Cinéaltaí*. The eccentric *fénnid* was competent in a fight but she'd chosen him above the other candidates primarily because of his reputed *ríastraid* ability – that supernatural combat frenzy that rendered raw battlers impervious to fear, pain or reason. During the recruitment process for new *fénnid*, she'd been convinced of the benefits of such a resource in times of desperate circumstance. At the time, in her mind, that had outweighed his obvious peculiarities but now she wasn't so sure. Over the two years he'd spent with *Na Cinéaltaí*, Feirgil had displayed no ability to control, or even trigger, his supposed talent. That failure, on top of his erratic behaviour and inability to follow her commands, meant that she increasingly thought of him as a liability.

'Did someone send you to fetch me?' she suggested.

The warrior brightened at that. 'Yes! An Giobach sent me to fetch you.'

Liath Luachra waited but he just continued to stand there, beaming that insane grin at her. 'And ...' she prompted.

'Yes,' he repeated, his enthusiasm undiminished.

The woman warrior exhaled heavily, tempted to give up and walk away. She decided to try one last time.

'Did he give you a message for me?'

'He did.'

'So, what was it?' she snapped.

'I have no idea,' the warrior admitted. With that, he rolled his head back and brayed with laughter.

Startled by the raucous outburst, Liath Luachra took a hurried step back. She'd heard all the stories about individuals with the *ríastraid,* how they could, abruptly and unexpectedly, explode in a maelstrom of insane violence. If Feirgil's talent was about to kick in, she didn't want to be anywhere nearby.

Fortunately, the moment passed. Liath Luachra cursed herself for a fool as Feirgil's laughter subsided and he, once again, stood grinning gormlessly at her.

Turning on her heel, the woman warrior started back through the trees in the direction of the lake. Feirgil, his laughter subsiding, trailed acquiescently behind her. It was probably An Giobach, she decided sourly. Over the previous *fian* season, the big *fénnid* had grown increasingly fond of dispatching Feirgil to convey whatever non-urgent message he had to communicate, greatly amused by how much it irritated her.

Returning to where she'd dropped her belongings, Liath Luachra sheathed her weapon and strapped the belt loosely around her hips. Divesting herself of the cloak, she bent down to retrieve her tunic. When she rose again, Feirgil had moved in alongside her and was peering fixedly at her chest.

The woman warrior flicked him a warning glare although, in truth, the *fénnid's* behaviour didn't overly concern her. Over the two years they'd fought alongside each other, he'd displayed all the sexual curiosity of a six-year old child, another of the reasons she'd put up with him.

'Where are your breasts, Grey One?'.

'In a bag,' she answered crossly. A permanent point of discussion and interest as a result of the exaggerations in Bressal's *Amhrán Liath Luachra,* the woman warrior had little patience for any discussion related to the size of her breasts. 'They're hidden under a stone in Luachair. Why? Where's your *bod?*'

Perplexed, Feirgil raised his eyes to look at her. 'In my leggings, of course.' His forehead creased into deep, horizonal furrows. 'It's always in my leggings. If it wasn't, I wouldn't be able to piss.'

He laughed uncertainly then shook his head at the outlandishness of the query. 'You're addled, Grey One.'

Ignoring him, the Grey One pulled on her tunic. Her upper body was still wet and the light material stuck to her chest but the moisture did nothing to lessen the strong whiff of stale sweat. After bathing, she generally preferred to change into a fresh tunic and leggings but, given they were going to be running for several days, there seemed little point in ruining her only other set of clothes.

Wrapping her cloak about herself, the woman warrior regarded Feirgil with muted disapproval.

'Let's get back to the others,' she said.

***

The *fénnid* had set camp beneath two enormous pines on the lake's southern shore. Standing close alongside each other, the trees' branches had twisted and intertwined, merging to form a broad, sinuously distorted awning above the ancient stone firepits that looked impervious to the rain now tumbling from the darkened sky.

A cooking fire had been set in one of the firepits and, kneeling beside it, Biotóg had laid out a selection of the Briga supplies: small baskets of tubers, griddlebread, smoked meat preserved in lard and wrapped in leaves. In a metal pot above the flames, one of the pre-prepared stews was coming to the boil and its wonderful meaty flavour seeped out from beneath the lid. Drawn by the smell, the *fénnid* had gathered around, salivating in anticipation.

An Giobach looked up as Liath Luachra approached, unable to disguise the grin on his face. Responding with a scowl, she took a seat on the ground, doing her best to maintain her habitual distance from the other *fénnid* while also keeping as close to the fire as she dared. Her hair was still wet from the soaking at the falls and she was keen to get it dry. It was going to be a cold night and the last thing she needed was a damp head drawing the heat from her while she slept.

When Biotóg decided the stew was ready, he doled it out in wooden bowls, accompanied by a slab of griddlebread. Ravenous, each of the warriors grabbed their containers and tore into the meal with gusto, washing it down with fresh water from the lake.

As always, the woman warrior ate brusquely, perfunctorily scooping fingerfuls of the stew from the bowl and into her mouth. When the container was half-empty, she looked up to wipe her mouth with the back of her hand and noticed that most of the others had already finished their first serving. Exhausted from the day's exertion, they stared blearily into their bowls, considering the contents like a *draoi* staring into an animal's innards during a particularly complex augury.

Her eyes fell on a cluster of pine cones lying in the dust beneath the trees, a momentary reminder of the *Buaircíní Bó* she'd found by Cairenn's bed in Briga. Twisting her head warily, she glanced over at Murchú who sat with the others, quietly supping from a leather waterskin.

He worries for his sister.

Thinking of the abducted *Uí Loinge* girl, Liath Luachra could feel her facial features settle into a frown. Up to the moment she'd discovered the *Buaircíní Bó*, her commitment to the Seeking had been driven more out of her own desperation to avoid Luachair and the possible consequences of remaining than out of any true empathy for the kidnapped girl. The discovery of those childhood toys however had established a sympathetic connection she hadn't expected. Now, as a consequence, Cairenn was far more than just a name or the object of a tasking and the ramifications of failure were very much more real.

When he'd finished caring for his horses, Mochta came to join them by the fire. Accepting a serving from Biotóg, he moved to take a seat on the ground close to Liath Luachra, uncomfortably close from the woman warrior's perspective. He glanced at her as he plucked a morsel of meat from the bowl and slid it into his mouth, chewing in appreciation as he swallowed it down.

The woman warrior observed him from the corner of her eye, recognising some of the familial traits he shared with his cousin: the tangle of ragged, brown hair, the blue eyes and high cheekbones emphasised by a day's growth of facial hair. In physique however the two cousins differed. Mochta, less of a fighting man, was more slender and didn't have the compact musculature and broad shoulders his cousin had developed over his years with the *fian*.

'This is good,' he grunted suddenly, nodding his head at the bowl for Liath Luachra's benefit. She shifted her gaze a little to the left, avoiding his eyes as she focussed on her own meal. Unperturbed by the lack of response, the *Uí Loinge* man made a second attempt to engage her.

'Can I ask you a question, Grey One?'

She didn't look up until she'd cleaned the bowl and had licked the last drop of grease from her fingers. When she did deign to consider him, her features were creased in an undisguised frown.

Murchú, noting the potential for conflict, took the initiative of sidling over from his own position and placing himself on the ground between them to deflect his cousin's interest. 'Ask me', he suggested.

Mochta looked at him in surprise, glanced over at Liath Luachra who seemed fascinated by some object in the bottom of her empty bowl, then shrugged indifferently. 'Why didn't we commence the Seeking at the spot where Cairenn was taken? Wouldn't it have made more sense to follow the *díberg* tracks from there?'

Murchú supped from the waterskin he was carrying and replaced the stopper before giving his answer.

'My father and I had already searched that area before I left for Luachair. While I was returning with the Grey One, An Giobach and the others combed that same piece of ground and came to a similar conclusion: the *díberg* was headed south-east, towards *Clann Baoiscne* territory.'

Briefly shaking the waterskin to assess its remaining content, Murchú laid it carefully on the ground alongside him.

'Travelling back to the site of Cairenn's abduction would have been a waste of time. And cost us another day or more.'

'But we're not following the *díberg's* tracks,' Mochta pointed out. 'We're simply following the trail to An Mám Liath. How do you know we're travelling in the right direction?'

'Because we know where the *díberg* was headed. This section of the Great Wild is harsh and rugged, the traversable routes few and the practical ones even fewer. The *díberg* travelled south-east and they were forced to continue in that general direction for the terrain restricts them from veering off until they reach An Mám Liath – The Grey Pass – just south of Poll an Iubhair.'

The warrior pointed across the lake to where the low mountain range was now little more than a blur against the descending gloom. 'Those mountains stretch south-east for at least another two days' travel. The *díberg* might have sought a route through them of course but it would have been a hard task and they'd have lost several days in the process – not a wise approach in enemy territory. Meanwhile, the lake drains into marshland directly south of here, difficult terrain that extends east for several days. Caught between the two, the *díberg* have no choice but to follow a route that eventually takes them through An Mám Liath.'

Mochta grunted and nodded his head as though satisfied. His next question however, suggested his curiosity had not been entirely sated.

'Is it possible the *díberg* are *Clann Baoiscne?*'

Murchú tapped his fingers against his knees as he considered the question. 'It's possible ...' he began, but then he paused and considered it further. 'But ... it's unlikely. For all their raging puff talk, *Clann Baoiscne* are just as eager as us to avoid a real confrontation. There are no clear victors arising out of a war between the tribes. Although ...'

He raised his hand to squeeze his lip between thumb and forefinger as he thought the matter through.

'It does seem strange that the *díberg* carried out no other raids while in *Uí Loinge* territory. It's a long way to come, travelling all that distance, only to ...'

Liath Luachra listened as the warrior's voice trailed off, struggling to find a satisfactory conclusion to his own conjectures. Evidently, he shared her misgivings in relation to the *díberg's* odd behaviour although, like her, he'd refrained from voicing them up to this point.

The woman warrior thought about it as she used her tongue to probe a sliver of meat lodged between her molars. They needed to relocate the *díberg's* tracks. That was essential. Tracks had a way of revealing truths the person making them often ignored or tried to conceal. Until they found some sign therefore, she would keep an open mind on the *díberg's* motives.

Mochta's eyes drifted back towards the warrior woman.

'You're quiet Grey One. You have no opinion on the *díberg?*'

An awkward silence followed the question and, once again, it was left to Murchú to intervene.

'The Grey One tends to keep her thoughts to herself, cousin. She'll share them when she's ready.'

Mochta chewed on a crust of griddlebread as he regarded the other *Uí Loinge* man. His expression was one of subdued amusement, nevertheless, on this occasion, he seemed to appreciate the woman warrior's reluctance to engage. Throwing the crust aside, he abruptly got to his feet. 'I'll see to the horses one last time before I retire,' he said. 'I wish you both a pleasant rest.'

With a quiet smile, he turned and walked away from the fire.

Murchú watched his cousin go then, with a sigh, reached down to pick up the waterskin. Liath Luachra assumed he was about to depart as well but, instead, he shifted closer so that he could speak to her without being overheard.

'Grey One.' The *Uí Loinge* man hesitated and awkwardly shifted position. 'Cnes' accusations at Briga ... they were cruel and ... unfounded. You deserved far better than such a poisoned welcome.'

Liath Luachra regarded him blankly. The apology seeming oddly incongruous given how close she'd come to spilling his woman's blood. Then again, he had been absent during those crucial moments.

She quietly put her empty bowl aside. 'Perhaps we should discuss how best to gain your uncle's consent for the Seeking.'

Thrown by the sudden and clumsy change of topic, the *Uí Loinge* man's fingers reached out to fret at the stopper of his waterskin. 'Yes,' he said slowly and gave her an uncertain glance. 'The Elders' condition is yet another action I regret, Grey One.'

'We could simply avoid him,' she said, ignoring the response. 'We could disregard the Elders' stipulation, skirt Poll an Iubhair and make directly for *Clann Baoiscne* territory.'

Murchú shifted uneasily. 'I can't imagine the Elders would be pleased with such a course of action,' he said at last.

'And you imagine me pleased at the prospect of confronting Bressal, of bending the knee for an invented slight?' Despite her best attempts to keep her voice steady, Liath Luachra heard some of her anger leaking through.

'I know of the troubled ... history between you and my uncle, Grey One. And I understand your distaste for the Elders' condition. I'm ashamed but also grateful for the sacrifice you endure for Cairenn's sake.'

'You can keep your gratitude for the time being,' she answered coldly. 'I agreed to consider it. I was serious about skirting Poll an Iubhair.'

Deep lines etched their way along the *Uí Loinge* man's forehead. 'Your reticence isn't unreasonable but ... but there'd be consequences to disregarding the Elder's directive. And don't forget, you won't stand alone before Bressal. *Na Cineáltaí* and I will be alongside you.'

'You think Bressal gives two flaccid shits about *Na Cineáltaí*? Their presence will stir all the interest of a three-day old cow-pat. His focus will rest on me alone.'

'Be that as it may, I'll stand at your side. Any hand raised against you will face contention from myself and the other *fénnid*.'

Liath Luachra lapsed into a troubled silence, even more concerned now with the realisation that any support from *Na Cineáltaí* could potentially result in a mindless bloodbath.

'Do you propose a plan, then?' she asked, desperate to change the direction of the conversation.

'I've thought of little else since leaving Briga. I've viewed the problem from every angle and …' His voice trailed off.

'And?'

'And no single approach presents itself. None with any likelihood of success, at least.' He noisily exhaled his frustration through his teeth.

'Perhaps it's best just to confront him directly. Man to man. He is my uncle, after all.'

Liath Luachra thought about that for a moment. 'He may be your uncle,' she admitted. 'But, first and foremost, he is Bressal.'

***

As soon as her hair had dried, Liath Luachra retreated to her bedroll at the edge of the overhead branches, slipping beneath the blankets with muted relief. Prolonged interactions with the *fénnid* tended to strain her, particularly when the *fian's* established routines and dynamics were upended as they'd been on this occasion. Glancing back towards the fire, she saw that everyone but Murchú had retired for the night. The *Uí Loinge* man was sitting alone prior to taking his turn at guard duty, staring deep into the flames as they licked and crackled at his internal ponderings. Half of his face was shrouded in deep shadow, half discoloured by the flickering yellow of the fire.

Watching him from the shadows, the warrior woman once again reflected on Cnes's behaviour. Over the course of the day, her fury had diminished but the incident lingered as a subdued seething. Murchú's woman had lashed out in the mistaken belief she was competing for her man's affections, fearful of the ramifications any such relationship might have for her ambitions and standing within the tribe. Given Liath Luachra's own disinterest in any such relationship, that could only mean Cnes' fears had been prompted by another source.

Murchú?

The Grey One chewed on the inside of her cheek as she considered that possibility. Was it conceivable Cnes had discerned some deep-rooted affection towards her by the *Uí Loinge* man?

Rolling onto her back, she stared at the dark tangle of twisted branches above.

It seemed unlikely. Over their time together with *Na Cinéaltaí* she'd never noticed any evidence of such an attraction, although she was realistic enough to know she wasn't the most perceptive when it came to

52

such matters. Her general assumption was that people either disliked her or simply wished to use her. There was a vague third possibility in there of course but not one to which she gave much consideration.

Still! Murchú promised to stand alongside me if the worst came to the worst. And that offer was genuine.

Which meant nothing, of course. Murchú had made the offer because it was the honourable thing to do and Murchú was an honourable man. His personal values and his sense of gratitude had prompted him to do so. It had nothing to do with any romantic notions towards her.

She ground her teeth in irritation. Dealing with people and trying to decipher their intentions always drove her to distraction.

Cursing under her breath, she rolled away from the fire and closed her eyes.

If there was any truth to the possibility that Murchú had feelings for her, that was a complication that she – and the *fian* – could ill afford on a tasking.

Which meant that if it reared its head, she'd have to stamp it down with the all the empathy of a boot heel to an unnoticed insect.

***

As always when engaged on a tasking, the *fénnid* rose before dawn. Stoking the fire back to life to counter the cold, they boiled a potful of hot porridge and ate quietly as they waited for Father Sun to crack one eye above the horizon and illuminate the trail before them.

The woman warrior ate sparingly, swallowing little more than four or five mouthfuls of porridge, then slipping two boiled tubers inside her tunic for later. With another day of running ahead, a full belly would result in her throwing up what she'd swallowed. From her own experience she knew it was far better to nibble on smaller morsels over the course of the day whenever they stopped to snatch a few moments of rest.

The *fian* departed Loch na nEasa as the first rays of light seeped in over the eastern forest. Fortunately, as the dewy light improved, so too did the trail it revealed. Rugged forest opened out to grassy meadows that ran between the densely timbered mountainsides, broad paths for the woman warrior to set a solid pace.

For the better part of the day, Liath Luachra's mind was consumed in the physical immediacy of running: the breathlessness, the relentless pound of her heart and the strain in her lower legs banishing any other mental consideration. That night, massaging the ache from her feet, she consoled herself with the knowledge that, once again, they'd gained ground on their quarry. Once again, they'd edged a little closer to Murchú's sister.

On the morning of the fourth day, despite the muted grumblings, Liath Luachra led the *fian* off at an even more gruelling pace, determined to reach An Mám Liath by noon, a feat Murchú believed possible if they were able to sustain that punishing speed.

The *Uí Loinge* man's speculation proved remarkably accurate for, sweating and ragged, they arrived at An Mám Liath just a little after mid-day. A stark gully through the eastern hills, the pass was well named, consisting of little more than a barren avenue between two bare rock faces. Crooked granite cliffs enclosed them on either side, void of vegetation apart from the trees that crowned them. Over time, some, growing too heavy or too broad, had toppled over and tumbled into the gully below.

Negotiating these fallen obstacles took the *fian* longer than anticipated, particularly with the need to pick their path while managing the horses through the treacherous ground. At last, exhausted, they emerged on the far side of the passage, into a wide clearing enclosed by the saturating greens of the forest.

In the lee of the hills, that grassy space was nicely sheltered but held enough open ground for the sun's weak rays to warm it with relative ease. To the Grey One's surprise, clumps of *sabhaircíní* – primroses – dotted the damp ground in the dappled shade of the trees, their glimmering yellow blooms a strong indication of an early Spring. Approaching the nearest cluster of flowers, the woman warrior stooped low to pluck one free, raised it to her nose and inhaled its sweet perfume as she looked around and considered their options.

For the most part, the eastern forest was impassable, the spaces between the endless rows of stark winter trunks locked with twisted woody debris and entangled shadows. Fortunately, two obvious trails carved through that vegetation, one leading to the north and the other veering away to the south-east. The latter stretched for forty or fifty paces before curving sharply out of sight. The northern trail, by contrast, looked more regularly utilised. Broad and surprisingly linear, it stretched directly towards a low hill in the distance until it too faded into the vegetation at its base.

Tossing the flower aside, Liath Luachra looked around at the *fénnid*, who'd spread out to stand and catch their breath. 'It's a long pursuit before us,' she said at last. 'No point burning wood for want of heat on a warm day.'

Although surprised by the decision to extend their halt, the *fénnid* were too relieved to question it. Most chose to flop onto the ground where they stood. Feirgil stretched out in the long grass and started waving his arms and legs to make odd shapes in the flattened pasture.

While the others laughed at the eccentric behaviour, the Grey One sidled closer to where Murchú was sitting and gestured loosely towards the north-eastern trail. 'That's the route to Poll an Iubhair?'

The *Uí Loinge* man's face looked strained and exhausted, nevertheless he made the effort to nod. 'About half a day's walk. Possibly a quarter of that at our current pace.' He didn't seem too enamoured by the prospect.

The woman warrior looked around the clearing, paying particular attention to the shadows between the oaks at the closest treeline. 'This clearing marks the intersection between the trail to *Uí Loinge* lands and *Clann Baoiscne* territory.'

'Yes.'

'And yet, I see no *Uí Loinge* presence.'

Murchú laughed. 'Don't be fooled. My uncle will have men stationed somewhere.' He jerked his thumb in the direction of the hill to the north. 'Probably up on a secure viewpoint like that hill. It's more than likely they're watching us as we speak.

Liath Luachra grunted softly in acknowledgement then turned her gaze to the south-east. From the corner of her eye, she noticed An Giobach watching her closely. Conscious that the observant *fénnid* had overheard the conversation, she suspected he'd already guessed her intent. The subtle nature of his subsequent comment confirmed it.

'This is a pleasant respite.'

'Yes,' she agreed.

Unable to glean anything from that response, the big *fénnid* decided on a less subtle approach.

'Do you intend to tarry here, Grey One?'

She shrugged. 'It is a pretty spot. Perhaps I'll pick some flowers.'

By now, noting the obliqueness of their conversation, the other *fénnid* had turned to listen. 'Are we really picking flowers?' Feirgil wanted to know, but no-one took any notice of him.

'I think,' said An Giobach, 'you've made the decision to avoid Poll an Iubhair.' He plucked a blade of grass, sniffed at it, and tossed it aside. 'You intend to bypass Bressal and the need for his consent.'

He nodded slowly, as though in agreement with his own conclusion.

'Which is the wisest choice.'

Liath Luachra chewed silently on the inside of her cheek, concealing her irritation at the *fénnid's* pre-emptive deduction. An Giobach was a canny man, too canny at times for, having just come to that decision, she wasn't prepared to discuss it just yet.

Murchú looked at her intently. 'Is that true?' he demanded.

Liath Luachra flipped her hand in irritation, put out at being pushed onto the back foot. 'If we travel to Poll an Iubhair, we lose a day, possibly two with the extra travel and talk. We also lose all the ground we've managed to make up to this point.'

'I thought we'd talk further on how best to approach my uncle.'

'We've talked enough. The plan you proposed didn't please me.'

'And you think this is a better plan?' The *Uí Loinge* man could not disguise his mounting anger.

She bit her lower lip. 'It's no worse,' she answered at last.

Murchú got to his feet to face her directly.

'And what of the condition to seek Bressal's consent?'

'We'll adhere to the condition.'

Murchú stared at her. 'What do you mean? How will we adhere to it? You've just said we're going to skirt Poll an Iubhair and avoid Bressal.'

'Because we'll do it on our return. Once we've recovered your sister.' She glared at him in warning, silently cautioning him against pushing her too far. 'The Elders made no stipulation as to when we had to seek Bressal's consent, did they?'

Murchú numbly shook his head. 'No, but ...'

'So if we've succeeded or even failed in our tasking, it's hardly going to make a difference.'

'But they ...' Murchú paused, stared at her. 'The Elders ...'

He paused, then to her surprise, he let out a chortle so infectious it was taken up by the other *fénnid*. A loud peal of rugged laughter ran through the clearing for the proposal appealed to the men's rough humour and their resentment at the smug tribalism of the *Uí Loinge* Elders.

'It is a deft solution,' Murchú admitted once the merriment had died down.

'*An glic,*' sniggered An Giobach. Very sly.

'Pick yourselves up, then,' said Liath Luachra. 'We have a *díberg* to catch.'

***

The *fian* left the clearing in a far more ebullient mood than when they'd arrived, lifted by Liath Luachra's innovative interpretation of the Elder's condition but also buoyed by the prospect of further reducing the *díberg's* lead. With Mochta's horses and supplies dispensing with the need to hunt or forage, the *fénnid* could travel unburdened and continue to cover ground at a rapid rate.

Despite their optimism however, no-one was under any illusion as to how challenging the remaining pursuit would be or how much sweat and hardship it was likely to entail. They had made good progress but the raiders still had a five- to eight-day lead. With the *fian* now advancing into unfamiliar territory, where the key routes of passage were unknown, the risk of losing their quarry's trail had also increased substantially.

Liath Luachra celebrated the *fian's* elevated morale by slowing their pace, although she had a double motive for that decision. After several days of rapid travel, the *fian* were weary and in need of respite. In addition, as the south-eastern trail was rarely travelled, there was a greater likelihood of encountering the *díberg's* sign and, to ensure they didn't miss it, they had to move at a more controlled pace. For the remainder of the day therefore, the *fian* trudged through the endless forest, skirting hilltops and treeless ridges, following a trail that grew so faint that at times it threatened to disappear altogether.

That night they camped in a twilight ravine as a chill mist formed over the ridges above them, waiting for the last sliver of blue to fade from the sky before lighting a fire so that the smoke couldn't be detected. The chances of someone tackling a well-armed battle group like *Na Cinéaltaí* were slim and they were still too far behind the *díberg* to be overly concerned, but out in the Great Wild it paid to remain vigilant. Raiders weren't the only threats to be found in the wilderness.

Once again, Biotóg took it upon himself to make the evening meal and the *fénnid* dug into a fresh feast of stew and griddlebread, using up the last of the preserved meat before it spoiled. When she'd finished eating, Liath Luachra retired with her blanket roll to a cluster of pines at the edge of the ravine, hidden in the shadows ten paces or so from the others still clustered about the fire.

Wrapping herself in her cloak, she leaned back against the pine trunk, folding into the shadows as she tried to make herself comfortable. While she relaxed, she watched Biotóg clean up, washing the bowls in rainwater caught in a basin-shaped rock at the base of the cliffs.

A pale youth with a shock of curly, black hair, Biotóg's features were dominated by a pair of unusually large and protruding eyes which tended to give him a dull, fish-eyed appearance. Although he was one of the original members of *Na Cinéaltaí,* and despite their years of fighting alongside each other, the Grey One had never really warmed to him or even established a meaningful connection. She recognised of course, that this was probably a hangover from her first few years as a *fénnid,* a time when her age and gender left her vulnerable to abuse from her fellow comrades. Biotóg had never threatened her in the same manner some of the previous *Na Cinéaltaí* members had. Neither had he participated in the actions they'd taken against her. Nevertheless, he'd never attempted to prevent them either. Instead, he'd just sat and watched, observing her with the same impassive scrutiny he observed her with today.

A flicker of movement left of the fire drew the woman warrior's eye and she spotted Mochta walking across the rocky ground from where the two horses were tethered, a leather satchel slung casually across his shoulder. Instead of joining the others, he too veered towards the shadows and ended up settling between the buttresses of a large oak just six or seven paces from her own position. Dazzled by the light from the fire, he remained oblivious to her presence.

Laying his blanket on the ground, the *Uí Loinge* man sat on it and wrapped his cloak about him. As the woman warrior continued to watch, she saw him glance furtively towards the fire before carefully withdrawing a small leather pouch. Dipping his fingers inside, he pulled something from it and palmed it quickly into his mouth.

Returning the pouch to his bag, he tossed both aside, sighed and slowly eased back against the tree, by chance turning his head in her direction.

Their eyes locked.

Startled, the *Uí Loinge* man jolted upright then swiftly turned away, lying on his side with his back towards her, his still form radiating extreme discomfort.

Liath Luachra exhaled slowly. It didn't take much to guess what he'd taken.

Beacán scammalach.

She felt the old hunger herself then, her hand unthinkingly dropping to pat the inside pocket of her tunic where she normally kept her own supply, grimacing when her fingertips pressed against its empty flatness. She'd exhausted that supply in Luachair.

Easing onto the uneven ground, she curled into a ball, cocooned by the heavy cloak and blanket. Ignoring the cold air on her face, she let the weight of fatigue drag her down, the ragged hunger nibbling the edges of her consciousness as she plummeted to sleep.

Chapter Four:

A further three days' travel took the *fian* south-east through rough, uneven forest and wide stretches of marshland unfamiliar even to the *Uí Loinge* men. On the morning of the fifth day since leaving Briga, An Giobach questioned the distance they'd covered, pondering aloud whether they might already have reached *Clann Baoiscne* territory. Murchú, however, was adamant the land was untamed wilderness. Although admitting he'd never actually travelled the route himself, he insisted it was common knowledge amongst the *Uí Loinge* that *Clann Baoiscne* territory was six days travel south-east of An Mám Liath.

Unless they'd expanded that territory of course.

Increasingly cautious now that they were in unfamiliar ground, each of the *fénnid* carried a javelin, with a second or third close to hand. The Grey One also took the precaution of having a pair of scouts travel ahead of the main party, not only to provide advance warning of any potential danger but to scan the ground for tracks without the distracting bustle of the larger group.

For the most part, the route they adhered to tended to follow the most accessible contours of the land. Occasionally that route intersected with other potential travel-ways coming from the north or south but at none of those points did they encounter evidence of the *díberg's* passage.

On the morning of the tenth day, Liath Luachra and An Giobach took the scouting duty, leaving the others to pack up and break camp while they ventured ahead to assess the lay of the land. Accustomed to working together, there was little talk between them as they followed the most likely trail, the big *fénnid* taking the lead and scouring the ground while the woman warrior remained several paces behind, scanning the treeline with her javelin at the ready. Most of the forest in that area was lichen-stained ash or elm, the trunks leafless and winter stark, their dark bulk matched by muddy leaf debris or the occasional cluster of rotting shrubs. The miserable character of the land was further emphasised by an icy breeze that whistled eerily through the trees and a leaden cloud layer hanging over the forest like a subtle menace. The morning had started foggy and cold and the dreary film of moisture from overnight showers still soaked the vegetation. Wading through ankle-high forest debris, the two warriors had soon felt their toes grow numb from the cold despite the insulation of their oil-treated boots.

It was late morning when they entered a broad valley with mist-coated hills visible above the trees to the north-east and south-west. By then, the trail had reduced to little more than a deer path, barely distinguishable from the reduced winter scrub to either side. While they were following the rocky contours of the terrain, An Giobach suddenly halted, dropping to an awkward, spread-eagled crouch behind the scant cover of a waist-high tree stump. Twenty paces to his rear, primed to respond to such an occurrence, the Grey One dropped to one knee and arched her javelin back, feverishly scanning the treeline for a target.

But no target presented itself.

As time stretched on without any sign of attack, the woman warrior glanced fretfully towards the big *fénnid,* surprised to see that he wasn't preparing to defend himself but staring at the ground directly in front of him with unnatural interest. Frustrated, the woman warrior waited, her arm aching from the strain of holding the javelin aloft and the *suaineamh* – throwing strap – at the ready. An Giobach continued to squat, staring fixedly at the ground, finally deigning to raise his head and wave at her to come forward.

Annoyed by the needless alarm, Liath Luachra remained stubbornly in place and it was only when the *fénnid* continued to signal that she finally relented, loosening the *suaineamh* and lowering her weapon with a scowl. Advancing at a crouch, she sank sullenly into the shadows two paces to his rear. There, her eyes dropped to the patch of muddy ground in front of him and she understood what he'd been looking at.

A footprint.

Faint, barely half-formed around the heel, but a footprint nonetheless.

Dropping flat onto the ground, Liath Luachra wriggled forward to examine the imprint, chewing the inside of her cheek in wordless concentration. The depth and size suggested it had been made by a man, an individual larger and heavier than herself but smaller than An Giobach. From its placement, that individual had been travelling in a similar direction to the two warriors.

Lowering her nose over the print, the woman warrior sniffed at it, detecting no scent apart from the familiar earthy aroma of drying mud. Pulling back slightly, she dipped her right hand into the little depression and ran her fingertips along its inner contours, assessing the crumbling texture of the compressed soil's outer surface. It felt slightly dry, suggesting it hadn't been exposed to the air for long. Which meant, of course, that the track had been made some time after the previous night's showers.

Pulling back, she rose to a squat and regarded the imprint thoughtfully.

'Well?' asked An Giobach.

She glanced up at him. 'This print was made earlier today.'

He dipped his head in agreement, her assessment apparently aligning with his own. Deep lines etched their way across his forehead as he mulled over the obvious ramifications. 'The *díberg* would have passed through here several days ago,' he pointed out at last.

Liath Luachra sniffed and scratched absently at her knee but said nothing. Given the time difference, it didn't seem likely the track could have been left by the raiders. Not unless they'd decided to pause their flight and remain in the area. Raising her head to consider the stark, inhospitable terrain, she found that possibility a hard one to entertain.

'A traveller, then,' suggested the *fénnid*. 'A hunter.'

Liath Luachra made no answer as she retrieved her javelin and rose to her feet. The big warrior was merely thinking aloud and besides, it wasn't possible to draw any meaningful conclusion from the evidence of a single footprint. She gestured sharply up the trail, indicating they should continue to search for more.

An Giobach grunted unhappily. Muttering inaudibly under his breath, he stood up and moved forward to take the lead again, this time with even greater caution.

While she waited for him to establish some distance between them, the Grey One arranged several stones on the ground in a pattern that would alert the *fían* to the presence of a potential threat. By the time she'd finished, An Giobach had already made it to a slight curve in the trail by a cluster of windblown pines. Glancing back to make sure she was ready to support him, he carefully started to edge his way around the trees.

Gripping her javelin, Liath Luachra started after him, appreciating his steady, careful advance. Over the previous two seasons she'd grown to trust the big man's competence … in as far as she ever trusted anyone. There was a certain irony to that of course, given how little she knew about An Giobach beyond the fact that he displayed greater intellect and morality than she'd experienced with most other *fénnid* to date. In the reality of battle of course, such qualities rarely mattered. When the blood lust was up and fear-fury blossomed inside your head, the only thing you needed to know was that you had a capable fighter at your side.

The two warriors proceeded cautiously for another eight hundred paces, An Giobach scanning the ground for tracks, Liath Luachra covering him from the rear. A little further up the valley, they paused again, listening to the sound of flowing water which had grown perceptibly louder as they advanced. Looking towards the rugged western hills – much closer now – Liath Luachra briefly wondered if the source of that noise might be a waterway draining those heights of the previous night's rain. Several hundred paces further, that hunch was confirmed when they stumbled out of the trees and onto a ledge overlooking a steep gully. A swollen river thundered through the narrow passage below, hurtling downstream from the western hills. Spilling out from a series of enormous rock pools, the white water tumbled onto moss-coated boulders and slammed through the gully's black cliff faces as it surged towards the east.

Both warriors glanced uncertainly along the rocky bank to either side. The height of the gully walls suggested the waterway wasn't flowing to full capacity, but the current was running strong and looked too dangerous to cross.

Liath Luachra grimaced at the froth of bubbling white. 'Make your way east along the bank,' she instructed An Giobach. 'I'll take the west. If you find nothing after eight hundred paces, work your way back and, if I'm not waiting here, follow my trail. If you're not here when I return, I'll do the same.'

Leaving the other *fénnid* to work anything else out for himself, the woman warrior abruptly walked away.

Proceeding along her chosen path, the Grey One soon found the slope steepened sharply and realised they'd edged far closer to the western hills than she'd originally believed. Because of the dense forest growth, it was difficult to work out a practical path up the sharpening incline, a task made more challenging due to the patches of rotting leaf debris that threatened to break away underfoot and slide downhill at any moment. To make matters even worse, sections of the slope were strewn with obstacles, large slabs of wood, boulders and other ancient debris cast out from the waterway thundering loudly four or five paces to her right.

Pausing to catch her breath, the woman warrior glanced back to gauge the distance she'd travelled but found the trees below prevented her from seeing the bottom of the hill. There was no sign of An Giobach, of course. The big man was well out of sight by now, the path he'd taken completely obscured by the forest as well.

Considering the treacherous slope below, it suddenly struck her that the terrain had become far too dangerous for the horses. Even with assistance, she doubted the animals could scale a hill this steep.

Which meant the *fian* would have to bid farewell to Mochta.

The woman warrior pursed her lips at that, surprised to find herself a little saddened at the prospect. She didn't really mind losing the company of Murchú's cousin of course, but she'd come to appreciate the practical utility of the horses and the effective manner in which they'd transported the *fian's* supplies across the Great Wild.

Liath Luachra continued her ascent, the steepness of the slope occasionally obliging her to scramble on all fours, fingers tingling from grasping cold rock and low-hanging branches for support. Unable to count in paces, she attempted to estimate the distance she'd covered in her head and was close to turning back when she suddenly stumbled on a sweep of tracks marking the passage of several people.

The Grey One immediately slipped sideways, sliding into a gap between two close-growing pine trees. Wedging herself in place to avoid sliding downhill, she remained completely still, feverishly studying the terrain above her. Clotted with trees and large rocks, it looked an ideal spot for an ambush.

It took a long time for the woman warrior to satisfy herself that she was alone. Only when she was completely certain that no-one was hiding or watching from the shadows, did she finally ease from her shelter to examine the tracks: a jumble of smeared footprints, scuffed patches of mud where someone had slipped and a cylindrical hole where the base of a spear haft had been used for leverage or balance.

Dropping to her knees in the soggy soil, she regarded the messy spread of indentations. Whoever had left them had made no effort to conceal their passage but then, scattered on this isolated slope, that was understandable given the minimal chances of anyone happening upon them.

Unless they were being actively sought after, of course.

At first the woman warrior moved carefully from one track to another, studying each print in detail as she worked out the different patterns. By the time An Giobach finally caught up with her, panting from the climb, she'd worked out the characteristic traits of different individuals and could recognise their distinctive prints.

An Giobach propped himself against a lichen-stained trunk to keep his balance on the uneven ground. He looked worriedly uphill before turning an inquisitive eye towards the woman warrior.

'Five travellers,' she said before he could ask. 'Four male, one female.'

An Giobach pulled silently on his beard as he eyed her and she could tell what he was thinking. That numbering matched his own estimate from the tracks the raiders had left near Briga.

'The female's young. And she's a prisoner. Her hands are bound so she struggles to keep her balance. When she slips, she can't break her fall and hits the ground hard.'

An Giobach was tugging his beard even harder now. 'Why?' he asked aloud, a distinct trace of vexation in his voice. 'Why would they remain here in this … pig's arse of a place? They should be at least three, four days ahead of us.'

Liath Luachra shrugged. She couldn't offer him any answers. All she could do was read the story the tracks were telling her.

'What do you want to do?' An Giobach asked.

'Go back and fetch the others. But have them set camp at the bottom of the hill. The horses won't climb that slope.'

'And you?'

Liath Luachra considered the tracks again before responding.

'The tracks are recent but if there's a fresh downpour we could lose them again. I'll follow their trail and once I've satisfied myself they've settled for the night, I'll work my way back.' She glanced briefly uphill before returning her eyes to the *fénnid*. 'Have the others alert and ready. If all goes well, there's a chance we might have Murchú's sister safe with us this very night.'

An Giobach sighed. He looked a little dubious about her decision but he also knew better than to question it. With visible reluctance, he pushed himself off the tree and started downhill, the big bulk of him slipping and sliding precariously on the damp patches of forest litter.

Liath Luachra waited until the warrior's hefty silhouette had faded into the trees before she started moving again, working her way uphill at an angle to the slope. This approach meant the climb took longer, but it also made it less steep and easier to keep her balance. More importantly, it allowed her to avoid following the tracks directly. If it had been the raiders making those tracks – something that looked increasingly likely – she didn't want to risk being seen, particularly if they'd left a warrior to watch their rear.

To her surprise, the remaining ascent was a lot shorter than expected. The summit turned out to be little more than thirty paces uphill from where she'd stopped to examine the tracks, the flat stretch of it concealed by the thick array of trees until she was almost on it. Scrambling up onto the flat ground, she found herself on a broad plateau although, once again, it was too thickly forested to tell how far back it extended. Carefully scanning the ground ahead for any potential threat, she moved forward to study the area where her quarry had crested the hill.

Her reading of the tracks suggested the group had paused to rest at the plateau's edge: the four men clustered together, the girl sitting alone off to the side, in the natural confines of a nook created between two buttresses of an enormous oak. On the ground alongside that tree, she found segments of a flax rope, the fibres neatly sliced by a sharp blade indicating that the raiders had finally relented and cut their prisoner's hands free.

Crouching to examine the ground some more, the woman warrior also discerned the imprint of the girl's buttocks. To the left and right of that imprint, little more than a hand's width in front of it, two other indentations in the earth were visible, unusual shapes made up of four shallow, but parallel furrows.

Curious, Liath Luachra considered the indentations for a time, struggling to work out what might have caused them. Prompted by some intuitive inspiration, she twisted about and backed into the confined space between the buttresses, settling back against the trunk in the same position the *Uí Loinge* girl would have occupied.

She remained in that position for a time, sitting calm and still while she tried to imagine what the girl had been up to. Looking down at the two depressions to either side, she instinctively stretched out both hands and discovered that her fingers settled almost perfectly into the curving furrows.

Sudden comprehension caused the woman warrior's chest to tighten. The girl had gouged her fingers into the earth with such force, she'd left a perfectly formed imprint in the mud.

She's terrified.

Pushing herself upright, Liath Luachra hurriedly hauled herself out of the little cavity, her breathing ragged, a metallic taste at the back of her throat. Shaken, she stumbled towards another tree, and took a seat on one of its exposed roots. Pulling *Gléas gan Ainm* free of its scabbard, she started to scrape the blade with a whetstone, over and over and over again, incessantly grinding the pits and tiny abrasions until its surface was smooth to the touch and its edge had a keen and hungry bite. As always, there was a release to be found in the mechanical repetition, the familiar routine that steadied her thoughts and loosed the tension tightening up inside her. Two years earlier, as *fénnid*, she would have used that same tension to bolster her battle frenzy, encouraging it to coil tighter and tighter so that when she was finally unleashed, she'd lunge mindlessly at the enemy, smashing into them with unstoppable momentum.

And the blood would flow.

As *rígfénnid*, of course, that kind of physical release was no longer an option. Leading others meant she couldn't give into the temptation of such mindless actions, succumb to a blood fury that, even after all these years, still simmered vehemently inside her. Nowadays, her responsibilities meant that old hunger had to be suppressed or diverted through occasional bouts of *béacán scammalach* or *uisce beatha*. Deep down however, she knew that part of her still craved that carnage, the driving, endless bloodlust for something – or someone – to hack from existence.

When her mind had quietened, Liath Luachra replaced *Gléas gan Ainm* in its scabbard. She briefly considered sharpening the knife in the hidden scabbard as well then decided against it. She'd already wasted enough time. She had to go and find the *díberg*.

Despite coming to that conclusion, the woman warrior remained where she was, listening to the creak of the branches overhead, inhaling the musty smell of damp leaves and rotting humus. Such uncharacteristic reticence surprised her, and she wondered whether it had been triggered by the marks she'd discovered. The casual cruelty of raiders was something that still had the power to stir up old ghosts. As she looked at the different traces of *díberg* sign on the ground around her, the warrior woman wet her lips, conscious of a cold patch spreading along her spine.

Something about this Seeking felt off. Ever since leaving Briga, she'd been unable to shake that sensation and although she'd ignored her instincts up till that point, those same intuitions had become more insistent. There was more to the raid than a simple abduction.

Frustrated by the continued sense of restlessness, the woman warrior angrily pushed herself off the root and onto her feet. Pushing forward into the trees, she set her jaw, determined now to follow the tracks, to find the mysterious *díberg* and ...

Succumb to the blood fury once more.

Up on that elevated plateau, the forest was exposed to the full force of the wind. Raked by relentless squalls that caused the upper boughs to shudder wildly, the violent rustling of leaves and the creaking of branches drowned out every other sound. For Liath Luachra, the effect of passing beneath that strident agitation was like a sustained and prolonged assault on the senses and she was relieved when she finally emerged at the far side of the plateau.

A chaotic jumble of angled boulders at the plateau's southern lip offered an elevated vantage point over the land to the south. Clambering onto the nearest of them, the Grey One worked her way up its smooth, wind-eroded height and pressed against its surface as she peered south for any sign of the raiders. Because of the wind and the shuffling forest canopy, it took a few moments to spot the stunted plume of smoke rising from the trees some distance from the hill's southern base.

The Grey One chewed silently on the inside of her cheek.

They've camped early.

That prompted a frown. Darkness was still some way off and yet it seemed the raiders were feeling secure – a behaviour she struggled to understand. Hampered by a prisoner and trespassing in *Clann Baoiscne* territory, she'd have expected them to tread more cautiously and, certainly, to display more circumspection when it came to revealing their presence.

Marking the location of the smoke, the woman warrior slid from her perch and started down the hill's southern slope, an incline just as rugged and steep as its northern counterpart. By the time she reached the bottom, the forest had once again closed in around her, obstructing her view of the smoke. Given the clear trail of the raiders' tracks and her own mental fix on the campsite's position however, she felt confident she'd find it easily enough.

Opting for caution over speed, Liath Luachra took a more south-easterly course, veering away from the raiders' tracks with the intention of swinging back to the south-west later. Such an approach would take her in a wide arc around the raiders' campsite, bringing her in from the south, the direction they'd least expect any pursuer to approach from.

The damp forest floor meant she travelled almost soundlessly as she slipped from shadow to shadow, traversing the forest at a low but rapid crouch. Reaching a decayed tree stump that had decomposed to form a shape similar to that of a human head, she estimated that she'd travelled far enough and switched direction back to the south-east. Advancing another six hundred paces, she caught the faint whiff of woodsmoke on the breeze seeping through the trees to the north-west.

The raiders' encampment was nearby.

Dropping to all fours, the woman warrior started north, crawling on her belly until she heard the thin murmur of voices. Freezing in place, she listened carefully until she was sure of the direction they were coming from, then started forward once more, using the tree and the low-lying foliage to conceal herself. Finally, when the voices were distinct, she crawled to a pair of hazel saplings and, parting them carefully, peered through to catch her first glimpse of the campsite.

The raiders were settled in a narrow clearing with a broad lake running along its western edge, a large body of water she'd somehow missed from the height of the escarpment. A surprisingly thick water-mist hung in the air just off the western shore, a bulging wall of cloud that stretched its full length. At the southern edge of the clearing meanwhile, less than thirty paces from where she lay concealed, the raiders' campfire crackled noisily, the smell of burning wood now far stronger. A grizzled warrior, the right side of his face marred by an ancient gash, was standing by that fire, turning a makeshift spit with the carcass of a roasted hare. Squatting beside him, watching the revolving hare with undisguised avarice, was a youth with a cruel mouth and a purple birthmark down his right cheek. Every now and again, when the warrior paused to rest, the youth would lean forward to carve a sliver of meat from the carcass, grinning in challenge at the bigger man as he slipped it between his lips.

Edging further around to the left of the saplings to get a better view of the clearing, Liath Luachra spotted a third figure stretched on the ground to the right of the fire. Apart from a pair of furred winter boots poking out from beneath one edge, this individual's body and face were entirely obscured by the bulk of a thick woollen blanket.

Cairenn?

Liath Luachra bit down on her lower lip to quell her mounting excitement. At this distance and with the cumbersome blanket, it was impossible to tell for sure.

Two more.

Keeping very still, she scanned the campsite for the missing warriors, eventually spotting the first of them in the shadows of the northern treeline. Lean, dark haired and heavily bearded, the manner in which he'd concealed himself suggested that he'd been placed there to monitor the approach from that direction, the very one she'd have come from had she followed their tracks.

Intrigued by the raider's behaviour, she continued to watch him. Despite his sentinel responsibilities, he shifted about with a nervous energy, erratically raising and lowering his javelin, as though seeking an excuse – any excuse – to cast it.

Unable to make sense of the agitated figure, Liath Luachra returned her attention to the two men by the fire and examined them more carefully. Like their comrade in the northern trees, both wore heavy furs against the cold and carried weapon belts around their waists. All three looked seasoned warriors.

One more.

Given the relatively unobstructed view of the clearing's northern treeline, it struck her as likely that the fourth man was closer, probably screened by the trees to her immediate left. Shifting cautiously around to the right therefore, she worked her way over to an enormous pine that had fallen to lie in an east-west alignment. Wriggling along the side of the trunk so that she was concealed from view from the clearing, she spotted the first distant blue-green splinters of the lake appear between the western trees as she reached the tangle of exposed roots. Merging into the shadows of that woody mesh, she lay still and studied the clearing from that new perspective.

Ansin! There!

The last member of the raiding party was standing at the shoreline of the lake, less then forty paces from her own position. A tall figure in a hooded wolf-skin cloak, he had his back towards her as he stared out at the ethereal curtain of wispy tendrils offshore, his silhouette crisp against the mist's eerie half-light. Staring at that sinister profile, the woman warrior felt a disconcerting rush of panic and it suddenly became difficult to breathe. Bewildered, but forcing herself to continue studying the distant figure, she struggled to ignore a mounting and inexplicable sense of revulsion, even as sweat broke out on her skin and bile bubbled up in her stomach.

Distressed and close to vomiting, Liath Luachra was finally obliged to yank her eyes away. Scrambling backwards, she flipped about and scurried back the entire length of the fallen tree, regaining the shaded shelter between the branches of the rotting leaves in its flattened upper forks.

Huddled in those dark shadows, hands trembling and gasping for breath, the Grey One fought a rising nausea from the flush of adrenaline through her veins. Forcing herself to breathe deeply, it took some effort before the queasiness and the sweating subsided and she could start to take stock of her astounding and irrational reaction. Although she knew she should return to her position at the roots to study the *díberg* further, for some reason the thought of doing so was enough to make her skin crawl. Frustrated and fearing the return of those physical symptoms, she started back into the forest at a crawl instead, without once glancing to her rear.

Retracing her steps, the Grey One finally got to her feet when she was at a safe enough distance. She started walking, following the round-about route back to the ridge that would avoid any proximity to the *díberg* campsite.

A tall figure in a hooded wolf-skin cloak, his back turned towards her.

Recalling the individual by the lake, Liath Luachra felt her heartbeat quicken once again and struggled to make sense of the visceral physical reaction the mental image had triggered. There'd been no obvious threat of any kind – at least none she'd been able to detect – yet the sight of that figure had prompted a baffling sense of panic and revulsion that also triggered her flight instincts.

A glacial tremor ran down her spine but she ignored it, bowing her head as she continued towards the ridge. Whatever had caused that reaction, it had confirmed her own conviction that this wasn't a group she wanted to tackle alone.

***

Conscious that the *fian* would be hidden at the base of the hill by the time she returned, Liath Luachra made sure to create plenty of noise during her descent of the northern slope. Better to risk the low likelihood of discovery she reasoned, than the possibility of a miscast javelin.

Hitting the lower ground, she advanced swiftly into the trees, guided by the sound of the river thundering through the gully away to her left. Although anticipating the *fénnids'* appearance, when two figures suddenly detached themselves from the shadows it still caught her unprepared and she barely restrained herself from grabbing her sword as Murchú and An Giobach's familiar features materialised out of the gloom.

'Did you see her, Grey One?' Murchú asked urgently. 'Did you see Cairenn?'

Liath Luachra regarded the *Uí Loinge* man sourly. Despite his understandable concern for his sister, covered in mud, exhausted from a double scaling of the ridge, and still shaken at her own inexplicable reaction to the *díberg*, she was in no mood to engage with him or anyone else for that matter.

'She's weary, Murchú,' said An Giobach. 'Let her get fed and rested. She'll tell us what she knows once she's caught her breath.'

The *Uí Loinge* man glowered at his comrade but then grudgingly nodded his agreement. Beckoning for the woman warrior to follow, he turned and led them deeper into the trees, away from the river churning noisily to their rear.

Although they seemed to be taking an unnecessarily twisted route, Liath Luachra posed no questions as Murchú clearly had a destination in mind. Her patience paid off some moments later when they arrived at that destination: an ancient stone circle that had been swallowed up by the forest. Closely enclosed by trees to every side, the structure's interior had been savagely invaded by a chaotic sprawl of twisted roots, some so big they'd upended two of the stones on the south-eastern side. Wrapped in heavy cloaks, Biotóg and Feirgil looked to have made an

70

effort to settle themselves in, but that serpentine root system, the cramped leg space and the lack of a fire had apparently proven too much of a challenge. Both *fénnid* looked cold and miserable, the scattered bowls and other residue evidence of a recent but joyless meal.

Too hungry to care, Liath Luachra scooped up a chunk of griddlebread and a bowl of cold soup. Ignoring the others, she stumbled across the mesh of roots to the opposite treeline to take a seat on an oak root as wide as her thigh. There, turning away so she wouldn't have to look at the *fénnid,* she managed to scoff down two mouthfuls before a soft whinny from the trees drew her attention. Twisting her head to peer into the forest, she caught a glimpse of the two horses munching placidly between the trees on a tiny patch of open grass.

Mochta.

She shook her head. Ever attentive to the needs of his horses, the *Uí Loinge* man had apparently requisitioned the only available section of flat ground so the animals could feed.

Returning her attention to her bowl, the woman warrior softened the griddlebread by soaking it in the greasy soup but was still obliged to chew furiously to break it down in her mouth. Fortunately, the soup had enough flavour to make the resulting phlegm-like substance slip down her throat without too much of a battle.

As always, she ate quickly and quietly, dropping the bowl onto the ground when she'd finished. Swivelling about on her buttocks, she faced the *fénnid* who'd been talking quietly amongst themselves, watching her from the corner of their eyes with ill-concealed impatience.

'They're camped on the far side of the hill,' she told them. 'At the edge of a lake, several hundred paces out from the foot of the ridge.' She sniffed, used the back of her hand to smear a spatter of soup from her chin and wondered whether she should make some mention of her unease about the man in the wolf-cloak. Almost immediately, she decided against it. She was still struggling to understand what it was about this *díberg* that unnerved her and there was no point in spooking the *fénnid* over something that was probably a simple case of nerves.

'There's four men and they all look formidable fighters. They're warriors. Chary and on their guard. They won't go down easy.'

'Was it the Briga raiders?' asked Feirgil, with uncharacteristic coherency.

'Who else could it be?' snorted Mochta. 'If it wa-'

'Did you see, Cairenn?' Murchú interrupted. 'Was she the prisoner?'

'I couldn't see the prisoner's face,' Liath Luachra admitted. 'Besides, your sister's features are unfamiliar to me.'

'She has a spiral tattoo on her left shoulder blade, a ...' His voice trailed off as he realised the improbability of the Grey One observing that tattoo under such trying conditions. 'Well, it hardly matters. If there's a single prisoner, it could be no-one else and ...' He paused, struggling to control his emotions, then looked intently at the warrior woman. 'We should strike now, Grey One. Take the raiders before they get a lead on us again.'

An Giobach leaned forward and gave the *Uí Loinge* man a comradely slap on the back.

'Murchú, your concern for your sister is admirable but your desire for haste distorts your reasoning.' The big man pointed skywards where dark clouds were roiling. '*Féach thuas.* Dusk tumbles over the Great Wild. Night would be on us well before we neared the *díberg* camp. If they're as alert as the Grey One says, they'd hear us blundering through the forest darkness and make their escape well before we could even get close.'

Murchú's frustration was evident from the stiffness of his stance, nevertheless his silence confirmed that he recognised the logic of what An Giobach was telling him.

'We'll strike out before dawn,' Liath Luachra told them bluntly. 'It'll take time to climb that ridge in the dark but once we gain the summit there'll be light enough to slip down the far slope. We'll reach the *díberg* before they break camp and, if we're careful, should hit them with their wits still dull from sleep.'

'That's another night Cairenn remains a captive,' Murchú pointed out.

Liath Luachra looked at him silently then turned her head away. She had no words to soften that truth.

A quarrel broke out amongst the *fénnid* at that point with Murchú proposing alternative courses of action, Biotóg and An Giobach countering with proposals of their own. Feirgil sat off to the side and looked eagerly from one *fénnid* to the other, following the argument like an excited puppy. Mochta, shaking his head in disgust, got up and walked away, treading carefully across the root-strewn ground in the direction of his horses.

Liath Luachra, too, left the *fénnid*, rising silently to slip into the trees, and away from the campsite. She knew there was no real substance to the quarrel. Tired and cranky, the warriors were simply venting their frustrations and any residual vexations would fade once they'd calmed and realised the shortcomings of their proposals.

Pressing deeper into the forest, the woman warrior passed the point where she could no longer hear the voices and then kept on going. Consumed by her thoughts, she'd probably have continued even further if an owl hadn't suddenly flown across her path, the stuttered flutter of wings in the otherwise silent forest causing her to freeze in place.

Breathing in deeply to still her heart, Liath Luachra watched the bird disappear into the higher branches and wondered briefly at the fate of the owl and chicks she'd left behind in Luachair.

Most likely dead. In Luachair, everyone dies.

Closing her eyes, she cursed aloud. Thinking of Luachair had been a mistake, for it stirred shadows from her own past that invariably invited comparisons with Cairenn's situation.

That's another night Cairenn remains a captive.

The Grey One gritted her teeth.

Shit on you, Murchú. What did you expect?

Conscious that she was veering dangerously close to a place she didn't want to go, Liath Luachra forced herself to breathe, to exhale the tension from her chest. Since committing to the Seeking, she'd sought to approach it with dispassion, to make decisions based on calculated practicalities and avoid responses based on emotion or a misdirected desire for vengeance. From her experiences in Dún Beag she knew that once you ventured down that particular route, it was much harder to venture back.

Leaning against the creased, lichen-stained trunk of the nearby pine, she pressed her head against its trunk, comforted somehow by the coarse touch of bark against her forehead. This Seeking was starting to affect her, she realised. Every fresh exposure of Cairenn's plight leached into her darkest parts, undoing the fragments of calm she'd managed to establish over the years, causing her to question her own judgement.

She inhaled and exhaled, inhaled and exhaled, her breathing regular and controlled, her mind flailing for the softness of dream mushroom and its unfailing ability to smooth out the ragged wrinkles in her mind.

Mochta! Mochta had beacán scammalach!

Straightening up, she pushed herself away from the pine and hastened back towards the grove where she'd left the others, retracing the marks of her earlier passage. The distance back to camp seemed far shorter on the return and it was as though mere moments had passed when she caught sight of the horses, amending her direction to make her way to their little patch of grass. Mochta, happily, remained in the clearing, cooing affectionately in the roan's ear as he brushed its mane gently with a metal comb. Alerted by the soft step of the Grey One's approach, he swung around, his eyes widening in surprise.

'Grey One!'

'Mochta.'

Coming to a halt before him, the Grey One hesitated, struck by a sudden sense of awkwardness and unsure of what to say. 'We seek to retrieve your cousin tomorrow,' she blurted at last then abruptly lapsed into silence. As that silence extended, she could see the curiosity flowering in his eyes.

'Your horses cannot travel with us,' she added quickly.

Mochta regarded her uncertainly. 'That poses no issue, Grey One. The animals can be hobbled and left in safety here. If you're trying to suggest I remain behind with them however, I -'

Liath Luachra shook her head quietly but Mochta persisted. 'I've travelled all this distance to rescue Cairenn. I do not intend to be absent from the very battle that frees her.'

The woman warrior regarded him mutely, unsure how to respond to the *Uí Loinge* man's misinterpretation. Finally, bereft of ideas, she dipped her head in weary acknowledgement as though that had been her intention all along. The slim *Uí Loinge* man regarded her with curiosity as she continued to stand silently before him.

'Was there something else?'

She shifted position, opened her mouth to speak but then closed it again and glowered at him. An awkward silence followed.

Mercifully, Mochta somehow seemed to grasp her unspoken plea for he turned to his bag, reached inside and withdrew the small leather pouch she'd seen him conceal the night before. Untying the leather thong, he poured several slivers of *beacán scammalach* into his palm and held them out to her.

Liath Luachra cast him a wary glance then quickly scooped the mushrooms into her own palm before he changed his mind.

Mochta appeared unperturbed by the somewhat feral behaviour. 'Hunger knows hunger,' he said simply, then, refastening the leather thong, he replaced the pouch in his bag. Turning his back on her, he continued grooming the roan.

Liath Luachra fled the little clearing, the *beacán scammalach* clasped tightly in her palm. Although desperate to bolt into the forest with her prize, she first – reluctantly – returned to the campsite to retrieve her bedroll. Fortunately, by then, the *fénnid* had finished their arguing and most of them appeared to have dispersed to sleep elsewhere. An

Giobach alone remained within the stone circle, a blanket wrapped around his shoulders as he stared glumly at the trees.

'I'll be sleeping deeper in the forest tonight,' Liath Luachra grunted by way of explanation.

An Giobach gave an indifferent shrug. 'We'll all seek to sleep in the forest tonight. There's little enough space here for a man to stretch out. Besides, no one sleeps easy in the sites of the Ancient Ones.'

Liath Luachra nodded shortly, glancing impatiently towards the trees. 'Set a guard to the south tonight,' she instructed him. 'There's little chance the *díberg* could learn of our presence but …'

She shrugged and left the obvious unsaid.

The *fénnid* nodded. 'Very well.'

He coughed and pulled his cloak tighter but Liath Luachra thought to detect something in his manner suggesting he already knew where she was going and what she was about to do.

Or, more likely, she was simply reading too much into the blunt response.

Angry and embarrassed, and angry at her own embarrassment, the Grey One turned and walked away from the camp without another word.

***

There was a familiar sense of failure at finding herself back in the forest, lured once again by the draw of the *beacán scammalach*. A familiar sense of failure but also one of weary resignation. Following the events in Gort na Meala and Sean Fergus's passing, she had thought to have lost her taste for dream mushroom, falling instead on the harsh mattress of *uisce beatha* when her despair or loneliness proved a burden too heavy to bear. The grim winter confines of the Luachair valley had put paid to that assumption, of course. In Luachair, the cloud mushroom's grip had revealed itself even stronger than she'd imagined, the cold loneliness of the winter cave reawakening old cravings she'd thought far behind her.

Fortunately, on a small patch of flat ground beneath a drooping oak, her earlier, fatalistic realisations were eroded with the first tender kiss of *beacán scammalach*. As her intellect faded, Liath Luachra felt her physical senses unlock. Coughing, she wiped sweaty palms on her leggings, her heightened sensitivity making her ever more conscious of her pounding heart, the damp sensation of sweat leaking from her pores, the residual meaty flavour of the soup swelling on the back of her tongue.

All around her the forest throbbed, vibrant with life despite the darkness. Stretched beneath the trees, cocooned in her cloak and blanket, she felt the Great Mother reach out to grasp her, to draw her in and absorb her in that wild enormity.

And that was when the full effect of the cloud mushroom kicked in. The Grey One could actually perceive a softening to the air, a palpable heaviness as the Great Wild paused in mid-breath. Shafts of streaming light breached the darkness of the forest, angled beams of bright yellows, vibrant reds and succulent greens, all the summer colours from the fields of her childhood in Luachair.

'Can you feel it, Grey One?'

Although surprised by the voice, the dampening effect of the mushrooms meant the woman warrior wasn't overly troubled by this unexpected presence. She was calm, as she eased her head around to consider the fair-haired young woman sprawled languidly at the foot of an ash tree, two paces to her left. Fresh and slender, the newcomer had about twenty years on her. Her eyes, bright blue, glinted intelligence and playfulness and a wilful streak that seemed at odds with the long legs stretched lazily out before her. Her silver-blond hair was braided up in a style favoured by the *Éblána* women.

'Muirenn?'

'Can you feel it, Grey One?' the fair-haired girl asked again. Strangely, despite the weather, she was clad in the same clothing she'd worn when Liath Luachra had first set eyes on her; a green *léine* that showed the best of her slender figure, a thin silver torc, no footwear to speak of. The woman warrior felt her mind struggling to make sense, both of the young woman's presence and the meaning behind her words.

'Can I …' She swallowed nervously. 'Can I feel what?'

'The soil brimming with life beneath your toes. The loam, teeming with worms. The tree roots, strangling the bones of the dead.'

The woman warrior wet her lips, troubled by the prospect that there might be some hidden meaning behind the question but unable to offer any kind of reasonable answer. 'I don't understand,' she said at last.

The fair-haired woman smiled shyly then shook her head kindly, as though to suggest the matter was of little consequence. Prising herself off the ground she slid across to Liath Luachra, lowering herself onto the blanket alongside her, so close their hips were touching.

'Your absence was a cold void in Dún Mór over Bealtaine.' Muirenn reached one hand over to press down on the woman warrior's knee. 'And you missed a great feasting: succulent roast lamb, salted pork bones and water cress.' She closed her eyes, her tongue blissfully licking the full length of her lips. 'Wild mushroom in butter, hot tubers in meat broth.'

Liath Luachra could feel her own mouth salivate at the talk of such food. She'd grown increasingly weary of travel fare.

'And there was music! At night, we danced about the bonfires, twisting, merging …'

She sat up suddenly, raising both hands to demonstrate as she performed a dextrously sensual weaving movement before laughing and dropping her arms to her side. Reaching over, she pressed her lips to the warrior woman's ear and whispered softly.

'We supped on *uisce beatha* and danced and held each other close till Father Sun's red glow burned the morning sky.'

You and Barra.

Liath Luachra abruptly pulled away, freeing herself from the Éblána woman's touch. Sitting up, she cleared her throat.

'Whispers of the *Éblána* drifted south to *Uí Loinge* lands last summer.'

'Whispers?' With her eyes still glazed from memories of Bealtaine, Muirenn appeared to be only half-listening.

'Rumours that the *Éblána* chieftain's woman was heavy with child and …' Liath Luachra's voice broke off at the visible brightening in Muirenn's eyes.

'Yes! That was my daughter!'

It was impossible to mistake the delight and affection in the *Éblána* woman's voice. Watching her, Liath Luachra felt a sudden, inexplicable sense of loss, a growing yearning for something she didn't fully understand.

'She has my mother's eyes and Barra's cheeks.' With a grin, Muirenn leaned close again and pressed the Grey One's thigh. 'And I do believe she has your spirit.'

'Then Fíne Surehands will be happy,' said Liath Luachra, struggling to keep the bitterness from her voice. 'You've not only raised her status, you've guaranteed her progeniture through Barra's reign. No-one can argue you've not fulfilled your duty to the *Éblána*.'

To her surprise, Muirenn laughed gaily at that. 'I suppose as *éclann* you couldn't really understand. One's duty to tribe is never fulfilled.'

She reached down to pat her belly with a tender hand. 'I'm already with my second child. This time it will be a boy – an heir for Barra.'

Liath Luachra's stared at the *Éblána* woman's midriff but, to her eyes, that abdomen was as taut and smooth as on the beach near Gort na Meala where they'd once swum together. She attempted to raise a smile in response but the effort cost too much and she was obliged to let it drop.

'What is it, Grey One? Your eyes have softened. I can smell sorrow on your breath.'

Liath Luachra shrugged, struggling to swallow the choking lump in her throat before she could speak again. 'Is any of this real? Have you truly had a child with Barra? Do you truly carry his son or is this some whim of the *béacán scammalach* to twist and provoke my unease?'

The fair-haired girl leaned over and wrapped an arm about her shoulder, pressing her head softly against the warrior woman's.

'Do not, despair, Liath Luachra. I haven't forgotten you.'

With that physical proximity, Muirenn's hand seemed to grow heavier on the Grey One's knee, the brush of her breath increasingly moist and warm in her ear. The woman warrior felt a tangible light-headedness slip over her as a pleasurable warmth blossomed in her groin.

As though in response to the woman warrior's arousal, Muirenn raised her right hand, tracing her fingertips along Liath Luachra's neck, under her jaw and then up to stroke her cheek, igniting the skin wherever it touched. Her left hand, meanwhile, slid down inside the Grey One's blanket and came to rest on the tightness of her waist. As Liath Luachra trembled, the *Éblána* woman's hand dropped lower, inside her leggings to cup the warmth between the legs. This time, the Grey One groaned, shivering violently as Muirenn's fingers delicately prised her lips aside and slipped inside.

A violent shudder racked her body.

'Grey One.'

Somehow, through the arousal, the woman warrior thought to hear her name being called: hard and urgent. As the *Éblána* woman continued to caress her however, she cast such idiotic notions aside, submitting completely to the pleasure lapping her up from the inside. Exhaling in light, feathery sounds, she squeezed her hips and groin around Muirenn's fingers but even as the pleasure swallowed her up, she heard it again.

'Grey One.'

Persistent. Insistent. Tugging at the abraded underside of her mind.

For a moment – for a single snap of coherency – she was back in the winter woods, the air chill against her flesh, her eyes flush with darkness.

But then she was falling again. Back to the joy, back to the summer lands. Back to oblivion where nothing and no-one could touch her.

Chapter Five:

The reality of the Great Wild seeped through the dullness with a relentless insistence. Oozing in first through subtle dribs and drabs – a subconscious sense of unease, a persistent itch of subtle irregularity – these were quickly followed by more tangible physical sensations: a gnawing hunger, the musty smell of forest debris, the discomfort of a stone poking into her side.

Liath Luachra's first conscious awareness was the frigid touch of air against her face. Her second was the pressure of the hand enveloping her waist, the weight of the leg hooked over her hip, the nose against her shoulder blades breathing warmth into her back.

?!

She lunged from the blankets in mindless panic, instinctively scrambling for the trees and the deepest sanctuary of the Great Mother's womb. Breathless, flailing, and grazed from the sharp edges of protruding branches, she was finally forced to slow her terrified flight in the pitch black of the shadows and try to work out where she was. It was only as the clouds opened and moonlight filtered through the ragged canopy that she realised her panicked evasion had terminated in an almost perfect circle. Directly ahead lay a small patch of flat ground and the drooping oak from which she'd just fled. Swaddled in the blankets she'd so recently occupied, a prostrate figure stirred and rolled over, his face revealed in the silver blush of the moon.

Murchú!

Liath Luachra gaped in confusion, straining to draw sense from what she was seeing even as a tumultuous rage filled her head, the red scald of it blistering the edges of her vision. Unthinking, she yanked the knife in her belt from its hidden sheath, rushed towards the stirring figure and slammed the blade deep into his throat. As she pulled back with trembling hands however, the silver glow of the moon revealed the weapon wasn't embedded in the *Uí Loinge* man's gullet but in the ground alongside it, so close its edge had parted a layer of skin from which blood now dripped freely. Somehow, at the very last moment she'd turned her hand.

Murchú was staring up at her in horror. Although the rip of her original lunge from the blankets must have roused him, any remaining wisps of doziness had entirely fled with the touch of cold steel. Flinging the woman warrior's blankets from him, he scrambled frantically backwards, drawing up against the leaf-strewn incline at his rear.

'Great Mother's tit! Grey One! What are you doing?'

The Grey One's response was a full-throated snarl as she lunged again, slamming him hard against the earth, sweeping the blade up at an angle to curl under his jaw. Noses practically touching, she roared into his face: a savage, blood-curdling bellow that caused the *fénnid's* moonlit features to blanch even further.

'I heard you cry out! I came to see you safe!'

In desperation, the *Uí Loinge* man grasped the only defence he had to hand: succinct statements of explanation. Oblivious to the stuttered avowals however, the warrior woman maintained an even pressure on the blade, keeping the weapon so steady its edge lay evenly across his jugular, biting sliver-deep through the skin of his throat.

'You were in the dirt! Unravelled from your blankets! Crazed from cloud mushroom!'

Liath Luachra maintained her vicious glare, eyes swollen, lungs bellowing, breath hot with bloodlust. Somewhere deep inside however, a sick realisation had begun to blossom and, as always when confronted by something that scared her, she reverted to her most feral, baring her teeth and growling incoherently.

By then however, driven beyond the limits of his fear, the *Uí Loinge* man's sense of self-preservation had transformed to anger.

'Shitsmear on you then, Grey One. Your body was cold to the touch. Had I left you, you'd have frozen to death.'

Although the hand that held the knife did not so much as tremble, Liath Luachra's head spilled over with bloody visions of plunging the blade home, of stabbing the *Uí Loinge* man again and again and again.

But her hand refused to do so.

Somehow, getting a leash on her anger, she drew the blade back a fraction, enough for Murchú to reach up and press against her wrist, tentatively pushing the weapon away.

Numbly accepting the fact that she wasn't going to kill the *Uí Loinge* man, Liath Luachra slid off him and stepped back, the substance of her rage peeling away in the shadows. Murchú wasted no time scrambling to his feet out of reach of her blade. Breathing deeply, hand clutched to the sliced skin at his throat, he regarded her with a mixture of incredulity and rage.

'Should you truly wish to open my throat perhaps you could hold your hand till my sister is safe.'

Without waiting for a response, he reached down to yank his blanket free from hers and, stuffing it under his arm, stalked off into the trees.

Liath Luachra watched him fade into the shadows, the veins in her temple still throbbing, the knife in her hand dangling loosely by her side.

All about her, the forest had grown silent, the wildlife cowering in response to her violence, the subsequent hush emphasised by a background breeze in the upper canopy that stretched and creaked the higher branches.

The woman warrior hoicked up a gob of saliva. Her throat and mouth reeked with the acrid aftertaste of mushroom slivers, the same sour whiff in the sweat seeping through her pores and coating her body like a fetid second skin.

The coherency that came with consciousness offered little solace to her disarray. Standing in the moon-strewn fragments of light, Liath Luachra trembled and gnashed her teeth, appalled – even through the miasma in her head – by what she'd almost done, even more appalled by the careless exposure of her own vulnerability.

Stirred by the cold bite of the night air against her skin, she gathered her cloak, wrapped it about herself and sat in a patch of grass illuminated by a silver shaft of moonlight. Shivering, she struggled to coalesce her thoughts, to make sense of what had happened. Her last coherent memory was a passionate embrace with Muirenn but even as her groin tingled at that recollected pleasure, she could feel the memory crumble into a blur of dreamlike ecstasy that ….

It wasn't real. It was the béacán scammalach.

Numbed by that bleak realisation, the woman warrior sat quietly, struggling to absorb its significance. In all the years she'd used cloud mushroom, she'd never experienced hallucinations of such overpowering eroticism and it terrified her to find how easily her innermost frailties and sexual desires had been exposed.

Realising that she still held the knife in her hand, the woman warrior flung it violently at the tree trunk directly opposite, experiencing a bitter satisfaction as the blade sank into the trunk with a *thunk*, the handle quivering from the force of the impact.

Although pragmatic enough to know that physical needs had the capacity to slip into one's dreams, Liath Luachra had always believed that in her own case such cravings remained deeply buried. As female *rígfénnid* to a group of brutal male warriors, sexuality was a weakness she couldn't afford to consider and, since her abduction in Luachair, not one she'd ever sought to explore. This had been her reality for so long she'd never even considered any alternative.

Now, however, it turned out that grave was far shallower than she'd envisaged. Freshly exhumed by *béacán scammalach*, she was unsure that particular corpse would ever go down quite so easily again.

With a grunt, she got to her feet to retrieve her knife, forced to tug the haft several times before she was able to yank it free. Standing beside the ancient oak, she glanced sideways at the crumpled heap of her blankets, struggling to contain the bile of dismay.

Once again, her hunger for *beacán scammalach* had left her vulnerable and open to harm, but this time, too desperate to lose herself, she hadn't bothered to take her usual precautions. Her sole good fortune was that she'd been discovered by someone who meant her no harm, someone whose kindness she'd rewarded with a response as insane as it was savage.

She stamped her feet to warm them against the creeping numbness in her toes and, pulling her cloak a little tighter, looked up at the sliver of moon, disturbed to see it so far to the east. Soon, she realised, she'd have to lead her *fian* – including Murchú – to do battle with the *díberg*. If she hadn't regained her equilibrium by then, or if she wavered in her resolve, everything they'd achieved up to this moment would be threatened.

Wiping cold sweat from her brow, the woman warrior stood and shook off the burden of lethargic detachment to concentrate on her preparations. Humiliating though it was, there was simply no time for shame.

Removing her tunic, she ignored the air's cold touch against her back as she rummaged through the backpack to retrieve the leather battle harness. Pulling it on over her head, she strapped it snug and tight. The strengthened leather provided no real warmth however, so she also pulled her cloak about her before starting back to rejoin the others.

Even with the intermittent moonlight, the trip back to the stone circle was far slower for she was obliged to tread with care in the darkness, stopping completely whenever the moon was engulfed by clouds. By the time she finally made it back, the other *fénnid* had already gathered at the centre of the circular alignment and despite the subdued sense of men just woken, she could detect an underlying pre-fight tension amongst them.

From the shadows at the treeline, she watched An Giobach and Biotóg sharpening their blades while Mochta adjusted and readjusted the tightness of his sword belt. Feirgil, seated on one of the roots, was pulling his sword blade in and out of its scabbard over and over again, as though fascinated by the mindlessly repetitive mechanics of the action.

Murchú, too, had returned but he sat apart from the others, his shoulders hunched in anger. He glanced at her coldly as she left the trees and made no comment as she entered the overgrown stone circle.

Glancing towards him, the woman warrior's guilt merged awkwardly with her relief. From the other *fénnid's* lack of response, it was obvious he'd made no mention of her behaviour in the forest and for that she felt immense gratitude.

For a moment she faltered, intending to move towards the *Uí Loinge* man until she realised An Giobach was regarding her with an odd expression, possibly picking up on the tension in his fellow *fénnid's* reaction. Flustered, she made instead for the tree where they'd stacked the javelins, grabbed two of the missiles, strapped them together and slung them over her shoulder.

Looking around, she found all the *fénnid* waiting.

'*Ar aghaidh linn*,' she said. Let's go.

***

The Grey One was relieved she'd already travelled the ridge ascent. Even with the intermittent moonlight and the helpful reference point of the thundering waterway, she'd have struggled to find a practical route in the pre-dawn darkness without that prior knowledge of the terrain. Fortunately, *Na Cinéaltaí* made the ascent without mishap, cresting the summit just as dawn was breaking and pausing briefly to rest at the edge of the escarpment. Once they'd caught their breath, Liath Luachra led them swiftly through the upper forest and down the precarious southern slope, halting in the shadows at the base of the ridge while she determined their exact position.

Once she'd worked out her bearings, the woman warrior gathered the *fénnid* about her and whispered a brief description of the terrain they'd be traversing. Given the caution she'd seen the *díberg* display with respect to the northern approach, she proposed skirting the camp once again and making for a point somewhere south of the raiders' position. There, they could arrange their battle formation in preparation for the attack. If the raiders were up and moving, the *fian* would cast a volley of javelins at her signal and follow that up with a full assault. If they were still abed, the *fénnid* would slink in and overwhelm them, dispatching any guard in advance if possible.

To Biotóg, Liath Luachra designated responsibility for taking out the guard, covered by the protective javelins of An Giobach and herself. To Murchú, she assigned the task of locating and protecting the captive, a responsibility he accepted with a nod but no other sign of acknowledgement. Feirgil and Mochta, the two members in whom she had less confidence, she assigned to the flanks, as far as possible from the most likely centre of the fighting. Feirgil would take the flank bordering the lake shore. Mochta, the least experienced amongst them, she'd keep close to herself on the eastern flank.

With the plan of attack clarified, the Grey One paused and looked towards the north.

A tall figure in a hooded wolf-skin cloak, his back turned towards her.

She shuddered and quickly pushed the memory from her head.

'These men,' she told the *fénnid*. 'They're dangerous. When you encounter one, spill his blood without pause. You can reflect on the rights and wrongs of it later.'

The *fénnid* nodded, confirming their understanding, but she eyeballed each of them to drive the point home, wincing inwardly when Murchú looked away and refused to meet her gaze.

Mallacht ort, a Murchú. Don't fail me.

Taking a deep breath, Liath Luachra examined her weapons for flaws or weaknesses one final time, then led the group off in single file, moving at a crouch as they retraced her steps – as far as possible – from the previous afternoon. With the grey light of dawn now filtering through the trees, it was far easier to work out their path, any noise produced by their careful advance dampened by the wet mulch of the forest floor or swallowed in the deafening chatter of the riotous dawn chorus.

The birdsong screened them for the better part of their passage then, just as it began to fade, the Grey One recognised the head-shaped stump she'd seen the previous afternoon. Adjusting their path, she led the *fian* sharply to the southwest for another several hundred paces, until she was certain they'd bypassed the *díberg* camp. Coming to a halt in a tiny hollow, she dropped to a squat, noiselessly gesturing for the *fénnid* to spread out and turn towards the north.

As the warriors dispersed to their positions, Liath Luachra unravelled a javelin from the two strapped to her back and removed the *suaineamh* from inside her tunic. Looping the leather strap about the base of the shaft, she ran the remainder back up the other side, tightly wrapping the leftover leather about her throwing hand. Setting up for a more powerful and controlled javelin cast in that manner limited her ability to respond quickly to close quarters combat but, given their advantage of surprise, she considered the risk warranted.

The woman warrior looked around one last time prior to moving forward only to realise that Feirgil was still crouched in the trees four or five paces to her rear. Exasperated, she was just about to snap at him when something about the *fénnid's* demeanour made her pause. Watching him closely, she realised that he was gesturing strangely with his hands, whispering fiercely as though engaged in an argument.

Despite the absence of any other participant.

'Feirgil!' she hissed.

The *fénnid* twisted his head to look at her in a furtive, sideways manner and the Grey One started in surprise. Although the warrior's eyes were bright, they were wild with an uncharacteristic maliciousness and a dark, canny knowing. Observing her reaction, his lips curled into a wolfish smirk and he poked out a triangular-shaped tongue, making a rapid licking motion that was undeniably sexual in nature.

Liath Luachra stared at him in shock, repressing the sudden shiver that ran through her. By then however, Feirgil had abruptly lost interest in her. Shifting back to his original position, he reverted once more to the urgent gesturing and muted whispering.

The woman warrior swallowed nervously, wondering if this bizarre behaviour might be some early expression of the *ríastraid*. Even as she watched however, the *fénnid's* shoulders slumped in on themselves and when he twisted around once more to glance in her direction, there was a hesitancy, a timidity very much at odds with his earlier deportment.

Conscious that the others would already be moving towards the *díberg* camp, Liath Luachra pushed her fears aside and hissed urgently in an effort to regain control of the situation.

'Feirgil! Shift your speckled arse!'

The *fénnid* looked around again, his expression sheepish and noticeably less assured. Nodding apologetically, he grabbed his javelin from where he'd dropped it then scurried off in the direction of the lake, quickly disappearing into the trees.

Shaking her head, Liath Luachra gave the *fénnid* a few moments to get into place, then crawled to take up her own position between Biotóg and Mochta, the latter now several paces off to her right. Seeing the warrior woman slide into view, the *Uí Loinge* man grinned conspiratorially and waved the hand-axe he was holding in his right hand. Disregarding that off-putting eagerness, the woman warrior gave her signal and the *fian* advanced at a crawl.

The ground between the trees was slick with gritty leaf litter and wet patches of stunted grass. As a result, it wasn't long before Liath Luachra's battle harness and leggings were greasy with moisture, any patches of exposed skin stinging from the cold. Ignoring that chilly discomfort, the woman warrior continued her advance, counting on the *fénnid* to maintain alignment with her as they continued northwards.

After they'd traversed a distance of almost forty paces, the woman warrior caught the smoky whiff of the raiders' campfire and, glancing to her left, saw Biotóg nod at her, confirmation that he too had smelled it. Liath Luachra felt her belly muscles tighten as the pre-battle tension clamped her insides.

Another six paces and she caught a glimpse of the lake, a brief sliver of blue-grey through the trees off to the left. Five paces further and she finally caught sight of the clearing, now less than twenty-five paces away and …

It was empty.

Liath Luachra pressed flat against the cold earth, her mind reeling. After a moment had passed, hoping she'd simply imagined the deserted clearing, she raised her head again, carefully peering through the trees, scrutinising the open ground for any sign of the raiders, any evidence of their presence.

But there was nothing: no baggage, no possessions, no cooking equipment, nothing but the low, smoking fire.

They're gone!

Stunned, she lay flat again, struggling to work out what might possibly have happened even as her body shuddered with the impact of slowing the bloodlust that flooded her system. Could the *díberg* have moved on since she'd left them the previous afternoon? She bit her lip. She couldn't imagine why. When she'd left the *díberg* camp, they'd looked bedded in for the night and, in any case, the presence of the smoking fire belied that possibility. Although it now looked close to going out, someone had to have been feeding it wood until recently and, given the absence of cooking equipment or utensils, it seemed unlikely it had been maintained for cooking purposes.

Which suggested it had been kept going uniquely for *Na Cinéaltaí*.

They knew we were coming!

Her initial reaction was to dismiss that possibility, nevertheless as she mulled it over, she could think of no alternative explanation. Somehow, the *díberg* must have discovered they were being pursued. Outnumbered, encumbered and in hostile territory, the last thing they'd have wanted was to engage in combat so they'd used the fire as a diversion, a lure to draw the *fian* while they made their escape in another direction.

The woman warrior cursed under her breath, the earlier adrenalin surge now fuelling a growing infuriation.

How could they have known?

She forced herself to try and think calmly as she worked thorough any mistakes the *fian* might have made, anything they might have done to give their presence away. For one brief, heart-clutching moment, she wondered whether her own use of the *béacán scammaclach* might somehow have contributed to their exposure but, on reflection, discounted it. Partaking of the cloud mushroom had been foolish and self-destructive but, at night, isolated in the forest on the opposite side of a steep hill it seemed ludicrous to think it might somehow have caused the *fian's* presence to be detected.

Glancing to the left, she saw Biotóg rise, peer carefully from one side of the clearing to the other then drop again. She couldn't see the other *fénnid* beyond him but she imagined they'd be experiencing a similar agitation. Having fired themselves up for bloodshed, their bodies would be raring for violence and it'd be a hard task to control or curtail that nurtured bloodlust, particularly when it remained unclear if the *díberg* were still in the environs. Turning to look in her direction, even Biotóg's dull and bulging fish-eyes couldn't disguise his restless anger.

She signalled for everyone to stay where they were, to maintain their position flat in the dirt. As time passed however and the absence of any activity in the clearing became ever more obvious, Liath Luachra knew she wouldn't be able to keep the strung-out warriors in place for much longer. Despite her misgivings, she gestured for Biotóg to send the western-most warriors forward to examine the lakeside campsite while he, Mochta and herself remained in reserve should the need arise.

Biotóg passed her message down the line but because of the trees she couldn't see what was happening until An Giobach suddenly appeared at the lakeside edge of the clearing, advancing at a crouch with his javelin ready to cast.

'Grey One!'

The call from her right pulled her eyes to where Mochta lay hidden in the withered undergrowth. Seeing that he had her attention, he raised both hands palm outwards and shrugged, evidently seeking some update on what was happening. When she ignored him, he started to shuffle across towards her until she firmly signalled for him to remain where he was.

Annoyed by the distraction, the woman warrior returned her attention to the clearing where An Giobach, Feirgil and Murchú were now warily searching the remnants of the *díberg's* presence. After a time, leaving the others to continue searching, An Giobach started back through the trees towards them, his angry expression a clear indication of his displeasure.

'They're gone,' he called. 'Their tracks show them headed south.'

Still lying flat in the dirt, Liath Luachra exhaled and angrily slammed the haft of her javelin against the earth. To her left, Biotóg got to his feet with a contemptuous snort, his pimpled features peering curiously towards the empty clearing. Even at that distance, the remains of the dying fire and the flattened grass where the captive had been lying were plainly visible.

Prompted by the return of the other *fénnid*, Mochta too got to his feet and started back to join them. From his perplexed expression, he had no idea what had occurred. 'Is this normal?' he called to Liath Luachra. 'I'm no seasoned warrior like you and the others but it strikes me that …'

Suddenly he stopped in mid-step, looked at her quizzically and cocked his right ear upwards. 'What's that noise?' he asked.

Liath Luachra looked at him blankly but then she too heard it: a long, tinny, high-pitched whistle.

'Flat!' she roared.

Mochta was still staring at her in surprise when the javelin slammed into his chest, the missile's downward momentum causing it to strike him with such force, the metal head and a finger's length of wooden shaft erupted from his back in a spray of crimson.

The Grey One watched in horror as Mochta was whipped off his feet, barely even registering the two other javelins that slammed into the ground to either side of him. The *Uí Loinge* man hit the ground like a misshapen sack of grain. His head lolled onto one side, blood spilling from his mouth, sightless eyes staring directly at her.

A cry to her rear, yanked Liath Luachra's attention back to where Biotóg was also down, his face white, his right hand clutching a gruesome gash in his left shoulder. Blood was spurting from between his fingers and a bloody-headed javelin lay strewn on the ground alongside his own weapon. The hafts from three other javelins protruded upwards from the earth around him.

Shaking off her shock, the woman warrior edged backwards towards the wounded warrior, unconsciously working through the elements of the attack as she did so. The raiders had targeted the *fian's* right flank, peppering the two warriors closest to them. She'd escaped harm only because she'd remained on her belly, unseen by the casters.

They're to the east! On our eastern flank!

Despite a burning urge to retaliate, she fought the temptation to raise her head and cast her own javelin. The raiders had planned their trap well and almost certainly had *Na Cinéaltaí's* measure. By fighting back now, she'd only reveal her own position and prompt another javelin volley.

An Giobach, Murchú and Feirgil had already gone to ground but obscured by the trees and the undergrowth, she couldn't tell whether they'd been hit or not. Drawing closer to Biotóg however, she was greatly relieved to see An Giobach wriggle in from between the trees behind the stricken warrior, clamping a beefy hand over the moaning *fénnid's* mouth to silence him and prevent drawing a fresh fusillade on them. A moment later, Murchú appeared just a little to his left. Creeping up beside the big warrior, he stared over at the corpse of his fallen cousin with eyes that were flat and cold.

Practical as ever, An Giobach plugged Biotóg's wound with moss while the woman warrior monitored their eastern flank, her javelin poised to cast. Taken completely by surprise and with one third of their force eliminated, *Na Cinéaltaí* were on the back foot and very vulnerable should the *díberg* make a full assault. Feverishly scanning the trees, she couldn't see any sign of movement but that didn't mean the raiders weren't closing in around them.

An Giobach had come to a similar conclusion. 'We need to withdraw,' he growled. 'Find a defensible position.'

Biotóg gave a muffled curse in response as the big *fénnid* bound his makeshift bandage with a flax tie.

'Stop bawling. You'll draw them on us.'

'I think they already have a fair notion where to find us,' Murchú hissed bitterly.

Just then, Feirgil crept out of the western trees, quickly crawling across the leaf-strew earth to join them. He looked blankly from one to the other until his eyes found Mochta's corpse and settled on it.

Liath Luachra poked the wounded *fénnid* in the leg. 'Biotóg, they have us trapped against the lake. You'll have to eat the pain while we move you.'

'Where are we going?' asked Feirgil.

'Well, we can't go north,' the Grey One answered. 'Crossing that clearing will have us exposed.'

'I think we can assume they'll have someone to the south as well.' An Giobach regarded the warrior woman with ill-concealed anger. 'Grey One, there were more than four raiders in that attack. I counted three javelins on Mochta, four on Biotóg. That's a volley of seven javelins which means seven raiders. More if they were keeping a man or two in reserve.'

'So where did they come from?' snarled Murchú. 'Do raiders bud from the winter trees now?'

Liath Luachra glanced back at him and didn't know what to say. They were in a bad position, fortunate only in that the raiders had chosen not to launch a full assault to follow the javelin volley.

'However many they are, it's more than enough to take us down. An Giobach has the right of it. The best we can do is retreat, find a better position to hold off a frontal attack.'

Murchú breathed deeply. 'There's a wide oak grove back towards the water. Fifty paces or so. It arcs around in a half-circle against the lake so the rear's protected. The trees would give a solid defence against another javelin volley and there's a short stretch of open ground between it and the main body of the forest. If we had javelins enough, the raiders would pay a hefty price trying to cross that ground.'

Liath Luachra looked at him. 'How many javelins do we have between us?'

'Ten, counting Biotóg's.'

'Eight,' Feirgil piped in. 'I lost mine.'

Murchú stared at him, infuriated. 'How did …' He paused and shook his head in frustration. 'Never mind. We have to move. Now.'

Conscious that they had few options left to them, Liath Luachra was quick to nod her assent. 'Good enough. Feirgil, help Biotóg back to the trees but stay low. Murchú, you and An Giobach can gather the enemy javelins, that'll give you another six – she looked at the one protruding up into the air from Mochta's chest – another seven missiles.'

An Giobach looked at her closely. 'And what about you? Where are you going?'

'I'll cover your backs while you withdraw. Once you're in safety, I'll move south to outflank them.'

'They'll have men to th-'

'I'll get past them,' she snapped. 'Once I do, I'll come around from behind and try to whittle the odds. Now, shift your arse. We move.'

***

Na Cinéaltaí's luck held while they carried out their retreat with no further sign of the *díberg*. Relieved at their good fortune, Liath Luachra kept watch as the *fénnid* hurriedly gathered the enemy javelins and helped a white-faced Biotóg to his knees, supporting him in a clumsy crawl through the trees in the direction of the lake. Holding her position, arm aching from the effort of keeping her javelin aloft, she waited until the *fian* had disappeared into the trees, then a little longer until she was sure they'd reached the shelter of the oak grove.

Taking advantage of the *díberg's* continued absence, the Grey One dropped to her belly and started wriggling through the ragged undergrowth between the trees, slowly but surely working her way southeast. She covered fifty paces in a laborious and wary crawl, then another fifty paces, pausing regularly to lie still and listen or scan the surrounding forest. After another fifty paces she was beginning to wonder at the raiders' continued absence when a bird call sounded somewhere to her right, a bird call that rang false to her ears. A moment later that call was answered by another, similar, call from the trees less than ten paces to the left of where she was lying. Gingerly adjusting her position, she started another painstakingly slow crawl in the opposite direction.

Moving with care, she managed to work away from the hidden raiders without being detected. When she got to a distance where she judged herself safe, she took a moment to think through the situation. It disturbed her that the *díberg* hadn't followed up on their javelin volley. Although grateful for the respite, the most rational action from their attacker's perspective would have been to swarm in immediately after launching their javelin volley, taking advantage of their opponents' confusion to finish them off while they were at their most vulnerable.

And yet, despite their unexpected increase in numbers, they hadn't done that.

She gnawed at the inside of her cheek.

And that was another issue. When she'd left the *díberg's* camp the previous afternoon, there'd been no more than four warriors. Now there were at least double that number. So, where had they come from?

Do raiders bud from the winter trees now?

She ground her teeth in frustration. Perhaps Murchú had the right of it. It made as much sense as anything else. Since their initial abduction of his sister, little of this *díberg's* behaviour had made any sense.

Conscious that these were issues she had no chance of resolving any time soon, the woman warrior pushed them from her mind and started crawling again. After a short distance, finding her route blocked by a fallen tree, she slithered around to its left side where she discovered a shallow gully running off to the southeast, barely discernible amongst the tangle of overgrown, winter-burned vegetation that shaded it on either side. Slithering down into that narrow culvert, she started wriggling forward, following it for almost three hundred paces, the movement of her body producing soft squelching sounds in the thick black muck congealed at its base.

Emerging from its southernmost end, she clambered up into a tangle of dead fern beside a flat patch of open ground that created a natural passage through the trees. It was on that patch of muddy ground that she found her first confirmation of the *díberg's* greater numbers: tracks for at least six men moving north towards the lake, the wide spaces between the individual footprints indicating that they'd been moving at speed.

Although tempted to follow the tracks, the woman warrior's instincts prompted her to proceed along the raiders' backtrail. The *fénnid* were secure in the oak grove by now, a refuge as safe as any for the time being, and she needed a better understanding of the force she was up against before she dared attempt direct action against them.

Rising to a low crouch, Liath Luachra advanced into the trees, the forest shadows darker and quieter in the early morning light, its stark character even more eerie due to the thin mist floating at knee level above the cold, damp earth. At ease in the familiarity of the Great Mother's mantle however, the warrior woman slipped sinuously through her musty surroundings.

Guided by the raiders' footprints, Liath Luachra continued south and soon noticed a brightening in the upper canopy some distance ahead, a dull glow suggesting the edge of the treeline or a large clearing. Spotting a jumble of misshapen, lichen-coated boulders off to the left that seemed to be located at the edge of that bright area, the woman warrior left the trail and cut away at an angle towards them.

Approaching the boulders, Liath Luachra discovered that they were far larger than she'd thought. Slipping closer to the nearest of them, the woman warrior pressed against the hard, lichen-sodden surface as she shifted around its granite bulk. A few paces beyond the boulders, the trees opened abruptly to reveal a long, roughly rectangular clearing with yet another grey-watered lake along its eastern side. Strewn with rough stretches of flat, grey rock, interspersed with wide patches of sickly-looking grass, the clearing had a cold, unwelcoming air and her eyes were drawn naturally to the brightness of a fire crackling beneath the broad boughs of an enormous oak that stood alone in the open clearing, closest to the westernmost treeline. On the far side of the flames, directly in front of the trunk, was a pair of young girls.

Cairenn?

The woman warrior froze, thrown not only by the fact that there were two girls but that both were completely naked. Sinking low into the undergrowth, she peered more closely then felt something sink deep inside her. Both girls had been shackled to the tree trunk, their hands encased in iron manacles.

Fearing another trap, Liath Luachra feverishly scrutinised every stretch of the treeline but no matter where she looked, the upper branches shifted serenely in the morning breeze, the birdlife chatter remained strong and untroubled. Confident that the girls couldn't free themselves, it looked as though the *díberg* had simply deserted them in their rush to confront *Na Cinéaltaí*.

But why leave them completely naked?

The answer to that question came to her quickly enough. It was the cold. Even had the girls managed to free themselves, without clothing or the heat of the fire to warm themselves, they'd quickly freeze to death. Their lack of clothing was just another means of imprisoning them.

Conscious that she was potentially wasting valuable time and that the raiders might return at any moment, the woman warrior edged cautiously towards the western treeline which, free from the restrictions of the lake, offered the best option for flight should the need arise. Advancing slowly, she stopped every five paces or so to listen, straining to distinguish any irregularity to the background sounds of the forest, but unable to detect anything out of place. If anyone else was in the forest, they weren't close by.

Nearing the tree, Liath Luachra paused to study its prisoners again, this time close enough to make out that both had not only been chained but gagged as well. She could also see that the girls' skins were covered in subtle spiral tattoos, complex patterns of twisting greens, yellows and blues that coated their torsos – front and back – from their necks to their groins.

The woman warrior blinked. The patterns were quite beautiful, but she'd never seen their like before and they looked nothing like *Uí Loinge* tattoos. The placement also struck her as oddly impractical.

Meanwhile, in stark contrast to the vivacity of their colourful body patterns, the prisoners slumped slack and limp against the roots of the tree. At first, on observing that listless demeanour, Liath Luachra imagined that they'd simply given up, resigned themselves to their helpless situation. Then she noticed the marks about their wrists, the bloody wounds where they'd struggled against the iron manacles and realised that, although they might look subdued now, they'd fought ferociously to escape their fetters.

Teeth clenched, the woman warrior continued her careful advance until she reached the treeline directly west of the giant oak, separated from it by a stretch of open ground around fifteen paces in length.

Squatting in the undergrowth, she once again scrutinised the clearing and the treeline to either side, nervous at the prospect of leaving the safety of the forest cover. Finally, unable to put it off any further, she rose to full height and, with one last look around, stepped warily into the open.

She covered several paces before she was noticed and, unsurprisingly, it was the nearer of the two captives who spotted her first. Head bowed in silent misery, the girl's attention was drawn by the flicker of movement. Raising her head, at first she regarded the woman warrior with numbed disinterest then, realising that the newcomer wasn't one of her captors, her eyes widened and she leapt up to strain against the manacles, her desperation visible through the wet creases of her eyes.

Roused by her comrade's sudden activity, the second girl also looked up and, seeing Liath Luachra, jumped to her feet as well. Desperately trying to speak to her, the two prisoners yanked at their chains, their voices muffled and incomprehensible behind the stifling gags.

Liath Luachra disregarded the girls as she approached the tree, her focus on where the links from both chains had been jointly driven into the trunk by an enormous metal peg. Staring at that substantial restraint, she experienced a sudden frisson of panic. The peg had been hammered in with great force and was deeply embedded in the trunk. Pulling it free with nothing more than her hands and weapons was going to be a challenge.

A sudden weakness flowered behind her knees and a burning sensation flared down through the scars on her back. Doing her best to disregard the muffled pleas from the desperate girls, she pulled her knife from its scabbard and started jabbing its blade at an angle into the trunk, targeting the wood directly around the peg.

The bark was thick, the angle difficult and it was frustratingly slow work, but she kept at it with manic concentration, breaking off tiny chunks of woody material to expose more and more of the shiny metal peg. Focussed uniquely on widening that hole, she ignored the girls, ignored the loud crackle of wood from the fire, ignored the woods, ignored everything but the tree trunk in front of her.

It was the steadfast focus allowing her to carve with such efficiency that also proved her undoing. With the sound of the fire, she never heard the muffled yelps of the girls, never heard the subtle tread of feet, never heard – or noticed – anything until a blade pressed against the right side of her throat.

'I see you, Grey One!'

An undiluted terror flowed through her at the sound of that soft-spoken voice. Wordless horror crammed her head with a vacuous white that suppressed all intellectual function. Somehow, like a disinterested bystander, she felt her body go rigid while her bowels, conversely, loosened and she barely had the wherewithal to avoid soiling herself.

A loud whinny of laughter sounded from her rear but the man holding the blade to her throat made no response. Clamping her left shoulder with a painful grip, he quietly shifted position, transferring his weight from one foot to the other.

Some intangible quality in that simple movement alerted the warrior woman. Somehow, intuitively, she knew he was going to hit her.

Reacting on instinct, she pulled her head to the left, away from the blade just as she was struck with the hilt of his weapon. That single movement saved her from the worst of the blow, but it still connected with force, shooting shards of silver up through her eyes. For a single heartbeat, the world tipped sideways. She felt herself falling, tumbling for what seemed a long time before hitting the ground hard, hot fire razing across her vision. Lying on her side, fading in and out of consciousness, she was somehow still aware of the shadowed figure crouched low beside her.

'I'd thought you passed, Grey One.'

The tone of the voice was mild, cordial and gentle. Kindly yet petrifyingly familiar. Even as her vision blurred, she saw, once more, the silhouette on the shore and everything suddenly made a terrible sense.

A tall figure in a hooded wolf-skin cloak, his back turned towards her.

'I'd thought you passed at Dún Beag. I truly had. With Garrad Mór and his inbred offspring.' A hand came to rest on her rump, slid down to cup the curve of a buttock. 'And now, what do I find here? Why, some dear old friends!'

Even through the stupor, Liath Luachra could feel her body tremble, heard the man chuckle, misinterpreting it as some involuntary pleasure response from his touch. A hand reached down to take hold of her jaw, gently lifting her head and turning it from side to side. Although her eyes were open, they were unfocussed and blurred with tears. She could make out little more than a dark shadow but there was no doubting who it was.

Dead! You're dead!

'Garrad Mór always was the lazy one. Taking his reward from An Draoi Dubh – The Dark Druid – but then too busy humping his prize to fulfil the tasks assigned him.'

The figure grabbed a handful of her hair and used it to tug her head a little higher. She felt a sawing motion and numbly realised he was cutting through the strands then, abruptly, she was released and her head lolled back onto the ground.

'Wat you kill tha for?'

Another male voice: boorish, thick with phlegm. Whether it came from off to the right or the left, she couldn't tell.

'What troubles you, Cerball? You developed a taste for boyish meat now?'

'Just a waste, tha. Slicin' her out. Just a waste.'

'Aaah, you know what Cerball's like.' A third man's voice chipped in at that point. Nasal and high-pitched, it grew louder as he spoke, as though he was drawing closer towards her. A foot kicked her hard in the ribs but she was still too dazed to feel pain.

'Makes no difference to him,' the nasal voice continued. 'Any meat with a sheath of flesh, Cerball's *bod* will poke it.'

The shadowed figure beside her snorted. '*Tá súil agam go blas feoil lofa a thaitin leis, mar sin. Is marbhán atá againn anseo.*' I hope he likes spoiled meat then. It's a corpse we have here.

'And what of the …?' the nasal voice asked. His words were swallowed in an indistinct mumble as though he was engaged in some strenuous activity, but it sounded like he'd said 'metal men'. Flitting in and out of consciousness, the woman warrior was in no state to care.

Roused by a soft rustling sound, Liath Luachra became aware that the shadowed man was wiping his hands in a patch of dewy grass next to her head. When he'd finished, he dried them on the loose material of her leggings, apparently keen to remove all taint of her hair.

Slowly, he got to his feet and there was a shuffle of grass as he stepped away.

'They'll have no interest in her,' he told them dispassionately. 'And neither should we. There's more important tasks to concern us.' He hawked up a lungful of phlegm and spat. Liath Luachra felt a wet spatter on her cheek.

'*Feoil lofa,*' he repeated. Spoiled meat. 'Cerball, dispatch her and we'll go t-'

He was interrupted by the violent wrenching of wood and an exclamation of victory from the nasal-voice man. Apparently, he'd succeeded in yanking the peg free from the tree.

The soft-voiced man took two or three steps away from the warrior woman but then paused as though he'd stopped to look back.

'Cerball, dispatch her,' he repeated.

There was a short silence.

'I want to see. For myself.' Cerball's voice, crude and coarse, had a distinct edge of petulance.

His protest was answered with an exasperated snort. 'Very well. Settle your curiosity. But put a hurry on it and when you're done, slit her throat. There'll be plenty of sheaths to sate your appetite where we're going.'

The Grey One blacked out at that point but she couldn't have been unconscious for long as she was roused by the muffled cries of the two girls being dragged away. Weak and almost incoherent from the pain in her head, she still managed to crack one eyelid open in time to see them being hauled into the trees. One of the girls glanced back at the fallen warrior woman, her eyes wild with panic. She was abruptly yanked into the undergrowth and disappeared from sight.

Liath Luachra was close to blacking out again when a hand attempted to force its way inside the top of her battle harness. The rigid firmness of the treated leather across her chest however, meant little more than a pair of fingertips managed to slip inside.

'Mo goblach sabhlásta. Aaah, mo goblach sabhlásta!' My tasty morsel. Aaah. My tasty morsel.

Defeated by the inflexibility of her body armour, Cerball's hand moved instead to the inside of her thigh and slipped up to grab her crotch.

Struggling to rouse herself thorough the stupor of pain, the Grey One attempted to open her eyes but before she could do so, was rolled roughly over, face down in the grass. This time, the raider's hands grabbed the bottom of the battle harness and tugged it up while also yanking down the heavy material of her leggings, stretching the two items of clothing so that her lower back was exposed.

She was confused then for her assailant gave a snort of disgust and punched her brutally in the back, as though holding her accountable for some irrational disappointment. This time however, the pain from that blow was sharp enough to cut through the cloud in her head.

Feigning an unconsciousness that wasn't far from reality, the woman warrior remained limp as she was flipped over again, this time onto her back. She felt the weight of Cerball as he climbed on top of her, straddling her hips.

Her eyes flickered open and she caught her first look at him: a greasy mop of lank hair, a crooked nose, faint scars on the left cheek, thick lips – not one of the *díberg* men she'd seen in the clearing. Reaching down to draw a knife from the scabbard at his belt, some instinct alerted the scar-faced raider and his eyes flicked to hers even as he pulled the weapon free. Liath Luachra's breath caught in her throat as those dull brown eyes regarded her with dispassionate purpose. He bared a mouthful of broken, yellow teeth and she understood immediately.

He wasn't going to assault her. He was going to kill her.

Somehow, without prompting, her body responded. Punching up with her right hand, fingers locked into a fist, she smashed his larynx with what force she could muster. It wasn't a strong blow, nevertheless she felt the exposed lump of cartilage crumple under her knuckles.

The *díberg* raider grunted in shock, a pained, panic-stricken choking sound emerging from his throat as he dropped the knife and raised both hands to his throat. Liath Luachra snatched the weapon from where it landed on her chest and, belatedly realising his mistake, Cerball barely had time to look alarmed before she thrust it upwards, spearing the blade through the raider's hands, deep into his throat.

The spray of blood from the resulting wound gushed over the Grey One's face and hair. Repulsed, she twisted, throwing the dying man off her. That sudden movement prompted a fresh surge of pain in her head. Everything blurred, then she was vomiting.

She blacked out again.

When she struggled back to consciousness a few moments later, her body was trembling violently, her face, hair and battle harness coated in drying blood. The *díberg* warrior was lying on his back on the ground alongside her, his skin grey and discoloured, bled out from the puncture wound in his neck.

The woman warrior forced herself to her feet and staggered against the broad girth of the oak, clinging to its mass to prevent herself from falling. Pressing herself against the rough bark, she did her best to ignore her throbbing head, the cloud building up behind her eyes as her vision distorted and faded. Conscious that she was in no state to pursue the *díberg*, she also knew that she had to act quickly and get away. It was almost certain at least one of the raiders would come back to see what was delaying their comrade.

Taking a deep breath, the warrior woman straightened up and stumbled forward to the raider's corpse. Bending down, she grabbed the dead man's ankles. Taking another breath, she straightened up slowly and, this time, with a mighty heave, hauled Cerball's corpse towards the treeline.

She succeeded in dragging him several paces into the forest before she collapsed from exhaustion, her head fogging from the pain the effort had provoked. Squatting by the body, she kept her eyes closed until it was bearable to open them again, then waited a little longer to recover her strength, staring back at the javelins she'd left propped against the isolated oak. Breathing slowly, she rubbed her head and, massaging her skull with her fingertips, felt the coarse stubble where a hunk of her hair had been sliced away.

A tall figure in a hooded wolf-skin cloak, his back turned towards her.

The wound from the blow was making it difficult to think clearly, to absorb this shocking new element to the Seeking. Reluctant and unable to gather her thoughts into a coherent whole, she focussed her attention on the raider's corpse, wondering at his background, his history, how he'd ended up with a *diberg* in the Great Wild. In a physical sense there seemed little to differentiate him from most other violent men she'd encountered. Dressed in furs and torn wool leggings, his clothing showed a level of wear that matched his weapons. Both the knife she'd stabbed him with and the short sword at his waist bore nicks and notches along the blades, signs of carelessness that would have irked her under normal circumstances. The raider's corpse, meanwhile, indicated that he'd led a violent, outdoor lifestyle, evidenced through the scars on his legs and the two fingers missing from his left hand. Rifling through his clothing for anything useful, the Grey One found a stale knob of tuber inside his tunic but little else. Whatever kit he'd carried was apparently with that of the other raiders.

Conscious that it wasn't safe to delay any longer, the woman warrior unsteadily got to her feet. Stumbling back towards the tree, she was disturbed by the watery feeling in her knees and the physical effort it took just to take several shaky steps. The blow to the head had been more serious than she'd thought and if the *diberg* returned, she knew she'd struggle to defend herself.

Arriving back at the solitary oak, the woman warrior glanced at the fire, reduced now due to the lack of fuel but still crackling away happily. Staggering over to the spot where Cerball had been lying, she kicked dead leaves and forest litter over it so that the bloodstained ground couldn't easily be discerned. No point in making it easy for the *diberg* if they came back to look for him.

Returning to the tree, she retrieved her javelins but, too weak to slide them over her shoulder and into their quiver as she'd usually do, she was obliged to pull the quiver off and insert them, one by one, before slipping it back over her shoulder again.

'Cerball!'

A ghostly grip clutched the warrior woman's heart. The call from the forest was angry and urgent but more concerningly, it had come from the treeline directly to the west, meaning she wouldn't make cover in time even if she'd been able to run.

Lurching back to the tree, she stumbled awkwardly around to its western side, positioning herself so the trunk concealed her from the direction in which the newcomer was approaching. The crunch and crackle of someone barging carelessly through the winter undergrowth grew louder. The woman warrior pressed close against the rough bark, hoping against hope that whoever turned up would simply see an empty clearing and leave.

'Cerball, you shit-licker! Where are you?'

She recognised the high-pitched nasal voice of the *díberg* warrior immediately, her left hand unconsciously dropping to touch the ribs where he'd kicked her. Peering carefully around the trunk, she saw him step out of the trees, surprised to find that he looked almost exactly as she'd imagined: lanky, scruffy-bearded, a pale face with cruel lips.

'He's gone,' said Liath Luachra.

The gangly warrior stumbled to a halt and stared. His jaw dropped in astonishment as she strolled around the left side of the tree trunk and out into the open, his eyes widening as he absorbed the bloodstained mess of her.

'I ate him.'

She patted her stomach.

'Yum-yum.'

She grinned fiercely at his fearful reaction, the blood clots cracking on her cheeks where the creases split. Swallowing, the raider took a worried step backward, hand on his sword, unsure whether to fight or run.

'Yum-yum.' Liath Luachra repeated, this time licking her lips.

She took a sudden step forward and the raider reacted with startling alacrity, spinning on one heel and launching himself into a dash for the trees before the flat of her foot had even pressed against the earth. Watching him flee, the woman warrior roared in his wake. 'Tell your leader I'm coming for him, little man! Tell him Liath Luachra's coming, that she's forgotten nothing. That she's going to slit his throat and watch his life spill onto the ground in front of her!'

When it was clear the raider had no intention of returning, the woman warrior stumbled towards the lake, soul-sick and spent.

Foolish!

Kneeling at the water's edge, she considered her likeness in the still surface, struck by the savage blood-spattered reflection she made. At first, angered by the image gazing sullenly back at her, she glowered irrationally in return then slapped the water violently to obliterate it.

Dipping her head into the water, she washed the worst of the raider's blood from her face and hair and smeared it off her clothing, dully noting the brief pink stain it left in the shallows. As her image reformed, she scowled but found herself reassured by its more human aspect.

Foolish.

It had been foolish to confront the raider but driven by her compulsive, overriding fury, she couldn't have responded any other way.

Groaning softly, she touched the back of her skull, aching still from where the blow had caught her. Bruises were also forming on her ribs but it was the deep-rooted throb in her back, the spot where Cerball had inexplicably struck her, that hurt most. Jaded and in pain, she felt dampened, sapped at her failure to save the girls, and yet she burned at the memory of the soft voice beneath the oak tree.

I see you, Grey One.

She'd recognised the voice at once of course, just as she'd unconsciously recognised the profile at the lakeside the previous day. Seared into her memory, that voice was a tone and timbre that would remain with her until she merged with the clay.

Oh, yes, Gadra, I remember you.

Even now, in her battered state, the memory of that voice and the odd way its softness swelled in conjunction with the speaker's cruelty, hollowed her from the inside, evoking a confusing blend of emotions that ranged from futility to despair, from unchecked terror to unquenchable fury.

The *Uí Cailbhe* raider's shocking reappearance, in such unrelated circumstances, had completely upended her and was all the more harrowing as she'd believed him dead or, at the very least, expunged from her existence. After Dún Beag she'd never imagined the possibility of crossing paths with any of the *Uí Cailbhe* raiders again, certainly not having Gadra reappear like a ghost to whisper in her ear and rekindle ancient traumas.

'Garrad Mór always was the greedy one. Taking his reward from An Draoi Dubh but then too busy humping his prize to fulfil the tasks assigned him.

The Grey One shook her head in bewilderment. And what was all that about? An Draoi Dubh? She knew of no-one with such a name or title and couldn't understand the comment's relevance.

Raising her hand to nurse the pain in her head, the woman warrior's fingers touched the rough patch where he'd cut her hair away, keeping it, no doubt, as some twisted trophy. She recalled how, afterwards, he'd cleaned his hands in the dew, wiping away the touch of her like so much tainted dirt.

Aye. And she remembered that from Dún Beag too.

She sat with her knees drawn up to her chin, her heart torn and roiling. Part of her wanted to curl up in despair, to embed herself deep in the forest, to never venture forth again. Another part however hungered to maim and spill *díberg* blood, and it exhausted her to try and reconcile such dramatically conflicting sensations.

Staring down at her reflection in the water, she studied the coldness in her eyes, the tightness of her lips, the patch of stubble where he'd shorn her hair away. With a surge of fury, she wrenched her knife from its scabbard and started cutting, hacking at the long black strands until the shorn patch was completely indistinguishable from the rest of her roughly cropped hair.

Plunging her knife into the earth, she lay her head down, physically and emotionally spent.

And passed out.

***

When Liath Luachra finally came to, her head still ached but the fuggy cloudiness from the blow had finally faded. Numb and cold, she got to her feet and, casting one last glance at the patch of ground where she'd dispatched the raider, started north, her movements awkward and stiff from the pain in her back and her ribs.

Despite her own traumatic engagement with the *díberg*, she felt relatively confident the *fian* would be safe in their oaken stronghold, the limited conversation she'd overheard suggesting the raiders had been under pressure to leave, driven by priorities and tensions she couldn't begin to guess at. Either way, she'd certainly got the impression they had no intention of engaging with *Na Cinéaltaí* in open battle.

Once again slipped away in the forest.

She grimaced, frustrated and angry but also knowing that, for the moment, like so many other disturbing aspects of this tasking, she'd have to put such frustrations aside and focus on getting safely back to the *fian*.

Although hampered by her injuries, it didn't take too long to reach the hidden gully and, from there, the area where she'd heard the false bird calls. Coated in slime from the gully's muddy base, she remained hidden in a cluster of pines, nursing the rekindled ache in her ribs and studying the activity of the wildlife until she was satisfied the raiders had departed. Finally, emerging from the undergrowth, she shakily headed towards the north.

By the time she reached the site of the ambush – pinpointed by the javelin poking up from Mochta's body – she had warmed sufficiently to work the worst of the aches from her body, although certain movements continued to make her wince. Easing past the corpse at a crouch, the woman warrior determinedly avoided looking at the *Uí Loinge* man as she continued to work her way west until, finally, the fortress-like semi-circle of oak trees that Murchú had described slid into view. A curving wall of more than thirty oaks, framed by the dull stretch of the grey-green lake to its rear, most of the trees had grown so closely together that little space remained between them. Like the trees at *Loch na nEasa,* their upper branches had also merged to an impenetrable woody mesh.

Coming to a halt at the edge of the forest, Liath Luachra stared across the open ground separating her from the oak cluster. Observed from that perspective, the contours of the cluster looked unnatural and, combined with the unusual stretch of flat ground surrounding it, its positioning had the air of human influence.

Crouched in the shadows, she raised two fingers to her mouth and whistled. Several silent moments passed without any response, without any sign of activity.

That's not good.

Moving position, she edged her way south along the treeline for twenty paces, pausing to lie flat at the foot of a pair of stark, leaf-denuded elms. There, raising her fingers to her mouth, she whistled a second time. Once again, there was no response.

Exhausted and in pain, the woman warrior stared towards the oaks, uncertain how to proceed. Had the *fénnid* been present, they'd surely have heard her whistle and responded in turn. The fact that they hadn't suggested that they'd either left the area already or had …

Any further opportunity to ponder the mystery was abruptly thwarted as a shadowy figure slid out of the trees to her immediate left and levelled a spear point at her. Flat on her belly, muscles too stiff to react with alacrity, Liath Luachra could only stare helplessly up at her aggressor, surprised to see how young he looked. *An óglach* – an unblooded young warrior – he had a pale face, a shadowed fuzz of hair above his upper lip and the appearance of no more than fifteen years on him.

Even as a number of desperate possibilities passed through the woman warrior's mind, she heard the sound of fresh footsteps to her rear. A rough pair of hands grabbed her shoulders and expertly patted her down, removing both *Gleas gan Ainm* and the knife in the scabbard alongside it while the *óglach* kept the spear point on her.

'Get up.'

Rising painfully to her feet, the Grey One turned to face the new arrival, a man with at least thirty years on him, clad in a rough leather tunic and a deerskin cloak. Crowned by a head of shaggy bronze hair, his strong jaw was visible through the thick bush of red beard. Folding his arms, he stood back on one leg and regarded her with cold disdain, the creases under his eyes deepening as though displeased by what he saw.

'You took your time,' he said at last. 'We've been waiting for you the better part of the afternoon.'

He paused, looked at her carefully and then a cynical smile split across his face. 'Oh, and welcome to the territory of *Clann Baoiscne.*'

Chapter Six:

The two warriors directed Liath Luachra towards the oak grove at the edge of the lake, guiding her with an occasional grunt or a prod from the points of their spears. Moving as rapidly as her aches and pains allowed, she hobbled forward towards the widest and most obvious gap in the grove's almost palisade-like wall, one of the few spaces between two of the close-growing tree trunks not clogged by saplings and woody debris. Entering the gap – less than two shoulder-widths wide – she pushed her way through the layers of undergrowth. After several paces, she emerged into a small semi-circular clearing adjacent to the lake shore which had been completely invisible from the exterior.

Her initial suspicions that the oak grove had been associated with some form of human influence were confirmed by the presence of a weathered *gallán* at the centre of the clearing, its basalt surface pocked and stained with yellow-green patches of lichen. Liath Luachra's eyes weren't drawn to the standing stone however, but to a patch of grass beyond it where An Giobach and Feirgil were on their knees tending to the prostrate Biotóg, overseen by another pair of armed *Clann Baoiscne* warriors. The skinny *fénnid's* wound was bleeding badly again and his comrades were attempting to staunch it with a fresh dressing. Spotting the little group's arrival, An Giobach glanced fleetingly in her direction and started when he recognised her, eyes widening at the sight of her savagely cropped hair. Distracted by a moan from the wounded *fénnid* however, he quickly returned his attention to Biotóg, holding the *fénnid* down while Feirgil applied a poultice of green moss.

Flanked by her escorts, Liath Luachra was marched briskly past, towards the treeline at the far side of the clearing where a sturdy figure with brown hair tied in a topknot, leaned casually back against the trunk of a fallen oak tree. The superior quality of his green *léine* and the distinct tattoo above his right eye immediately marked him as a tribal member of authority and the probable leader of the *fian*. He was supping silently from a steaming bowl as they approached, looking across a tiny fire to where a scowling Murchú was on his knees, hands tied behind his back.

'Crimall!' the red-haired warrior called as they drew closer. 'You have a new visitor.'

Turning his head to regard the newcomers, the thickset man watched quietly as the woman warrior was pushed forward then forced to her knees alongside the bound *Uí Loinge* man. As her escort moved to take up position on either side of him, the *Clann Baoiscne* leader supped again from his bowl, then raised a hand to wipe liquid from a several-days old growth of beard. Solidly built, the warrior had a broad chest and his shoulders were firmly muscled. Liath Luachra estimated his age at a little more than twenty years.

Murchú glanced sideways at her, his nostrils flaring as he struggled to control his anger, which appeared to be directed at the *Clann Baoiscne* men rather than at her. To the Grey One's relief, his face bore no signs of bruising and she could see no other obvious signs of ill-treatment.

Crimall laid his bowl on a flat section of the trunk and as he turned back to face the woman warrior, his dark brown eyes bore into her, inspecting her carefully for several moments before he finally deigned to speak.

'You must be the leader of this sorry band. Your warriors told me they were a mercenary *fian* led by a *banfénnid* but, in truth, I didn't believe them.'

His lips curved up on one side to form a cynical grin.

'And to speak plainly, I remain unconvinced. A *fian* led by a woman …' He chuckled dismissively. 'An entertaining possibility, although one that would seem to contradict the feminine nature, not to mention the established wisdom of our Elders.'

He redirected his gaze across the fire at the fuming Murchú.

'Unless, of course, the *Uí Loinge* now have their women do battle for them.'

'You may wish to question the established wisdom of your chieftain,' Liath Luachra cut in quickly, fearful that Murchú would respond in anger and aggravate their captors. 'Tréanmór not only entertained that possibility but sought a tasking of us some two years past.'

Crimall's lips tightened a little at that and she could tell she'd got his attention. Regarding her quietly, he scratched at the budding beard on the right side of his face as he thought her answer through. 'You are *Na Cinéaltaí*?'

'Yes.'

'Then you would be the one they call The Grey One.'

'That's the name on me.'

The *Clann Baoiscne* man grunted but he considered her now even more keenly. For all his easy bluster there was a sharp intelligence behind those eyes and the Grey One could tell the man was no fool.

'I had assumed the stories of *Na Cinéaltaí* were fantasies, tall tales spawned from the lips of bored old women.' He sniffed and wiped his nose with the back of his hand. 'But there's a sliver of truth to what you say. Tréanmór did entertain the possibility of sending for *Na Cinéaltaí* at one time. I hadn't realised he'd gone so far as to propose a possible tasking.'

Adjusting his position against the fallen trunk, he folded his arms once more. 'What, then, of this one?' He jerked his jaw at Murchú. 'I know him as *Uí Loinge*. He's Murchú, son of Congal.'

'That's the name he bears but he's also *fénnid* to *Na Cinéaltaí*. As *fénnid,* he answers to the *rígfénnid* and, as such, I speak for *Na Cinéaltaí*, not him.'

The warrior continued to observe her in silence, his lips curled in an expression that was neither smile nor grimace but more a twisted expression of reservation. 'If that's the way of it,' he said at last, 'Then you're the one responsible for leading your men into an ambush.'

It was a low blow, a sly blow but Liath Luachra offered no response. The *Clann Baoiscne* man was baiting her, poking at her as he'd poke a stick in a burrow, hoping to provoke a panicked reaction from the animal within.

'You have no answer?' he prompted.

'You asked no question.'

Crimall's lips tightened a little at that and Liath Luachra reminded herself she had to temper her answers. The *Clann Baoiscne* man wasn't used being spoken to in such a manner, particularly by a female and she was in no position to risk confrontation. Bowing her head, she stared hard at the ground. Fortunately, the submissive behaviour appeared to mollify the bristling warrior.

'If you are a mercenary *fian*, as your men claim, then …' The *Clann Baoiscne* man continued to stare fixedly at her. 'Then the *Uí Loinge* must have engaged you for a tasking.'

The statement was issued in a challenging manner, as though he'd caught her in some deception. Liath Luachra didn't respond to the bait. She'd already decided there was no point in lying. Murchú was known to the *Clann Baoiscne* and it simply wasn't feasible to bluff their way out of the situation.

'Yes.'

He nodded slowly, satisfied with the honesty of her answer.

'No doubt because they, themselves, fear traversing *Clann Baoiscne* land.'

The woman warrior raised her head, forcing herself to regard him with as much passive authority as she could muster, conscious that Murchú too was listening intently to every word she said. Unaccustomed to such prolonged, thorn-riddled conversations, she could feel the sweat breaking out on her back as her mind floundered to find words that would cause no offence but which, at the same time, implied no weakness.

'The *Uí Loinge* are mindful of causing offence to the people of *Clann Baoiscne*. A great injury was done upon them and passage through *Clann Baoiscne* lands was a necessary step to cauterise that wound. Unfortunately, the circumstances allowed no opportunity to seek consent in advance.'

Crimall sucked thoughtfully on the molars to the left of his mouth but a gleam of curiosity flickered in his eyes. 'What great injury?'

'Cairenn, daughter of Congal, was abducted by a *díberg* on *Uí Loinge* lands. That *díberg* currently traverses *Clann Baoiscne* territory which is why *Na Cinéaltaí* are in pursuit.'

Crimall continued to watch her carefully. His eyes displayed no surprise at the odd news of a winter raid but a *loinnir glic* – a crafty glint – overlaid the half-smile that followed. 'And the *Uí Loinge* dispatched you on the suspicion it was *Clann Baoiscne* men who led the raid.'

Although it wasn't phrased as a question, Liath Luachra shook her head to deflect it. 'We know it wasn't *Clann Baoiscne* men.'

This time she caught a distinct flicker of surprise in the dark-haired warrior's expression. Beside her, she sensed Murchú stiffen, then lean imperceptibly closer as though to listen with even greater concentration.

'Oh? And how did you come to this conclusion?'

'Because you're chasing them as well.'

There was a startled silence from all four men, a brief respite for her to assemble her thoughts. In truth, she'd had no idea they sought the same *díberg* until the words were almost out of her mouth. Somehow, just as she'd made to speak, the different elements of the tasking – the raiders' great urgency, the presence of the *Clann Baoiscne* warriors, the converging of the three different groups – had all coalesced in one part of her mind to arrive at the obvious conclusion.

'Is that true?' asked Murchú. He stared directly at Crimall. 'Are you truly in pursuit of the same *díberg*?'

The left corner of the *Clann Baoiscne* man's mouth tugged down in a dissatisfied frown. He looked coldly at the *Uí Loinge fénnid* before pointedly returning his attention to Liath Luachra.

'I thought you said you were the one who spoke for *Na Cinéaltaí*.'

The woman warrior feigned a nonchalance she didn't feel and slipped a lazy shrug from her right shoulder. 'You know what the sons of chieftains are like. They have … airs.'

All three *Clann Baoiscne* men looked at her strangely then suddenly erupted into harsh laughter. Startled by the reaction, the warrior woman regarded them carefully, struggling to make sense of their good humour. 'And what of me, Grey One?' Crimall asked her. 'Do you think I have airs?'

She stared at him in confusion until the red-haired warrior explained.

'Crimall is son of the *Clann Baoiscne rí*, Grey One.'

Liath Luachra frowned. 'Tréanmór's son has the name Cumhal on him.'

'That's Tréanmór's eldest son.' The warrior chuckled. 'Crimall is his second son.'

Although she attempted to hide her surprise behind a face of stone, the woman warrior couldn't conceal the tension in her posture, which only seemed to make the three men laugh even more.

Bristling inwardly at their mockery, the Grey One attempted to drag the conversation back to the matter at hand. 'Given our mutual interest in this *díberg*,' she suggested, 'Perhaps we should share our knowl-'

Crimall held up his hand, palm outwards, to stop her in mid-sentence. 'There is no mutual interest, Grey One. We do not pursue the same *díberg*. The coincidence of interaction is curious, I grant you, but you pursue a *díberg* that's raided *Uí Loinge* lands to the north-west. *Clann Baoiscne* interest rests with the *díberg* that raided one of our farms to the north-east. They are not the same.'

'Do *díberg* grow on the winter trees, then?' asked the Grey One, echoing Murchú's earlier exasperation. 'One *díberg* in the winter season is a rarity. But two? And both working their way to this exact spot in *Clann Baoiscne* territory?' She shook her head vehemently. 'No. That is a contrariety.'

Crimall frowned, his brows clenching in vexation.

'What are you saying?'

'I'm saying that the *díberg* we were following have merged with the *díberg* you pursue. There were two groups and now there is one. I'd wondered at their decision to remain in the area and to reveal themselves so openly with a campfire. Now, I understand they were waiting, marking their placement for the second *díberg* to find them. That second group must have come across our tracks, alerted their comrades and then set an ambush to prevent any further pursuit.

And they'd probably have massacred us if the Clann Baoiscne fian hadn't turned up on their heels.

Not that she had any intention of admitting that.

The *Clann Baoiscne* leader inhaled heavily. 'Tell us, then, of the *díberg* you pursue,' he suggested, an audible trace of irritation in his voice.

'The group we're chasing comprises four men – all seasoned warriors – and a single captive. They had a ten-day start on us from Briga. Our use of horses and the burden of their captive meant we were able to reduce that lead.'

She paused then, offering Crimall the opportunity to reveal some insights of his own. Although willing to share information if it helped to improve relations with *Clann Baoiscne*, she expected some contribution in return.

Crimall appeared to be juggling similar considerations for he bought himself some time picking up his bowl and supping from it repeatedly before he finally delivered his response.

'The object of the *Clann Baoiscne* pursuit comprises six men. We haven't been close enough to determine much more but their tracks show them young and fit.' He paused. 'They attacked a farm to the north of our territory and slaughtered its inhabitants. According to the single survivor, they snatched two young women who travel with them still.'

'What?' exclaimed Murchú. 'This *díberg* raids and abducts women from any territory without qualm?'

Crimall glanced at him and looked to make a testy response but then his expression unexpectedly softened.

'Therein lies the mystery, *Uí Loinge* man. The raiders appeared out of nowhere, slaughtered and burned, and then fled back to the wilderness like ghosts. We've had raids before of course, but this one was different. Less … opportunistic. The raiders not only took captives but, when we followed their trail, we found sign where they'd stockpiled supplies of food and water. The attack had been planned well in advance.

Liath Luachra sat quietly, taking advantage of Murchú's interjection and Crimall's subsequent explanation to think the matter through. On top of Gadra's distressing reappearance, this new revelation sent the linear nature of the Seeking spinning off on a new and tangled tangent. Garrad Mór's old comrade-in-arms and his raiders were operating on a scale she'd never encountered before and the coordinated strikes across two separate territories, plus the presence of stored supplies, displayed a level of organisation unlike any *díberg* of her experience.

What despair do you sow now, Gadra?

'Grey One?'

With a start, she realised the *Clann Baoiscne* man was regarding her testily. A perceptive man, he clearly suspected that she'd kept something back and, now having made his own contribution, was impatient for reciprocation.

'There's little else to say. What I can tell you is that when I separated from my *fian*, I worked my way south in the hope of taking the raiders from the rear. In the forest I came across two girls chained to a tree but the raiders returned before I could free them. I was forced to flee but downed one of my pursuers in the skirmish.'

'And these men, these raiders … Were they familiar to you in any way? Did they have any markings, anything that might suggest a tribe or a region of origin?'

She shook her head.

Crimall continued to stare at her intently, as though sensing her equivocation. As the woman warrior endured that penetrating gaze, the lie burned so fiercely inside her chest, she felt certain he must see through her. Just as she felt her nerve begin to fray, the *Clann Baoiscne* man abruptly slumped back and grunted, shaking his head in frustration.

'This is very strange. We pursue a force whose motives remain unclear. Even worse, if what you say is true, the *díberg's* numbers now surpass our own.' He paused then, clicking his teeth quietly together and from the vacant look in his eyes she could tell he was working through the numbers once again, reassessing the scale of the challenge. The *Clann Baoiscne fian* numbered six men, not enough to pose a substantial threat to the fleeing raiding party.

'We should combine our forces,' she said.

Crimall glanced down at her in surprise. He shook his head. 'I think not. This is a *Clann Baoiscne* matter.'

'It is also an *Uí Loinge* matter,' insisted Murchú. 'If our positions were reversed and the *díberg* travelled through *Uí Loinge* lands, you'd demand similar consideration.'

The *Clann Baoiscne* man glared at him but said nothing. Liath Luachra decided to press the argument further.

'The numbers speak for themselves, Crimall. The *díberg* number ten able fighting men. You have six and we have four.'

Crimall looked unconvinced but he continued to offer no response as he thought the matter through. Unable to come to any obvious conclusion, he turned to the red-haired warrior standing quietly on his right. 'Néde. You have an opinion to offer?'

The warrior clucked his tongue softly, assembling his thoughts before he spoke.

'Neither our *fian* nor *Na Cinéaltaí* have the force to defeat this *díberg* alone,' he said at last. 'But, even merging our forces, there's the issue of experience to consider. Combined, we might equal them in numbers but if the Grey One has the right of it – and the skill of the raiders' ambush suggests she has – these men are seasoned warriors. Three of our own number are *óglaigh* – unblooded youths. They've yet to experience the hot rush of blood in battle.'

He paused to think, touching his lips with the tip of his forefinger.

'There's also the matter of supplies. Through their stockpiles, the *díberg* are well replenished. We're down to our last morsels. We cannot sustain an extended pursuit. And …' His voice faded.

'And?' prompted Crimall.

The warrior hesitated before speaking again. 'It seems to me that there's something more complex at hand. I have the sense of a threat hidden deeper in the woods beyond the treeline and I think …' He regarded his leader with a grave expression. 'I think we need to alert our people.'

Crimall considered his comrade's words in silence then abruptly grunted.

'As ever, Néde has the right of it. We cannot tackle a *díberg* of this size with any certainty of defeating them. He also has the right of it in that we need to prepare our people for whatever menace this *díberg* – and any other that appear – may pose.'

Pushing himself off the fallen tree trunk, he stood up straight and tossed the dregs of his bowl onto the ground.

'Néde, free the *Uí Loinge* man. Return the Grey One's weapons.'

He waited as the red-haired warrior slipped behind Murchú's back, slicing through his bonds with a simple flick of a knife. The younger warrior, meanwhile, returned the woman warrior's weapons, shyly avoiding her eyes as he did so.

Getting to her feet, Liath Luachra replaced her arms in their scabbards and turned to face Crimall, who'd moved around the fire to approach her directly.

'Grey One, I'll be leading our *fian* to Dún Baoiscne to obtain the supplies and extra warriors needed to continue the pursuit. That diversion will cost us three to four days but the alternative is to run out of supplies and be forced to abandon the chase when we're too far away to fetch the help we need. As for you, you have the choice of taking your *fian* and departing *Clann Baoiscne* lands or accompanying us to seek permission to join that pursuit. Our healers can tend to your wounded man there if that is your choice.'

'That delay would lose us the raiders' trail,' protested Murchú. The *Uí Loinge* man too had risen to his feet and stood facing the *Clann Baoiscne* leader, massaging his wrists where the bonds had cut into the skin.

Crimall shook his head. 'The risk is not great. The tracks indicate the *díberg* are headed south-east. That means they'll soon strike the sea and their route will almost certainly follow the coast in a southerly direction. That also means their trail will be easier to find again.' He folded his shoulders with a slightly smug expression. 'Nevertheless, just to be sure, Néde will trail them at a distance and leave markings for us to follow.'

'I'd propose an alternative,' said Murchú.

'You have my ear.'

'The *díberg* have but a short lead and flee with the burden of three captives. If we pursue them now, we could run them down easily, probably before nightfall. Three or four days from now, we risk finding the captives' bodies in the forest with their throats cut.'

Crimall's expression did not change. 'I'll not expose untested *Clann Baoiscne* warriors to the possibility of an unnecessary defeat. You've heard Néde outline our circumstances. At Dún Baoiscne we'll obtain the men and supplies we need to be certain of victory and seek further information of the *díberg* from my father. Little happens on *Clann Baoiscne* land that Tréanmór does not hear of.'

From the corner of her eye, Liath Luachra saw the *Uí Loinge* man glance towards her, silently pleading for support. Unfortunately, despite sharing his fears for Cairenn there seemed little she could do. Murchú's suggestion was sound and Crimall was being foolishly overcautious given the urgency to rescue the girls. Nevertheless, in *Clann Baoiscne* territory, the decision was his and he had enough of an upper hand to enforce it.

Feeling Murchú's eyes on her however, a frisson of guilt passed through her. She repressed a sigh.

'Crimall, I acknowledge your decision but Murchú's sister is *Na Cinéaltaí's* priority. We cannot take the risk of travelling to Dún Baoiscne only to be denied permission to continue the pursuit.'

The *Clann Baoiscne* man shrugged. 'I sympathise with the *Uí Loinge* girl's plight, Grey One, but you've been travelling through *Clann Baoiscne* land without consent. Your options are clear. Leave now or travel to Dún Baoiscne and take your chances.'

'Can you not provide the consent we need? You're Tréanmór's son. A senior *Clann Baoiscne* member.'

Crimall shook his head. 'Should you accompany us, I'll speak in your support but, as *rí*, it's Tréanmór's decision whether to let you continue the pursuit or not. He doesn't appreciate unconsented strangers travelling upon his territory but whichever choice he makes, my firm advice would be to abide by his judgement. To oppose him would expose you to his wrath and it would sadden me to have bloodshed between us, particularly ....' He gave an unexpectedly broad smile. 'When we could be such good friends.'

Having said all he wanted to say, the *Clann Baoiscne* man turned to address the red-haired warrior. 'Néde. Take what you need from our remaining supplies and follow that *díberg*. Keep a safe distance, mind, but whatever you do, don't lose them.'

Néde nodded silently and, without a word, moved back towards the gap in the trees through which they'd entered the clearing. A moment later, he'd disappeared from view, presumably making his way to wherever the *Clann Baoiscne* supplies had been secreted. Crimall, meanwhile, returned his attention to the warrior woman.

'So, Grey One. As *rígfénnid* of *Na Cineáltaí,* what is your decision to be?'

Liath Luachra held his eyes, conscious that Murchú was hovering at her right shoulder, fixed on every word she uttered.

'You leave us with little choice. *Na Cineáltaí* will accompany you to Dún Baoiscne. But before we can leave there are matters that need resolving. Our warrior Biotóg requires a litter and the *Uí Loinge* horses must be recovered.' She paused. 'And then there's the matter of Mochta, the member of our party slain in the ambush. He needs to be laid in the clay.'

Crimall dipped his head in satisfaction. 'It pleases me that you've chosen to show sense, Grey One. I look forward to our time together, however I intend to depart at once. If you truly wish to accompany us, I suggest you set to it.'

***

From the gap in the oak grove treeline, Liath Luachra watched An Giobach and Feirgil depart with the *Clann Baoiscne fian,* Biotóg stretched on the hastily constructed litter that they carried between them. As the larger party crossed the flat ground to the forest and entered the trees, the woman warrior's heart sank when she saw Crimall look back, raise a hand and smile at her before fading into the vegetation.

The eager hound anticipating its meal.

Beside her, Murchú had also caught the *Clann Baoiscne* man's gesture and he looked silently at her with an expression she found difficult to interpret. Although tempted to ignore it, she knew it was time to address the silence between them. She couldn't operate effectively with the *Uí Loinge* warrior while this unspoken tension remained.

Raising one arm, to prop herself against the nearest tree trunk, she felt the pain in her ribs flare to life at the movement and found herself oddly pleased by the physical distraction.

Focus.

She took a deep breath.

'Murchú, do you still bear an anger towards me? Because of last night.'

Murchú exhaled heavily, regarding her with an expression that carried more sadness than anger.

'I bear many angers, Grey One. My sister's been abducted, a rival tribe obstructs the only realistic chance of rescue. I must bury my favourite cousin in cold ground far from his people ...' His voice trailed off and he gave a listless shrug. 'My head is so full of anger and despair I cannot distinguish one from the other.'

The Grey One stayed silent, not knowing what to say.

'Last night, I thought you'd kill me, Grey One. And, yes, for a time I bore you a great anger.' He turned his eyes away to gaze across at the distant trees. 'But in the grey light of dawn, that anger competes with the gratitude I bear you.' He paused and glanced sideways at her. 'And the great tenderness.'

Thrown by this unexpected declaration, the Grey One dropped her eyes and stared fiercely at the ground, forcing herself to avoid all eye contact with the *Uí Loinge* man. Murchú, meanwhile, struggled with his own efforts to articulate his thoughts.

'Knowing what I know ... Knowing your history, Liath Luachra. I.... I know I've no right to ask but I wo-'

'Don't.'

The *Uí Loinge* man paused and stared at the woman warrior, now holding both hands up in front of her, as though to physically prevent any further words from reaching her.

'Don't talk, Murchú.'

The *Uí Loinge* man went deadly quiet then and, like her, he too turned his gaze away, staring back towards the distant trees with such intensity it seemed his very life depended on it. Finally, visibly shaken, he straightened up and cleared his throat.

'Of course. I understand. I won't trouble you again.'

He paused again, glanced across at Liath Luachra as though to try and catch her eye. The woman warrior was still staring steadfastly at the ground however, defying any hope of doing so. Murchú coughed, cleared his throat again. 'Perhaps ... perhaps, we should go and lay my cousin to rest.'

'Yes,' the Grey One agreed hurriedly. '*Ar aghaidh linn.*' Let's go.

Despite the *Uí Loinge* man's assurances and the desperate, unspoken – but mutual – agreement to avoid any further discussion, a palpable awkwardness remained between the two warriors as they returned to the site of the ambush where Mochta's body still lay, cold and lonely between the trees. Working in silence, they dug a shallow grave but as they prepared to roll Mochta into it, found themselves stymied by the javelin transfixing his corpse. Still solidly wedged in the *Uí Loinge* man's torso, neither of them was able to pull the missile free despite several gory attempts.

In the end, Liath Luachra had to resort to sawing the haft off at the point where it emerged from his back while Murchú watched on in stony silence. Reducing it to a ragged stump, she cast the remaining wooden shaft aside and got the *fénnid* to help her roll the body into the earth. It seemed an ignoble way for the *Uí Loinge* man to be put to rest given everything he'd sacrificed to help rescue Cairenn but, under the circumstances, it was the best they could do.

Once they'd laid Mochta down and covered him with soil, the Grey One retreated to allow Murchú privacy to make his final farewell. From a distance, she waited and watched in silence as the *fénnid* dropped to one knee, spread the last few handfuls of dirt over his cousin's resting place and wept. Still shaken and resentful at the *Uí Loinge* man's unsought declaration of affection towards her, she was nevertheless touched by the obvious fondness and grief he felt for his deceased cousin and the sincerity of those feelings caused something to twist inside her own chest.

Getting to his feet, Murchú looked down at his cousin's grave, wiped his hands on his leggings, then turned and started back to the waiting warrior woman. Moved by his stricken expression, Liath Luachra felt a need to say something, to offer the *Uí Loinge* man some expression of condolence.

'Murchú, your cousin …'

The *Uí Loinge* man looked at her in surprise.

'He was … he was a great man for the horses.'

The *fénnid's* blue eyes widened slightly and the woman warrior winced internally at her own clumsy, ham-fisted words. A glimmer of frost gleamed behind the *Uí Loinge* man's eyes but then, suddenly, his shoulders sagged and he sighed.

'Grey One, you know I hold you in the greatest respect but ...' He hesitated. 'Sometimes, I think you might have spent too much time alone in your cave at Luachair.'

Brushing past her, the *Uí Loinge* man made for the tree where they'd stacked their javelins. The woman warrior stared after him, stung by the rebuke and fighting to quell the flare of anger his words had sparked. To dampen her rising fury, she turned her mind to another matter, a practical matter over which she had more control and comprehension: the Seeking.

'Let's fetch the horses. We need to catch the *Clann Baoiscne fian* up.'

Holding a javelin in both hands, Murchú wearily shook his head. To the woman warrior, he seemed suddenly deflated, worn down by the loss of his cousin and the successive list of frustrations and barriers that prevented him from finding his sister.

And, no doubt, the brutality of her rejection.

Fortunately, the *fénnid* didn't attempt to revisit that shambolic interaction, his subsequent words focussing instead on a greater priority.

'Do you believe an alliance with *Clann Baoiscne* is wise? It seemed to me the fate of the abducted girls held little interest for Crimall and his *fian*. If anything, his priority seemed directed more to furthering his battle reputation.'

In a sudden expression of anger, Murchú slammed one of the javelins point first into the earth, the haft shaking furiously from the violence of the action. Liath Luachra looked from the *fénnid* to the quivering shaft and then back again.

'The worst of this situation,' Murchú continued, 'is that although Crimall's a pompous ass, he can at least be counted on to speak plainly. Tréanmór's deviousness is legendary. He cannot be trusted. No matter the circumstances, he'll seek to play us, even if it leads to the detriment of his own people and the abducted Dún Baoiscne girls.'

Liath Luachra shrugged awkwardly but she was relieved to be back on a topic of which she had at least some understanding. 'There was no choice, Murchú. To continue the Seeking and retrieve your sister, we need their help and goodwill. Besides, Biotóg needed attention an-'

'Yes, I had noticed that Grey One.'

She looked at him and bit her lip, reining in her anger, reminding herself once more that he had plenty of reasons to be angry at her. She paused for a moment, hoping that something would pop into her head, some words or wisdom that might soften the wedge her actions had created between them.

As usual, nothing came.

'Let's fetch the horses,' she said again.

***

By the time they retrieved the horses from where Mochta had tethered them and found a traversable path around the ridge, the *Clann Baoiscne* party had more than a half-day's lead. Even travelling at speed, riding the horses whenever it was feasible, it was almost dark by the time the two travellers finally caught them up at their campsite on the bank of a slow-flowing stream.

Weary and coated in dirt, they removed the packs from the horses' backs, hobbled the animals and released them a little upstream from the campsite. Stumbling back to where the two *fian* had settled, they found a solitary *Clann Baoiscne* guard to greet them, most of the warriors having already retired to their bedrolls.

Approaching the fire however, they found that Crimall too remained awake for he was sitting alone on a log, staring into its crackling depth, his face slack and thoughtful. Liath Luachra nudged Murchú in the shoulder.

'Make friends with him, Murchú. We need to work him to our side.'

The *Uí Loinge* man glanced sideways at her, surprised by the sudden instruction. Neither had spoken a word to the other over the long ride from the spot where they'd located the horses.

'Why should I make friends with him? Why don't you do it?'

'Because when he looks at you, he sees a peer to talk to. When he looks at me, he sees a hole to fuck.'

Murchú blinked at the vehemence in the woman warrior's voice but, alerted to their approach, the *Clann Baoiscne* man had looked up and now called out in greeting, putting an end to any possibility of further discussion. As the travellers took a seat on the rotting logs on opposite sides of the fire, Crimall lazily stretched out one leg to tap a metal stew pot in the embers with the tip of his boot. 'The evening meal was meagre,' he said. 'But we've saved you a portion.'

Muttering their thanks, Liath Luachra and Murchú helped themselves to the pot, pouring its watery contents into two wooden bowls that had also been left by the edge of the fire. The stew was insipid and tasteless and barely filled three quarters of the containers, nevertheless they wolfed it down, appreciating the warmth it brought to their frozen bellies.

Finally, with a belch, Murchú dropped his bowl onto the ground and sighed. Stretching his arms, his glance fell on the huddled shadows where the *Clann Baoiscne* warriors were sleeping. Peering at them for a moment, he turned to Crimall. 'You've lost some men since we separated.'

Crimall acknowledged the *Uí Loinge* man perceptiveness with a sharp dip of his head. 'Two men,' he answered. 'Nédé's left to follow the *díberg* and I've dispatched an *óglach* – our fastest runner – to Dún Baoiscne. Unburdened, he should reach the fortress a half day or more before us. That provides plenty of time for my father to be alerted, a call for more warriors to be dispatched and the preparation of supplies we'll need when we depart the following day.'

'Huh,' the *Uí Loinge* man grunted. He reached down to grasp a lump of wood and tossed it into the fire then, picking up a slender branch, used it to poke through the embers.

'You're not for your blankets?' asked Crimall. 'After your day of travel, I'd imagined you'd be straight for slumber.'

'Slumber escapes me,' Murchú explained. 'Unless my head's foggy with fatigue, I see Cairenn's face when I close my eyes. I cannot sleep for worrying of her plight.'

Crimall mumbled some vague, barely audible consolation then glanced across at the warrior woman who'd been listening in silence. 'And you, Grey One?' he asked. 'I'd imagine you a deep sleeper.'

She shook her head. 'Similar to Murchú,' she lied.

'Then Murchú's sister has the luck on her having two such warriors committed to her rescue.'

The woman warrior looked at him impassively but, in her mind's eye, saw two sets of parallel furrows in the earth where the *díberg* had set their prisoner.

Murchú's sister has the luck on her.

She dropped her bowl gently onto the ground and pushed it aside with her foot. When she looked up again, the *Clann Baoiscne* man's eyes were still on her.

'Grey One, I must confess you've lingered in my thoughts this evening. Your presence has stirred up some … curiosities.'

Liath Luachra regarded him warily. Conscious that he was waiting for her to ask why she'd been in his thoughts, she made a point of not doing so, obtaining a bitter satisfaction as the *Clann Baoiscne* man grew increasingly impatient at her silence.

'Tonight,' he tried again. 'I pondered the trail that leads a young woman to the status of *banfénnid*, a bloodied fighter on the *gaiscíoch* path. My curiosity in that regard remains unsated.'

She considered the *Clann Baoiscne* man carefully. The question seemed to have been earnestly posed but she considered it unlikely that he'd never come across any mention of her background, particularly given his father's interest in *Na Cinéaltaí.*

'You've not heard the song, then?'

Crimall snorted. 'I've heard many songs. Dún Baoiscne throbs with the sound of crooning voices, tunes of warriors who've slain wild boars with their teeth, ballads of foreign lands where honey flows from the cliffs in sweet waterfalls, warblings of women whose lust can sate a hundred men and even songs where …'

His dismissed the topic with a loose wave of his right hand. 'But, I'd be a fool to believe every tale those songs recount.'

'Before I answer, can I first pose a question of my own?'

Crimall smiled. 'As you like.'

'You mentioned Dún Baoiscne.'

'I did.'

'I wondered why you chose to travel to Dún Baoiscne now, why you didn't gather sufficient supplies prior to leaping into the pursuit of the *díberg*?'

Crimall's left eyebrow arched ever so slightly and although he displayed no other reaction, she could tell he was miffed by the abrupt – and complete – change of topic. Evidently, he'd been under the impression her question would relate more directly to himself.

'I didn't gather sufficient supplies at Dún Baoiscne,' he answered stiffly, 'because I do not dwell at Dún Baoiscne. I hold lands of my own to the north, not far from where the raiders struck. That's why I was able to assemble a *fian* and start a pursuit with such haste. Raiders often evade retribution because of the time it takes to discover their actions and organise the subsequent chase. Given the rare opportunity granted by a survivor alerting us of the *díberg's* action, I was determined not to let these raiders escape so readily.'

He smiled wryly then and shook his head. 'Of course, I hadn't anticipated the possibility the *díberg* might combine with another to create a force larger than my own. Neither did I imagine we'd encounter another *fian* bearing a similar objective.'

Murchú, who'd been toying with his empty bowl, now placed it on the ground beside his right foot. 'Your candour's appreciated Crimall, and although I cannot agree with your decisions, I understand your reasons.'

Nicely done, Murchú.

'In truth,' the *Uí Loinge* man continued. 'Given the evident mistruths I'd heard with respect to *Clann Baoiscne*, its pleasing to find a tribal leader so … judicious, so even-tempered.'

Instead of responding to the thinly veiled flattery, Crimall bent down to grab a fresh piece of wood and tossed it onto the fire. 'By mistruths, I assume you're referring to my father.'

Murchú's awkward and very obvious hesitation appeared response enough, for Crimall chuckled loudly at the *fénnid's* tongue-tied response. 'Be at your ease, Murchú. You're not the first man to hold such an opinion, certainly not the first to say it aloud. Tréanmór is as Tréanmór is. My father has his peculiarities and all of his decrees are by no means popular, but he's proven himself an effective leader to his people.'

'Is it true he talks to the dead?'

Liath Luachra had to restrain herself from glaring at Murchú. Fortunately, to her relief, Crimall took no offence at the *fénnid's* diplomatic misfire and laughed out loud at the question.

'Aaah! I see word of Tréanmór's discussions with *Na Cúig Cairde* – The Five Friends – has spread beyond *Clann Baoiscne* territory.' He leaned forward then, his hands held out with the palms spread wide to capture the heat of the fire.

'I suppose you could say there's some truth to the rumour. My father does talk to his dead 'friends' but as to whether they actually answer him or not, I couldn't say.'

Prompted by the heat of Liath Luachra's regard, Murchú hurriedly attempted an apology. 'Forgive the thoughtlessness of my question. No insult was intended.'

'And none was taken. I am not my father. I respect him and adhere to his judgements, but I have my own mind. I do not share his obsessive hostility to strangers on *Clann Baoiscne* land, particularly where we clearly stride with common purpose. I share your distress for what's happened to your sister. I too have a sister and she's as dear to me as yours is, evidently, dear to you.'

Relieved to find that he hadn't put his foot in it, the *Uí Loinge* man was more than happy to change the topic of conversation. 'What's the name on your sister?'

'Bodhmhall.'

Murchú nodded. 'Ah, yes, I've heard the name. Usually spoken with respect. Some say she has the beauty of the first ray of sunlight on a mid-summer's morning.'

'Even *Uí Loinge* people say this?'

Murchú smiled. 'Even *Uí Loinge* people.'

Crimall rubbed his hands together and lowered them to his knees. 'It's true my sister's a beauty. Alongside the fact that she's the smartest woman I've ever met, that makes me very proud. My father, for his part, believes that beauty dulled by her wilfulness and offers that as the reason she remains unbonded.' He chuckled again. 'This, of course, coming from a man more wilful than most.'

'Your sister remains unbonded?' Murchú sounded surprised at the possibility.

'Think it through, son of Congal. As Tréanmór's daughter it would take a brave or foolish man to step forward and risk such wrath for Bodhmhall's hand.' He grinned broadly. 'And yet, some years back there was one who shocked us all by doing exactly that and who …' His voice trailed off and he shrugged. 'But that was all for nought. The bonding between him and Bodhmhall lasted less than a year.'

He watched as Murchú returned to poking at the fire, his stick now scorched with a blackened tip. 'Perhaps you should seek her hand, Murchú. That would please Tréanmór no end.'

Both men laughed out loud at that.

'And you, Grey One,' Crimall continued, turning his attention to the woman. 'You could probably cheer my father further by accepting my brother Cumhal's hand and …' A sudden thought seemed to strike him then for he paused and looked from one of them to the other. 'Unless, of course, you're already paired.'

Both warriors stiffened at that. Murchú blushed. 'I'm bonded to an *Uí Loinge* woman,' he said hurriedly.

'A shame,' said the *Clann Baoiscne* man, shaking his head in mock dismay. 'Bodhmhall will be disappointed.' He looked across at Liath Luachra and winked. 'And Cumhal, of course.'

The Grey One made no answer although she struggled to restrain a scowl. She'd remained at the fire solely to maintain polite relations with the *Clann Baoiscne* man but, tired and in pain and still chafing from her strained relations with Murchú, she wanted nothing more than to retire to her blankets, a desire enhanced by Crimall's grating banter.

An awkward silence fell over the company and, for a time, all three stared quietly into the fire. It was Murchú who finally scattered the calm with a fresh question. 'This brother of yours. He resides at Dún Baoiscne?'

'Cumhal? Yes. As *tánaiste* and future leader of *Clann Baoiscne*, it's his responsibility to stay close and support our father. You'll meet him yourself when we get there. He's an impressive man. Broad of stature, noble of nature, wise of experience.' He winked at Liath Luachra again. 'And, like all *Clann Baoiscne* men, hung like a stallion.'

'And does he intend to accept the chieftainship from your father soon?' Murchú quickly interjected.

Crimall roared with laughter at that suggestion. 'Tréanmór retains a tighter grip on tribal leadership then an inflamed rectum on a swollen turd. He'll not surrender his position readily.'

Liath Luachra glanced at the *Clann Baoiscne* man, surprised by the unexpected causticity regarding his father given his earlier deference. As a general rule, tribal members didn't relinquish secrets on tribal strife to outsiders. To do so, in such a manner, suggested either a striking lack of tact or an underlying resentment not normally exposed to the air.

Too tired to maintain the effort of cordiality any longer, the woman warrior rose stiffly to her feet and bade the others a good night.

'Perhaps you'll dream of *Clann Baoiscne* men,' chuckled Crimall.

'Perhaps.'

'Then I wish you a restless slumber, Grey One.'

It was an effort to smile at the boorish humour so Liath Luachra didn't try. Acknowledging the comment with a neutral nod, she walked away from the fire, back to the horses where her belongings were located. Retrieving her bedroll, she headed towards the treeline, the murmur of the two men talking across the fire still audible from behind.

With the bedroll and cloak wrapped about her shoulders, the warrior woman pushed twenty paces or so past the treeline, deep into the forest until the fire was no longer visible and the voices couldn't reach her. Locating a clear patch of earth beside an elm tree, she spread out her bedroll, lay down with the heavy cloak wrapped around her and pulled its hood up to cover her head. At last, feeling safe in the depth of the Great Wild, she closed her eyes and relaxed.

It was on the verge of sleep, after her mind had loosened, that the traumatic events of the previous days slipped through her guard. Horrific visions filled her head: the furrows in the earth, the blood on Mochta's lips, the frantic eyes of the girls chained to the tree.

And the terrifying touch of Gadra's hand.

It was that last memory that yanked her upright: breathless, nauseous, chest heaving in panic as she fought the instinctive urge to run. The scars on her back had started to burn again when the tremors started, a violent series of shudders that rocked through her body and sent her muscles into spasm.

But that, too, eventually passed and huddled beneath her blankets, she clung to herself and shivered.

And waited in the forest dark for the promise of sleep to come.

***

123

It was late afternoon, two days later, when they finally entered Gleann Cuirreach. A sprawling valley of faded winter pasture interspersed with ragged patches of tilled fields, its secure location between two heavily forested ridges meant it had been used as a grazing site for the *Clann Baoiscne* herds for longer than anyone could remember. Looking around at the individual animals, Liath Luachra estimated between two and three hundred cattle, scrawny and slag-coated now after the hardship of winter.

Dún Baoiscne, the *Clann Baoiscne's* main settlement and tribal base, sat on a low, tussock-coated hill at the centre of the valley. Looking up towards its formidable outer earth embankment, topped with wooden palisades, the woman warrior recalled hearing that its defences included a deep ditch that encircled it completely, although from that distance and low-lying position it was impossible to tell. A worn path led up from the valley floor to a wide stone gateway in the eastern curve of the embankment. From the top of that gateway, three guards looked warily down towards them.

Making towards the fortress, the party halted at a cluster of three huts located about five hundred paces from the path at the base of the hill. Here, Crimall called the party to a halt, drawing surprised stares from *Na Cinéaltaí* members.

'Daithí!'

A bald old man with a greying beard that hung down to his chest, appeared tentatively in the doorway of the largest hut. Peering cautiously outside, he looked concerned at the sight of so many unfamiliar warriors but relaxed visibly when his eyes fell on Crimall. Wiping his hands on his tunic, he stepped forward with greater confidence, trailed by an impressive gaggle of at least seven yapping children of varying ages and gender.

'This is Daithí, my old retainer,' the *Clann Baoiscne* man offered by means of explanation. 'He and his family will offer *Na Cinéaltaí* their hospitality and fetch a healer to treat your wounded man.' He paused and cleared his throat. 'The Grey One alone will continue with us. Non-tribal forces aren't permitted inside Dún Baoiscne and the sight of an *Uí Loinge* man will only set my father's pulse racing. The rest of you can tarry here to await our return.'

'You seek to have the Grey One enter the wolves' den alone?' An Giobach demanded, an angry smile creasing his features. 'What kind of fools do you take us for?'

'Hopefully, the practical kind. Those are the only conditions in which a conversation with the *rí* of *Clann Baoiscne* will take place.'

Liath Luachra silently looked from Crimall to the high settlement and back again. Sensing her reticence, Crimall quickly moved to reassure her. 'You enter under my personal protection. On my head and by my name, you'll not be mistreated.'

He regarded her then with even greater intensity.

'Grey One, if you seek to obtain Tréanmór's permission to continue the pursuit, this is the sole means of achieving that goal.'

The woman warrior considered him without expression, fuming silently to find herself once again caught up in tribal powerplays without the power or the leverage to defend herself. 'Very well,' she said at last. 'Let us make a visit to Tréanmór.'

Murchú swiftly stepped forward, blocking her path before she could depart.

'A word, Grey One?' He looked pointedly at Crimall. 'For your ears alone.'

The *Clann Baoiscne* man merely shrugged. 'It's your decision, Grey One. Follow us when you're done. Or not. It makes little difference to *Clann Baoiscne.*' He hesitated. 'Although, personally, I'd be greatly disappointed of course.'

Leaving her with a suggestive smile, Crimall started towards the settlement, the remaining *Clann Baoiscne* warriors in his wake.

Murchú shuffled awkwardly as the Grey One turned to face him, her jaw tight, her expression hard. Even after two days, she continued to struggle in the *Uí Loinge* man's company and presented little more than a frosty face towards him.

'Entering that stronghold alone would not be wise,' he said.

Liath Luachra's lips tightened. This much she'd already worked out herself. 'Even if it meant your sister saved?'

Murchú went silent then, his expression stricken. Watching his obvious consternation, Liath Luachra felt a stab of shame. It had been a spiteful blow to offer such an impossible choice.

'I'm going up to Dún Baoiscne,' she said. 'For I can see no alternative. Can you offer one I've not considered?'

He shook his head.

'Well, then.'

Murchú's fingers strayed to the leather bindings around the hilt of his sword, toying awkwardly with them for several heartbeats. 'I'll not presume to warn you to be on your guard then, but I'd offer a word of advice.'

'Yes?'

'Be wary of Tréanmór. He's a strange one and my father says he speaks with the tenuous substance of an enemy in the mist. His words lunge out from nowhere in a manner that can seem erratic or strange, but which bears a depth of slyness. Listen when he speaks but be aware of what he doesn't say, for he'll try to upend you.' The *Uí Loinge* man paused. 'And if he invites you to see *Na Cúig Cairde,* you'd be wise to refuse.'

Liath Luachra's brow furrowed at that. 'Why? Have you learned more of *Na Cúig Cairde?*'

'No. But if these 'Five Friends' of his are truly passed and he's inviting you to see them, I'd feel more comfortable if you refused.'

She nodded shortly. That seemed sensible – if obvious – advice.

Taking a deep breath, the woman warrior looked around at the remnants of her *fian.* An Giobach looked furious, his bushy eyebrows agitated, his nostrils flaring. Although visibly unhappy with her decision to enter the *Clann Baoiscne* stronghold, he held his tongue, which meant – like her – he could see no workable alternative.

Feirgil, conversely, appeared to have lost all interest in the proceedings and was playing finger games on the ground outside the entrance to the nearest hut with Daithí's children. Beside him, lying unconscious on the litter, Biotóg remained blissfully oblivious to anything that was going on.

Liath Luachra sighed. *My glorious fian,* she thought morosely. *My famous and reputable band of warriors.*

'If I don't return by nightfall, feel free to slaughter any *Clann Baoiscne* you see, in honour of my memory.'

The woman warrior looked around at the *fénnid* but no-one responded to the weak attempt at humour. Shaking her head, she turned on her heel and started after the *Clann Baoiscne* men and, moving at a steady pace, soon caught them midway up the hill path. By the time they reached the large stone gateway, all were breathing heavily but she discovered that there was, indeed, a deep ditch at the base of the embankment, stretching off to either side along the curves of the fortification.

The gateway framed two massive oaken doors, pushed back against the interior walls of a dark stone passage. Following Crimall uneasily into that tunnel-like space, she matched his step for about twelve paces before emerging into the open air on a flat section of trampled grass sweeping forward to the base of a high stone wall: the settlement's second fortification. Like the ditch, this grassy section also curled off to either side, running in two wide arcs between the curved bulks of the embankment and the stone wall.

Liath Luachra stopped and stared, struck by the scale of the *Clann Baoiscne* tribal base, the level of activity and the diverse range of smells: woodsmoke, cooked meat, animal dung and, of course, people. Much of the grassy area was taken up with small huts and animal pens and a small crowd of about thirty men, women and children gathered around to watch the arrival of the little party. Wrinkling her nose, the woman warrior kept close to Crimall as he negotiated his way through the crowd, relieved to observe no open expression of hostility on the faces of those gathered. If anything, the people seemed curious, probably intrigued by the report from Crimall's messenger and keen to see the rarity of a *banfénnid* for themselves.

A second gateway further around the stone wall revealed another passageway, similar but shorter to the one in the embankment. Passing through it swiftly, the little party emerged onto the *lis*, the stronghold's circular, inner courtyard.

The fortress' pebble-coated interior had a large fire-pit at its centre. Following the curve of the eastern wall, four sturdy roundhouses faced a much larger, rectangular building with a sloped thatch roof on the *lis'* western side. Assembled on the ground directly in front of the larger building was a group of about ten men, mostly clustered by a solid wooden seat that looked to have been placed there specifically for the purpose of the interview. That seat was occupied by a man dressed in a bright blue *léine* and matching chequered leggings, who watched the arriving party with quiet intensity.

Liath Luachra felt her chest tighten.

Tréanmór, rí of Clann Baoiscne.

Crossing the *lis* towards the assembled men, Liath Luachra noted a heavily bearded figure break away from the others and advance directly towards the approaching party. A brawny, broad-shouldered block of a man, he looked to be at least a head above her in height and carried himself with the sharp, agile movements of an experienced fighter, an impression supported by the lumpy broken nose and a jagged scar above his left eyebrow. When he was within five paces of the woman warrior, he abruptly adjusted the direction he was moving in, effortlessly backfooting while maintaining that same distance between them. While he was doing this, he kept one hand conspicuously on the pommel of his sword, glaring at her coldly in a threatening manner.

'Ignore him,' whispered Crimall. 'That's Cathal Bog – Soft Cathal – my father's bodyguard. He enjoys marking his territory in his manner, like a dog pissing against a post. It amuses my father.'

Following the *Clann Baoiscne* man's advice, Liath Luachra turned her eyes away from the warrior, redirecting her attention to the man she'd come to see just as Crimall brought them to a halt in front of the gathered *Clann Baoiscne* men.

Even seated, Tréanmór of *Clann Baoiscne's* physical presence exuded an unmistakeable sense of supremacy. A handsome man, his features were composed and strong, flanked by a pair of complex grey braids and underset with a steel-grey beard that had recently been trimmed. Combined, they gave his face an unmistakeably authoritative air, one reinforced by the dazzling gold torc he wore about his neck.

Like Crimall, the *Clann Baoiscne rí* was somewhat heavy-chested, albeit in a muscular fashion. His eyes – like Crimall's – were dark brown but exuded a cold intelligence and a severity several levels above that of his son.

'I see you, Crimall. Welcome home to Dún Baoiscne.'

The *rí's* voice, deep and sonorous, rang impressively clear in the open area.

'I see you, Tréanmór, *rí* of *Clann Baoiscne.*' Crimall paused. 'It's pleasing to see you again, Father.'

The *Clann Baoiscne* chieftain nodded in a distracted manner, his attention already fixed on Liath Luachra. The woman warrior felt a frisson of unease at the intensity of that hooded gaze.

Although visibly disgruntled by the curt and somewhat inattentive welcome, Crimall gamely engaged once more. 'Did the runner deliver my message?'

Tréanmór nodded silently, his eyes still hooked on the Grey One's silent form. 'It was received.'

Recognising that the conversation had already moved on without him, Crimall grudgingly raised his hand to indicate the woman warrior at his side. 'This is the one they call Liath Luachra, *banfénnid* and *rigfénnid* of *Na Cinéaltaí.*

At the mention of her name, Liath Luachra immediately took a step forward, noting from the corner of her eye how swiftly Cathal Bog matched it.

'I see you, Tréanmór, *rí* of *Clann Baoiscne.*'

'I see you, Liath Luachra.'

The *Clann Baoiscne* chieftain's response to the ritual greeting seemed lethargically – almost insolently – delivered. Slouched back in his seat, he dangled one leg lazily over the armrest and appraised her with a shrewdness belying the affected nonchalance. Studying her features briefly, his gaze dropped to her chest and then down to her crotch where it remained for a moment before rising once more to latch onto her face. Focused on the purpose of her interview, Liath Luachra endured the in-depth carnal examination with her habitual stoicism.

'Great Tréanmór, *Na Cinéaltaí* seek your consent to pass through *Clann Baoiscne* lands to purs-'

'Yes, yes.' Tréanmór waved her explanation aside with an impatient gesture. 'The runner's already explained what you want. What I want however, is an explanation for your prolonged trespass of *Clann Baoiscne* lands.'

Liath Luachra looked at him in surprise. Having sent an account of their presence though his messenger, it seemed implausible that Crimall would have neglected to explain the reasons behind it.

'We follow a tasking set by the *Uí Loinge*, a Seeking to retrieve a young *Uí Loinge* woman abducted by raiders.'

'Come now, Grey One. Let's not be coy. You seek to retrieve *one* young *Uí Loinge* woman, in particular: Cairenn, daughter of my old rival, Congal.'

The Grey One studied the *Clann Baoiscne* leader closely, wondering why he was harrying her down these unrelated tangents, until she remembered Murchú's warning. Tréanmór was toying with her, playing games, just as the *Uí Loinge* man had forewarned.

Understanding then that there was probably no one answer which would satisfy the *Clann Baoiscne rí*, she lapsed back into silence, opting to offer none instead. For several moments, they eyed each other in complete silence. Finally, realising that she didn't intend to follow him down the path he'd laid out for her, Tréanmór broke the silence with a fresh diversion.

'I offered you a tasking some two years past.'

This being a statement she could confirm, the woman warrior nodded. 'Yes.'

'And you refused it.'

'Yes.'

'And, yet, you agree to a tasking set by my old adversaries, the *Uí Loinge*.'

'I had my reasons for tha-'

'So what then must a *rí* of *Clann Baoiscne* do that the famous Liath Luachra might deign to accept a tasking? Should I facilitate the abduction of my own daughter?'

A ripple of laughter ran through the assembled warriors. The woman warrior frowned uneasily. Tréanmór's outbursts had the air of crabby bleats from a cantankerous old man but thanks to Murchú's warning, she could now see that they were cannily timed and phrased to upend her. In that objective, he was greatly assisted by his control of the environment and the circumstances in which they were talking, that dominance allowing him to change topic or apply insult to outflank her without any real fear of reprisal.

Sensing that he'd nettled her, Tréanmór smiled broadly. 'I play you a joke, Grey One. I have no plans to have my daughter abducted. In truth, I'd pity any raider exposed to a lashing from Bodhmhall's tongue.'

He chuckled again and, taking advantage of that apparent softening, Liath Luachra attempted to herd the conversation back to the Seeking.

'Tréanmór, my request was sincere. *Na Cinéaltaí* have concerns for the girl's safety and we're eager to ensure her safe return. When we find the *díberg*, we'll seek to ensure the safe return of the *Clann Baoiscne* women as well.'

Tréanmór responded with a dismissive snort. 'We have no need of a mercenary *fian*, Liath Luachra. This *díberg* caused injury to *Clann Baoiscne* so it's *Clann Baoiscne* who'll deal retribution.'

'But we can help by offering …'

She stopped herself just in time. Caught up in the terse dynamics of the interaction, she'd come perilously close to blurting out her knowledge of the raiders' background. Furious at the potential mishap, she clamped her mouth shut. She had no intention of sharing such details, particularly to someone of Tréanmór's erratic guile. Gadra was, and would remain, her own dirty little secret.

Tréanmór however was now regarding her with renewed interest, his astute political instincts sensing her inadvertent exposure. Scrutinising her like a predator circling a wounded prey, he sought to sniff her secret out, scanning her face and body language for any tell-tale emotion. Thwarted by her impenetrable expression however, he was obliged to resort to a more direct approach.

'What can you offer?'

The question was thrown out carelessly, yet Liath Luachra sensed the devious intelligence behind it and tried to think swiftly.

'I've been close to the *díberg* that raided Briga. I've seen its warriors. When we locate them in the wilderness, I can confirm their identity.'

Tréanmór continued to watch her intently, sensing her deflection of his unspoken probing. Accepting that the moment and the opportunity had passed, he relaxed and laughed out loud at her proposal.

'I hardly think that's of great benefit, Grey One. It's true there's been a rash of *díberg* activity through *Clann Baoiscne* lands of late, but such events are rare. I don't doubt we'll find these raiders, even in the emptiness of the Great Wild. I certainly foresee no difficulty in identifying them.'

'Then I can offer you *Na Cinéaltaí's* experience and expertise of combat, of forest tracking, of b-'

'Again, Grey One, these have limited benefit. We already have such skills within our tribe.'

With sudden alacrity, the *rí* of *Clann Baoiscne* swung his foot down from the armrest and sat up to face her directly. 'The sad truth is you have nothing that *Clann Baoiscne* needs.'

Liath Luachra felt her heart sink.

Oh, Cairenn! Two steps closer, two steps sideways.

Tréanmór sighed. 'To be honest, the rejection of your service for the pursuit is one I regret,' he said suddenly. 'Unfortunately, the major resistance to your inclusion comes from my warriors here.'

He gestured expansively around at the gathered men for her benefit.

'They're not of the mind that a woman – well, a titless girl – could effectively lead a *fian.*'

Liath Luachra kept her features impassive. 'That did not seem a problem two years past, when you sent a message requesting a tasking.'

The *Clann Baoiscne rí* acknowledged her point with a shrug.

'That, I confess, was simple curiosity on my part. Like many others, I'd heard the song of the ferocious *banfénnid* and felt this was something I wished to see for myself. Given the tasking I required against our *Clann Morna* enemies, I -'

Tréanmór broke off with a chuckle.

'But that's talk of times past. I see now that my offer was misjudged. The sad reality is that your real accomplishments appear far less impressive than the obvious exaggerations in your song. The size of your *fian* was said to number twelve men or more yet, clearly, it's far less. The same, of course, can be said about the song's claims relating to the size of …' He held both hands, palms upward, in front of his chest. 'Your paps.'

Tréanmór shook his head with exaggerated dismay.

'You'll understand that … well, my warriors are a sceptical bunch. To have any hope of accompanying the pursuit, you'd first have to convince them of your abilities or competence. You'd have to pass … a test.'

Liath Luachra shifted uneasily from one foot to the other, keeping her emotions under a tight rein. She didn't like where the conversation was going.

'And what sort of test would satisfy you -. What sort of test would satisfy your warriors?'

Tréanmór put on the air of giving the question some serious consideration although it was obvious he already had an answer in mind. 'Well,' he said at last. 'Given the nature of the pursuit, I'd think a test of martial ability most apt. A test of one-to-one combat. If you're the first combatant to draw blood, you'll have proven yourself and then, of course, you'd be free to traverse *Clann Baoiscne* lands. If you're the first to bleed, however … well then, you and your *fian* would have to leave, depart back the way you came while passing my greetings to that dried out shit-stain, Congal, on your way.'

Liath Luachra looked at him in shock.

'You'd have me fight you?'

This time even the *rí* was startled. He blinked, then abruptly laughed out loud. 'Oh, no. I'm afraid the *rí* of *Clann Baoiscne* doesn't engage in combat with any random stranger who decides to visit Dún Baoiscne.'

'Then who would you have me fight?'

'Who?' Steepling his fingers, Tréanmór pressed his tips of his index fingers against his lips as his eyes trailed around the encompassing arc of *Clann Baoiscne* warriors. 'Well, it strikes me that Cathal Bog was the one most vociferous in his objections to your presence so perhaps you should prove the true level of your skills to him personally. Yes, that feels right. You can display your mettle against Cathal Bog here in the *lis* this very night. The outcome of that combat will decide in which direction you leave come the morning.'

Liath Luachra turned to regard the massive warrior. He looked back at her with a cold indifference that did nothing to belie his dangerous appearance.

'So, if I strike first blood, *Na Cinéaltaí* can freely traverse *Clann Baoiscne* land to fulfil their tasking?'

'If you defeat my champion, Grey One, you might as well lead the *Clann Baoiscne fian* while you're at it.'

The woman warrior mulled on that for all of two heartbeats. 'Very well. I accept.'

'Yes, well, there's one further stipulation, I'm afraid. It's a *Clann Baoiscne* tradition you may be unfamiliar with but it's one we align to strongly in deference to those who warred before us.'

The Grey One waited for him to get to the point.

'The combat will take place *faoi nocht* – naked.'

'*Faoi nocht*!' Liath Luachra stared at him, too appalled to conceal her horror.

'*Faoi nocht*,' he repeated.

'That's no tribal tradition I've ever heard of.' She threw a quick glance around the assembled warriors. From the startled expressions of bemusement, this was evidently a tradition they'd not previously encountered either.

'Would you resent us seeing you as you truly are, Grey One?' There was a distinct heat to Tréanmór's voice as he leaned forward in his seat, grasping the arms with a furious grip. 'The true individual behind the stories and the song.'

'As I truly am?' It was difficult to resist a sneer.

The *Clann Baoiscne* chieftain rose to his feet and glared at her. 'Through combat we'll see the truth of you, Grey One, whether you're a genuine warrior or a stripling maiden who wields a sword like a child's toy. After all, girls of your age are better placed bearing mewling brats for your spouses than storming through the wilderness, pretending to bear the makings of a man.'

With his true anger vented, Tréanmór sat back in the chair, breathing heavily at the effort of his outburst. 'If you don't wish to accept, you can return to the safety of your *Uí Loinge* friends at dawn tomorrow.'

The woman warrior looked from Tréanmór's reddened face to Crimall, who was now looking down at his feet, mortified and refusing to meet her eyes.

'Shit on your stupid tradition,' she said. 'I accept.'

Chapter Seven:

By the time Liath Luachra returned to the cluster of huts, the *fian* had settled themselves in for the evening, usurping two of the structures to lay out their bedding and supplies and hobbling the horses on the patchy grass nearby. A large fire was blazing in the central space between the three huts as the Grey One approached, creating a dramatic backdrop to where An Giobach and Murchú stood, javelins in hand, observing her advance. The expression on her face must have revealed her rage for both *fénnid* regarded her warily and made no attempt to greet her as she stormed past.

Approaching the fire, she pulled up a stool and sat close to the flames, poured herself a bowl of soup from the cauldron hanging above it and then grabbed a wooden spoon to agitate the broth. When it had cooled, she ate restlessly, mechanically spooning the liquid into her mouth, barely conscious of its taste as the fury seethed from her, radiating out to merge with the heat of the fire.

She'd made a grievous mistake. That realisation had sunk in even as she passed through the gates of Dún Baoiscne and started her descent along the angled pathway. By giving into her anger and standing up to Tréanmór, she'd stepped into a trap of her own making, assenting to conditions that would have outraged her under any other circumstances. It was only now however, with the gradual dissipation of her rage, that the true consequences of what she'd agreed to were starting to register.

The combat will take place faoi nocht.

Fighting an opponent almost twice her bulk in the *Clann Baoiscne* tribal centre, a place where every inhabitant's hostility would be directed against her. Exposed in her full vulnerability for the entertainment of a howling mob.

The woman warrior felt a sudden clenching in her gut, a rising taste of bile at the back of her throat, a …

Dropping the bowl, she fell to her knees and violently retched up everything she'd just eaten, heaving up mouthful after mouthful until nothing was left but sour strands of yellow bile. When the spasms finally eased and her gut unclenched, she collapsed back onto her haunches, her breathing ragged, her chest heaving, sweat seeping from her brow.

'Discussions with Tréanmór didn't go as you'd hoped, then.'

She looked up as An Giobach moved in to hook a stool with his foot and drag it over close to her own. Dropping his full weight onto it, the bulk of him was enough to make the entire space between the huts seem smaller and more crowded.

Too drained to feel any anger or shame, Liath Luachra exhaled heavily. Using the back of her hand, she wiped threads of vomit from her lips but offered no response. Reaching over to her own stool, she grabbed one of its legs to pull it closer and create some distance between herself and the seated warrior. Shakily rising to her feet, she flopped onto its flat wooden surface just as Murchú came to join them, pulling up another seat alongside his fellow *fénnid*. He looked at her wordlessly across the flames but she turned her eyes away, already dreading the thought of having to tell them what had transpired.

'In truth,' said An Giobach, 'I'd feared you wouldn't return. I wouldn't have put it past Crimall and his lot to ignore obligations of hospitality and slit your throat once they'd had their fu -' He broke off quickly and threw her an awkward sideways glance. 'Or worse,' he mumbled lamely into the depths of his beard.

Liath Luachra inhaled deeply, poked a toe into the earth by the fire. 'I had discussions with Tréanmór,' she said. 'He's decreed I must prove my worth through a test if *Na Cinéaltaí* are to be allowed through *Clann Baoiscne* lands.'

'A test?' Murchú's brow furrowed. 'But why? What would that prove?'

'Prove?' she repeated bitterly. 'It wouldn't prove anything. Nothing of substance, in any case. The test has no basis but to justify Tréanmór's malice. The existence of a *banfénnid* clearly offends the *rí* of *Clann Baoiscne's* sensibilities. His test is nothing more than an excuse to assuage that rancour while also preventing our passage on his land.

'And what does his ... test consist of?' asked An Giobach.

'A test of combat.'

That silenced them for a moment. Again, it was An Giobach who followed up with the subsequent question. 'Combat with who?'

'With Cathal Bog'

'Cathal Bog? Bodyguard to the *Clann Baoiscne rí*?'

She nodded.

An Giobach chewed on his lower lip. 'And is he a formidable opponent?'

Liath Luachra shrugged.

An Giobach said nothing but continued to chew on his lip. Unable to glean anything from the warrior woman's expression, he turned instead to Murchú. 'This Cathal Bog, Murchú. Do you know of him?'

The *Uí Loinge* man sniffed and rubbed his nose. 'By name only. I understand the appellation's something of a joke. By all accounts he's a giant of a man and a hardy warrior.' He paused. 'Given his role as bodyguard to Tréanmór, I'd hazard there's little soft about Cathal Bog.'

'A fighter, then.'

'A formidable one so they say.'

Both looked to Liath Luachra, but she'd already turned her eyes away. Neither of the warriors made comment but their unease was tangible and underlined her own mounting disquiet. In all her time as *fénnid*, she'd never been one for face-to-face combat, preferring to come at her opponents from the rear or from the side and using her natural speed and athleticism to best effect. The problem with one-on-one combat of this nature was that it dispensed with all skill or tactics, reducing everything to the pure physical fundamentals: brute strength, reach and staying power.

Although tall for her gender, Liath Luachra's slight – albeit muscular – frame meant she was at a serious disadvantage against the taller, heavier Cathal Bog. In addition, given what she'd seen of Cathal Bog, even her strongest advantages were matched, and possibly surpassed, by the warrior's own suppleness. The *Clann Baoiscne* champion moved like shadows beneath a windblown tree but, unlike those insubstantial shades, he had mass and muscle to boot.

Maintaining a neutral expression, the woman warrior looked around for something to distract herself from such reflections. She noted that, in addition to the food and accommodation, Crimall had also kept his word with respect to the healers. Two *Clann Baoiscne* women were now bent over the wounded Biotóg, murmuring some quiet supplication to the ancestors as they plastered a grey paste around his wound. Freshly woken, the young *fénnid* was staring up at them as though enraptured and allowed them to treat him without complaint.

To the left of the healers and their charge, Feirgil was entertaining Daithí's children, using some of their childish paints and tinctures to daub their faces with different shades of green dye. The detail of his manipulations gave their features a surreal, leaf-like appearance and provoked gales of merriment irritatingly at odds with her own mood.

'We could make a run for it,' suggested An Giobach, abruptly drawing her back to the conversation.

Liath Luachra looked at him then back at the litter where Biotóg lay smiling up at his caregivers. 'And leave Biotóg?'

It was obvious the skinny warrior wouldn't be running anywhere.

An Giobach shrugged. 'It's only Biotóg.'

The warrior's quick grin assured his comrades that his words hadn't been in earnest and yet, as she regarded him, the Grey One wondered whether there might have been some truth beneath the *fénnid's* harsh humour. She'd always had a sense that, like her, An Giobach didn't have full confidence in the pale-faced *fénnid*. Biotóg with his strange, off-putting ways was a hard man to like or, sometimes, even to engage with. As an inheritance from Bressal's war band, he'd always aligned strongly with their old *rígfénnid* and she occasionally wondered at his loyalties and whether he secretly passed information on her own activities back to his old leader.

'So!' An Giobach declared suddenly, yanking her back to the present. 'If I have the right of it then, you'll be fighting alone in the *Clann Baoiscne* tribal centre with no *fian* support permitted inside. Your opponent's an experienced warrior who exceeds you in size and strength and even should you somehow overcome him, there's no guarantee Tréanmór will keep his word with respect to the Seeking.'

Liath Luachra exhaled heavily. 'There is one other element I neglected to mention,' she said.

***

As the evening closed in about them, the Grey One withdrew inside one of the huts to prepare herself for the trial ahead. Sitting alone by the building's internal firepit, she fed little sticks to the flames, struggling to still her mind and control her fear, objectives hampered by the lack of any workable plan or line of action on which to frame her thoughts. The truth of the matter was that she didn't believe she could defeat the *Clann Baoiscne* champion and that conviction only served to undermine her confidence.

Leaning forward with her elbows on her knees, she stared into the fire, mentally working through a number of potential actions. Possibly, if she could distract Cathal Bog, somehow take him by surprise. Perhaps using her naked form …

She pulled back and scowled at that, disturbed by the desperation of falling back on such a feeble fantasy. During her brief encounter with Cathal Bog, she'd seen the bluntness in his eyes and had instantly recognised its origin. It wasn't sexuality that drove the *Clann Baoiscne* man but the thrill of violence, the physical exultation that came with overcoming an opponent, with defeating them brutally and completely. If he did defeat her, there'd probably be some subsequent display of domination of course, some sexual humiliation or degradation for the amusement of the *Clann Baoiscne* people and one which they were unlikely to oppose.

She raised a bowl of warm water to her lips and sipped but her hands were trembling so much she had to replace the container on the hut's dirt floor.

But this was all prevarication of course. Focusing on the combat with Cathal Bog meant she was essentially ignoring the issue that truly terrified her; the requirement to present herself before the *Clann Baoiscne* assembly … *faoi nocht*. That prospect chilled her heart, made it difficult to breathe and threatened to crush her spirit completely. It also made the combat with Cathal Bog fade into insignificance.

You could run!

She dispelled that thought through the physical action of rising to her feet, kicking her stool aside and drawing *Gléas Gan Ainm* from its scabbard. Bending her knees lightly to take up a defensive stance, she held the weapon out flat before her, as though confronting an imaginary attacker. Tightening her grip on the hilt, she adjusted her stance, lunging forward in a series of different offensive movements, but no matter how many times she tried, she couldn't ignore the fact that the tip of her blade was wavering perceptibly.

Disgusted, she dropped the weapon to her side and grunted. Even if Cathal Bog failed to smell the fear on her when she first presented herself, he'd certainly see it when she raised her weapon.

'Grey One!'

A muffled call from the other side of the doorway's heavy fur flap alerted the woman warrior to Murchú's imminent entrance and she grunted in displeasure as he brushed it aside. As the *fénnid* pushed his way into the little structure, she glared at him, annoyed at the interruption. She needed solitude to work out a plan and had no time for fruitless discussion.

'*Scuab leat, a Murchú.*' Piss off, Murchú.

'Ignoring her, the *Uí Loinge* man advanced even further into the hut's interior and faced her across the little firepit.

'I don't want you to do this, Grey One. I don't want you to go ahead with the combat.'

The woman warrior chuckled bitterly at that. 'I don't want to do it either Murchú, but the alternative is to lose any chance of saving your sister.' To still her growing anger, she turned away, sliding the blade of *Gléas gan Ainm* back into its leather sheath.

'Does my sister really mean so much to you?'

That snagged her attention. Turning back to consider the *fénnid* in silence, she waited for him to explain, unsure where he was attempting to lead the discussion. The thought of abandoning Cairenn and leaving her in Gadra's possession was a genuine anchor, one that helped prevent her giving into her fear and fleeing the Cuirreach Valley. It wasn't the only one of course.

'You've never met my sister, Grey One. Endearing though she is, that lack of familiarity means you couldn't possibly bear the same sense of responsibility I bear her.' He sighed softly. 'For that reason alone, you should slip away into the forest. Leave An Cuirreach Valley. Turn your back on this place and depart without looking to your rear.'

Liath Luachra felt the embers of anger rouse deep in her belly.

'I may not know her, Murchú, but I've sat in her place. I've seen her terror carved into the forest floor. I've also seen girls tethered to a tree like cattle, helpless and terrified at the fate awaiting them. I've seen all this, Murchú. And seeing it, I know your sister in a manner you never will.'

And I know Gadra.

She slumped back, exhausted by the rare outburst of emotion. Murchú however, had barely noticed. Intent on his own aspirations in her regard, his ears were closed to anything she'd said. 'You don't have to do this,' he insisted. 'I relinquish any claim of loyalty, any debt you feel you owe to me or to *Uí Loinge*. I want you to leave. I'll proceed alone through *Clann Baoiscne* territory. Rescuing Cairenn is my burden. I should never have asked you to help.'

'You'll fail. Go by yourself and you'll fail.'

He chuckled wryly at that. 'Who's to say. There's certainly a chance but one man can travel with a stealth a *fian* cannot match. Besides, An Giobach or Feirgil might yet accompany me.'

Liath Luachra looked at him and suddenly she felt exhausted, wearied and worn out by the fear churning inside her.

'Leave me be, Murchú. I've made my own decision, for my own reasons. There are no more words to be said between us.'

To her surprise, the *Uí Loinge* man simply looked into the flames and nodded acquiescently. 'In my heart,' he said, 'I was certain you'd not grasp the lowest-hanging branch.' He gave a sad chuckle and shrugged. 'But, I had to ask.'

He looked up at her then, his eyes still bearing the heat from the flames. 'That's why I also turned my mind to a plan for upending the smugness of *Clann Baoiscne*, to giving you an edge before you face Cathal Bog.'

She laughed cynically at that. 'You have the means then to get me through Dún Baoiscne unscathed, to have me face Cathal Bog on equal terms?'

'No,' the *Uí Loinge* man admitted. 'But I believe that Feirgil does.'

***

When she could put off the moment no longer, the woman warrior wrapped the heavy cloak about her and rose to her feet, drawing the scabbarded *Gleas gan Ainm* free from the pile of clothing beside the fire. Grasping the weapon's hardened leather covering for reassurance, she advanced toward the doorway, brushed the flap aside and stepped out into the night.

It was dark outside of course, but the darkness had a far more solid quality than she'd expected due to the thick cloud layer that blotted out all trace of the stars. The three able-bodied *fénnid* – Murchú, An Giobach and Feirgil – were standing by the fire and they turned their heads towards her when they heard the sound of footsteps. Moving into the circle of light thrown out by the fire, she watched their reactions, noting how An Giobach, and even Murchú, stiffened in surprise, taken aback by the gruesome fierceness of the pattern Feirgil had painted across her features. Earlier, she'd studied the skinny *fénnid's* handiwork herself using the reflection from the surface of a bowl of water. Despite her lack of expectation, she'd found herself impressed. Using a dark-green tinted base to startling effect, Feirgil had somehow imbued her fine features and high cheekbones with far greater substance, creating a foundation so dark it looked completely black in the flickering light of the torches. More impressive however, were the white circles he'd daubed about her eyes and the ragged white line smeared across her lips that resembled a jagged, powdered wound. In stark contrast to the dark green which absorbed the flickering light, those white patches reflected it, imbuing her features with an ethereal hue.

'I don't know about Cathal Bog,' said Murchú. 'But looking at you makes me want to shit in fear.'

Feirgil, pleased with their reaction to his work, chortled and clapped his hands in delight.

Taking a moment to consider the *fénnid*, the Grey One realised, with a start, that all three were armed to the teeth. 'What's this?' she asked, suddenly alert. 'You look ready for battle.'

'Your escort,' answered An Giobach stiffly, still recovering from his initial shock at her appearance. '*Clann Baoiscne* may not allow us to enter but they cannot prevent us from escorting our *rígfénnid* to their gateway.'

Liath Luachra shook her head. 'No,' she said.

An awkward silence followed that steadfast refusal.

'You should probably prepare to leave,' she told them. 'The likelihood of Murchú's plan succeeding is tenuous at best and, if I lose this fight, I'll not be fit to lead a *fian* again.'

She paused and kept her eyes on the ground.

'You'll be better off following your own path. As soon as I pass through the gateway of Dún Baoiscne, *Clann Baoiscne's* attention will focus on me. If you're quiet, you'll be able to slip away. And ...' Her eyes flicked across the fire to Murchú. 'Whatever actions you decide to take, you'll be safer far from the Cuirreach Valley. But you'll have to move fast, particularly if you're bringing Biotóg with you.'

None of the *fénnid* spoke. Liath Luachra glanced past them, her eyes drawn to the hill by the flicker of flaming torches marking either side of the path leading up to the *dún* entrance. The gates of the embankment passage remained ajar, the rectangular outline glowing slightly through that darkness, illuminated by the soft light from the interior. Due to the absence of wind, the irregular throb of voices up at the stronghold was audible, intermittently punctuated by shouts of excitement or the cackle of hysterical laughter. Spilling out over the palisades, it rolled down the hill towards them.

Confronted with the reality of the great crowd awaiting her arrival, the warrior woman felt a ripple of terror cut through her. Tréanmór was intent on using her humiliation as an entertainment, and possibly a subtle warning, for his people.

'There's been people coming and going all afternoon,' said An Giobach, as though reading her mind. 'More coming than going. Well over a hundred people up there now by my reckoning.'

Too tense to speak, Liath Luachra nodded brusquely. She felt her knees soften and, for a moment, feared they'd give way beneath her.

'Oh, and I managed to get what you asked for, although it took some threats and promises.' The big *fénnid* raised a leather waterskin in his right hand, the brusque movement causing the liquid to slosh around inside. '*Uisce beatha.*'

Numbly accepting the container, Liath Luachra tucked it under her left arm, keeping the hand free to clutch the material at the front of her cloak while her right hand grasped her sheathed sword. Pulling the hood of the cloak up over her head, she turned and started walking in the direction of the settlement. If she remained any longer, it would only make the departure that much harder.

The night chill had settled and a fresh breeze eased in from the west as she made her way across the flat terrain towards the hill. Low and cold on the open ground, it tugged and wrinkled the material of her cloak and seeped up beneath the lower hem to lick against the bare skin of her buttocks and thighs.

Striding barefoot through the ankle-high grass, she ignored the bite of the first grass frost against the soles of her feet, ignored the lump in her throat, the nausea in her guts and the almost overwhelming desire to shit, driving herself onwards despite the hollowness in her chest. Thirty paces got her to the darkest patch of ground between the fire at the cluster of huts and the torch-illuminated path leading up to Dún Baoiscne.

You should run.

That thought stopped her dead in her tracks. Despite her best attempts to ignore it, her fear had swollen and taken root and now threatened to overwhelm her.

Murchú's plan is a joke. Feirgil's finger-painting will do nothing but provoke Clann Baoiscne laughter.

She shook her head in a vain attempt to dislodge her mounting despair.

No-one would see you go in this shadow. No-one would know you'd run.

But the *fian* would know.

What of it? By the time they work out what's happening, you'll be long gone.

And why do you care what they think? You're nothing to them. They're nothing to you.

By then, the terror was rippling through her, the space in her head swimming with the enormity of the insurmountable task ahead. Despite the chill, her skin had broken out in a cold sweat. Her heart was beating fiercely, her chest tight from labouring to absorb each breath. Closing her eyes, the woman warrior drew up her memory of the indentations in the forest floor where the *díberg* had paused to rest, the shallow furrows in the earth where Cairenn's terror had scarred it.

Lifting the waterskin, Liath Luachra yanked the stopper free and, took two long *sliogs* to smooth herself out. The *uisce beatha* was harsh and abrasive against the back of her throat.

But the caustic burn of it was soothing.

Reaffixing the stopper, she continued to stand, quiet and unmoving in that darkest patch of the night, breathing deeply, conscious of the many sets of eyes peering into the shadows to catch sight of her.

Bolstered by the *uisce beatha*, she somehow managed to take a step forward. And a second step. And a third. And, by then, she had enough momentum to push herself onwards, her eyes locked onto the distant glow of the gateway, her mind set and blinkered.

Although her fear still bubbled beneath the surface, by the time the woman warrior had reached the torches at the base of the hill path, she felt more in control, her fear clamped beneath a cap of fierce determination. Striding purposefully up the ascending path, it didn't take long to reach the gateway and step directly into the gaze of the two *Clann Baoiscne* guards on the stone lintel above it. From the eager intensity with which they examined her, the woman warrior could tell they'd been tracking her ascent from the moment they'd spotted movement in the light of the lower torches. Now however, in the flaring light of the nearby torches, their faces were twisted in scowls of irritation. With a start, she realised they were disappointed, put-out by the fact that she'd clad herself in the concealing mass of hood and cloak.

Stepping into the gateway passage and out of their line of sight, the Grey One paused, cowed by the noise of the *Clann Baoiscne* crowd echoing down the passage towards her. The stones lining the far aperture glistened red from the light of the torches, mottled with the flurried shadows of people moving just beyond. The woman warrior's mouth felt thick with mucus, her hands clammy and awkwardly cold.

Too late to turn back now.

Taking a deep breath, she strode towards the end of the passage and heard confirmation that the guards had signalled her arrival when the noisy hubbub and laughter abruptly ceased. Drawing closer, that muted air of heightened expectation was punctured by a sudden outburst.

'It's her! She's coming!'

A fresh wave of sweat broke over her body as she emerged from the passage and into the initial press of bodies.

More than a hundred men and woman had gathered to watch her arrival. Standing in a rough arc, some of them were holding skins like her own and displayed obvious signs of inebriation. Others were chewing silently on freshly cooked pork cutlets sourced from trestles to the left of the passage which bore further servings of meat and other edibles.

An unnerving silence filled the first internal ring of the *dún* as the *Clann Baoiscne* people stared at the hooded figure in their midst. Taking advantage of that startled calm, the woman warrior moved forward, keeping her hooded head low to conceal the face paint. Unsure what to expect, the crowd backed uneasily out of her way, involuntarily creating a corridor through which she could pass. Nearing the great stone wall, however, she encountered a group of men and women more vocal and belligerent than their fellow tribal members, and who greeted her with hoots of derision and scornful laughter. One old crone stepped aggressively into the Grey One's path, forcing the woman warrior to raise her head and draw up abruptly to avoid a collision. As the *Clann Baoiscne* woman opened her mouth to deliver some further invective, she caught sight of the painted features framed against the black cave of her hood. Startled, she abruptly stepped back in alarm, the intended words falling unspoken from her lips.

'*Marbhfháisc ort!*' she managed to splutter fearfully, before hurriedly retreating into the crowd. Bad cess to you!

Ignoring her, the woman arrior drew on her anger once more and brushed indifferently past, leaving the disconcerted *Clann Baoiscne* members in her wake, wondering at the old woman's reaction.

Despite the distracting presence of the crowd and the confusing flicker of torches, Liath Luachra succeeded in working her way along the curving inner wall until she reached the second gateway to the stronghold's interior. As with the embankment entrance, a pair of guards were stationed there. Unlike their comrades at the outer gateway however, they were standing directly in front of the passage which had been sealed by two solid-looking wooden gates. The combat, it seemed, was reserved for the eyes of the *Clann Baoiscne rí* and key members of his inner sanctum.

Both guards eyed her warily as she approached, noting the scabbarded weapon in her right hand.

Understanding that they'd refuse to let her enter until she dropped her hood and identified herself, she consoled herself with the satisfaction of seeing their startled expressions when she did so. Striding past the two stunned men, she pushed one of the gates open, entered the passage and sealed it behind her.

Checking to make certain the guards couldn't see her, she took a deep breath, slowly undid the fastenings of her cloak and shuffled it from her shoulders. As the heavy covering dropped to the passage floor, she lifted the waterskin, undid the stopper and took one quick swig of *uisce beatha* before liberally splashing the remnants of the container's contents over her arms and chest and patting the last drops gently onto her face. When she was done, she stood, her skin chilled by the combination of the liquid and cold breeze running through the passage.

Taking a deep breath, Liath Luachra started down the length of the stone corridor, the scabbarded sword swinging loosely in her right hand as she added a little lurch to her step to mimic inebriation. To keep a tight rein on her fear, she fixed her gaze on the distant opening, focussed uniquely on that rectangular patch of brightness while keeping her mind free of any other distraction.

When a tall female figure entered the passage through that aperture therefore, a part of the woman warrior's mind noted the new arrival but she otherwise dismissed it. Oblivious to the woman warrior's presence because of the darkness, the newcomer continued swiftly towards her and it was only as they closed at its centre that she realised another person was present. Startled, the *Clann Baoiscne* woman shrank back against the wall in alarm, staring wide-eyed as the naked woman warrior swept past. Despite her indifference to the other woman's presence, the Grey One still registered her reaction with relief and satisfaction. On this occasion at least, Murchú's plan seemed to have achieved the desired effect. The far end of the passage however, was where the true test would begin.

Nearing the entrance to the *lis*, it quickly became apparent that, as with the embankment gateway, the occupants here, too, had been forewarned of her imminent arrival. Slowing to a halt in the final shadows, she looked out at that central area to find herself confronted by a silent crowd of at least fifty onlookers, all staring expectantly towards the passage entrance. The major proportion were gathered outside the hall where Tréanmór's chair remained in a prominent position, however two ragged lines of spectators stretched out on either side of a marked-off circle at the far side of the blazing firepit where the combat was to take place.

Before the hall entrance, the *Clann Baoiscne rí* was leaning forward in his seat as he peered eagerly towards the passage, Crimall standing silently to his left. Off to their right, at the edge of the combat circle, Cathal Bog stood alone, an immoveable pillar of muscle and sinew, his white skin gleaming yellow from the flames of the fire. Like the Grey One, he was completely naked, his *bod* hanging loosely in the cleft between his legs like a giant eel poking out of the reeds.

There were several intakes of breath, exclamations and grunts of surprise when the woman warrior stepped out of the shadows, the light from the torches in the *lis* revealing the full clout of Feirgil's body painting. Using the same dark green foundation to cover every morsel of the woman warrior's skin, the *fénnid* had skilfully overlain it with thick, horizontal white lines that sinuously encircled her torso, arms and legs in an erratic series of rings. Offset against that gleaming white, her breasts and genitals were indistinguishable in the flickering light from the torches and fire.

Moving forward, she stumbled loosely towards a vague point somewhere between Tréanmór's position and the combat circle where Cathal Bog awaited her, conscious of, but paying no attention to, the whispered mutters and twitching nostrils of the spectators she passed. The *Clann Baoiscne* onlookers were reacting to her presence with a mixture of anger and bewilderment, confused and unclear as to what they were seeing. Anticipating a humiliated *éclann* obliged to present herself in a vulnerable state of undress, they instead found themselves confronted by a frightening figure who exhibited a tangible air of contempt through the inebriated swagger in which she moved. That sense of confusion was further exacerbated by the prominent symbols adorning the woman warrior's abdomen and back, powerful symbols and designs normally associated with milestone rituals for hunt preparations, death, birth, isolation and sexual abstinence. The confusing portrayal of such significant symbols upon the woman warrior's body had the unusual effect of changing how it could be perceived, for the inability to separate the symbols from the body they adorned meant it was transformed to the status of a desexualised living canvas.

Advancing towards Tréanmór, Liath Luachra was satisfied to see that the *rí,* too, had been overwhelmed by the impact of the bodypainting. Dumbfounded, he'd risen to his feet, jaw hanging loose as he watched her stumble unsteadily to veer off in Cathal Bog's direction. Cathal Bog, for his part, observed her erratic approach without any apparent expression, however the series of lines forming across his forehead revealed the extent of his own consternation.

Moving towards him, conscious of the strong reek of *uisce beatha* that preceded her, the woman warrior tottered into the circle and waved the scabbarded sword at him. *"seo!"* she slurred tossing the weapon carelessly into the air towards him. Here!

Caught off guard by such an unexpected and clumsy action, the warrior responded instinctively, reaching up to grasp the heavy weapon before it fell to strike his head. The instant he raised his hand however, the Grey One moved with swift precision. Stepping forward in one perfectly balanced movement, she swung her right foot up and kicked him high between the legs, her muscled foot connecting solidly with the soft flesh of the *Clann Baoiscne* man's ball sack. Cathal Bog's eyes widened, his face ballooned into an expression of agonized bewilderment and, as his knees gave way, he crumpled to the ground like a tumbled oak.

The *Clann Baoiscne* audience gasped collectively as their champion curled into a huddled, whimpering pile and a subdued silence slowly filled the *lis.* While the stunned onlookers continued to watch, Liath Luachra stepped forward and retrieved her sword from where the groaning warrior had dropped it. Yanking *Gléas Gan Ainm* from its sheath, she dispassionately stabbed him in the left buttock with the tip of the weapon. Already consumed by pain, Cathal Bog didn't even notice this new discomfort.

Checking to make sure the point of the blade retained a crimson stain, Liath Luachra turned and walked towards the *Clann Baoiscne rí*, any facade of drunkenness now completely discarded. Tréanmór stared, his left eye twitching involuntarily, still too shocked to react. Two of his warriors however, stepped forward to bar the woman warrior's way, so she held the blade up where no-one could fail to miss its bloodstained point.

'First blood!' she shouted.

Holding the weapon at an angle, she swung around in a semi-circle, eyes blazing in challenge for anyone to deny her claim. After a moment or two had passed, and no-one had stepped forward, she rounded back on Tréanmór.

'I claim first blood and victory over your champion.' She spoke clearly and distinctly, having no need to shout in the absolute hush of the *lis*. 'I also claim the right for *Na Cinéaltaí* to traverse *Clann Baoiscne* land freely to fulfil its Seeking.'

She paused, then looked the *rí* of *Clann Baoiscne* squarely in the eye. 'And I accept your generous offer of leading the *Clann Baoiscne fian* to retrieve your womenfolk.'

Tréanmór's expression was apoplectic, the protracted humiliation he'd planned upended and countered in less than two heartbeats. Nostrils flaring, he eyed her in cold but helpless fury, conscious that having openly offered that option in front of his supporters, he could not go back on his word. Never expecting for a moment that she'd be in the position to accept such an offer, it seemed that – like her – he too had stepped into a trap of his own making.

Retrieving her scabbard, Liath Luachra sheathed her weapon and turned her gaze around the onlookers.

'*Na Cinéaltaí* will be leaving the valley at first light. Any members of the *Clann Baoiscne fian* who wish to join the pursuit, can gather at the huts before dawn.'

Without another word, the woman warrior turned on her heel and stalked back towards the passage. Entering the dark stone aperture, she disappeared from sight.

And left a stunned hush in her wake.

***

Later, she wouldn't remember much of her departure from Dún Baoiscne. There were vague memories of retrieving her cloak and sullen stares from the *Clann Baoiscne* occupants but, mostly, all she could recall was the head down, plodding sensation of forward movement. Emotionally overwhelmed by the events in the *lis*, her mind had closed down, reduced to its most basic functions.

The single event she did recall was the depth of her relief at finding Murchú waiting outside the embankment gateway. Having convinced herself that the *fian* had already departed, the sight of the young *Uí Loinge* man wrapped in a cloak against the cold, one hand on his sword pommel as he glared up at the guards, was almost enough to make her weep. Wracked with tension, by then her body was close to shutting down and she was obliged to grab his arm for support, refusing to give the guards the satisfaction of seeing her stumble as he subtly guided her downhill.

Back at the cluster of huts, the other *fénnid* were standing by the structure she'd claimed for her own, awaiting her arrival with visible concern. An Giobach, in particular, looked torn, his face tight, his expression indecipherable as he looked from her to Murchú and back. Realising that he was waiting on her news, she somehow found the energy to speak.

'Tomorrow,' she muttered. 'We recommence the Seeking at dawn.'

Ignoring the big man's dumbfounded reaction, the woman warrior stumbled forward, brushed the flap aside and staggered into the little hut, making straight for the single mattress of bundled straw. Lying down without pausing to remove the paint, she rolled onto her side and curled into a ball.

For a time, her exhausted mind struggled to accept the reality of what she'd achieved, that Murchú's plan had actually worked, that Feirgil's skills had been up to the test, that she'd escaped Tréanmór's vindictive designs for her. Consumed by the marvel of her own survival, although a part of her remained furious for what she'd been forced to endure, another part was exhilarated by her own audacity, by the fact that she'd somehow managed to bluff her way through.

The power. The power of the symbols.

Huddled in the dark, she thought back to how she'd grudgingly endured Feirgil's touch earlier that evening. As he'd smeared the dark green dye upon her shoulders, she'd snarled fiercely when his hand had veered to less tolerable areas and, in the end, had confiscated the tints to apply them herself under his direction.

Despite her ill-concealed resentment, she'd sensed a power to the symbols she was painting, a kind of familiar intensity that she recognised but didn't fully understand. Sensing her confusion, the slight *fénnid* had nodded his head obliquely as though somehow able to read her mind. 'A person without symbols,' he said suddenly. 'Is a person invisible to the ancestors.'

At the time, the *fénnid's* comment had made little sense but now, having seen the impact of those symbols for herself, the woman warrior sensed a deeper truth to the powerful association they held. Even if it was one she didn't – and probably never would – completely fathom.

Chapter Eight:

The *Clann Baoiscne fian* emerged from the shadows just before dawn the following morning and they made an unhappy sight. Ten shaded figures in lumpish cloaks, they were barely distinguishable as they trudged gloomily down from the *dún* in the murk of the early morning. Moving desolately in single-file behind their leader, a freshly-shaven Crimall, each warrior carried a wicker backpack of supplies, some visibly heavier than others.

Advancing towards the fire where the *Na Cinéaltaí* had gathered with the elderly Daithí, Crimall nodded a muted greeting while his men gathered in a half-circle behind him. Although wrapped in her own cloak with the hood drawn up against the chill, Liath Luachra could feel the scrape of the *Clann Baoiscne* man's eyes as he scrutinised her for traces of the body paint he'd seen the previous evening. Beneath that obvious curiosity however, she also detected a distinct cooling in her regard, the warrior's previously open ardour displaced by a frostier formality. It seemed her new reputation within the tribe meant she was now strictly off limits for any *Clann Baoiscne* with political or leadership aspirations.

'I see you, Liath Luachra.'

'I see you, Crimall. You have a strong *fian* at your back. Are your warriors ready for the pursuit?'

'They are.'

The *Clann Baoiscne* man paused and adjusted his stance, his fingers playing awkwardly with the bone fastenings of his cloak. Clean and well maintained, the garment was one of great quality and, regarding it enviously, Liath Luachra knew its manufacture must have taken someone a great deal of time and effort.

'You should know, Grey One …' Crimall hesitated once again before continuing. 'The *Clann Baoiscne fian* will follow your leadership only so long as the *díberg* remain in *Clann Baoiscne* territories. Should the pursuit extend beyond the limits of our land, my father's instructions are for the *fian* to return to Dún Baoiscne.'

Liath Luachra eyed him coldly. 'And your women? You would leave them to the *díberg*?'

Crimall regarded her without answering, leaving his silence speak for itself. The Grey One continued to observe him but she refrained from comment. The *Clann Baoiscne* man was visibly embarrassed by the shit-tainted instructions imposed upon him so there seemed little point in rubbing his nose in them, particularly given her dependence on his familiarity with the territory to be traversed.

'Then before we depart, I'll seek your permission to leave our wounded *fénnid* in the care of your healers. Biotóg's eager to continue the pursuit but his wounds are such that he'd only slow us down.'

She glanced over to the entrance of the hut where the young warrior sat, attempting to eat from a bowl of gruel. Although he must have heard his name mentioned, he steadfastly avoided looking towards her.

'With your permission I'd have him remain here at the huts. With Daithí's help, he can care for the *Uí Loinge* horses until our return.'

Assuming we return.

'Of course,' answered Crimall. He turned to address the elderly *Clann Baoiscne* man. 'Make sure you see to that, Daithí. The Grey One's man is to be treated as a guest and his care falls on the hospitality of you and your family.'

Daithí, methodically adding blocks of wood to the flames, kept his head low as he responded with an acquiescent nod.

'Well, then,' said Liath Luachra. 'I see nothing to delay us further.' She coughed and cleared her throat. 'Perhaps you can choose one of your men to lead the south-west trail.'

'I'll lead the way myself.'

Apparently deeming this a great honour for *Na Cinéaltaí*, Crimall turned to face the *Clann Baoiscne fian*.

'Ready yourselves, men of *Clann Baoiscne*!' he addressed them loudly. 'Ready yourselves, for this is our time to confront those who'd threaten our people, who'd attack us in our homes and abduct our women. This is our time to stare those raiders down, to hold their eye boldly and say, "Enough!'

He paused to look at each warrior in turn, although with their hoods up and the murk closed in about them, it was impossible to make out their features.

'So ready yourselves, *Clann Baoiscne* men. Ready yourselves to make your people proud, to make yourselves proud. This is our land and we'll deal this *díberg* a blow so loud your grandchildren will listen to its echo in song, long after we lie stretched beneath the sod.'

Without waiting for an acknowledgment to this rousing call to arms, Crimall turned and set off at a trot. His warriors reacted almost immediately, each one moving forward in turn to slip smoothly into position and create a single line that followed silently at his rear.

As he watched that adept manoeuvring, An Giobach chuckled softly. 'Very neat.' He turned to offer his comrades a cynical grin. 'I suppose this is our time too. We'd better follow our hosts and make ourselves proud.'

Liath Luachra shrugged. '*Ar aghaidh linn,*' she said wearily. Let's go.

Moving to retrieve her backpack, the woman warrior raised it off the ground, making sure her javelins were fixed firmly in place before slipping her hands through the hoops and settling it onto her back. By the time she'd secured the fastenings, the others too had retrieved their backpacks and stood ready to depart.

As *Na Cinéaltaí* moved off in the wake of their hosts, Feirgil paused to wave back at Biotóg. 'Don't eat the horses,' he yelled. 'The *Uí Loinge* will want them back.'

***

Despite the early-morning gloom, the *Clann Baoiscne fian's* in-depth knowledge of the land meant they were able to maintain a steady pace as they followed an indiscernible path towards the south-west. *Na Cinéaltaí* for their part, guided by the movements of the warrior directly ahead, had little difficulty keeping up.

With the dawning of the day, Father Sun rose, cracking like a golden egg upon the jagged outline of the Eastern hills and spreading a viscous, yellow light across the land. That initial promise of sunshine was short-lived, however. No sooner had its glowing bulk cleared the mountain tops than a nebulous cloud bank swept in from the west, completely engulfing it and smearing the sky with muddy streaks. The rain came moments later, a merciless downpour of cold, unctuous drops that quickly drenched the travellers. Within a short space of time, despite their greased cloaks and hoods, the warriors were soaked through, anything not saturated by the incessant rain, sodden from sweat trapped beneath the heavy cloaks.

With the improved – albeit limited – daylight, Crimall subtly increased the party's speed so that they were moving swiftly through the thinly forested terrain, slowing only when they encountered fallen trees or other obstacles that had to be skirted with care. Because of the rain, the going was hard. By mid-morning, any low-lying terrain was saturated, the ground increasingly boggy and mire-like. It wasn't long until the warriors were layered with coats of grime, their clothing smeared with sludge and filth, their boots coated with a thick, mucky casing.'

It was an effort to drive through that incessant rain, to ignore its cold discomfort and the mounting fatigue as the sticky ground sapped their strength. Pushing through the shadows of the forest however, they ran until late-morning, emerging from the treeline at the upper slopes of a rugged valley with a wide, fast-flowing river at its centre. As Crimall led them towards a long stretch of riverbank lined with willows, it became clear he intended for them to pause by the river, to rest and snatch a mouthful of food before continuing the pursuit once again.

Forging down the steep incline, Liath Luachra noted a *Clann Baoiscne* warrior, in a distinctive herringbone-patterned cloak, stumble twice on the greasy forest litter before clumsily regaining his balance. The corners of her mouth creased as her lips turned down. Over the course of the morning, she'd noticed several similar signs of clumsiness from that same warrior, in addition to a persistent lagging behind the rest of the *Clann Baoiscne fian*. It seemed obvious to her that he was struggling to maintain the pace.

She put such thoughts aside as they approached the flat ground alongside the river and the warriors spread out to seek shelter from the rain. Liath Luachra took refuge beneath a moss-coated willow with boughs that seemed to extend far wider than the others, sighing with relief to be out of the downpour. Leaning against the gnarled trunk, she sucked air into her heaving lungs. Smearing moisture from her face, she regarded the rippling puddles on the waterlogged ground around the tree, vexed by the knowledge that any trace of the *díberg*'s passage must now surely be washed away.

She moved to one side as An Giobach pushed in beneath the cover of the boughs to join her, using his massive hands to flick the worst of the raindrops from his shoulders. Stepping a little closer, he muttered softly so that the warriors sheltering beneath the neighbouring trees couldn't hear.

'That one's not well acquainted with the *fian* trail.'

The Grey One looked at him in surprise before following his gaze to one of the more distant trees. There, the *Clann Baoiscne* warrior with the herringbone cloak was standing alone, hood and cloak drawn up about him as he stared miserably out at the tumbling rain.

There seemed little to add to the *fénnid's* comment, so the woman warrior maintained her habitual reserve.

'See how he keeps his own company,' An Giobach continued. 'He avoids the main body of warriors, the *fénnid* you'd expect to be his comrades and friends.'

To support this observation, he raised his right hand and gestured towards another sprawling willow several paces to the right where several of the *Clann Baoiscne fian* had taken shelter and were talking quietly amongst themselves.

'That one's not a regular *fénnid* of the *Clann Baoiscne fian*.'

Conclusion drawn, the massive warrior reached down to pluck a blade of grass from between the tangled roots of the tree and popped it into his mouth, grinding the moist stem noisily between his molars.

'You should step wary in the shadows, Grey One.'

Liath Luachra looked at him coolly. 'Spit out the gristle that troubles your tongue, An Giobach. Speak clearly. What is it that ails you?'

The big *fénnid* stretched, causing his shoulders to pop softly. Liath Luachra continued to watch him, sensing an uncharacteristic tension to the man she hadn't ever noticed before.

'That *fénnid*. It could be that Tréanmór's placed one of his own within the *Clann Baoiscne fian*. It could be that he's decided to dispose of an irritant out in the solitude of the Great Wild where none would notice.'

'You believe Tréanmór would …?' Liath Luachra paused to glance back at the solitary *Clann Baoiscne* warrior, seated now on the protruding root of the willow, his back still towards them. An unbidden recollection of the seething *Clann Baoiscne rí's* face momentarily filled her mind but she discarded it with a shake of her head.

'No.' She shook her head again, more firmly this time. 'That makes no sense. Disposing of me would undermine the Seeking, weaken any hopes of retrieving the *Clann Baoiscne* women. The loss of face from such a failure would be abhorrent to a man such as Tréanmór.'

'More abhorrent than the loss of face you made him suffer before his key supporters?' An Giobach regarded her, one eyebrow curved in a sceptical arch. 'But perhaps you have the right of it. Perhaps Tréanmór's of solid enough character to stay his hand for the benefit of his stolen womenfolk. Perhaps he'll let you travel to rescue them unhindered.'

The big man paused to suck air through his teeth, creating a soft whistle as it passed through the ragged gaps.

'But on our route of return … Huh? On the way back …' He shrugged and brushed dirty rivulets of rainwater from his sodden shoulders. 'Perhaps it would be the wise man – or the wise woman – who'd have a care.'

***

Rested and somewhat revitalised, the party did not overly delay, although it was with some reluctance that they responded to Crimall's call. Grudgingly, they emerged from their shelters, back into the downpour which hadn't weakened since they'd stopped. Weaving their way up through the more solid ground of pine forest that coated the valley's southern ridge, Liath Luachra noticed they were moving at a reduced pace. At first, she wondered whether Crimall had intentionally slowed for the benefit of the rearmost *Clann Baoiscne* warrior but almost immediately discounted that possibility. The early morning sprint had served two separate purposes: reducing the *díberg's* lead but, more importantly, boosting the morale of the two *fianna* with the satisfaction of having covered an impressive distance. With that latter objective successfully achieved, despite the excruciating weather, Crimall had settled them into a more practical pace so they could retain their strength for the longer pursuit.

By late afternoon, the rain was still falling and the light faded early. Everyone was greatly relieved therefore, when Crimall finally called a halt at a site perfectly suited to the weather: a pair of caves in an east-facing cliff face, separated by a narrow stretch of rock less than seven paces in length. Although both caves were relatively shallow, a broad overhang protruding from the cliff face above provided some additional dry space and a sheltered passage between them.

As the smaller group, it made sense for *Na Cinéaltaí* to occupy the more compact cave. Warily leading the *fian* inside, Liath Luachra was pleased to find the stone floor – extending seven paces into the rock at its deepest point – was dry and strewn with the accumulated debris of leaf litter blown in by the wind. The copious bundles of kindling and firewood stored at the cave's rear indicated it was a refuge frequently used by the *Clann Baoiscne*.

Divesting themselves of their backpacks and shuffling out of their sodden cloaks, the warriors immediately set to work, the Grey One and Murchú building up a fire while Feirgil and An Giobach unpacked beef and vegetables supplied from the Dún Baoiscne storehouses. Liath Luachra looked ruefully at the meat. This meal would be one of their last with fresh food for the next few days at least. From this point on, the Seeking would consist of a hard pursuit with neither pause nor comfort and little opportunity for hunting or foraging to supplement their hard tack diet. None of the warriors had any delusions about what lay ahead. When the combined *fianna* weren't running, they'd be resting in preparation of running. Swiftness and distance would be their entire existence until they closed on the *díberg* and there was a final resolution, almost certainly terminating in violent action.

Draping her cloak over a rock as close to the fire as she could set it, Liath Luachra left the others to complete the preparations for the meal while she passed through the cave mouth to stare out at the descending night. From the shelter of the overhang, she watched as it settled over the land, an oppressive haze draining all colour and form from the world and reducing substance to dark obscurity.

The Grey One kicked at the rocky floor, fretfully stubbing its notches with the toe of her boot._Something in the dismal view had stirred despair inside her, a sensation she countered with a surge of resentful anger.

Where are you on this wet night, Gadra? Do you sit by a fire? Do you lie drowsy in your blankets, dreaming of waking to the touch of my blade on your throat?

Looking down, she realised that her hands were shaking, a frustrating frailty that paradoxically spurred her to even greater fury. Clamping both hands into fists, she folded her arms and locked them within her armpits. Glaring out at the night, she breathed deeply to repress the complex mix of fear and rage spiralling up inside her, struggling to contain it before it broke free and transformed to more violent expression.

Somewhere out in that darkness, the *Uí Cailbhe* man and his *díberg* would be sheltering from this storm, looking out at that bulk of black murk, possibly wondering at the fate of his man Cerball.

And what of Cairenn? And the two Clann Baoiscne girls? Where will they be sheltered?

Depressed by the sense of helplessness such thoughts provoked, the woman warrior unthinkingly stepped forward to the outermost point of the overhang. Stretching out her right hand, she closed her eyes to appreciate the touch of rainwater streaming cold and wet along her palm, the cool slickness of it as it slipped between her fingers. Breathing deeply, she closed her eyes and focussed on the slippery sensation of liquid against her hand, slowly feeling her anger wane.

The scrape of a boot on stone caused the Grey One's eyes to snap open. Turning her head, she looked towards the *Clann Baoiscne fian's* cave, surprised to spot the warrior with the herringbone cloak occupying a space in the shelter of the overhang. Freshly emerged from the shelter, he too appeared absorbed in contemplation, staring out at the darkening world with an apprehensive bearing that seemed to mirror her own. As Liath Luachra continued to watch, the warrior turned, glancing back towards the cave in response to a bellow of laughter from the *Clann Baoiscne* warriors. Some level of hesitancy in that movement however, gave her the strong impression that the warrior was reticent, or reluctant, to rejoin his fellow *fénnid*.

Without warning, the distant figure suddenly shifted position and turned towards her, stiffening in surprise when he noted the Grey One's presence. Startled, both peered at each other through the enveloping murk although, once again, the warrior's raised hood made it impossible to make out his face. As they continued to stand there, neither willing to be the first to turn away, Liath Luachra slowly eased her hand towards the knife scabbard at her belt.

In the end, it was the *Clann Baoiscne* man who ceded, turning on his heel to move back inside the cave and out of sight. Curious to see if he'd return, Liath Luachra remained where she was but after a few moments it became clear he had no intention of doing so. With a sigh, the warrior woman considered the gaping mouth of her own refuge, the outline of the rocky interior glowing dully from the light of the flames. Despite a similar reluctance to rejoin her own *fian*, the weather left her little choice. It was too dark now to seek an alternative shelter for the night, too cold to remain beyond the heat of a fire for long.

With a soft grunt, Liath Luachra returned inside, joining the *fénnid* around the now blazing fire. Accepting a bowl of stew, she sat back from the flames, uneasy at their close proximity as she ate in silence, chewing on the boiled meat while she listened to their chatter. Of the *Clann Baoiscne fian,* there was little to be heard beyond an occasional bout of muffled laughter, but soon even this grew faint, drowned out by the sound of the rising wind and a fusillade of hail the size of small pebbles.

Liath Luachra had just put her bowl aside when Crimall appeared abruptly to the left of the cavemouth. Entering the cave proper, he raised a hand in greeting and approached the fire, settling himself onto the ground in a space between Feirgil and Murchú.

'Well!' the *Clann Baoiscne* warrior declared with great heartiness, emphasising the word with a loud clap of his hands. 'Here we are, once again travelling the *gaiscíoch* path together.'

Crimall beamed happily at each of the *fénnid* in turn but, discomforted by his unexpected and intrusive arrival, all bar Feirgil declined to show any interest.

'I think,' continued Crimall, unruffled by their lack of enthusiasm, 'I think we can be confident this pursuit will be one of short duration. By tomorrow's eve, we'll have reached the sea. The following day, once we've veered south, we'll strike Nédé's trail. Unlike the *díberg*, we run unhampered by prisoners, so I expect our union of *fian* to overtake the raiders within two to three days of striking the coast.'

'It'll be a short union,' Murchú muttered sourly, 'unless your man Nédé marks the *díberg* trail. 'And even if he does, his markings risk being obliterated in this weather.'

Crimall dismissed such concerns with an airy wave of his right hand. 'Nédé is *Clann Baoiscne's* greatest tracker and a warrior of renowned experience. Rest assured, any marking he leaves will be prominent enough that we won't miss it.'

Murchú, unconvinced, returned his attention to the flames and lapsed into silence. Crimall looked around the little group, as though seeking further queries.

'Do you have all your teeth?' asked Feirgil.

Crimall looked at him in surprise, a vein at the side of his forehead pulsating fiercely as he strove to find sense in the *fénnid's* query.

'What lies to the south-east?' asked An Giobach, ignoring Feirgil's contribution. 'It's not terrain we have a great knowledge of.'

Crimall was quick to grasp this lifeline to saner topics. 'It's a wilderness,' he answered hastily. 'It's true I don't speak from experience, but our Elders say little lies in that direction but wild land and even wilder beasts. There are rumours of tribes further south along the coast but ...' He shrugged. 'The distance is such that we've never had connection with them.'

An Giobach nodded slowly as he mulled over the *Clann Baoiscne* man's words. Using his fingernails, he teased a sliver of gristle from between his teeth then flicked the greasy sinew into the shadows.

'My father had land south of *Clann Baoiscne* territory. Like you, he never ventured to the south-east, but he was always of a mind that the land there was rugged and harsh for the unwary traveller.'

'South of *Clann Baoiscne* territory?' Crimall scratched thoughtfully at the dark stubble of a freshly growing beard, regarding the *fénnid* with fresh interest. 'Then you must be of *Uí Laoire* stock.'

An Giobach tapped the base of the bowl on his knee. 'I have affiliation to *Uí Laoire*,' he admitted.

Liath Luachra raised her head to look at the big *fénnid* in surprise. In all their time together, An Giobach had never once made mention of any tribal affiliations. If what he was saying was true, it was a sobering revelation for it meant she was the only true *éclann* within *Na Cinéaltaí*. Murchú was of the *Uí Loinge*, Feirgil had *Uí Laoichre* and *Uí Carraige* connections through both parents, and even Biotóg had a *Clann Morna* tribal affiliation.

Crimall had paused to chew on his lip as he regarded the powerful *fénnid*. 'Then why do you dawdle with *Na Cinéaltaí*? Why do you not support your own tribal *fian* instead of tarrying with an *éclann* grouping?'

There was an audible air of bewilderment to the *Clann Baoiscne* man's voice, the possibility of anyone preferring alternative company to their tribe beyond his ability to comprehend.

In response, An Giobach turned his head and spat onto the ground. Crimall glanced down at the bubbling spittle then back at the *fénnid* but diplomatically kept his words and opinions to himself. Evidently, there were tensions between An Giobach and his people that the big man had no interest in explaining.

Murchú utilised the ensuing silence to pose a question of this own. 'Could the raiders have come from one of those tribes to the south-east?'

Liath Luachra quickly dropped her eyes to the ground, retreating into a guilt-ridden silence. She'd still revealed nothing of Gadra to the other *fénnid*, disclosed nothing of their interaction and, as such, couldn't reveal that the *díberg* – or at least the leader of the *díberg* – originated from an area far closer than they imagined.

Oblivious to the woman warrior's concerns, Crimall responded with a lazy shrug. 'That's a query for which I have no answer but I imagine we'll discover the truth for ourselves over the coming days. When we overtake the raiders, I'll lead our combined force in an encircling manoeuvre to ensure that none escape. Once they're overwhelmed, we can question them to our hearts' cont-'

'There'll be no encircling manoeuvre,' Liath Luachra cut in, regarding the *Clann Baoiscne* man with a glacial chill. Murchú, it seemed, had had the right of it after all. Keen to make use of the Seeking to further his own battle reputation and confident because of his superior number of warriors, Crimall was already vying for leadership of the pursuit.

'The decision to engage the *díberg* is mine alone,' she reminded him. 'For *Na Cinéaltaí* but also for the *Clann Baoiscne fian*. Are you going to challenge me on that?'

They glared at each other for several heartbeats but, in the end, Crimall had no choice but to drop his eyes. A challenge would have meant a fight with the Grey One and a direct contradiction of his father's instruction; neither of which he was willing to risk.

'Once we find their trail,' the woman warrior continued, 'we'll keep our distance until we have a full sense of their numbers and their purpose. We'll not underestimate them.'

Crimall's lips tightened into a thin line, stung by the woman warrior's unsubtle reminder of who was in charge. 'I'm aware how dangerous they are, Grey One. And I don't underestimate them. After all, it wasn't my *fian* they took down in ambush.'

It was a malicious jab of course, but having anticipated such a response, it deflected harmlessly off the Grey One's impervious silence.

A brief hush followed the acrimonious exchange but before the conversation deteriorated further, a fresh movement at the cave mouth drew the warrior's attention. Despite the darkness and the flickering light thrown out from the flames, Liath Luachra immediately recognised the herringbone pattern of the newcomer's cloak and her hand instinctively slid behind her back to the knife concealed in her belt. Fingers curling smoothly around the bone handle, she watched the *Clann Baoiscne* warrior's approach, struck by the easy manner in which he sauntered towards a group that – although allies – were still complete strangers.

Sidling up behind Crimall, he waited as the *Clann Baoiscne* leader shuffled obligingly to one side. When there was enough space, he settled easily onto the ground, sitting cross-legged on the hard rock beside his comrade. As the *fénnid* watched, he raised both hands to tug back the hood of his cloak.

An Giobach's startled curse underlined the stunned silence of the other *Na Cinéaltaí* members. The face revealed by the dropping hood wasn't that of a hardened warrior, but of a young woman with less than twenty years on her. Strikingly attractive, her features were delicate but bolstered by a firm jaw, strong cheekbones and a pair of determined brown eyes. As they watched, the young woman reached one hand up to pull a wooden pin from her hair, causing a cascade of long, very black strands to spill down about her neck and shoulders.

Crimall cleared his throat. 'Liath Luachra, *fénnid* of *Na Cinéaltaí*, I present my sister Bodhmhall.'

The dark-haired woman nodded shortly in greeting. Dropping her hands into her lap, she lowered her eyes, acquiescently letting her brother speak for her.

'Bodhmhall's a healer of some renown,' he informed the dumbstruck *fénnid*. 'She's also one of the few *Clann Baoiscne* members to have travelled close to the south-eastern territories. Her knowledge of that section of the trail should prove helpful in our travels.'

In the awkward silence that followed, Liath Luachra somehow managed to mumble a grudging response that was more vague acknowledgment than greeting. Glancing towards An Giobach, she caught his bewildered look and the helpless shrug he returned.

Crimall, meanwhile, was grinning smugly, clearly enjoying the shocked reaction his sister's presence had provoked. Just as he was opening his mouth to speak again, Feirgil leaned across him to address his sister.

'Would you like me to paint your body?'

The *Clann Baoiscne* woman regarded the wiry *fénnid* with a look of disbelief then, to everyone's surprise, snorted loudly, hurriedly raising one hand to her mouth to smother the laughter that threatened to erupt. Crimall however, was aghast, his eyes widening with outrage at Feirgil's presumption.

'I helped paint the Grey One,' Feirgil continued, leaning even closer. 'It was my idea to paint the black strip across her ti-'

'Feirgil!' barked Liath Luachra.

The skinny warrior snapped upright, recoiling to his original position. Disconcerted by the anger in the Grey One's voice, he looked at her across the fire, tilting his head backwards as though trying to make her out her more clearly through the flames.

'Grey One, can I ge-?'

'Shut your beak!' she growled.

Cowed by her ferocity, Feirgil shrank back inside the copious folds of his heavy cloak, Drawing the hood up about his head so that his face could no longer be seen, he shuffled backwards on his buttocks, pulling away from the fire.

Crimall glared furiously at Liath Luachra. 'Is that *fénnid* of yours completely muddle-minded? Does he ha-'

The feral snarl that erupted from the Grey One's throat was completely involuntary but undeniably effective in shutting the *Clann Baoiscne* man up, mid-sentence. Thrown by the sheer ferocity of that primal, almost bestial, bellow, he recoiled and stared at her in shock, at a complete loss how to react.

Another awkward silence followed, stretching interminably until it was mercifully broken by Bodhmhall clearing her throat. 'It grows late,' she said with admirable calm, her voice clear but bearing an unexpected huskiness. 'I regret the distress my presence has prompted.'

As the others watched, the *Clann Baoiscne* woman rose gracefully to her feet, pulling her cloak about her shoulders. It was only as she stood upright that the Grey One fully appreciated how tall she was. Easily as tall as the woman warrior herself, with the bulk of her cloak and her face hidden, it was little wonder she'd been mistaken for a man.

Offering them a silent nod of farewell, Bodhmhall ua Baoiscne turned to leave. Six lithe steps took her to the left of the cavemouth, which she rounded smoothly and abruptly vanished from sight.

With a deep sigh, Crimall, too, got to his feet, an action that prompted *Na Cineáltaí fénnid* to rise as well. 'My sister has the right of it,' he declared, a trace of resentment in his voice as he looked at Liath Luachra. 'We have another full day of running ahead of us tomorrow. We should to our beds.'

Leaving the others to clean and repack the cooking utensils, Liath Luachra escorted the *Clann Baoiscne* man towards the cave entrance, following him outside along the sheltered stretch of ground beneath the overhang.

'A word, Crimall.'

The stocky warrior turned to regard her with a wary expression. 'Yes?'

'Why is your sister here? On the *gaiscíoch* path. She's no *banfénnid.*'

The *Clann Baoiscne* man regarded her thoughtfully. 'Why do you ask, Grey One? Do you fear a competitor for the young *Uí Loinge* man's affections?' He chuckled wheezily at his own wit, although the chortles faded as he noted her souring expression.

Crimall sighed. 'Very well. I see you have no temper for humour. The truth is Bodhmhall browbeat me into letting her accompany the *fian* in secret. In doing so, she defied our father's wishes, but ...' he shrugged. 'My sister has a way of getting what she wants.'

'She slows the *fian.*'

Crimall frowned. 'Do not concern yourself in that regard, Grey One. Bodhmhall runs sprightly when the need demands. As a child, she outran me often enough.'

'And now? Can she outrun you now? I see scant evidence of it.'

The *Clann Baoiscne* man's brow furrowed as he returned her gaze and, for a moment, it looked as though he might argue the point. He apparently thought better of it however, for he raised both hands in a conciliatory gesture.

'Very well. I'll have her burden shared amongst the others. Tomorrow you'll see her run spry and light without that weight.'

He attempted a reassuring smile but the obvious strain sapped it of conviction.

'Then she can run spry and light back to Dún Baoiscne.' Liath Luachra's face retained the hard texture of stone. 'She has no place here.'

Crimall's eyes narrowed and when he spoke again there was an audible edge to his voice. 'You shouldn't underestimate my sister, Grey One. It's true she's no *banfénnid* but she has other skills and knowledge that could contribute to our success.'

He paused then, glancing back towards the cavemouth as though to make sure they couldn't be overheard.

'Bodhmhall has the *Gift*. She can see people's life flame and her early talent with *imbas forosnai* was of a measure to set her apart as a child. Before she was bonded, she was personally chosen for tutelage by Dub Tíre, the *Clann Baoiscne draoi*. Through him, she learned things tha- '

'I have no need of a *draoi*,' Liath Luachra cut him off sharply. 'I have need of warriors who'll cleave a skull or pierce a torso at my command. No more, no less.' She glowered at him, parted her lips to speak once more but then paused, struck by a sudden suspicion.

'Is this a trick? Some scheme of Tréanmór's?'

The furrows in Crimall's brow deepened even further but then, to the Grey One's surprise, he snorted loudly.

'Hardly! My father's rage would scorch the land were he to learn of Bodhmhall's presence with the *fian*. His plans to extend *Clann Baoiscne* influence include her future bonding and he likes to have her close where he can keep a wary eye on her. As it was, she had to resort to duplicity and the deceit of visiting a sickly cousin to excuse her absence from Dún Baoiscne.'

'Which completes the circuit of my unanswered question. If the risk of discovery is so great for your sister, why is she here?'

Crimall's lips pressed together in irritation and she could almost sense the tension rising in him as he worked to hold his temper in check.

'One of the kidnapped *Clann Baoiscne* girls is Bodhmhall's closest childhood friend. Having overheard Tréanmór's instruction, she feared the *fian* might renege on the Seeking and believed her presence might strengthen our resolve, shame us into not surrendering her friend to her fate.'

Liath Luachra couldn't help herself. 'And will it, Crimall? If your sister wasn't present, would you leave her friend to the *díberg*?'

Crimall's angry expression took on a smouldering intensity.

'You press too far, Grey One. I've fulfilled my duty to my sister as best a brother can. I supported her false motives for leaving Dún Baoiscne, I found her a place within my *fian,* and believing it unfair to conceal such secrets, I shared the truth with you as soon as we were a safe distance from Dún Baoiscne.'

The stocky warrior paused and glowered at her and although the woman warrior thought he'd run out of words, he quickly continued where he'd left off.

'I've fulfilled every duty to my best ability so now the burden of this disclosure falls to you. As *rígfénnid,* you can choose to let Bodhmhall accompany us and make use of her skills or you can order her back to Dún Baoiscne where her return will almost certainly be noted. I'll adhere to whichever choice you make but my father won't have forgotten the humiliation he suffered at your hand. It's more than likely he'd make use of Bodhmhall's actions against you.'

A malicious glint flared in his eye. 'But, naturally, as leader of this Seeking, any such decision is yours alone to make.'

Having delivered this final vengeful jab, the *Clann Baoiscne* man started towards the second cave, the darkness now so thick about them that by the time he'd taken four steps, Liath Luachra could no longer see him.

'I bid you a soft sleep on your hard bed.' The words echoed out from the dark without any visible form to accompany them. A moment later, they too had faded.

Too angry to make a retort, the woman warrior glared helplessly into the dark, infuriated to have her leadership circumvented by actions over which she'd had no control or knowledge.

Crimall, you gutless hound!

Unfortunately, loath though she was to accept the *Clann Baoiscne* man's words, she suspected he had the right of it. If his sister returned to Dún Baoiscne, Tréanmór would almost certainly learn of her departure with the *fian* and twist events to suit his own machinations. It was even possible he'd raise a second *fian* just to seek vengeance on her.

The woman warrior ground her molars furiously, chewing fretfully on the soft tissue of her inner cheek as she worked through her options. She could, potentially, dispose of Crimall's sister after five or six days' travel. With such a head start, the goal of the Seeking would most likely have been achieved by the time the *Clann Baoiscne* woman made it back to her home territory at Dún Baoiscne.

Or failed completely.

But Crimall would never agree to abandon his sister. He'd insist on taking the Clann Baoiscne fian back with her.

Liath Luachra closed her eyes and groaned. She had no choice. She was stuck with Bodhmhall ua Baoiscne.

For the time being at least.

Moving back towards her own shelter, still glowing warmly from the ruddy light of the fire, the Grey One found Feirgil standing guard inside the entrance, his still damp cloak draped about his bony shoulders. After the cold air of the exterior, the reek of woodsmoke and the pungent stink of dried sweat was a harsh assault on the nostrils. On the ground beside the fire, Murchú and An Giobach were distinguishable only as two shrouded lumps within the shadows, their snores reverberating softly in the rocky confines. Pausing, the Grey One considered them briefly before returning her attention to the skinny *fénnid*.

'Feirgil.'

'Yes, Grey One?' Recalling her earlier anger, the *fénnid* faced her like an excited puppy, desperately eager to please.

When this Seeking is done ...' She paused, struggling to draw up the words. 'When we've returned to Briga ...'

'Yes?'

'I'd have you leave *Na Cinéaltaí*.'

'Leave.' Feirgil looked at her in vague perplexity. He repeated the word, scratching the stubble of his bearded chin. 'Leave.'

'There's no longer a place for you in *Na Cinéaltaí*, Feirgil. Your behaviour grows erratic, your judgments falter. As a non-tribal *fian,* our position's precarious as it is, but the mad-talk you spout makes our existence all that more perilous.'

And after what I saw in the forest before the ambush, I don't entirely trust you.

The *fénnid* stared at her with dawning comprehension. In contrast to his earlier enthusiasm, he now looked beaten, his eyes dull and his shoulders slumped. For one horrible moment, she thought he was about to cry.

'You have my gratitude for your help at Dún Baoiscne,' she added hurriedly. 'I'll not see you leave emptyhanded or disadvantaged but ...' She hesitated. 'I will see you leave.'

Without waiting for a response, the Grey One brushed past him. Retrieving her cloak from where she'd hung it by the fire, she settled down by the wood pile at the back of the cave. There, wrapping the cloak about her, she turned her back to the world, closed her eyes and almost immediately succumbed to sleep.

***

The following morning, dawn edged over the horizon with a gleaming crispness, the delicate clarity of the light a sharp contrast to the dreariness of the previous day and the thundering deluge that had lasted the better part of the night. Beyond the cave entrance, the waterlogged earth was a stark reminder of that particular reality.

After a hurried breakfast of cold porridge and water, the party did not delay. By the time the first fragile rays of sunlight filtered through the forest canopy, the warriors had already ventured from the caves and started up the steep, wooded slopes of the eastern hills.

To his credit, despite the previous evening's bitterness, Crimall's guidance took on an even greater sense of urgency on leaving the campsite and he drove the two *fian* hard. Continuing south-east at a breakneck pace, they traversed interminable stretches of dark forest, crossed rivers swollen from the rains or negotiated their way through the hills alongside those waterways to safer fords that were known to the *Clann Baoiscne*.

Despite her initial scepticism, the Grey One was relieved to see that Bodhmhall Ua Baoiscne kept pace with the rest of her *fian*, assisted in no small measure by the length of her step, her long legs giving her a stride equal to that of her male companions. Still smarting at having been outflanked by her and her brother's machinations, Liath Luachra stayed clear of the *Clann Baoiscne* over the course of the day, conscious that any interaction had the potential to provoke a reaction she'd have cause to regret. Fortunately, the pair were easily avoided. The party spent the better part of the day running, with little individual contact. On the few occasions they did come together as a group to rest or eat, each *fian* sat apart from the other.

During one of these occasions, when they paused to rest at the bank of a slow-running river, the woman warrior perceived worrying indications of an internal fraying within her own *fian*. Despite the achievements at Dún Baoiscne, Murchú had withdrawn into a dismal fug and, worn down by fears for his sister, refused to engage with anyone. Feirgil, as a result of their discussion, was also more subdued than normal and sat quietly by himself, exuding an almost tangible despondency. Even An Giobach, normally the most steady member of the company, exuded an atypical stiffness, the reasons for which became clear soon enough.

Joining the big *fénnid* on a flat stretch of the stony riverbank where it was possible to fill the waterskins without stirring up silt, the woman warrior finally lost patience when he regarded her with an expression of open irritation.

'What?' she demanded. 'What chill breeze stirs the embers of your rancour?'

An Giobach held her gaze coldly for several heartbeats. 'You told Feirgil he was to leave the *fian*.'

The accusation hung like a storm cloud in the air between them.

'I did.'

'Why? Why would you do that?'

Liath Luachra frowned, wondering at the purpose behind the warrior's query. The answer seemed blatantly obvious. 'Feirgil's rambling nonsense provokes trouble for the *fian*. We can ill afford a *fénnid* who's loose mouth makes difficult circumstances more trying.'

'Hah!' snorted An Giobach. 'I've seen many *fénnid* worse than Feirgil. People aren't so foolish they can't tell he means no harm.'

The woman warrior grew quiet, picking at a loose thread on the inner knee of her leggings. Rough wear had caused a small portion of the seam to split and it now revealed a pale patch of smooth skin beneath. She frowned then, unsure whether she should share that part of the eccentric *fénnid* she'd seen prior to the ambush several days earlier. It was true she'd observed no further expression of that nature, but that wasn't to say it wasn't happening when she wasn't present or hadn't been looking.

'There's another trait to Feirgil that ... one that is best avoided.'

'A trait? You mean his supposed *ríastraid*?'

Having filled his skin, An Giobach stoppered it and stood up to slip it into his backpack.

'I wouldn't place trust in rumours, Grey One. I've heard such gossip myself but in all the time we've spent or fought together, I've yet to see Ferigil display any trace of the *ríastraid*. Besides, he's *fénnid*, a member of *Na Cinéaltaí* and, therefore, one of us.'

Liath Luachra stoppered her own skin as she regarded the broad-shouldered *fénnid*, hearing the words but sensing a deeper, meaning behind their apparent simplicity. The unintended obscuration stirred the embers of her own anger.

One of us!

What did An Giobach mean? Did he see *Na Cinéaltaí* as some kind of comrade-based grouping? An emotional substitute for the tribe he'd rejected?

Swollen with a sudden, inexplicable anger and fearing to unleash it with further talk, the woman warrior turned and walked away, the heat of An Giobach's gaze searing into her back. Locating a resting place at the base of large boulder, she'd just sat herself down when Crimall made the call and had them up again. Casting a resentful glance at the big *fénnid*, she waited for the line of Crimall's warriors to pass her by and then slid into place behind them. Despite her immersion in the physical and mental effort needed to follow the *Clann Baoiscne* lead, it took a long time to drive the conversation from her mind.

∗∗∗

They struck the coastline later that afternoon as dusk gathered its dark skirts in over the land. Emerging from the trees on the summit of a broad hill, the unrestrained horizon opened out abruptly before them, the vast breadth of the sea framed against the bulk of the sky. In the fragile light of the incoming dusk, the water had taken on a dark hue, its shifting blue-green bulk faded to grey, speckled here and there by splotches of white where a breeze whipped the wave crests. That same salt-encrusted breeze reached the warriors on the hilltop, rustling the leaves of the forest to their rear and creating an eerie rattling noise that seemed to roll down the length of the coast.

Trembling from the strain of the day's exertion, Liath Luachra looked out at the dark expanse, the sight of the rolling waves and the churning foam along the sandy shore below lifting her spirits in a way she hadn't expected. It'd been a long time since she'd last seen the sea. A long time since she'd felt the sharp tang of sea air at the back of her throat.

A long time since Gort na Meala.

Since Muireann.

A lifetime ago.

Sprawled across the open ground, the exhausted party soaked in the view while they recovered their breath. Too soon however, Crimall sought to rouse them once more, reminding them of the distance still to be covered before they could halt for the night. Despite her weariness, the Grey One rose on shaky legs and gestured for him to take the lead. Starting down the steep slope, the *Clann Baoiscne fian* grudgingly followed in his wake. Once they'd passed, Liath Luachra too started downhill with *Na Cinéaltaí* at her rear.

A line of undulating sand dunes at the base of the hill – four or five dunes deep – separated the party from the sea but it only took moments to clamber over them and access the long beach they'd observed from the summit. Advancing towards the damp sand near the water's edge where the surface held more firmly underfoot, they ran the beach's length to the forested promontory that marked its southernmost tip. Here, rather than leading them up the steep slope as the Grey One had expected, Crimall instead veered right, cutting back in through the dunes

168

to a hidden clearing nestled between the leeward side of the sandy mounds and the woods at the base of the hills. Dotted with clusters of *muiríneach* – marram grass – the clearing contained a number of round, wind-smoothened boulders and a patch of flat rock with a freshwater pond fed by a tiny stream flowing down from the hills.

Staggering towards one of the boulders, the *Clann Baoiscne* leader stumbled to a halt. Divesting himself of his backpack and, wheezing for breath, he slid down the rocky surface until he was lying flat on the ground, completely spent. This, then, the Grey One realised, was where they were going to pass the night.

Once again, Liath Luachra had to appreciate the *Clann Baoiscne's* choice of campsite. The bulk of the dunes shielded them from the sea breeze while the freshwater pool offered a convenient supply of drinking water. If the weather turned for the worst – unlikely given the absence of clouds during the day – it would be an easy matter to retreat to the shelter of the trees.

The woman warrior's head was swimming with exhaustion when she dropped to her knees on the gritty rock at the water's edge, the other warriors scattering out around her to find their own space within the clearing. Leaning forward, she dipped her hand into the still pool, scooped up a palmful of water and splashed it over her face and neck, appreciating the delicious coolness of it against her skin. On the sandy ground alongside her, she noticed a fine set of prints leading down from the trees: tracks from a fox that'd snuck down from the woods to drink. In addition to one or two other tiny indentations at the water's edge, a fresh line of similar prints led straight back to the trees, the depth of the departing imprints suggesting the animal had bolted on hearing the *fian's* approach.

That evening, given the party's collective fatigue, they elected to set a single campfire and share the food preparation. Although not overly comfortable with the proposal, Liath Luachra was too weary to argue against it. Instead, she resisted the temptation to succumb to sleep while numbly watching a *Clann Baoiscne* warrior carve up some smoked meat and fry the slices in a metal pan with a combination of tubers and water cress.

Salivating, she accepted the share served up to her on a flat strip of bark and retreated to a patch of sand between two clumps of *muiríneach* to enjoy it in peace. Sitting quietly, she inhaled the savoury aroma and forced herself to eat slowly, knowing that if she gorged it down, she'd pay for it with stomach cramps later in the night.

While she ate, the woman warrior also took stock of the various aches throughout her exhausted body: the muscle pains, the bruises and the swelling of joints that invariably followed such extended exertion. Dull-eyed, she then did her best to ignore them, distracting herself by focusing instead on the strong beefy taste of the meal.

She was down to the last few morsels when she saw Crimall and his sister leave the larger group and start walking towards her. Popping a segment of beef into her mouth, she chewed on it patiently as they drew closer, her expression offering little in the way of welcome when they finally came to a halt before her.

'Grey One,' said Crimall. 'We should speak of tomorrow's path for the Seeking.'

Both the *Clann Baoiscne* siblings were visibly weary and swaying with exhaustion. Reluctantly, the woman warrior gestured for them to take a seat on the sand alongside her and waited silently while they settled themselves.

When he was comfortable, Crimall sighed loudly. 'Well, we've made a good distance these past two days.'

Liath Luachra sucked tolerantly on a hard segment of rind clamped between her lower left molars and the soft tissue of her left cheek. Although wary now of any attempt by the *Clann Baoiscne* man to supplant her leadership of the Seeking, in this situation at least, she saw no reason to dispute his claim. They'd covered an enormous distance in a remarkably short time.

'The route we've followed,' Crimall continued. 'It's the only passable route to the south-east, particularly with the recent rainfall. Last night's downpour may have washed the *díberg's* tracks away but combined with previous downfalls, the flooded rivers and wetlands have effectively blocked any other potential route.'

He glanced at her as warily as though expecting her to argue this point. When she made no response, he was quick to continue.

'Unfortunately, this beach marks the extent of my familiarity with the southern lands. Bodhmhall fortunately, has travelled a little further.'

Although she could feel the weight of the *Clann Baoiscne* woman's eyes upon her, Liath Luachra did not look her way and focussed her attention on running the tip of her forefinger along the bark strip, swabbing up the last smear of meat grease.

'Tell the Grey One what you know, Bodhmhall,' her brother urged.

The *Clann Baoiscne* woman looked uneasily from the woman warrior to Crimall and then back again. She coughed and cleared her throat.

'Two years ago, I followed this route with Dub Tíre to gather rare herbs at Inbhear Ciúin; an estuary that lies further to the south. That trip took almost five full days of walking to reach this site, a distance we've covered in two. From this beach, it took another six days to reach our destination.'

This time, licking the smear of fat from her fingertip, Liath Luachra allowed her gaze to drift slowly in the *Clann Baoiscne* woman's direction.

'What lies beyond the promontory?'

Despite her mud-spattered face and the layers of trail filth coating her feet and clothing, Bodhmhall retained a surprising air of sedate gentility. Brushing a loose strand of black hair from her eyes, she regarded the woman warrior with equable insouciance. 'It's not a promontory so much as a headland. Admittedly, the view's deceptive from here but it marks the start of a series of cliffs and other, narrower, headlands stretching south for five days at a rapid walk. From there, the land drops sharply to Inbhear Ciúin, a broad estuary that empties into the sea and which has swampland to its rear.'

Her lips compressed as she dragged her memories to the surface.

'Were we to continue at the pace we've been travelling, it may be possible to traverse the distance to Inbhear Ciúin in little more than half that time.'

The Grey One glanced down at the hands that lay settled in the *Clann Baoiscne* woman's lap. Despite the casual manner in which she'd relayed the suggestion, they were trembling fiercely. The dark-haired woman might make a brave face of it, but she was clearly exhausted and, Liath Luachra suspected, dreading the prospect of yet another day's running.

'And beyond the estuary?'

This time, Bodhmhall's response was a shrug that caused the dark curls to bounce softly on her shoulders. 'The herbs we sought are found on this side of the water. We had no need to travel further.' She grew quiet for a moment, her gaze turning inward.

'I remember the terrain looked dangerous, too dangerous to traverse directly. I think we'd struggle to find a path through that swampland.' She hesitated and bit her lip. 'If we cut further inland to bypass the wetlands, we might find another route.'

Liath Luachra held her eyes for three heartbeats before redirecting her gaze to Crimall. 'If the *díberg* passed his way, there must be a route they had in mind.

'There is.' The *Clann Baoiscne* man answered confidently. 'It's just a matter of locating it. And we'll do that by continuing south until we strike Nédé's markings. Once we find the markings, we'll find the *díberg* trail and the route they followed.'

'You place a heavy trust on your man Nédé's shoulders, Crimall. If he fails, any hope of relocating the *díberg* sign is lost.'

Crimall's forehead creased in resentment. 'Nédé will not fail us. We'll not miss his marking. On this, you have my word.'

Liath Luachra regarded him silently, repressing her own anger behind a face of stone as she breathed smoothly through her nostrils. It infuriated her to be dependent on the *Clann Baoiscne* man but until they reconnected with the *díberg* trail she had little choice but to follow his lead.

'Very well. Tomorrow we follow the coastline south, but we'll do so at a slower pace. The *fénnid* need rest and I don't want to risk an encounter with the *díberg* if our warriors are too tired to fight.'

Or your sister falling dead from exhaustion.

Crimall acknowledged the directive with a grudging nod. From the dark hollows around his eyes, Liath Luachra suspected he was only too happy with her decision but hadn't suggested it himself for fear of appearing weak.

'Then that's all there is to say.'

Tossing the bark strip aside, the woman warrior rose to her feet and strode away, desperate to put some space between herself and the *Clann Baoiscne* siblings. Despite her unruffled demeanour, the conversation had confronted her again with the potential reality of losing Gadra's trail, a possibility that stirred up a panic-stricken sense of urgency.

Bad cess to Clann Baoiscne! Bad cess to them all!

Moving towards the dunes, she spotted the dark silhouette of An Giobach atop the nearest mound, facing mutely out to sea. The water was beyond her line of sight, but she imagined that it had to be too dark by now to see it clearly from his raised position, although the repeated surge of the waves was audible through the stillness of the night.

Hearing the grainy crunch of her feet on the sand, the big *fénnid* twisted about and, although he looked surprised to see her, traces of his earlier anger remained embedded in his features.

'You should take your ease,' she told him. 'I'll take the first watch.'

An Giobach acknowledged her with an ill-natured grunt but seemed in no hurry to leave.

'I saw you talking with the *Clann Baoiscne* leaders. Is Crimall still confident we'll find his man's markings?'

Liath Luachra nodded shortly, uncomfortable with the warrior's uncharacteristic surliness towards her.

An Giobach muttered under his breath, making no effort to hide his scepticism. Another awkward moment passed, however the *fénnid* remained where he was, standing quietly alongside her. Staring out towards the sea, the Grey One did her best to ignore him, wishing he'd leave so that she could be alone with her thoughts.

'Grey One.'

She kept her eyes straight ahead, staring out at the darkness.

'I lack the energy for further argument, An Giobach.'

The big *fénnid* was silent for a moment, thinking his next words through. Finally, with a sigh, he too looked out towards the sound of the invisible surf.

'Do you tire of the *gaiscíoch* path, Grey One?'

This time, the woman warrior turned to look at him, genuinely thrown by the question. After five years with *Na Cinéaltaí,* a life outside the *gaiscíoch* path wasn't a concept she could easily envisage, the possibility of an existence beyond the *fian* season and her winter cave in Luachair, one almost impossible to fathom.

She eyed the *fénnid* warily, unclear where he was leading the conversation but feeling no less uncomfortable for that.

'What do you mean?'

An Giobach pulled a heel of griddlebread from inside his tunic, took a bite out of it and chewed while thinking through his next words.

'When it comes to the *gaiscíoch* path there are but two certainties, Grey One. The first is its inevitable ending. The second is the brutal nature of that ending.' His lips tightened and the corner of his mouth turned down. 'But perhaps that's the way of it. Perhaps like the *gaiscíoch* path, every *fian* has its time of high valour before its inevitable decline.'

He turned his head to look at her with an expression of unexpected softness.

'There'd be no fault in recognising that, no fault in moving on to avoid the drag of such an inevitable burden.'

Liath Luachra stared openly at him now, completely at a loss. 'What are you asking me, An Giobach?'

'I thought it clear enough. I'm asking if you intend to step down as *rígfénnid.*'

Liath Luachra felt herself take an involuntary step back. 'Why would you ask such a question?' she demanded, a burr of anger on the edge of her voice.

'Because I know of the relations grown between you and Murchú.'

Thrown by this new accusation, the woman warrior could only stare, too dumfounded to make an answer. Misinterpreting her silence for confirmation, An Giobach quickly moved to reassure her.

'There's no shame in seeking comfort with another, Grey One. In truth, it pleases me to see you find comradeship, even if its timing rubs me wrong.'

He paused, and this time it was he who seemed embarrassed.

'Unfortunately, *Na Cinéaltaí* is a small battle party with a simple hierarchy. There's room for a single *rígfénnid* to lead and the sad truth is you can lead a man, or you can fuck a man, but you can't do both.'

The woman warrior felt her entire body stiffen and her two hands balled into fists. When she finally spoke again, through clenched lips, it was an effort to keep the snarl from her voice.

'There are no relations grown between Murchú and I. Murchú is *fénnid,* I am *rígfénnid.* That is the extent of our relations.'

An Giobach sighed. 'It saddens me you don't have trust enough to tell me straight of it, Grey One.' He shrugged. 'Given the tribal complexities, I can understand your reticence to discuss such matters, but the simple truth is that I saw you. The night before the *fian* was ambushed, I saw you and Murchú lying together in the forest.'

'Then you saw wrong, An Giobach. You ...' Confronted with the realisation that this was a story too complex and too painful to unravel, Liath Luachra faltered, completely overwhelmed. In desperation, she attempted denial through a different route.

'Murchú already has a woman.'

'Cnes?' An Giobach laughed out loud at that. 'Yes, of course. But I know of their fractious union just as I know Murchú would drop her like a hot stone for you.'

He sighed.

'*Éist, a Liath Luachra!* Listen, Grey One! I don't say this out of jealousy. Murchú's a good man and I don't doubt his affection for you is real. Truth be told, you'd do far worse than settle with a man of his calibre and standing. As for his family and *Uí Loinge* expectations, they can be appeased easily enough. Squeeze out a few whelps to satisfy their dreams of dynasty and they'll warm to you in time, particularly if you ...'

His voice trailed off as he saw Liath Luachra walking away.

'Grey One! Where are you going? I hadn't finished.'

'Since you hold Murchú in such high regard,' she snarled back over her shoulder. 'I suggest you squeeze a few whelps out of your own arse for him. While you figure out how to do that to his family's satisfaction, you might as well take the fucking watch!'

Chapter Nine:

The morning sun broke like fire against the sky, a crimson backdrop to a skein of wild geese winging their way towards the west. Roused before dawn by an ache in her knees, Liath Luachra had already been awake for some time and glanced disinterestedly at the passing birds before returning to the task of massaging her leg muscles. With the stiffness subsided, she rose from her bedroll and climbed to the summit of the dune where Feirgil had relieved An Giobach over the course of the night. Taking the skinny *fénnid's* place, she ignored his wounded expression as he left her to descend to the campfire where the others were stirring.

Turning her face towards the beach, the woman warrior settled into the feeble shelter of the *muiríneach* clumps and shivered from the cool breeze sliding in from the sea. Gazing out at the enormity of that shifting green mass however, she found an unexpected calm in the subtle variation of its movements and the more regular pattern of waves crashing down the length of the beach.

Turning her head towards the south, she stiffened when she caught sight of a distant figure on the foreshore, moving slowly from the direction of the promontory. As she was about to get to her feet however, she paused, recognising the broad set of the shoulders and the individual's distinctive gait.

Murchú.

Liath Luachra frowned and chewed on her lower lip, pleased the dim light made her indistinguishable among the *muiríneach* clumps. Tugging a sliver of grass free, she crushed it between her teeth and chewed on it as the *Uí Loinge* man drew closer, strolling with his hands behind his back, feet immersed in the water where the waves lapped upon the sand. The *fénnid,* she noticed, was moving with his head down, shoulders hunched stiffly as though burdened by thoughts of a weight too heavy to bear.

Nearing the dunes, Murchú veered away from the water and headed for an opening in the sandy mounds where the rugged path to the camp began. Before he could enter however, a second figure in a familiar herringbone cloak, suddenly emerged from that narrow channel. Startled, both pulled up short and faced each other in surprise.

As Liath Luachra watched, she saw Murchú make a tentative movement to the side as though to allow the *Clann Baoiscne* woman to pass him by, then pause in mid-step as she addressed him. Although too far away to make out what she was saying, the woman warrior could see that Murchú was listening intently before he, too, responded in turn.

The exchange continued for a time, accompanied by nods and easy hand gestures then, to the Grey One's surprise, the *Clann Baoiscne* woman stepped forward and gently touched the *Uí Loinge* man's arm in an apparent gesture of sympathy.

At that touch, Murchú stiffened, his shoulders momentarily braced but Liath Luachra could tell he'd been moved for, a moment later, he too reached out to touch the *Clann Baoiscne* woman's shoulder in an apparent expression of gratitude.

Intrigued, the Grey One continued to observe the two figures but, even as she watched, they concluded their discussion, parted and continued on their separate ways.

As Murchú disappeared from view behind the dunes, Liath Luachra transferred her attention to the *Clann Baoiscne* woman, who was now advancing towards the waterline. Coming to a halt just out of reach of the surf, she stood staring out to sea, her back towards the dunes. Watching that slim, statuesque profile, Liath Luachra couldn't help but wonder what the woman was thinking, whether she was pondering her recent interaction with Murchú or whether there were topics of far greater significance passing through her mind.

For some reason, she found herself convinced it was the latter. Even within the constraints of their limited and terse interaction, it was obvious the *Clann Baoiscne* woman was a deep thinker. Crimall certainly hadn't exaggerated with respect to her intelligence, just as he hadn't exaggerated with respect to her beauty. Over the previous evenings, Liath Luachra had noticed how the men's gaze would latch onto her when she moved about the camp, the deft movements of her shapely form and her striking features drawing eyes in her wake.

A fresh flare of pain in her left knee drew the woman warrior's attention and, kneading the responsible ligaments with her fingers, she became distracted. By the time she remembered the figure on the foreshore, the *Clann Baoiscne* woman had moved out of sight and whether she'd travelled further up the beach or back through the dunes, the woman warrior couldn't be sure.

Getting to her feet, the Grey One brushed sand from her thighs and buttocks, wincing slightly as her belly growled from hunger. By her reckoning, the *fian* had received sufficient respite and she was keen to recommence the pursuit. That could wait a few moments however, while she grabbed a mouthful of porridge.

'Grey One.'

The woman warrior turned at the unexpected call, surprised to see Crimall stumbling up the slope of the dune towards her, his cloak flapping behind in the onshore breeze.

'Are *Na Cinéaltaí* of a mind to depart? The *Clann Baoiscne* men have had their fill of rest and your *fénnid* seem … well … subdued.'

'They're tired, Crimall. They've been traversing the Great Mother's mantle far longer than your *Clann Baoiscne* warriors.' She took three paces down the slope, into the lee of the dune to get out of the wind. 'But have no fear. With this late rising and an unrushed breakfast, they'll be ready when it's time to go.'

'And when will that be?'

'When I've decided it is.'

'I see. And you still intend to take the lead?'

'I do.'

'Very well.' Crimall coughed and stood a little straighter. The Grey One thought to sense a subtle resentment in the stiffness of his stance but couldn't be sure if she was simply reading too much into it. The *Clann Baoiscne* man made as though to leave but then he paused and looked sharply back at her. 'Last night … after our discussion…'

'Yes.'

'I took to thinking about this Seeking, about certain aspects to the *díberg* that … troubled me. Perhaps there's some *Uí Loinge* insight to which I'm not privy but …'

He paused as though expecting her to contribute something but continued swiftly enough when she displayed no inclination to do so. 'In truth, I struggle to make sense of the *díberg's* motives.'

Liath Luachra regarded him stonily, infuriated by this sudden interest in concerns he'd so steadfastly ignored when she and Murchú had attempted to raise them. A hot anger swelled in her belly and she suddenly imagined thrusting a knife blade into the *Clann Baoiscne* man's chest, could almost feel the meaty resistance against her fist as she drove the blade in past his ribs to pierce the heart.

'Let us consider the matter in full,' continued Crimall, oblivious to that bloody reverie. 'Here are a group of raiders, more numerous than any encountered before. Emboldened by the size of their force, they decide to strike in two separate tribal territories.'

He scratched irritably at the thickening stubble on his chin.

'But here's the strange thing. Not only were both strikes carried out in winter – poor timing for any foray – but situated a great distance apart. Even stranger, both appear to be a vast distance from the raiders' final destination, wherever that may lie. Travelling all that distance, in late winter, through unknown terrain and territories …' He let his voice trail off. 'These do not seem the actions of a typical *díberg*.'

Although wary of the *Clann Baoiscne* man's fresh interest in the *díberg's* origins, Liath Luachra concealed her thoughts behind a lethargic shrug. 'And?'

'What do you think they were doing when they regrouped?'

'I cannot say. Perhaps they were comparing booty.'

'Ah yes! The booty. Two girls from *Clann Baoiscne*, one girl from *Uí Loinge*. Why do you think they took the girls?'

'Slaves,' she answered curtly. She couldn't think of anything else to say, didn't want to think of anything else to say.

Crimall frowned. 'Perhaps. And yet, that would seem a meagre reward for all the effort involved, the risks taken, the great distances traversed. Apart from the girls, the raiders took almost nothing of value. Cattle from the *Clann Baoiscne* farmstead were left where they were. The farmstead occupants were slaughtered yet their more valuable belongings – their tools and weapons – were left untouched. As for the strike in *Uí Loinge* territory, that wasn't even a raid so much as a simple abduction. In fact, it seems …' He paused to offer her a look of aggrieved confusion, both hands held out in the manner of a man who remained unconvinced. 'It seems the only bounty sought was … two girls from *Clann Baoiscne*, one girl from *Uí Loinge*.'

With this conclusion, Crimall regarded her keenly, making no attempt to disguise his misgivings. Liath Luachra returned that scrutiny with her habitual dispassion, now recognising in Crimall some elements of his father's slyness, less obvious and less venal though their expression might be. Like Tréanmór back in Dún Baoiscne, Crimall was suspicious. Compared with his father however, his efforts at eliciting information were far less effective in that his strategy seemed to consist of poking at her blindly in the hope of provoking some involuntary revelation.

'When we first crossed paths, you spoke of your encounter with the *díberg*, of your attempts to release the *Clann Baoiscne* girls and of the raiders untimely return.'

Liath Luachra eyed him coldly. 'Yes.'

'And of killing one raider during your escape.'

Deciding there was nothing worthwhile to say, Liath Luachra said nothing.

'I have a wrinkle in my head, Grey One. A crease of curiosity that allows me no ease. Perhaps you could smoothen that wrinkle out by satisfying my curiosity.'

'What is it you wish to know?'

Crimall cleared his throat, briefly adjusting the sword belt around his waist. 'During your flight from the *díberg*, did any of the raiders speak or shout?'

Liath Luachra felt the hairs rise on the back of her neck. 'What do you mean?'

'It's a simple enough question. Did the raiders say anything of relevance: a name, a destination, some indication of their origin?'

She shook her head.

'You have no doubts?' he persisted, regarding her with an expression of mild disbelief. 'Amid all that bustle and violent activity, the raiders didn't utter the merest whisper!'

This time, the woman warrior responded with a sour expression. 'I've already told you what I know. The *díberg* warriors barely spoke.'

'Aaah!' Crimall exclaimed, grasping onto her words like a drowning man to flotsam. 'You say they "barely" spoke, which suggests they must have said something, no matter how trivial. What exactly did they say?'

Liath Luachra lips compressed in anger. 'The only one who spoke was the man I killed, and in truth I heard but a single word. One that, given the events, was difficult to decipher.'

'Yes, yes. But what was it?'

The woman warrior regarded him coolly then abruptly dropped her head to one-side and opened her mouth, her tongue lolling out.

'Aaarrgh.'

Straightening her head again, she regarded the *Clann Baoiscne* man with stony dispassion.

Crimall considered her in frosty silence for the space of several heartbeats. 'We'll depart when you give the word,' he said at last and stiffly walked away.

***

With the assistance of Bodhmhall ua Baoiscne, the party located a workable path on leaving the campsite clearing, one that allowed them to scale the steep slope of the promontory with relative ease. Cresting its summit, they found the landscape exactly as the *Clann Baoiscne* woman had described. The promontory did, indeed, form the northern edge of a headland that steepened to cliffs as it curved away to the south. Further in that direction, through the morning haze, they could make out a second protrusion from the coastline which, she assured them, was the next in the series of five headlands marking the route to Inbhear Ciúin.

179

Moving *Na Cinéaltaí* to the front, Liath Luachra led the party southwards, guided by the run of the coastline to their left. From time to time, the party was forced inland to circumvent natural obstacles that barred its path but never lost sight of the sea for any significant period of time. The woman warrior kept them moving at a consistent, if slower pace, to scrutinise the ground for sign of the *díberg's* passage or Nédé's promised markings. Both, however, remained frustratingly elusive.

At mid-day, the Grey One halted to allow the party to rest, taking the opportunity to talk with the two *Clann Baoiscne* siblings who sat chatting on a fallen tree trunk. Noting the woman warrior's approach, Bodhmhall nudged her brother. Crimall looked up and observed her with an expression of polite tolerance. 'Grey One,' he greeted her as she came to a halt before him.

'Are we on the stray?'

Crimall frowned. 'On the stray? Of course not. My sister's already confirmed we travel the correct path.'

'The correct path is the path leading to the *díberg*. I've yet to see any trace of them.'

'Hah!' exclaimed Crimall. 'It's too early to see such traces yet. Besides, the track they must have followed along this length of coast is obvious. Nédé's probably saving his efforts for when he feels we'll need them. Don't trouble yourself. I'm sure we'll see his markings later this afternoon or early tomorrow.'

But they didn't see Nédé's markings later that afternoon. Nor over the course of the following day. At noon on the third day following their departure from the beach, the woman warrior approached the *Clann Baoiscne* leader again, very concerned at this point by the continued absence of sign. On this occasion, although he fobbed her off with his usual bluster, she sensed an unsettling nervousness behind the strained assurances.

Dependent still, on *Clann Baoiscne* goodwill, the woman warrior decided to bite her tongue and repress her frustration for the time being. That night however, while sheltering from yet another heavy downpour, she determined to confront Crimall directly and take matters into her own hands if no sign or markings were detected before reaching Inbhear Ciúin.

As it turned out however, she was spared such a confrontation for evidence of the *díberg* passage finally came to light before noon the following day. Leading the party towards a high ridge that formed part of the final headland before Inbhear Ciúin, Liath Luachra was surprised to find An Giobach – dispatched on scouting duties earlier that morning – awaiting them in a clearing on the slope of a low-lying hill. Although the big *fénnid* remained silent as the party filed in about him, he considered the Grey One with a grim expression, then wordlessly raised one hand to indicate a V-shaped gap in the ridge ahead. Although still some distance off, a small cloud of fluttering black shapes could be seen swarming erratically above it.

Na fiacha dubha. Ravens.

The warriors from the combined *fianna* spread out to study the distant sight.

'Well,' muttered Crimall under his breath. 'That does not bode well.'

'The cleft marks a pass,' said Bodhmhall. Surprised at this unexpected contribution, the warriors turned their gaze towards her and the *Clann Baoiscne* woman momentarily wavered under their concentrated attention. 'The cleft marks a pass,' she repeated, this time a little more nervously. 'It's the only route through to Inbhear Ciúin.'

Liath Luachra regarded her sharply.

'You're certain?'

She nodded.

The woman warrior exhaled heavily, glanced towards the swarming birds then back at her again. 'What form does the pass have?'

'It's more a gully than a true pass. It starts between two sections of crumbling earth at the base of the ridge but as it cuts deeper, the earth's replaced by rock. Run-off from the ridge drains into it so there'll probably be water streaming through after last night's rain.'

'How far does it stretch?'

'The first section runs a short distance through the cliffs but then it curves and broadens out. At the far side of that open space, it narrows again and there are several other bends before it opens on the southern slope above Inbhear Ciúin.'

The Grey One nodded. '*Agus na fiacha dubha?*' And the ravens?

Bodhmhall shivered. 'I don't know. The pass is mostly stone and rock. There are some trees where it first widens but I can't think of anything that would draw such numbers of birds.'

'Well, something's drawing them.'

Even as she uttered the words, Liath Luachra felt the weight of Murchú's gaze press upon her. She didn't need to turn and look at him to know what he was thinking.

'We'll send a smaller group to scout the pass,' she decided. 'An Giobach …' She regarded the big *fénnid,* conscious even now of the unresolved tension that still hung between them since the discussion on the dune. 'An Giobach, you'll come with me. And you, Crimall. But bring two of your warriors in support.'

Finally, knowing she had to offer him some duty to distract him from thoughts of his sister, she turned to the *Uí Loinge* man who was watching her quietly, his face tight and pale. 'Murchú, have the other men spread through the trees, placed to launch a full javelin volley. Should we come running back this way with enemies at our heels, you'll need to be ready to stop them short.'

The *Uí Loinge* man regarded her bleakly but nodded in acknowledgment. As he moved off to organise the remaining warriors, Liath Luachra divested herself of her backpack, looped her javelin haft into its leather *suaineamh,* then gestured at the others in her advance party.

'Ar aghaidh linn.' Let's go.

She led the four warriors off at a run, moving cautiously, but swiftly, through the forest until the bulk of the ridge appeared through the foliage of the trees directly ahead. Arranging the warriors into a wide, triangle-shaped wedge, she placed herself at its head, set Crimall and An Giobach to either side at her rear and had the two *Clann Baoiscne* warriors – Usna and Odrán – take up the rear flanks. Satisfied with the arrangement, she led them off once more, moving slowly forward to the treeline where the forest ended, thirty paces or so from the foot of the ridge.

Coming to a halt, the warriors spread out and concealed themselves in the shadows as the Grey One studied the cleft directly ahead: a deep gully running between two steep, badly eroded banks of earth. A small stream, littered with woody debris and small stones, emptied out from its base, flowing off sharply to the right where it followed the ridge before being swallowed up by the trees. From where she was crouched, Liath Luachra could see the gully penetrate further, deep into the heart of the ridge where it squeezed between two high cliffs of grey, lichen-stained rock. Even from that distance, those narrow confines had a dank and menacing air, their ominous character exacerbated by the hollow gurgling sound produced by the stream running through them.

Signalling for the others to remain in place, Liath Luachra stepped out of the trees and crossed the flat ground at a run, her feet sinking into the earth where it became soggy with spill-off from the stream. Closing on the gap between the two banks, she slowed and dropped to a crouch, javelin up and ready to cast. Glancing up the channel to make sure the route was clear, she cautiously stepped forward, into a flow of water less than two fingers' breadth in depth.

Peering up the eroded channel between the banks to where it entered the ridge proper, she saw that the narrower passage created between the cliff faces was strewn with individual heaps of rock and debris. Twenty-five paces or so beyond the entrance, it veered sharply to the left and although she couldn't see beyond that point, harsh squawks resonated down towards her, amplified by the closeness of the rock faces. Whatever had drawn the ravens lay somewhere just beyond that curve.

Gesturing for the others to follow, Liath Luachra started up the gully and entered the passage, lifting and placing her feet with care to avoid splashing against the flow of the shallow water. Conscious that, if confronted, she'd have no option but to fight, she kept her javelin poised, her arm muscles aching softly from the continued strain of keeping the missile aloft.

The frantic clamour of the birds grew louder and more piercing as the woman warrior closed on the bend and she could feel her stomach muscles clench from the tension. Slowing to a stop within five paces of her goal, she waited for the others to catch her up, javelin at the ready, eyes fixed on the stony curve. Finally, hearing the soft splash of careful footsteps to her rear, she started forward once more and, reaching the corner, pressed her left shoulder against the damp rockface. Slowly, carefully, she edged her head around it. Behind her, the other warriors remained completely silent.

Beyond the bend, the passage continued for approximately twenty paces then abruptly widened out to form a broad section of open ground, encircled by high cliffs of jagged grey rock. Although the main passage swung around to the right, narrowing where it continued through the ridge, innumerable years of erosion had created a semi-circle of raised ground to the left which was occupied by a small wood of sickly-looking elms.

It was within that small wood that the riotous cloud of ravens had converged, a squawking mass of undulating black feathers and yellow beaks that tore and pecked savagely at an object attached to the moss-coated bough of the nearest tree, the clamour of their noisy feasting ringing through the rocky enclosure.

Lowering her javelin, the woman warrior slid around the curve and splashed her way towards the trees. When she was within ten paces, a number of the ravens – more timorous than the others – hurriedly took flight. As she continued forward, the remaining mass of birds took to the air, fluttering furiously around the clearing, squawking in outrage at the intrusion. Ignoring the raucous outcry, Liath Luachra came to a halt less than two paces from the tree and stared.

The object which had drawn the birds was human, or rather it had been human. Now it was a slab of meat strung upside down on a head level branch, fastened to the bough by its ankles. Despite dangling naked in front of her, it took the woman warrior a moment to identify the corpse as male, for it had been heavily mutilated even before the ravens had got to it. The genital area had been sliced to shreds and a vicious wound rent the chest from waist to throat, exposing bloody ribs, white globules of fat and striated shreds of muscle ripped apart by the ravens. Much of the head had also been battered, and dried shreds of brain leaked out through bloody wounds. Both eyes had been plucked from the sockets and the empty spaces stared hollowly at her.

On the ground directly below the corpse, any blood seeped into the soil had long since washed away. There were lumps of old tissue that looked like trails of intestine but, so heavily picked at, it was hard to be sure.

The woman warrior looked to Crimall who was also regarding the body, his face deathly pale.

'Is it Nédé?'

The *Clann Baoiscne* man swallowed and cleared his throat several times as though struggling to breathe. Unable to answer, he settled for an awkward nod.

Liath Luachra said nothing. The raiders must somehow have spotted the warrior on their trail and captured him alive before stringing him up. She stepped forward to examine the corpse more closely, pressing her palm against her nose and mouth to stifle the stench of putrefying flesh. The flax rope used to fix the corpse to the branch made a soft creaking sound as it shifted slightly from left to right, brushed by the movement of air coming down the passage.

Studying the wounds, it seemed clear that Nédé had been cut before he died, most probably in an effort to make him talk. And looking at those ragged wounds, she had no doubt the *Clann Baoiscne* man had talked. Whatever he'd known, the *díberg* now almost certainly knew as well, which meant they had a far better understanding of their pursuers than their pursuers had of them.

As ever, the Grey One's stony expression concealed her true fury and frustration at being bested, once again, by the *díberg*. Despite their inauspicious start, since leaving Dun Baoiscne the two *fian* had been moving with an increasingly unified sense of purpose, encouraged in no small part by the definite gains made on the *díberg*. The discovery of Nédé's mutilated body however, now swept those achievements aside. From the state of the corpse, the *Clann Baoiscne* warrior looked to have been killed at least two to three days earlier, certainly before the previous night's rainstorm, which meant any tracks the *díberg* had left would be washed away. Without tracks or any certainty of the raiders' destination, it was impossible to work out which direction they'd taken.

Shit on your head, Gadra!

Exhaling heavily, Liath Luachra turned to Crimall, struggling to stifle the rage in her chest as she recalled his insistence on returning to Dún Baoiscne. 'It seems I misjudged you,' she said at last.

Crimall looked at her blankly.

'You promised that any marking left by Nédé would be prominent enough not to miss. I can't deny you haven't been true to your word.'

Unable to disguise her contempt, the woman warrior quickly turned away with the javelin over her shoulder and started back towards the passage, back to the larger party, back to share the good – and the bad – news with Murchú and the others.

***

Father Sun was well into his slow descent when the party emerged at the southern side of the pass overlooking the estuary of Inbhear Ciúin. Looking down at the broad spread of brackish water snaking out between the two headlands, Liath Luachra was tempted to continue downhill but called, instead, for an early camp. Reeling from the body blow of the mutilated *Clann Baoiscne* scout and deflated from the effort of burying him in the hard ground beneath the elms, the *fianna* spirits had soured. Like a grime-encrusted gash, the party's morale had gone on to fester, and the woman warrior knew she had to cauterise the wound before it was too late.

Murchú, as expected, had taken the news badly. Although he'd sagged with relief at the confirmation the corpse wasn't that of his sister, when he'd learned who it was, he'd immediately understood the ramifications. For a time, he just sat alone by the treeline at the top of the slope, looking down at the estuary with a stricken expression. Distracted by the need to secure their new campsite, the Grey One left him to his own devices, By the time she returned, he was gone, slipped away into the forest without telling anyone.

Preoccupied with her own responsibilities, the Grey One had little opportunity to go search for him, although she already suspected he didn't want to be found. Instead, setting Feirgil and one of the *Clann Baoiscne* warriors on guard duty, she sat quietly by herself, working

185

through options to salvage the Seeking as the fire was lit in the glow of a full moon and the evening meal prepared.

It took some deep contemplation but by the time everyone had gathered around the flames she had a clear idea of what she had to say. Forcing herself to overcome her natural reserve, she got to her feet and stood before them. Weary and disheartened, the warriors looked on, sceptical but willing to hear her out.

'This has not been a good day,' she began, conscious of the need to acknowledge the truth of their situation. 'Nédé was our greatest hope for recovering the *díberg* trail. Without him, it'll be a struggle to achieve that task but it's not one we'll shy away from.'

There was a snort of bitter laughter at that from one of the *Clann Baoiscne fénnid,* a stocky man with a shock of black hair, by the name of Guaire. 'And how do you propose we do that?' he asked sourly.

Liath Luachra glanced quickly at Crimall, situated a few paces behind his acerbic *fénnid.* Sitting alone, he displayed uncharacteristic diffidence as he observed her with a sour expression.

Choking on thwarted ambition, no doubt.

And the bitter knowledge it was all his own doing.

'By using what little knowledge we have,' the Grey One answered, turning towards the *Clann Baoiscne fénnid* as though to address him directly. 'The presence of Nédé's body – disturbing though it was – confirms that the *díberg* passed this way and descended to Inbhear Ciúin. Tomorrow, I propose that we too descend to the estuary.'

'For what purpose?' the *fénnid* interjected again. 'We'll find nothing. Any trail the *díberg* left will be two or three days old. Even then, it's most likely been scrubbed from the Great Mother's mantle by last night's rain.'

Liath Luachra impassively returned the *Clann Baoiscne* man's gaze, her lack of expression belying her irritation at the criticism. 'You have the right of it,' she admitted through gritted teeth. 'But you forget the two factors that work to our advantage. Firstly, the *díberg* is a large group, made up of at least ten warriors and three prisoners, the latter in chains. No matter how hard they try, they'll leave a trail. Yes, the rain will have obliterated their prints but it won't have touched the more enduring signs of passage: the broken branches, the badly trampled ground, the deeper imprints where the chained prisoners might have fallen.'

'That may be,' the warrior Usna commented. 'But such signs will be few and far between. Locating them in the vastness of the Great Wild will be a big ask.'

'True. Which brings us to our second advantage. Because of the prisoners and their chains, the *díberg* move far slower than us, half our fastest pace over the course of the day by my estimate. Last night's rain may have washed away the tracks they made leaving Inbhear Ciúin but, moving at our fastest pace, we could strike their tracks within a day or a day and a half at most.'

She looked around at the *Clann Baoiscne fénnid*, listening now with far more interest. Someone – she couldn't see who – snorted. 'We don't know which way they've gone. Their tracks could lie one to two days in any direction. You'd have us chasing phantoms!'

'Hear me out!' she growled, struggling to keep the exasperation from her voice. 'I have a scheme for that.'

She waited until they'd settled down into silence again, curious as to what she was about to propose. 'Tomorrow morning,' she began. 'We descend to Inbhear Ciúin to locate the most likely route of departure towards the south-east, for that's clearly the direction in which they're headed. Using that area as our central point, we'll split the party and spread out in every direction on a south-eastern arc. For a full day, we'll each travel from that point in a straight line at our fastest pace. On the morning of the second day, we'll continue those lines but slow our pace to search the ground for tracks of passage.'

She paused then, noting how the *fénnid* were working the timing through in their own minds.

'Most of us will find nothing but empty wilderness but one of us, one of us should find some trace of their trail on the afternoon of the second day. Once the trail's discovered, it's the responsibility of the person who finds it to light a fire to alert the rest of us and draw us all towards him. We'll also keep one of our party here at Inbhear Ciúin to watch the horizon for smoke. Once a smoke column is seen, he'll light a second fire to alert those who've travelled too far to see the initial smoke. The remaining *fénnid* can then work their way towards the point where the trail was discovered and regroup there.'

There was a silence as the *fénnid* thought her proposal through and although there were some mutterings and grumbles, she could tell they were giving it serious consideration. There'd be some justifiable scepticism, of course. In rugged terrain, keeping a straight course was difficult at the best of times. Trying to maintain a straight line in forest while searching the ground for tracks would be ten times more difficult.

But it was possible.

She decided to pre-empt the inevitable arguments by addressing the most obvious, keen to undermine the warriors' resistance to her idea before they ganged up in opposition against it.

'I'll admit this approach is one of desperation. But it's a sound one. You'll find its key weakness when you try to scan the ground on the second day while also striving to travel a straight course. If you have the luck of it, the ground you cover will be rugged, for rugged ground reduces the number of potential routes. If you find more than one route, use your judgement to choose where the Great Wild sets the most natural path. Those are the routes the *díberg* would be most likely to abide by.'

She cleared her throat, her mouth dried out from such unaccustomed and extended talk.

'I'll not lie to you, men of *Clann Baoiscne*. This will be no easy task but there's good cause to believe in its success. The alternative is to concede defeat and that's not something I'm prepared to do. I'll understand should you choose to return to Dún Baoiscne with your tails between your legs but *Na Cinéaltaí* will fulfil the Seeking alone if we have to.'

Having said everything she'd wanted to say and knowing she couldn't maintain the facade of confidence for much longer, Liath Luachra abruptly left the campfire. Ignoring the curious faces of the *Clann Baoiscne fénnid,* she moved swiftly towards the gloomy refuge of the treeline and there, huddled in the silent shadows, she looked back at the consternation she'd left in her wake. The *Clann Baoiscne* warriors were talking loudly now, some aggrieved at her questioning of their courage but most arguing over their own interpretation of her proposal and the associated practicalities.

Of all the *Clann Baoiscne* men, Crimall was the most conspicuous and that was because of his silence. Although his warriors were clearly awaiting direction, he sat apart with his sister, eyes to the ground as he ate his meal, in no apparent hurry to share his thoughts or engage on the matter.

The woman warrior's gaze slid across to the *Cinéaltaí fénnid* – An Giobach and Feirgil – who also sat apart observing the *Clann Baoiscne* reaction with a guarded air of interest. Watching them, she felt a fresh tremor of guilt, conscious now that somehow, over the course of the pursuit, her *fian* had fallen apart. Mochta was dead, Biotóg lost to injury, Murchú disappeared. She'd exacerbated the situation further by dismissing Feirgil and now even An Giobach remained distant since their acrimonious exchange. Chewing bitterly on the inside of her cheek, she realised that her limitations as a leader meant she'd not only missed the *fian's* slow disintegration but had contributed directly to it. Now, she was stuck with the consequences and no idea how to undo the damage.

Perhaps like the gaiscíoch path, every fian has its time of high valour before its inevitable decline.

Further depressed at that prospect, the Grey One turned away and stepped deeper into the forest, eager to get away from the braying arguments of the *Clann Baoiscne.* Walking aimlessly, without direction or purpose, she followed a natural dip that sloped away from the ridge and allowed herself to be directed downhill, walking without hindrance in the light of the full moon. Emerging suddenly from a grove of pines, she found herself on an unexpected flat almost entirely taken up by a wide pond encircled by drooping willows. Although choked with reeds and leaf litter at its western-most edge, the greater part of the surface lay placid and clear, reflecting the moon perfectly without a single visible wrinkle.

Approaching the edge of the pond, Liath Luachra knelt on the gritty mud and looked down at its still waters. Although tempted to wash the day's filth from herself, when she dipped her fingers into that black liquid, the skin-tingling chill prompted a rapid change of heart. Instead, she settled for splashing drops on her face and wiping the worst of the grime from her cheeks and forehead.

Sitting back on her haunches with her arms on her knees, the woman warrior stared up at the moon and wondered what the *Clann Baoiscne* men had decided in her absence. Despite the plan she'd outlined, it seemed inevitable they'd relinquish the Seeking. Crimall's lack of concern for the captives – except as a means to boost his own battle reputation – had been obvious from the start. As for the *Clann Baoiscne fénnid,* she had little faith in their reliability. With no real connection to the abducted *Clann Baoiscne* women beyond tribal affiliation, unlike her they had no genuine motivation to partake in the Seeking.

Prying Cairenn free of Gadra's noxious grasp.

Conscious then that her hands were trembling, the Grey One clasped them together and shivered. Her jaw clenched at the thought of the scars on her back, the blistered burn of them flaring just as fiercely as they had all those many years ago.

Of the *Uí Cailbhe* raiders, Gadra had always been the one she'd feared the most. Ironically, despite his mild manner and quiet voice, the *Uí Cailbhe* man had had a callousness to him that made the brutal antics of his comrades pale in comparison. With a malignant cruelty that surpassed every boundary she genuinely never knew if she'd survive his solitary visits to the cave where she was held captive, for the absence of others allowed him free rein of depravity.

She stared at the surface of the pond, her hard, white features reflected glacially back at her.

On one occasion, intrigued by the scars along her back, Gadra had taken to them with a knife while taking her from behind, using the blade to slice through the hardened tissue so that the blood had flowed freely down her back. That same time, he'd also beaten her so badly even the brutal Garrad Mór, drawn by the sound of her screams, had felt compelled to intervene, banning the warrior from making use of her again for another full moon.

Fortunately, she'd escaped before Gadra had returned but her fear of him had been such that memories of him had haunted her for the better part of a year, leaving her with nightmares that shook her awake at night, choking for breath and wracked by phantom pains that stayed till daylight. By the time she'd joined *Na Cinéaltaí,* those nightmares had fortunately faded, her memory of him buried and far behind.

But now, like a malevolent ghost, he was back.

She smacked the water violently, the splash of it gleaming silver in the moonlight. The coldness of the liquid did nothing to cool her fury at the easy way he'd subjugated her, once again reducing her to the creature she'd been.

Dropping her head, she closed her eyes tightly, washed by a breeze sweeping in across the water.

But not even that cold gust could blow those memories away.

Sighing, she opened her eyes and dipped her fingers into the pond. Scooping up water in the palm of her hand, she slowly raised it to her mouth.

'You shouldn't drink that.'

Startled, the woman warrior spun around on one knee, the water spilling to the ground as she surged upright, drawing *Gleas Gan Ainm* from its scabbard. She froze then as her eyes latched onto the female figure in the trees several paces to her right, the perpetual herringbone cloak enveloping her shoulders.

Bodhmhall ua Baoiscne regarded her steadily, her expression offering no indication as to how long she'd been standing there. Although shaken at being taken by surprise, Liath Luachra managed to return the stare with affected calm. 'Why not?' she demanded.

The *Clann Baoiscne* woman gestured towards the moon's reflection on the surface of the pond. 'See for yourself. The moon's tainted the water and left its sparkling residue. Drink from it and you risk losing your mind.'

The woman warrior glanced towards the water then back at the dark-haired woman. 'That's a child's tale,' she said, her voice layered with a dusting of scorn.

Bodhmhall laughed at that, the same wholesome husky laugh the Grey One had heard back in the cave in response to Feirgil's inanities. 'Perhaps. Perhaps not. That's what the Druidic Council tell us, although, truth be told, I've never entirely believed everything the Druidic Council say.' She regarded the woman warrior with a somewhat cynical mien. 'Never believe what a druid wants you to hear. That's my advice to you.'

Liath Luachra continued to observe her quietly, intrigued by the *Clann Baoiscne* woman's undisguised disdain for that revered group yet angered too at the careless intrusion on her privacy. 'Leave me, Bodhmhall. I have no patience for *Clann Baoiscne* games tonight.'

'Then our thoughts align, Grey One. I didn't slip away from camp to play games. I came to speak of two matters that prey upon my thoughts.'

Liath Luachra regarded her without expression. 'What matters?'

'Tomorrow we reach the extremity of *Clann Baoiscne* territory. Inbhear Ciúin marks the furthermost territory under the tribe's influence.'

'You're concerned Crimall will fall back on Tréanmór's command, abandon the Seeking.' The woman warrior grunted bitterly. 'Given the discovery of Nédé's corpse I'd have thought that matter already …'

Her voice faded in mid-sentence as the ramifications of Bodhmhall's words suddenly struck her. The *Clann Baoiscne* hadn't yet declared a final decision on whether to abandon the Seeking or not.

The *Clann Baoiscne* woman regarded her thoughtfully, evidently wondering at that sudden pause. 'Don't judge my brother too harshly, Grey One. Like all men, Crimall has his pride and his weaknesses, particularly where it relates to pleasing our father. Nevertheless, he's also very dear to me.'

'Pleasing your father? How's that a weakness?'

'Because my father's not a man to be pleased. Tréanmór has a singular scheme – growth of the *Clann Baoiscne* powerbase – and that scheme consumes him entirely. With the exception of my brother Cumhal – who he believes will continue his obsession – his offspring hold little value for my father.' The *bandraoi* compressed her lips then, her eyes dulling in inner reflection before she gave a dismissive shrug of her shoulder, abruptly shuffling such thoughts aside.

'Except, perhaps, as chattel to serve his scheme.'

'He respected Crimall's abilities well enough to let him take the *Clann Baoiscne fian*,' the Grey One countered

'A *fian* in harness to an *éclann* leader? There's no tribal honour in that. Don't take offence at my words, Grey One. I merely speak the truth as it stands. Crimall accepted this poisoned undertaking in the naive hope of impressing our father. That and because he saw the Seeking as an opportunity to make his name – Crimall has his own ambitions too, of course. Now, however, with Nédé's death and his plans usurped, my brother finds himself ... disheartened.'

Liath Luachra repressed a bitter smile at that. 'And to save face, he'll fall back on the excuse of his father's instruction, he'll leave your friend to her fate.'

Bodhmhall held her gaze, her expression torn. 'Yes,' she said at last.

'So why bring your tale of family woe to me, Bodhmhall Ua Baoiscne? What is it you want?'

'Your consent.'

Liath Luachra looked at her blankly. 'My consent?'

'I seek your consent to join in the continuation of the pursuit. If my brother learns I intend to complete the Seeking he's relinquished, he'll be too ashamed to leave.' A cynical half-smile creased the left side of her face. 'Particularly if there's even the slightest chance of its successful conclusion.'

Liath Luachra breathed softly through her nose, unsure how to respond. She didn't trust the *Clann Baoiscne* woman and *Na Draoithe* had a reputation for being fluid with the truth. *Bandraoi*, in particular, were said to have skills to beguile or possess a mind through the clever use of language. With one as comely as Bodhmhall ua Baoiscne, any such threat would have to be doubly dangerous.

'Given the obstacles put in our way by *Clann Baoiscne*, why would I possibly agree?'

The dark-haired women drew herself up, the movement so slight it was barely perceptible, nevertheless when she spoke again, she exuded a poise and an authoritative grace that was impossible to ignore.

'Because if the *Clann Baoiscne fian* leaves, you lose three-quarters of your force. More importantly, when you commence your search for tracks at Inbhear Ciúin tomorrow, you'll have but four sets of eyes to cover the terrain instead of fourteen.'

Liath Luachra shifted awkwardly from one foot to the other, unsettled by the *Clann Baoiscne* woman's perspicacity. The two issues Bodhmhall had raised were the very same issues she'd fretted over prior to making her appeal at the campfire. The woman warrior frowned, wondering if there was some truth behind the rumours that a *draoi* had the ability to read your silent thoughts.

'Very well. You may accompany *Na Cineáltaí*. Until such time as I consider you a burden I'm unwilling to bear.'

'*Go raibh maith agat*,' Bodhmhall said simply. Thank you.

The two women regarded one another in silence.

'You mentioned there were two matters preying on you,' Liath Luachra prompted.

'So, I did.'

The Grey One said nothing, waiting silently for the *Clann Baoiscne* woman to get to the point.

'That second matter concerns your *fénnid*, Murchú of the *Uí Loinge*.'

The woman warrior's eyes narrowed at that. 'What about Murchú?'

The *Clann Baoiscne* woman frowned, hunched her cloak higher up over her shoulders. 'I ...' she began but then paused before starting again. 'I like Murchú.'

Liath Luachra grunted softly, unsure where this discussion was headed.

'He's a man who speaks the truth and who follows through on what he says. In these times – in any times – such qualities are rare, but ...'

'But?'

'He bears a heavy burden of grief.'

'Of course, he does. His sister was abducted, his cousin killed. He's had to deal with obstruction from your people and th-'

She paused as the *bandraoi* raised one hand to silence her.

'I fear the burden on him might have been greater than you suspect. Grief turns easily to despair and unchallenged despair can poison the mind. If ...'. Noting the cynicism in Liath Luachra's eyes, the *Clann Baoiscne* woman paused and attempted an abrupt change of tack. 'Knowing Crimall, I'm sure he'll have bragged to you about *An tíolacadh* – my *Gift*.'

Liath Luachra nodded cautiously, intrigued by the direction this new tangent was taking. 'He said you see ... fire. That you see people on fire.'

'I see flames,' the *bandraoi* corrected. '*An tíolacadh* offers me sight of the life flame in all things, but, most of all, in people. When men or women experience anger or happiness or fear, I can see their flames grow. When burdened with sadness or despair, I see those same flames dwindle and diminish and, sometimes, come dangerously close to snuffing out.' She bit her lip. 'That is how Murchú's flame now looks to me.'

The Grey One continued to stare at her, her expression giving nothing away. 'I don't understand. What are you saying?'

'I believe Murchú needs a friend, a friend to challenge the despair, to coax his flame back to life.'

'A friend?' Liath Luachra's voice was brittle. 'Murchú is *fénnid*. I am *rígfénnid*. We are not "*friends*".'

Bodhmhall held her gaze but her expression didn't so much as flicker. 'Well, then I suppose you will not miss him.'

'What do you mean by that?'

'I mean you may not see him again.'

'Why would you tell me that? Is it your meaning that he'll not return tonight?'

'If something or someone doesn't rouse his flame at the time he needs it most then, yes. I fear there's a strong likelihood he may not return.'

The woman warrior snorted. *Ráiméis!* Nonsense!

At that, the *Clann Baoiscne* woman drew herself up again, somehow managing to appear even taller. '*Éist, a Liath Luachra,*' she said, an unmistakeable urgency to her voice. Listen, Liath Luachra. 'Given your poor experience of Dún Baoiscne I understand your distrust, but I gain nothing from this. I'm not one to recount a lie and I wouldn't have approached you had I not thought the matter a serious one.'

The woman warrior considered her doubtfully. 'Then why don't you go see him? You claim to like him. And what do I know of ... rousing flames?'

'I do like him. But Murchú doesn't know me or like me well enough to be influenced by anything I say. He likes you. He ...' The *Clann Baoiscne* woman's voice momentarily faded. 'When Murchú looks at you, his flame rouses most brightly.'

The Grey One regarded the other woman in silence, her expression completely unreadable. Despite the *bandraoi's* earlier calm, there were now distinguishable cracks in her composure where tremors of emotion roiled beneath the surface. At the same time, the Grey One could detect no trace of deceit or duplicity in her features.

'Very well.'

Bodhmhall released a sigh of relief. 'Thank you,' she said again.

'Don't thank me yet. I've agreed to go and find him but, in truth, I have few words for Murchú.'

Bodhmhall reached in under the hem of her cloak and withdrew a small leather waterskin. 'Here,' she said, holding it out to Liath Luachra. 'You can take this with you and start by offering him a drink. Drink's a good thaw to any conversation.'

Liath Luachra regarded the container suspiciously but then grudgingly accepted it. She shook it, listening to the contents splash around inside. 'What's in it?' she asked.

'Enchanted water.'

Arching one sceptical eyebrow, the Grey One pulled the stopper free and raised the container to her nose to take a cautious sniff. Despite herself, she gave a cynical chuckle.

'Uisce beatha.'

The *Clann Baoiscne* woman shrugged.

'Tell me, Bodhmhall ua Baoiscne. These flames that you see. Can you observe such flames in me?'

Bodhmhall held her gaze but the Grey One detected a slight hesitation before she responded.

'Yes.'

'And what do you see?'

This time the tall woman looked distinctly uncomfortable but, after a short pause, she quietly answered the question.

'Around you I see a darkness, a joyless draping of shadow that swallows the light. And yet, within that darkness I also see a flame, a flame burning with a ferocity that terrifies me.'

Reaching up to clasp her cloak, Bodhmhall drew the thick material of it closer about her shoulders as a cold breeze slid past, stirring the perfect surface of the pond.

'I think, Liath Luachra, were you to release that flame, the fire you start would engulf the world entirely.'

***

The Grey One found Murchú at the base of the ridge, sitting by the foreshore of Inbhear Ciúin. In truth, locating the *fénnid* hadn't been an exacting task. Concerned by the weak flicker of his 'flame', Bodhmhall had watched him leaving the camp and could therefore advise the Grey One on the direction he'd taken. Moving downhill from the pond, the terrain had soon funnelled her into the sole practical path leading down to the water. On hitting the shoreline, she'd turned left, again taking the advice of the *bandraoi* who'd informed her that the route to the right, leading to the marshlands, was too treacherous to travel at night, even under such a brilliant moon.

The glaring moonlight imbued the terrain with a silver-black clarity that allowed the woman warrior to follow the shoreline with relative ease and it hadn't been long before she spotted the *Uí Loinge* man sitting on a low rock, staring out at the water with his forearms resting on his knees. Approaching to within twenty paces of the *fénnid's* position, Liath Luachra paused, struck by a sudden and unexpected vacillation. Now that she'd found him, she realised she had no idea what to say to him.

Oblivious to her presence, Murchú sat silently, his posture morose and listless. That dispirited stance disturbed the Grey One for in it she recognised a familiar brooding, the recurring soul sickness that still frayed the edges of her own existence. Confronted with that reflection, her initial instinct was to turn and run, to flee back to the campsite and claim she hadn't found the *Uí Loinge* man. She dismissed the idea almost immediately. Bodhmhall would hardly be fooled by such a weak lie but, more importantly, she couldn't leave Murchú in such a potentially perilous state. Over the two years since claiming the role of *rígfénnid* from Bressal, the young *fénnid* had kept the *Uí Loinge* from her back, despite his loyalty to kin and tribe. With An Giobach, he'd always formed one of the two critical pillars of support that held *Na Cinéaltaí* together in her name. Notwithstanding the awkwardness created by his affections towards her, she owed him this much at least.

Sighing, she took a tentative step forward.

'Murchú!'

At the sound of her voice, the *Uí Loinge* man stiffened but he twisted about with far less urgency than she'd have expected from a man in such potentially hostile territory. 'Oh,' he said quietly when he saw her.

Liath Luachra frowned, disturbed more by the listlessness of the *fénnid's* reply than by its curtness for it seemed further confirmation of the warrior's despair.

Advancing quickly, she moved around the rock and took a seat beside him. The *Uí Loinge* man didn't look at her.

Raising the skin, she yanked the stopper free with her teeth, shook it to attract his attention, then held it out to him.

Drawn by the sound of the sloshing liquid, Murchú considered the skin for a moment then slowly reached out and took it. Lifting it to his lips, he took a sip, swallowed and wordlessly passed it back to her.

Struggling for words, Liath Luachra fumbled awkwardly with the container, then abruptly recalled the gesture she'd seen the *bandraoi* make on the beach. Reaching out her hand, she touched the *fénnid* gently on his shoulder. Murchú looked down in surprise at the woman warrior's hand then back at her. 'What are yo-,' he began, but then he paused. 'Oh, you're trying to be nice.'

His voice sounded empty, disinterested, yet after the prolonged silence even that involuntary barb felt like a success.

'You have to put it aside, Murchú.'

The *Uí Loinge* man looked at her. Confused, he glanced down at the skin in her hand.

'Your grief,' she clarified. 'The guilt and the sorrow that burns you from the inside. If you want to save your sister, you must find the strength to fight it for, unchecked, it'll consume you.'

She broke off again, groping for better words.

'I have a plan, Murchú. A plan to find the *díberg* trail. We can still find your sister. Find her and return her safe to Briga.'

Although Murchú gave no indication that he'd heard or was even listening, she sensed that she'd hooked his attention so briefly summarised the plan she'd outlined earlier that night back at the campfire. When she'd finished, the *fénnid* remained silent, expressionless.

Because there were no other words left to share, they sat in silence for a long time, taking it in turns to sip from the skin, saying nothing. Although she had expected the situation to grow increasingly awkward, the woman warrior was surprised to find that, if anything, their mutual silence had calmed her and she no longer felt under pressure to talk. It was a long time later, therefore, before she spoke again.

'Will you come back? Back to camp. Tomorrow we'll rise early to go find your sister.'

Murchú remained quiet and still, his emotions impossible to discern through the shadows. In the gloom, the shake of his head was all but imperceptible, but she caught it all the same.

'I can't,' he said suddenly, his voice strained and quiet as a whisper. 'Not tonight. In the morning I'll … Tonight I'll wait here. Watch the stars. Listen to the sea.'

Liath Luachra nodded. 'Not tonight,' she agreed. 'I'll wait here with you.'

Chapter Ten:

At mid-day, the Grey One had halted on the south-facing slope of the highest hill she could find. Removing her backpack, she placed it against the base of a moss-encrusted oak, using its frame as a support to step up and haul herself onto the tree's lower branches. Slowly, and very carefully, she clambered her way up past the midpoint of the oak's full height. There, straddling a south-facing bough, she shuffled out as far as she dared from the central trunk and peered at the view stretching into the distance.

As far as the eye could see, the land was blanketed in forest, an undulating stretch of endless green, intermittently shadowed by the dark indentations of valleys and other depressions or broken by the occasional hill or isolated ridge. Far to the south-east, there was a hill with a distinctive narrow summit, crowned with an unusual cluster of what looked like enormous rocks. Whatever they were, the Grey One decided, the eye-catching peak would serve as her point of reference for the remainder of the afternoon, the bearing she'd use to continue the line of travel commenced that morning at Inbhear Ciúin.

Working her way back to the trunk, the woman warrior drew her legs up and leaned against the coarse bark. Once she'd secured herself to her satisfaction, she relaxed, slipping a hand inside her tunic to withdraw a half-empty water-skin and a lumpy tuber from the interior pocket. The latter, resting in that warm nook since the day they'd left Dún Baoiscne, had taken on a stone-like consistency. To eat it, she had to break off small chunks with her molars and chew laboriously until they were soft enough to swallow.

She finished off the entire tuber in this manner and, hunger sated, retrieved the waterskin. Undoing the stopper, she took a quick swig before pouring the remaining contents over her head. The liquid was lukewarm as a result of being carried so close to her body, but there was pleasure to be had from the sensation of its heavy wetness seeping through her hair, cooling her sweating skull and overheated brow. Replacing the skin inside her tunic, she pressed it flat against her chest, secure in the knowledge the recent rains meant no shortage of water over the course of the day.

With a sigh, the woman warrior rolled her head back against the rough bulk of the trunk and pondered the events of the morning. Even now, after so much running, it was hard to believe her plan was actually in motion, that at this very moment, thirteen other warriors were also travelling out in a tight arc from Inbhear Ciúin where Bodhmhall alone remained, watching the horizon for signs of smoke.

She had the *bandraoi* to thank for that achievement, of course. Returning to the campsite with Murchú before dawn, she'd been startled to find that Crimall had not only agreed to accompany *Na Cinéaltaí* but had his *fénnid* lined up and ready to depart at her word. It was only later, as they'd descended towards the estuary that Bodhmhall confirmed how, confronted with the choice of continuing the Seeking or being shown up by his sister, the *Clann Baoiscne* man had grudgingly opted for the least embarrassing option.

Just as the *bandraoi* had known he would.

The woman warrior closed her eyes for a moment, appreciating the touch of the sun against her skin, the brush of air across her face, and the flaky crackle of leaves underscored by the pounding of her heart. She'd missed being alone in the forest, she realised. She'd missed that unique and heady sensation of complete absorption, of being reduced to one more minute component of the Great Mother's vast plan.

Opening her eyes, she again looked towards the south-east. Determined to be the one to relocate the *díberg* trail, she'd assigned herself this specific course for, not only did it match the direction the raiders had been following up to this point, it 'fit' the kind of terrain she had in her head that the *díberg* would follow. Those were her own instincts on the matter, of course. There was no certainty she'd got it right and, up to this point, she'd seen no evidence to support such conjectures.

Sighing again, she breathed in deeply through her nostrils, wondering how the other members of the party had fared.

What's your hurry? You'll find out soon enough tomorrow.

And you may not like the result.

With a frown, the Grey One rose to her feet and started her descent. Back on the forest floor, she retrieved the backpack, strapped it on and started downhill with new urgency. By the time the ground began to level off, the thickness of the forest canopy meant the distant hill was once again obscured from view. By keeping one eye on Father Sun however, she was able to maintain her south-easterly route with a fair degree of accuracy, clambering up a tree every now and then to make sure she hadn't veered too far off track.

For the most part, the terrain she passed through was easy enough to traverse. The trees in that section of forest – oak, rowan and elm – were well spaced and although green shoots pushed through the debris of the forest floor, the more substantial undergrowth that might have hindered her passage had withered away over the winter. The resulting ease of access meant she was able to travel swiftly, but it also made it more difficult to guess the route the *díberg* might have taken. Had the raiders travelled this route, then veered off in a completely different direction, without the presence of residual tracks she would simply have no way of knowing. Frustrating though it was, her only option was to put faith in her plan and hope that she, or one of the other warriors, picked up the trail the following day.

By late afternoon, the woman warrior had covered a substantial stretch of ground and the occasional snatches of the hill's bulk glimpsed through the canopy revealed it much closer, eventually looming high over the trees of the forest ahead. Although she was still some distance from her goal, exhausted and conscious of the fading light, she decided to halt for the night at a natural shelter created where an oak had fallen at an angle across an enormous boulder. Long and wide of girth, the tumbled tree was firmly wedged in place, its dense upper branches slanting down against the earth like a wooden screen on either side.

Removing her backpack, the Grey One made the time to set a pair of snares before she entered the shelter. She wasn't greatly optimistic about catching anything, but the routine was a practical one she tended to follow out in the Great Wild when her food supplies were dwindling. Dropping to all fours, she wriggled her way through a gap in the branches, dragging the backpack on the ground behind her and working her way into the area beneath the slightly angled trunk.

To her surprise, the interior turned out to be far more spacious than she'd imagined. Although low enough to oblige her to remain in a sitting or a kneeling position, it extended almost seven paces from the gap where she'd entered to the rough granite surface of the boulder where it abruptly terminated. The thickness of the branches to either side meant the interior was dim and gloomy, although there were several small gaps where light penetrated. If it rained, it was unlikely to pass through those gaps unless a particularly morose Father Sun wept heavier tears than usual. If that was the case, she'd simply retreat closer to the boulder and shelter directly beneath the trunk itself. It wouldn't be the most comfortable of refuges she'd ever had but it wouldn't be the worst either.

Arranging the copious leaf litter into a makeshift mattress alongside the boulder, Liath Luachra unrolled her blanket and lay down, supplementing its heavy wrap with the extra layer of her cloak. For a time, she lay staring up through the gaps in the slanted 'roof' of branches, unable to see anything beyond those gaps except a dull, green blur that grew progressively duller with the encroaching darkness. Despite the cold, she felt snug and comfortable, certainly warmer than the previous night with Murchú. On that occasion, to counter the chill, she's acceded to sharing her cloak and body heat with the distressed *fénnid* … if little else.

She exhaled heavily, wondering how the *Uí Loinge* man was coping tonight, whether it'd been the wisest move to leave him on his own again so soon.

Not that there was anything she could do about it now.

Rolling onto her side, the woman warrior struggled to relax but, despite her fatigue, her mind persistently wandered to the weaknesses in her plan and the multitude of possibilities where it could all go desperately wrong. Despite the confidence of her assertions before the *Clann Baoiscne fian,* she was conscious her plan was little more than a desperate gamble, a last-ditch effort with no certainty of success. The simple truth was that if none of the *Na Cinéaltaí* or the *Clann Baoiscne* warriors found evidence of passage over the course of the following day, any chance of relocating the *díberg* trail, of rescuing Cairenn or confronting Gadra, was well and truly lost.

***

The Grey One must have fallen asleep for at some point during the night she woke, roused by a breathless sense of danger. As always on waking in the depths of the Great Wild, she came to full consciousness immediately and without making the slightest sound. Eyes open, ears alert and listening, she remained completely still, using the full range of her senses to reach out through the darkness and identify what had disturbed her. The cause of her abrupt awakening became apparent all too soon when a distant howl suddenly sounded, lonely and forlorn, through the forest to the north. A moment later, it was taken up and echoed by a second howl and then, by a third.

Na Mactíre. Wolves.

Fully alert now, the woman warrior sat up and looked around, struggling to reassess the murky interior of her refuge from a defensive perspective. Although conscious of the threat a wolf-pack posed after a harsh winter – when they were starving and desperate enough to challenge a healthy human – she didn't feel particularly threatened. To attack her, the pack would first have to come across her scent and, in the vastness of the Great Wild, the chances of that were quite slim. The howling was loud but such sounds could travel a great distance on a

201

windless night, particularly when the animals were positioned at a height. The wolves, therefore, were probably much further away than they seemed, possibly the full stretch of several valleys from her own location. Even if she did have the misfortune of the animals crossing her trail and following it back, she was well armed and confident in her ability to defend herself. With the rock at her back and the impenetrable mesh of the branches to other side, the only realistic option for the animals to come at her was through the same narrow gap by which she'd entered. With the extended reach of a javelin shaft, that gap was easily defended. When she had need to leave her refuge, those same javelins would also allow her to drive the animals off without any major risk to herself.

All the same, the woman warrior decided to take some precautions. Leaving the mattress of flattened leaves, she relocated to the boulder and sat back against its hard surface, one javelin resting across her knees as she faced the little entrance. Confident that her senses would rouse her again should any threat present itself, she leaned her head back and drifted off, lulled to sleep by the undulating chorus of desolate howls.

***

The following morning, the woman warrior awoke rested if a little stiff, her legs and thighs aching from the previous day's run. Pushing herself off the rock, she grabbed the wicker backpack and dragged it behind her as she exited the woody refuge on all fours.

Emerging into the subdued gloom of the pre-dawn forest, she rose to her feet and stretched the pain from her limbs and back, listening to the first tentative chirps of the growing dawn chorus. As the birdsong exploded, Father Sun emerged ponderously from the hills to the east. Despite its tepid appearance, the morning remained cold and patches of a thin frost layered the ground. The gloom prevented any study of the clouds but, cocking her ears, Liath Luachra listened carefully then sniffed the air before allowing herself a small sigh of relief. As far as she could tell, there was no trace of moisture to the air and not a breath of wind. It was going to be a good day for tracking.

Checking her snares, the woman warrior was delighted to find the corpse of a hare in one of them and, pulling it free, deposited it in her backpack, quickly followed by the snare itself. Hauling the weight of the wicker pack onto her back, she affixed it carefully then started towards the distant hill, the odd arrangement of boulders on its summit now clearly visible above the trees to the south-east.

202

Advancing through the forest, she soon struck a shallow river where she paused to refill her skin and took the opportunity to breakfast quietly on smoked fish and cold water. Hunger sated, she looked towards the hill and winced with the sudden realisation that, today, she'd learn with complete certainty if her plan had succeeded or failed.

And the consequences that entailed for the Seeking.

Continuing her path towards the hill, the woman warrior resisted the urge to hurry and, fearful of missing anything, forced herself to maintain a pace slower than the previous day. Although focussed on scanning the ground for evidence of the *díberg's* passage, as the morning progressed, she struggled to repress her mounting apprehension at its continued absence. She was encouraged however, by the fact that her route matched the general direction of the river, glimpsed every now and again through the trees to her left. Had the raiders come this way, their natural inclination would have been to remain close to the water, provided its flow didn't conflict with the direction in which they needed to travel.

Closing on the hill, she emerged from the trees onto a flat section of rocky ground where the base of the tree-coated slopes rose from the surrounding forest. Directly ahead, the hill's bulk dominated the immediate skyline, the boulders she'd originally seen on the summit barely visible from that lower angle. Now that she had a clearer view however, she realised that the 'hill' wasn't a hill but an escarpment, the extremity of a long ridge stretching back to the south-east before it curved sharply around to the right. Midway up the right side of that rocky mass, an enormous triangular outcrop pointed towards the east like a gigantic stone arrowhead.

Two routes were immediately discernible, one to either side of the escarpment. The route to the left led south, the one to the right further southeast. As she considered that fork in the trail, the woman warrior felt a sinking sensation in her stomach for she knew she'd reached an unavoidable juncture and that a critical decision now had to be made. With the barrier of the escarpment lying directly before her, she could no longer continue the course she'd been following since Inbhear Ciúin.

The Grey One champed on her inner cheek as she considered the two options available to her. The path to the left led into a broad valley that continued for some distance before curving out of sight. The river that had aligned with her own movements since she'd first filled her waterskin, also flowed in that direction, its glistening waters coursing loudly along the valley floor. It looked to have picked up several feeder tributaries prior to entering the valley for it had swollen significantly since the last time she'd caught sight of it.

The route to the right was smaller and less dramatic, little more than a curving stretch of rocky ground, enclosed on one side by dense forest and, on the other, by the steep slope of the escarpment and its trailing ridge. Apart from its narrowness relative to the valley route, the limited section of the path that she could see bore no other distinguishing features.

Liath Luachra frowned. Under other circumstances, had she been travelling this way, the valley route – with its convenient water supply – would have been the most obvious one to take. If the *díberg* had come this way, it was also the route they'd most likely have taken. Unfortunately, she had no way of knowing whether it offered the most direct path to their final destination or not. Given the potentially dire consequences of choosing incorrectly, she had no choice but to give both paths equal consideration.

Cursing softly, the woman warrior glanced anxiously towards the valley as she started along the south-eastern trail. Despite her conviction the *díberg* would have taken the former, she couldn't commit to that path until she'd explored the lesser route further, investigating it sufficiently to discount it at least.

Taking off at a run, she followed the long curve of the rocky ground, making no effort to search for tracks as the hard, irregular surface retained no imprints. By the time she'd closed to within a hundred paces of the outcrop, she was breathing heavily and already considering the possibility of turning back. She decided to press ahead however, continue a little further to the stretch of rough ground directly beneath the outcrop's bulk.

Stumbling into the shadowed space beneath the looming rock, she paused briefly to catch her breath and look around, her eyes immediately falling on a small scatter of debris on the ground ten paces or so from where she'd halted. Unable to work out what it was, she peered at it curiously before trotting a little closer. It turned out to consist of several grey, cord-like lumps, tapered at one end and unquestionably biological in origin.

Wolf droppings.

Most likely from the very pack that had disturbed her sleep the previous night.

Another good reason to turn back.

Picking up a nearby stick, she crouched to poke at one of the larger turds, splitting it apart and spreading the faeces to reveal individual strands of hair and several bone fragments within the dark matter.

Not that hungry, then.

Tossing the stick aside, the woman warrior straightened up again and looked back the way she'd come, studying the stretch of treeline for any sign of the animals. Running her eyes along the trees, it struck her then that she was looking at another long ridge, one far lower than the escarpment to her rear but almost indistinguishable beneath the blanket of forest.

Turning her gaze towards the south, she considered the treeline of the route ahead, her eyes coming to rest on a section of dark shadow three hundred paces from where she was standing. Clucking her tongue softly, she continued to stare then slowly started towards it, breaking into a run after several steps.

It was only as the woman warrior drew closer that her suspicions were confirmed. The 'shadow' was a break in the treeline, a distinct cutting into the trees at the base of the ridge. Coming to a halt in front of the narrow gap, she discovered an overgrown trail that cut directly up the lower slope for twenty paces or more before commencing an increasingly twisted path up the ridge's steeper incline.

The Grey One considered the trail with a frown. Although intrigued by this unexpected evidence of human activity in such an area of wilderness, she was conscious that exploring it further might be a waste of time. The trail was an old one that looked to have been created many years earlier. More importantly, it showed no signs of recent passage, at least none she could see.

Inhaling deeply, she considered the possibilities. The well-established nature of the trail suggested some permanent occupation or habitation nearby, even if no-one had used this specific path in the last few days. If someone resided in this area however, there was a good chance they'd have noticed at least some sign of a party as big as the *díberg's* passing by.

Presuming of course that they'd come this way.

She bit her lip. That question at least, was one a local inhabitant might be able to confirm, one way or the other.

Stepping through the gap, Liath Luachra proceeded swiftly up the trail, maintaining a steady pace as she ascended the incline. Mid-way up the slope, she found herself at a series of cliffs that ran along the western side of the ridge. Following the path at the base of the cliffs, she struck a wide aperture that cut through the rock face and led into a narrow canyon grown thick with pine and underlying forest scrub.

Passing through that constricted opening, she worked her way through the tightly crowded trees, skirting a small marsh that had formed on the canyon's lower right side. After an extended stretch up another gentle incline, the trees finally opened out to reveal a small clearing containing several axe-dropped trunks and weathered stumps. Watching from the shadows of the pines, Liath Luachra considered this new evidence of human occupation, noting the furred nature of the axe scars on the trunks, something that suggested some time had passed since the trees had originally been cut.

Continuing onwards, past the clearing for a hundred paces, the trees opened out again and the canyon terminated abruptly at a curving arc of high, steeply slanted cliffs. Although crowned by green mountain ash, the rocky crags were completely bare of vegetation and gave the area a stark and hostile appearance.

On the flat ground to the west of the cliffs, Liath Luachra discovered the source of the water feeding the lower marsh: a compact but natural stone catchwater pooling runoff from the surrounding slopes. In a heavy downpour, rainwater would overflow from that stony catchment and stream down the western side of the canyon. At present however, that flow had been reduced to a trickle.

More interesting from the Grey One's perspective, however, was a domed roundhouse of wicker and thatch a little further left of the catchwater pool. To the woman warrior's eyes, the structure had a dilapidated and hoary appearance. The heavy fur flap that sealed its doorway had greyed from exposure while the building itself showed signs of many sporadic repairs since its initial construction. The strip of ground separating the hut from the pool held a soot-stained fire pit and a line of four, head-high wooden poles with flax filaments fastened to the tips. Several items were attached to the filaments, mostly small, dried out fox and hare skulls but also withered feathers and ragged pieces of grey cloth.

Staying in her refuge among the pines, the Grey One hunched down to study the roundhouse more closely, one hand resting on the pommel of *Gleas Gan Ainm*. The structure's obvious age, the established infrastructure of the fire pit and the fallen trees suggested the canyon had been inhabited over a prolonged period, however the unmistakable look of neglect suggested those same inhabitants had deserted it.

The woman warrior bit her lip as she ran her eyes around the compact semicircle of rock to the rear of the canyon. The open ground and the absence of vegetation meant there was no realistic concealment apart from the trees where she was currently hidden or the interior of the roundhouse. Conscious of passing time, yet driven by instincts to explore a little further, she rose and stepped out into the open.

'I see the hut!'

Her greeting rang loud in the rocky confines and although she waited, she saw no reaction to her call, no movement or activity of any kind. Moving with care, she started towards the hut, eyes locked firmly on the fur flap, ready to charge forward if it made the slightest twitch.

Six paces from the structure, she paused and called again.

'I see the hut!'

Once again, she was answered with silence, a solitary hush emphasized by the eerie rattle of the skulls against the poles as they shifted in the breeze. The fur flap blocking the doorway remained resolutely still.

Taking another step, she halted abruptly, thinking to hear a shuffle of movement from the hut's interior, but one so faint she wasn't sure if she'd imagined it or not. A chill trickled down her spine as she closed swiftly on the structure, positioning herself by the curved wall to the right of the entrance, confident the thick mud-daubed surface prevented her from being observed from within.

Carefully unsheathing *Gleas Gan Ainm,* she edged the blade forward, easing its tip under the edge of the flap. Sliding the blade mid-way down the doorway, she drove it in deeper and, with one deft movement, flipped the covering back onto the domed crest of the roof.

Heart pounding, the woman warrior gripped her weapon tightly, the sweat from her palms soaking into the pommel bindings as she prepared to respond or strike out at any threat emerging through the entryway. Off to her left, the clatter of the bones banging against the poles grew noisier and more insistent as the wind began to rise.

Observing no sign of danger, the woman warrior edged closer and glanced in at an angle through the structure's entrance. Despite the light streaming through the doorway, it was hard to see much of the interior beyond a bright rectangle of beaten earth floor.

Darting across to the other side of the doorway, she placed herself lightly against the curving wall. It was doubtful anyone could cast a javelin within that restricted space or effectively launch an attack through the narrow entrance, but she didn't intend to take any chances.

Once again, edging closer to the doorway, she cast a quick glance inside before yanking her head back. This time she managed to catch a glimpse of the other side of the interior, including a rough bed of moss and rushes with a skeletal pair of feet protruding from one end. Pulling back, Liath Luachra heard a sound like a soft wheeze or a moan. Whoever was stretched on that bed still breathed.

Reassured now that there was no real danger, the woman warrior plunged *Gleas Gan Ainm,* blade first, into the earth and drew the short-bladed knife free from the back of her belt. Still to taste blood, the weapon had no name on it and, although she didn't think she'd need it, previous experience had aptly demonstrated the usefulness of a sharp blade when you weren't entirely certain what you were stepping into.

Slipping through the doorway at a crouch, she held the knife at the ready, poised to defend herself from anything – or anyone – attempting to strike her. The only thing that did strike her however was the smell: a nauseating tang of an unwashed body mingled with the pungency of stale urine. As Liath Luachra's eyes adjusted to the gloom, she could make out the source of this stink more clearly: a figure lying flat on the crude rush mattress, cocooned and – apart from his feet – almost completely engulfed by a pair of threadbare blankets. With the exception of the mattress and its occupant, the roundhouse contained little else apart from an empty wooden bucket, a pair of flat, flameless fish-oil lamps, two metal pots and a wicker basket filled with tools and different cooking utensils. There was also a firepit that contained nothing but ashes.

The woman warrior's nose creased at the stench but she replaced the knife in its scabbard and shuffled a little closer.

'You,' she whispered. 'Are you alive?'

There was another vague wheeze, a minute shifting of covers but no other response.

Leaning forward, the woman warrior grasped the tatty blankets and pulled them down, starting with surprise as the figure's wizened head was exposed to the light. The skin was so thin it was almost transparent and, combined with the sunken eye sockets, gave the head a horrific skull-like appearance. That ghoulish aspect was further reinforced by threads of stringy, corpse-like white hair, crushed flat against the figure's patchy skull. Although the skin of the forehead was so thin it bore no wrinkles, the Grey One was still able to make out the faded trace of what had once been a gloriously ornate tattoo.

The eyebrows, the only part of the face to have any substance or colour, looked to have been painted on and, oddly, that indistinct paint appeared to have run for vague streaks lined both cheeks like the trail of dried-out black tears. Beneath a spindly neck meanwhile, the emaciated torso was little more than bare skin and bone, the former having all the texture of ancient spiderwebs, the latter skeletal and fragile. Miraculously, despite the deteriorated physical condition, the figure was indeed alive for a pair of grey eyes peered out at her through slitted eyelids. They looked glazed but seemed cognizant of her presence.

'Old Fath-,' she began but then paused. She wasn't entirely sure of this individual's gender and the age-damaged asexuality of those physical features did little to help.

'Old One, do you hear me?'

With no response forthcoming, Liath Luachra reached inside her tunic to retrieve the waterskin and yanked the stopper free with her teeth. Ignoring the smell, she slid a hand under the Old One's thin neck and shoulders and propped the ancient figure up, struck by the lightness, the fragility of that body. Raising the waterskin with her free hand, the woman warrior dribbled a few drops into the toothless mouth. As the beads of water slipped inside those desiccated lips, she saw them stir faintly.

Easing the genderless creature softly back onto the bed of soiled rushes, the woman warrior draped the blanket back in place, took one of the metal pots and exited the hut. Free of the stagnant air, she inhaled deeply, relieved to be out of the stinking confines. Tossing a quick glance back at the aging structure, she pondered at the Old One's presence in this solitary place, alone in the isolation of the Great Wild.

This will be your destiny one day, Liath Luachra.

If a blade doesn't take you first.

She shivered, unsure which of the two potential fates scared her most.

Fetching the hare from her backpack. The woman warrior set a small fire in the firepit by the pool. She filled the metal pot with water and placed it in the flames, skinning and boning the hare while she waited for the water to boil. Chopping the meat into little morsels, she dropped them into the pot, adding some watercress and whatever herbs she could find within the immediate vicinity of the pool. Finally, she sat by the fire as the stew slowly thickened, kept one eye on Father Sun's lethargic passage across the sky.

You don't have time for this.

Reaching down for some more pieces of wood, she added them to the fire.

Cairenn's life flitters between your fingers. Gadra slips further away with every breath you waste in this place.

This time she snarled at the vexing voice in her head. Bowing her head, she broke some wood for the fire into smaller pieces and did her best to ignore it.

Eventually, the water boiled off sufficiently to create a thin stew and, pouring the reduced mixture into a wooden bowl, the woman warrior returned to the roundhouse. There, putting the bowl aside, she lit one of the small, fish-oil lamps and although the dull, yellow light it produced did little to illuminate the interior, the burning smell of scented oil helped to smother the stench.

Tapping the ancient figure with her finger, the woman warrior received no sign of acknowledgement, so she waved the bowl under the Old One's face instead, allowing the meaty vapor to drift upward. This time, the Old One's eyes cracked wide open, the resulting slits revealing two dark and rheumy orbs with dried mucus at the corners.

'Have a sup, Old One.'

Using a wooden spoon from the basket, the woman warrior started to feed the ancient figure, scooping tiny portions of stew from the bowl then dribbling each one laboriously between the desiccated lips. After several such servings, her efforts were rewarded with a distinct stir and the greedy flicker of a tongue lapping at the meaty juice.

The Old One hasn't eaten in many days.

The Grey One spooned in a few more drops. That seemed to revive the Old One further for the eyes took on even greater awareness and, eventually, with her help, the decrepit figure was able to sit up, wrapped in the tatty blankets and lean back against the curve of the wall for support.

To the woman warrior's surprise, the Old One gave a satisfied, almost bliss-filled sigh then raised a bleary pair of eyes to regard her.

'There's nothing ...' The voice was a whisper. Faint and crackly, it petered out briefly before starting again. 'There's nothing that makes food ... so good ... as a great hunger.'

Liath Luachra considered the wizened form before her. 'Who are you, Old One? Why do you sit out here alone in the wilderness?'

The Old One grinned toothlessly at that, the shriveled features making the expression look more like a leer than a smile. 'I prepare ... for a journey.'

'It'll be a short journey,' she responded bluntly. 'You're wasting away from thirst and hunger.'

'That much I know,' the Old One snapped back, and Liath Luachra had to conceal the bitter grin that tightened the corners of her mouth. There were signs of life in that withered husk yet.

'I travel ... to the Dark Lands.'

The woman warrior grunted in sudden comprehension. The shriveled figure sitting with her was a *Marbhán* – a Lifeless One, isolated in the wilderness to prepare for what some called the 'Breathing Death'.

And she, in her ignorance, had blundered in, disrupting the final ritual, upsetting the Old One's painstaking preparations for passing.

Liath Luachra dropped her eyes to the ground and awkwardly picked at the threads of her leggings. 'I …' she began but then lapsed into clumsy silence. She had no idea what to say.

The Old One's head shook, two vague movements from side to side that were barely perceptible in the gloom of the hut. 'No … importance. The Dark Lands …' The voice trailed off as those labouring lungs struggled to inhale and exhale. 'The Dark Lands bear infinite patience. They are … unharried. People … the sole creatures to rush to their death.'

The shriveled creature shifted slightly, the blankets drawn closer about the bony shoulders. 'I fast my way to the Dark Lands. A growth in my chest. Of late … the pain grew piercing. I could feel … flesh rot from the insides.'

Liath Luachra said nothing. Given the smell emanating from the makeshift bed, the claim seemed plausible.

'My children are passed. My tribe are no more. There is no reason … to stride the Great Mother. Instead I set … for the Breathing Death.'

The Old One paused, visibly exhausted from the effort of talking. After several painful, protracted wheezes, the words came again.

'Three days into my final rest … my life began to fade … but so, too, did the pain. For that I am thankful.'

The ancient figure shrugged, the barest of movements beneath the thin fabric of the blanket. 'Now, dragged … back to the light. This corpse has not lost its taste for meat … still hungers for sweet …sweet, succulent fat. Even now … on the cusp … my body fights me … fights my decision … to end the pain. Despite the knowing that pain will return … as life returns, it hungers for life. And meat.'

The Old One sank back against the wall, completely spent. Liath Luachra awkwardly rubbed the back of her neck, eager to be free of this excruciating situation and to continue her search for the raiders, despite the increasing likelihood she wasn't on the correct path.

'You were sent,' the Old One declared suddenly. 'The ancestors sent you here.'

Liath Luachra looked at the corpse-like figure, her left eyebrow cocked in a skeptical arch. She very much doubted that.

'The ancestors didn't send me. I have my own reasons for coming here.'

'Yes. You seek … you seek … the *díberg*.'

Liath Luachra started in surprise. 'You've seen the *díberg*?'

'Yes.'

'How did you know I wa-'. Liath Luachra paused in mid-sentence. The question was a foolish one. Out in the wilderness, if the Old One had seen no-one for an age, then spotted a *díberg* and several days later, a warrior, the conclusion was all too obvious. 'Where were they travelling from?' she asked instead.

'From … the north-west. A group of … fourteen warriors.'

Fourteen!

Inwardly reeling at this latest escalation in numbers, the Grey One concealed her shock by filling the silence with another question.

'Can you tell me in which direction they travelled?'

'I can tell you that … and more.'

With that, the Old One lapsed into silence. Liath Luachra waited but it soon became clear no further words were coming.

'You seek an exchange for the sharing of knowledge?'

The Old One's red-rimmed eyes held her gaze.

Liath Luachra sighed. 'Very well. What is it you seek? I've little enough to offer you and you've already benefitted from the hare, the one item of worth that I carried.'

'As you benefit from … my shelter. My hospitality.'

Despite the fragility of that whispered response, there was an iron determination behind it that caused Liath Luachra to burst into laughter, a rare and airy tinkling very much at odds with her menacing comportment.

'That's hardly a fair exchange.'

'Reparation. For your intrusion. For dragging me back … from the Dark Lands.'

Liath Luachra exhaled in frustration. That was an argument she couldn't counter.

The Old One regarded the woman warrior through those rheumy, red eyes. 'You are a taker … of lives. A dealer of death. I smell … spilled blood … on your breath.'

Liath Luachra nodded. She was surprised the ancient figure could smell anything given the stench in the roundhouse but, again, this was something she couldn't deny.

'That is my price. My body … resists. I have no strength to ease … to ease back to Breathing Death.'

The Old One shifted slightly as though trying to find a more comfortable position. When the next whispers came however, there was a distinguishable tremor to the words.

'At night. I hear wolves … about the hut. Sniffing, poking at the edges. Until now … they have not tried … to force the flap. But soon

… their hunger will grow. I would be in the Dark Lands… before they feed.'

A fragile claw of a hand emerged from beneath the blanket and came to rest on the Grey One's knee.

'*An bhfuil margadh againn?*' Do we have an arrangement?

The Grey One considered that skeletal frame for a time. Finally, she dipped her head. '*Tá margadh againn.*' We have an arrangement.

Satisfied, the Old One raised the blanket once more, just below the protruding chin.

'When you leave this canyon… at the bottom of the ridge … there is an … escarpment.'

'Yes.'

On the far side … a valley. A river runs through it.'

Once again, struggling to breathe, the Old One had to pause before continuing.

'The waterway is wide … but shallow. Not difficult for one … of your limber frame. Three days past … I saw the *díberg*. On the far bank where …where the stream enters the river. They looked a cruel group.'

Liath Luachra's features hardened and she glared darkly at the ancient creature. 'Your ragged corpse hasn't breached the threshold of this roundhouse for several days at least. How could you have seen the *díberg* three days ago?'

'*An tíolacadh.*'

'*An tíolacadh!*' The woman warrior made no effort to hide the scorn in her voice. 'You're saying you …you have *An tíolacadh?*'

'The … final gift. An exchange … for sacrifice to the Breathing Death.'

Liath Luachra breathed deeply, her cold regard belying the fury she felt at having wasted her precious time on this deluded wretch.

'If my answer displeases, you can … always kill me,' the Old One whispered, a disturbing eagerness in its eyes.

'Treacherous creature. I'll stake you on the ground outside the hut, watch the wolves feed on you.'

A flicker of panic passed across the Old One's face, flittering on those haggard features like the ghost of an emotion. 'I do … not lie. I have seen … the ones you seek. Moving south. Following the valley. Had I looked again … I'd have seen them return … that same way. Yesterday.'

Although still raging at the Old One's lunatic assertions, Liath Luachra couldn't help but regard that wretched corpse in consternation. 'What do you mean they'd return yesterday?' she demanded.

The *díberg* travelled … up the valley. For more than a day. Only to find … the far end flooded, the route clogged with … marsh to either side. That's … that's always the way with rains at …With rains at this time of year. The ground … in that part of the valley … holds water. It takes … an age to drain. In winter … that route is closed. They'd have no choice … but to backtrack. Take … the south-easterly route … instead.'

Spent from the effort of talking, the Old One sank back against the wall once again. The woman warrior watched as the wizened figure struggled to inhale, the ruined chest beneath the tatty blanket rising and sinking in feeble movements.

'And you saw all this with …' Struggling with her unbridled cynicism, the woman warrior paused, unable to finish the sentence.

'*An tíolacadh*. It is … the truth,' he managed at last. 'The *díberg* … they had girls … girls in chains.'

Liath Luachra started in surprise. The Old One couldn't possibly have known about the girls …

Unless he had actually seen them.

'The warriors and the girls … travelled that same spot … yesterday. If you hurry … you could fi-'

Before the Old One could conclude that laboured sentence however, the woman warrior had lunged to her feet and was scrambling through the low doorway. Abandoning her backpack and javelins where they lay, she hurtled downhill towards the trees, using her momentum and the full weight of her body to slam vegetation and pine branches aside in her haste to reach the canyon entrance.

Achieving the rocky gap, she plunged through and onto the cliff path, retracing her steps along the overgrown trail at a run. Hitting the steeper incline, she increased her speed, ignoring the beaten path as she leapt into the scrub and slid precariously down the forested slope.

The bulk of the rocky escarpment loomed welcomingly into view through the treeline cutting as the Grey One reached the foot of the ridge. Pausing only to assure herself the way was clear, she lurched back onto the rocky trail, following it back to the triangular outcrop at breakneck speed, then onto the open ground at the far end of the escarpment.

She was panting painfully by the time she reached the fork in the trail where she'd paused earlier that morning. Chest heaving, she bent forward with her hands on her knees, trying to catch her breath while she stared towards the river. Scanning the nearest bank for any potential crossing points, she struggled to compress the complex mix of fear and excitement bubbling up in her chest.

In hindsight of course, she knew there'd been no real thought behind her response to the Old One's words, no consideration of how unlikely or implausible those claims had been. The reality was that having pushed her tracking skills to the limits, exhausted every trick in her arsenal, every potential alternative she could think of, she'd nothing left to fall back on. Nothing but instinct. Ultimately, she'd thrown everything into one final act of desperation.

The grim truth of course, was that the Old One had probably dispatched her on a fool's errand, possibly out of sheer vindictiveness at her disturbance of the *Marbhán* ritual, possibly out of an insane self-delusion brought on by his physical deterioration. Either way …

Driving those depressing possibilities from her mind, the woman warrior sucked in one last lungful of air and started to run.

Hurtling towards the valley, Liath Luachra followed the long stretch of it down the left of the escarpment, eventually working her way towards a wide depression in the riverbank, part of a wider basin that spread across to the far bank as well. Here, the river seemed much shallower due to its greater breadth, certainly less deep than that of the water before and after, where the banks were much narrower. All in all, it looked the most obvious and practical place to cross from the other side.

By the time she'd reached the depression, the Grey One was breathing heavily again but she ignored her fatigue as she dropped to a crouch and started examining the ground. Commencing at the area where the water surged into the low bank, she worked her way upwards, moving from side to side within that wide indentation to cover ground faster.

The earth nearest the bank revealed nothing: no prints, no obvious overturned stones, no unnatural depressions, nothing to indicate anyone had passed that way. Despite that demoralising absence of sign, the Grey One assuaged her fears with the knowledge the river would almost certainly have been far higher a day earlier due to the rains. If the raiders had crossed at this point, any trace of their passage in the lower section of the bank had probably been washed away before the water level dropped again.

Mid-way up the side of the bank however, the continuing absence of sign caused her confidence to waver further. Forcing herself to concentrate, the woman warrior continued to scan the earth, determined to keep searching right up to the area where the incline flattened out.

When she finally reached the lip of the bank however, and still with nothing to show for her efforts, the Grey One slowly straightened up and turned a glum eye to Father Sun, now hanging well beyond the midpoint of its daily arc.

They didn't come this way.

Her shoulders slumped. She breathed deeply. Thinking of the Old One, she felt a brief surge of bitterness but then forced herself to let it go, knowing that there was no-one to blame. The Old One was most likely insane and, as for herself, she'd done everything she possibly could. Now, there was no choice but to accept the fact that she'd never been on the raiders' trail, that it was up to one of her comrades to find any trace they'd left behind. All she could do was climb to a higher point and scan the horizon in the hope she'd see the signal indicating they'd been more successful.

Exhaling slowly, she started back towards the fork, moving far more slowly now, her pace steady but subdued. Leaving the river, she'd almost covered half the distance to the junction when the toe of her boot pressed down on something small and unexpectedly hard. Pausing to lift her foot, she looked down then crouched to examine the object she'd stood on: a short length of bone, tapered into a smooth triangular shape and sanded to a smooth finish. At its centre, it had two small holes cut alongside each other.

It was a button. A bone button.

Liath Luachra stared at it numbly for several heartbeats then picked it up and rolled its cool smoothness between her fingers. A common enough object in a settlement or other places where people gathered, it was markedly out of place here in the middle of nowhere and could only have come to rest on this spot by falling loose from a cloak or other clothing. The lack of any dust layer however, suggested it couldn't have lain there for very long.

Which meant that someone had dropped it recently.

And the only people likely to have passed this way recently …

Collapsing back onto the grass, the woman warrior released a croaky chuckle of relief.

The Old One wasn't insane. He'd truly had the right of it. The raiders had come this way.

And now they were little more than a day ahead.

***

216

Back at the roundhouse, the Old One displayed no surprise at the woman warrior's return, at least none that she could make out on those fiercely wrinkled features.

'It seems you had the right of it,' she said as she took a seat on the beaten earth alongside the bed. The *díberg* did pass this way. They retraced their path just as you described. It took me some time but I found their tracks again further along the southern trail.'

The Old One wheezed at the Grey One's report, the soft reedy exhalations barely audible even within the confines of the roundhouse. The woman warrior observed the impact of her news with interest, curious as to what kind of reaction it'd elicit. She had expected her confirmation of the raiders' presence to trigger some measure of smugness or vindication given her earlier scepticism, but nothing emanated from that crinkled corpse beyond complete indifference and resignation. As far as the Old One was concerned, the *margadh* had been fulfilled. Now, there was nothing of interest beyond her own honouring of that deal.

But Liath Luachra wasn't quite ready yet.

'Forgive me, Old One but I have need of further insight.'

The corpse-like figure returned her gaze with an air of overwhelming weariness but made no response.

'Can you tell me where the rocky trail leads? The trail to the south?'

The Old One's sigh was little more than an imagined whisper. 'Wilderness. Many days ... of wilderness.' An emaciated hand reached up to touch the faded forehead tattoo. 'Then ... territory of *Na Gréasaigí.*'

Liath Luachra frowned. *Na Gréasaigí* – The Illustrated People. The name wasn't one she was familiar with.

'Then... Lands of *Na Brígiantaí.* Fearsome warriors.'

Again, a name she didn't recognise.

The Old One's head dipped silently. 'This is ... all the knowledge ... I have to share.' The rheumy eyes raised once again to regard her fearfully. 'You will keep your word?'

Liath Luachra breathed deeply. 'Yes. The wolves will not have you.'

The Old One nodded faintly but whether there was relief or satisfaction on those ruined features, the Grey One could not tell. An awkward silence followed the exchange.

'Will you have some more stew?' the woman warrior suggested. 'I've given my word. You may as well sate your body's desire one last time.'

The Old One's eyes flickered greedily to the wooden bowl. 'Yes.'

'Very well.'

The Grey One dipped the wooden spoon back into the meaty bowl that she'd reheated on her return. Once again, she raised it to the Old One's lips. As the viscous drops dripped inside those grey lips, the old figure's head nodded, eyes closing in blissful pleasure.

'Meat!'

Liath Luachra poured a little more stew into the bowl. 'I'm not the best of meal makers,' she confessed.

'Good … enough.'

The Old One sipped a little more, a thin smile forming along the dried-out lips, eyes closing to appreciate the meaty flavour. That dreamy expression remained frozen on those wrinkled features as Liath Luachra withdrew her short knife from the Old One's heart. It came free with a single tug. There was hardly any resistance, hardly any blood.

And with that, the Grey One understood she finally had the name on her weapon: *Lann An Chroí Deannachúil* – Blade of the Dusty Heart.

Wiping the blade on the tattered blankets, Liath Luachra got to her feet and rearranged the fragile body back on the bed, tugging the blankets free and then using them to cover the brittle corpse. With one last glance at those shrunken remains, she sighed and exited the roundhouse.

Outside, the wind had dropped and the air was still. In the pine trees below the roundhouse, a single blackbird sang its slow and fluty song, the shrill, wide-ranging notes ringing loudly through the silence of the canyon, underscored by the slow, steady drip of the catchwater to the woman warrior's rear.

Liath Luachra breathed deeply and looked up at Father Sun, now beaming down warmly at her as though pleased by her actions. Sheathing her blade, she realised her hands were shaking badly, the compressed stress of the last two days finally finding an outlet.

Slumped, exhausted, on the ground near the blackened fire pit, Liath Luachra knew that by now, the other members of her party would be watching the horizon for any sign of smoke. Too tired to move, she wondered at the tangible change to the air. Just a little earlier, convinced the Seeking was over, the afternoon had pressed upon her like a gloomy burden. Now …

She looked around and sighed then slowly lumbered to her feet.

She had a fire to light. A *díberg* to catch. A girl to rescue.

And a ghost to kill.

This story will be completed in **<u>Liath Luachra: The Metal Men</u>**.

Historical And Creative Notes:

Liath Luachra: The Seeking is the first in a two-part story to be completed with the forthcoming *Liath Luachra: The Metal Men*. As usual, with these books I've used the available information on pre-historic Ireland (generally sourced from academic or archaeological sources) to recreate the natural and social world in which Liath Luachra and her contemporaries would have lived.

One of the aspects I delve into a little deeper with this book is the workings of 'tribes', at least in terms of how they related to ancient Ireland. The concept of 'tribe' (*'tuath'* or *'treibh'* in Irish) is one that most westerners are familiar with on an intellectual level. Due to the individualised, 'nation'-based societies in which we live however, most of us don't really have a practical understanding of how tribal systems function or how they might impact on human interaction and behaviour.

There are many different definitions of 'tribe' with most English-language explanatory texts usually defining it in the form of a human population that has the basic elements of:

- a common ancestry; and

- a common/homogenous culture

It's a fundamental part of human nature for people to come together, not only for social interaction but for the purpose of survival in threatening or trying circumstances. The established truth where human beings are concerned, is that over the longer term, groups of people operate (and survive) far more effectively than individuals. That's particularly the case where an established interdependency exists between their members and it's summed up nicely in the old Gaelic saying *'Maireann na daoine ar scáil a chéile'* – It's in the shadow of one another that people endure.

In ancient Ireland, where the population was substantially smaller than it is today, the most natural groupings would have been those based on familial bonds. Like all families however, once those groups reached a certain size (and the interdependency or internal bonds between people weakened), members would have 'moved out', splitting away from the larger group to form sub-tribes, some eventually growing large enough to be recognised by others as tribes in their own right. Certain tribes of course, would have gone the opposite way, combining with other tribes to form much larger tribal confederations.

One aspect of tribal life that many modern – particularly western – definitions tend to overlook, is the importance of a common geographical territory or 'homeland' in which tribes operate or over which they hold authority (even nomadic tribes have established routes they follow). This element is important as land 'roots' the society living on it. Over a long period of occupation, it allows the establishment of strong interactions with – and connections to – the land, that strengthen tribal identity. This is one of the reasons, tribal identity tends to be far stronger and encourages far greater loyalty than 'national' identity'.

Losing authority or control over a territory (as expressed by a tribe's continued occupation or presence on it) – would have had a deleterious effect in that it separated tribal members from their established cultural/societal history and stories – critical factors that defined them. Nowadays, many western nations struggle to understand tribal models as they don't fit neatly into their paradigm and/or systems of governance. As something that doesn't align with their concept of 'nationhood', some nations simply don't want to.

That's a short and very simplistic take on tribal dynamics, of course and, hopefully, it helps to provide some context around the ferocity with which tribes in these books defend their territory. These, and other tribal dynamics of course, would also have had major ramifications for an *éclann* like Liath Luachra – something I also try to cover in these books.

The not-so-true stuff:

Despite my best attempts to make my books as historically and culturally accurate as possible, some of the elements I've introduced are fictional. The *Marbhán* ritual, for example, described in the final chapter, is complete fancy on my part, based in part on rituals from other cultures that I've read about but of which I have no personal experience. Theoretically, it's possible such rituals may have occurred in ancient Ireland but there's certainly no evidence to suggest they did.

In addition, although I've mostly steered clear of the Fenian Cycle narratives to date with previous titles in this series, this book establishes clear links to them (and to my own Fionn mac Cumhaill Series) through the introduction of characters such as Bodhmhall ua Baoiscne, Tréanmór and Crimall – all members of the fabled *Clann Baoiscne*. It should be noted however, that in the original Fenian Cycle stories, all three of these figures appear in very limited forms, sometimes as little more than a name in a single sentence or as a passing reference. As a result, the characterisations and personification that appear in these books – as with those of Liath Luachra – are my own invention and should not be treated as historic.

Where to next?

This two-part story will be completed later in 2021 with the release of *Liath Luachra: The Metal Men* and although I don't intend to give too much of the story away, it will provide resolution for most of the plotlines in this book. After that, any further books in the series will depend how well the two books are received. Either way, I'd like to thank those of you who've followed this story this far and, in particular, those of you who've contacted me directly and made the effort to write a review.

Go raibh mile maith agaibh! (literally, a thousand good things to you!)

Brian O'Sullivan: Feb 2021

If you'd like to receive an update on when I'll be releasing the next Liath Luachra book (or any other project), you can sign up for the New Release email at the Irish Imbas website. This email only goes out 1-2 times a year.

Alternatively, if you're interested in more regular updates, aspects of the creative process, bits and bobs on Irish culture and history, reviews and other articles, feel free to sign up to my **monthly newsletter Vóg** *– also at the Irish Imbas website. This goes out 10-11 times a year.*

Liath Luachra: The Grey One

1st/2nd century Ireland: A land of tribal affiliations, secret alliances and treacherous rivalries.

The woman warrior Liath Luachra has survived two brutal years fighting with mercenary war party "The Friendly Ones" but now the winds are shifting. Dispatched on a murderous errand where nothing is as it seems, she must survive a group of treacherous comrades, the unwanted advances of her battle leader and a personal history that might be her own undoing.

Clanless and friendless, she can count on nothing but her wits, her fighting skills and her natural ferocity to see her through.

Woman warrior, survivor, killer and future guardian to Irish hero Fionn mac Cumhaill – this is her story.

A sample of what the reviewers say:

"In the legends of Fionn mac Cumhaill, Liath Luachra is an intriguing name with minimal context but in Brian O'Sullivan's adaptions she becomes a most fascinating and formidable character in her own right. Her backstory is a great read; brigands

and bloodshed, second-guessings and double-crossings. This is an Ancient Ireland that is entrancing and savage, much like Liath Luachra herself."

"I re-immersed myself in the very believable world the author creates and couldn't put the book down until I had finished it. It shed so much light on the character of Liath - her grim experiences and her strength in the face of adversity. I am now going back to reread the other books, which I am sure will be all the richer for a greater understanding of Liath. You don't often come across such a compelling hero(ine), written with such depth and understanding."

"This is a fast-paced traverse through bush trails and battles with a female heroine who is commanding and fascinating."

"As always, the plotting is riveting — full of twists and turns — and the action is full on, hell for leather. If you like Games of Thrones style dramas with a strong splash of Celtic culture, this is a book you'll enjoy!"

'Once again Brian O'Sullivan has created a thrilling historical drama. Liath Luachra provides strong ties to his other books (although each also stands alone very well). I think it's the depth of knowledge and research that adds the extra dimension that appeals to me, but I really liked the fast pace, the developed relationships and the writing style.'

Beara: Dark Legends

[The Beara Trilogy – Book 1]

Nobody knows much about reclusive historian Muiris (Mos) O'Súilleabháin except that he doesn't share his secrets freely. Mos, however, has a *"sixth sense for history, a unique talent for finding lost things"*.

Reluctantly lured from seclusion, despite his own misgivings, Mos is hired to locate the final resting place of legendary Irish hero, Fionn mac Cumhaill. Confronted by a thousand-year old mystery, the distractions of a beguiling circus performer and a lethal competitor, Mos must draw on his knowledge of Gaelic lore to defy his enemies and survive his own family history in Beara.

Beara: Dark Legends is the first in a trilogy of unforgettable Irish thrillers. Propulsive, atmospheric and darkly humorous, *Dark Legends* introduces an Irish hero like you've never seen before. Nothing you thought you knew about Ireland will ever be the same again.

A sample of what the reviewers say:

"A great tale with all the elements of a "Who dunnit" all woven into modern and ancient Irish history and mythology."

"Fantasic book - couldnt put it down. A 'MUST' read! original Irish thriller, historical novel, mystery novel, best book I've read in years."

"O'Sullivan has done an amazing job of introducing a culture that many would say is dying and using it as the basis for a unique and exciting thriller. I think I've learned more about Irish history and the Irish language in this one book than I have in many years of school and television, without it once feeling forced or jaded."

"A great mixture of a strong story and strong characters, dark (some very dark) themes and wonderfully evocative descriptions of the wild Irish landscape, interspersed with ancient Irish lore running throughout the book."

"Excellent story, very well though out, many twists and turns that weren't expected. Thoroughly enjoyed the main character Mos and his no nonsense-take no crap attitude to life, he says what most of us often probably think but are too polite to say, highly entertaining!"

"O'Sullivan's cast of international characters enliven this tale of archaeological intrigue, magic, murder and sex, set mainly in West Cork, Ireland. Dual story lines, across different time zones, reveal secrets of Irish spirituality, ancient lore and language."

Fionn: Defence of Ráth Bládhma:

[The Fionn mac Cumhaill Series: Book 1]

Irish Bestseller and SPFBO Competition 2016 Finalist

1st/2nd century Ireland: A time of strife and treachery. Political ambition and inter-tribal conflict has set the country on edge, testing the strength of long-established alliances.

Following their victory at the battle of Cnucha, Clann Morna are hungry for power. Meanwhile, a mysterious war party roams the 'Great Wild' and a ruthless magician is intent on murder.

In the secluded valley of Glenn Ceoch, a disgraced druid and a woman warrior have successfully avoided the bloodshed for several years. Now, the arrival of a pregnant refugee threatens the peace they have created together. The odds are overwhelming and death stalks on every side.

Based on the ancient Irish Fenian Cycle texts, the bestselling Fionn mac Cumhaill Series recounts the fascinating and pulse-pounding tale of the birth and adventures of Ireland's greatest hero, Fionn mac Cumhaill.

A sample of what the reviewers say:

"I loved this book. It's a very mature and culturally rich interpretation, a far cry from some of the Celtic pop literature that is around today. Well written and captivating, with a fair dollop of grit and wit. Strong characters, great development, excellent story telling. Worth more than the price of a coffee."

An Ireland of centuries ago, threaded through with myth and magic, but very 'real' for all that. Dark and at times violent, it is balanced by affirming friendships and relationships, and a very strong female cast."

"If you're sick of elves, chivalrous knights and arcane quests, this is probably the most exciting and refreshing book you'll read in a long time. Five stars!"

"Powerful female characters are all too rare in literature. The druid Bodhmhall, and her lover the warrior Liath Luachra will inspire current and future generations of women. O'Sullivan keeps a cracking pace in this, the first of his Fionn mac Cumhaill series.'

There's a nice mix of action, clever dialogue, and a mounting tension up to the dramatic finale but it's the touching relationship between the woman warrior (Liath Luachra) and the druid Bodhmhall (plus the little references to Gaelic/Celtic culture) that really made this surpass so many other books of the genre.

Review from 'Bookworm Blues' Speculative Fiction/Fantasy Review Blog

"You know how some books come out of left field and just shock you? Well, this was one of those. If you're looking for an action/adventure fantasy that is different than the normal, look no further. This book has some welcome diversity, and a story that is absolutely unforgiving. This is a novel based on some ancient Irish text and is full of myth and magic and I just loved it for that. The writing is tight and the book is well edited. I welcomed the strong female characters, the obvious twist on tropes, and the way the author genuinely owned the book he wrote."

Review from 'The Qwillery' Book Review Blog

"The characters were well developed, the plot was gripping and the characters were both realistic and interesting. It was however, the prose that really made this book. It was so very well written. Hats off to Brian O'Sullivan for telling this myth in a truly evocative way."

Printed in Great Britain
by Amazon